# Fearless

## BY: KRISTIN SMITH

*Fearless*
Copyright ©2018 Kristin Smith
All rights reserved.
Printed in the United States of America
First Edition: March 2019

Clean Teen Publishing
WWW.CLEANTEENPUBLISHING.COM

Summary: On the run from the government, Sienna and her Fringe companions seek refuge in the primitive Zenith Camp, until a government decree draws them out of hiding. They're ready to resist, but it may be too late.

ISBN: 978-1-63422-323-2 (paperback)
ISBN:978-1-63422-322-5 (e-book)
Cover Design by: Marya Heidel
Typography by: Courtney Knight
Editing by: Cynthia Shepp

COVER ART
© BRAM J. MEIJER / FOTOLIA
© THEARTOFPHOTO / FOTOLIA
© TOHEYVECTOR / FOTOLIA

Young Adult Fiction /Dystopian
Young Adult Fiction / Science Fiction / General
Young Adult Fiction / Action & Adventure / Survival Stories

For more information about our content disclosure, please utilize the QR code above with your smart phone or visit us at www.CleanTeenPublishing.com

FOR MY PARENTS

TWO OF THE MOST FEARLESS PEOPLE I KNOW—
THANKS FOR ALWAYS BELIEVING IN ME.

*"Progress is our future and perfection is our goal."*

-Excerpt from the
Official Decree of the Commonwealth of Pacifica

# 1
## Sienna

Death Valley is an appropriate name for this place. If anything is alive, it would be beyond a miracle. The heat glares down as our ragtag team treks through this vast, never-ending sauna on our way to the Zenith Camp. Sweat pools under my armpits and drips down my nose. I didn't know mirages could look so real until I saw one on the horizon—a trick of the eye making me think a large lake loomed only footsteps away.

It didn't.

It's been two days since we left Rubex. Two days since Zane left *us*. Even though we were apart for a month while I languished in that fecal-infested prison, I miss him. I miss *us*.

The only solace is having Trey with me again. We have a long way to go before we can get back to where we were. Before the government decided to drop a bomb on our Compound hideout and brainwash him. But we'll get there. I know it.

As for my father...

My chest squeezes at the thought of him, the laser bullets riddling his body—

*Stop*. I can't go there. My mind unwillingly plays his death on repeat, but I can't dwell on it. If I do, it's likely to consume me. I had him back for such a brief time, only to have him stolen from me once again. It doesn't seem fair, but then again,

I learned a long time ago life isn't fair.

"How's your shoulder?" Trey asks, referring to my gunshot wound. He's been walking at the front of the pack with Paige, probably getting a rundown on what it will be like at the Zenith Camp, but now that we're taking a break next to a boulder, he joins me.

I squat next to the oversized rock, then pull out my water bottle. The skin around my wound pulls, a biting pain stabbing my shoulder. "Better." The water is warm and not nearly as refreshing as I would like, but after weeks in that prison cell, I'm certainly not complaining. The more distance we put between myself and that fortress, the better.

"Still sore?" Trey's hands move to his hips as he stares down at me.

"A little." Closing one eye to avoid blinding myself— because let's face it, the sun is like a death ray—I peer up at him. His face is darker than it's ever been, his skin a deep copper from so many hours spent trekking in the sun. I'm jealous he can tan so well. My skin is a constant shade of pinkish red. "But I'll manage."

Trey crouches next to me. "You're burnt." He pulls a T-shirt from his pack, wets it a little with his water bottle, and places it on my forehead. "If you cover your head with this shirt, it might protect your skin."

Once the shirt is in place, his hand moves to my cheek. My face grows hotter, if that's possible. He's barely touched me since the train, since the night we left Rubex, the night we slept in each other's arms. I try not to let it bother me. We are, after all, fugitives who barely escaped with our lives. Perhaps he's focused on getting to the Zenith Camp, so we can reunite with the other Fringe members. Or perhaps it's something else entirely.

But I refuse to let my mind go there as well.

"Trey," Paige calls from a few feet away, "can you come here for a sec?"

Like a well-trained puppy, Trey rises to his feet. To his credit, he does throw me an apologetic look, but that doesn't stop him from being at her beck and call. I watch as she places a hand on his arm and steers him away from everyone, speaking in a low tone so no one will overhear. My mind gallops wildly, filling with scenarios and questions.

Trina flops on the ground next to me as I eye Trey and Paige. I'm not the jealous type typically, but something about the two of them rubs me the wrong way.

"I wouldn't worry about it," she says, following my gaze. "He only has eyes for you." She makes a face. "Trust me."

My mind flips back to when we were in the Compound—to when Trina confessed her feelings for Trey. Okay, so maybe I had to *force* it out of her, but still. I'm worrying I hurt her again when she gives me a teasing grin and wink. My chest loosens, relief coating my insides like a balm. A second later, Trina stops smiling and bites her lip.

"What's wrong?"

"It doesn't feel right. Not without him."

I know immediately she's talking about Curly. My chest knots up again, making it hard to breathe. His death has left a hole in us both. But I don't feel like I have the right to mourn him. It's because of me that he's dead. It's because of me that Trina and Curly came to the Capital. And it's because of me that we were captured by Madame Neiman and her cronies.

So, yeah, when you place a target on someone's back *and* pull the trigger, you don't get the privilege of mourning their death. Thankfully, Trina doesn't seem to blame me, but that's okay. I carry enough blame.

Rising to my feet, I wipe the dust off my shorts so Trina won't see the tears filling my eyes. I've found this to be a great defense mechanism—when I'm feeling guilty over another life I'm responsible for, I change the subject or walk away. It doesn't amount to very meaningful conversations lately, but there's not much anyone can say to comfort me anyway.

Which is why of the three Zenith members I've met so far, I like Asher the most. He's dark, steady as a rock, and doesn't require conversation. He's content to hike in silence, so I've found myself by his side for most of the journey.

Careful of my wound, I shoulder my pack and plod over to him. He gives me a silent nod. We may not talk, but there's something about the solidness of his presence that keeps me grounded.

"All right, folks, let's keep moving," Paige calls out. She and Trey break away from each other, then Trey strides over to me.

"Everything okay?" I ask in a low voice.

"Everything's fine." He readjusts his own pack. "Paige needed my opinion on something."

I don't want to be the prying type, but I can't help myself. "What?"

"The best route into the mountains."

"But how would you know? You don't even know these mountains."

He shrugs. "She wanted to run the different options by me. That's all."

"So what are the options?"

"We have to cross an open area of the desert. We'll basically be sitting ducks for any of the government drones that may be looking for us. She wanted to know what I thought about traveling through the night. Not stopping to make camp."

Since Trina and I are wanted fugitives who barely escaped our execution, it sounds like a safer alternative. "And what did you say?"

His eyes flicker briefly to my shoulder. "I told her I didn't think that was a good idea."

"Why? Because of me?" I take a step back. "I can handle it."

Trey's mouth curls up at the corners. "I know you can. But

you need rest. We all do. And we'll need our strength to climb the mountains tomorrow."

My eyes narrow. "You're only saying that because you don't think I can handle it. Is it because I'm the only one who's not genetically modified? Is that it?"

This hasn't been revealed to me yet, but I'm not stupid. Paige is a perfect shot, Asher is built like a tree trunk, and Grey looks like he could easily bench-press four hundred. Not to mention, they're all gorgeous in their own unique, rugged ways. And I've been around enough GMs at my old school, GIGA—the Genetically and Intellectually Gifted Academy— to recognize their enhanced qualities.

"Nash isn't, either," Trey says, basically confirming my previous assumptions.

"Right…" I say sarcastically. "Like I want to be in the same camp with Nash." He's Trey's obnoxious cousin who thinks everyone should refer to him as *Commander*. The two of us have never mixed. Not sure why Trey wants to compare me with him now.

Chuckling, Trey tucks a flyaway strand of hair behind my ear. "No, that's not it." His face grows serious. "You act like I'm different now that we know I'm a GM. But I'm the same person. I haven't changed." His hands grip my elbows, drawing me closer. "You understand that, right?"

My stomach flips, and I swallow hard, amazed a simple touch from him can still provoke these feelings. "Of course. I'm just—"

"Tired?" Trey finishes for me.

"Yeah."

"Sad?"

I sigh. "Maybe a little of that, too."

Trey pulls me close, kissing the top of my head. "Everything will be better once we get to Zenith. Your mother and sister are already there, waiting for you. We can start over. Together."

*Fearless*

I step back to look at him. "Is that what you want?"

A muscle in his jaw twitches. "Of course. Isn't that what you want?"

An image of Zane forces its way to the front of my mind, but I push it back. Far, far back to the dusty place where memories of GIGA and our house in the suburbs lie. And for the first time in days, I smile. "Yeah. It is."

# 2
# Zane

I don't look back.

Not when Geoff drives away, tires churning up a cloud of dust. Not while we're driving for hours on an endless highway that looks as if it hasn't been used in years. And not when I see Legas in the distance.

Instead, I tell myself, *She made her choice.*

Sienna could have told me she loved me, but she didn't.

Somewhere between one desert mountain range and the next, I've decided it's time to begin my life—the one I was born to live. I may not be Harlow Ryder's real son, but I'm the only one left to carry on his legacy. Once I'm home, I'll make everything right, with him and Arian.

When we're close to the city, I lean forward in my seat and instruct Geoff to take me to Arian's house instead.

It's a rambling structure made up mostly of sharp angles, glass, and stucco. I've only been here a few times.

Geoff lets me off in front, and I walk up the stone sidewalk, breathing deeply, trying to prepare myself for what I should say when I see her.

Her maid answers the door when I knock, giving me a knowing smile. "Miss Arian," she calls up the steps behind her. "You have a visitor."

"Coming," Arian calls back.

"She'll be right with you." The maid drifts off to the next room, a duster in hand.

As I wait, I stare at the floor. The entire foyer floor is made of glass and built over a pool of water so large that goldfish swim beneath my feet. Their shimmery scales catch the light from the afternoon sun, sending rays of color up through the glass.

Arian's footsteps are hesitant as she descends the curving staircase that hangs from cables so thin the stairs appear suspended in midair. "Hi," she says, her back straight, her tone cool.

"Hi." Why am I suddenly so nervous to talk to her? Maybe because the last time I saw her—over a month ago—I was a jerk and told her I was in love with someone else. Yes, that would probably do it.

"I didn't think I'd see you again." She stops halfway down the staircase as if trying to decide if she should go back up or come all the way down.

"I know. There are many things I need to tell you, but the most important is what an idiot I am."

"I would agree with that." Arian takes a few more hesitant steps, stopping on the last stair. "Is Sienna okay?"

Leave it to Arian to be concerned about someone else when she is hurting herself. I think Arian was given an extra dose of compassion in her genes—that's the only thing that makes sense.

"She's fine. She's safe." That's really all I can manage, especially since her location needs to remain a secret from everyone, including me.

Arian bites her lip. "She was almost executed. They're searching for her. It's all over the news—" She stops when she sees the expression on my face. "But, of course, you already know."

I nod.

She descends the last step until she's standing on the glass floor, right above the largest goldfish I've ever seen.

"So did you know? Did you know she was a member of the Fringe?"

I contemplate lying to her, pretending I didn't, but I'm tired. Tired of the deception. If I'm about to start a life and have a future with this woman, I want no lies between us.

"Yes, I knew. I wanted to help her."

Arian worries her lip between her teeth again. "And now? What do you want now?"

I close my eyes. *For all of this to be over. To forget Sienna exists, so I can go back to my boring life. To pretend all is right in our world when I know distinctly it is not.*

Instead, I open my eyes and say, "To be with you."

Some may think I'm playing her, that I'm so fickle if I can't have one woman then I choose another. And maybe I *am* the biggest jerk in the world. I treated Arian like crap, and now I'm here, standing in her foyer, begging for another chance. The truth is, I've always cared about her, from that moment in the ice cream shop when she laid her hand over mine and said, "I'm nervous too."

Any man would be lucky to have her, but she wasn't chosen for any man. She was chosen for me.

Arian's face flashes through several distinct emotions—hurt, confusion, and surprise. And suddenly, all I want to do is kiss away her pain. I reach for her, attempting to tug her into my arms. She resists at first, which isn't surprising, but then gives in, her body loosening under my touch.

"I'm sorry," I whisper. "I'm sorry I hurt you."

Her eyes are full of tears. "Do you still love her?"

"I'm trying not to." When she doesn't say anything, I add, "But I want to be with you. I want to *marry* you."

Tears slip down her cheeks. "You do?"

"I do. And to prove it to you—" I pause because I haven't

really thought this through, but who cares? I'm tired of thinking things through. My entire life has been carefully planned and laid out, and I'm ready to do something spontaneous. "And to prove it to you," I continue, "I think we should get married as soon as possible. Does two weeks give you enough time?"

Her mouth parts, but no words come out. "Are you—are you sure this is what you want?"

I rest my forehead against hers, and my heart soars. *Yes, this is what I want.*

Instead of answering, I decide to let my lips do the talking. Her eyes connect with mine as I lean in, her body stiffening. I think it's a good sign when my lips touch hers and she doesn't push me away. Instead, she relaxes in my arms. I try to put a month's worth of *apologies* into that kiss.

When I pull back, her eyes are a little glazed over. "Does that answer your question?" I whisper.

She blinks slowly, her eyelashes practically hitting her cheeks as she does. "Yes." Then she smiles. "Two weeks is plenty of time."

# 3
## Trey

Sienna's different. She's like a smaller, inverted version of herself. I understand it will take some time to get her strength back after being in that hellhole of a prison for a month—and after being shot—but I only hope they didn't break her.

She even looks at me differently. I don't know if it's because I betrayed her while I wasn't in my right mind, or if it's something else entirely. Then again, maybe I'm the one who's different. Maybe I'm the one who's changed.

One thing I do know, my feelings for her haven't. Before, I didn't want anyone to know we were together, but I now realize how short life can be. Especially this kind of life we're living. I want to make the most of each moment. I want Sienna to know how I feel, and I don't want to fear others knowing the truth. I told her once that being with her made me weak…

I was wrong. It makes me strong.

When we've gone as far as we can for the day—and when Sienna's face is knotted in pain, yet she doesn't complain—we set up camp. I help Sienna roll out her bedroll—of course, she protests she can do it herself—while Nash and Grey start building a fire with the brush and yucca leaves they've collected. Trina wanders off to find some privacy, probably to use the bathroom. Even though he's busy trying to get a fire started,

Grey's eyes follow her as she walks away. Looks like Trina has an admirer.

Sienna straightens up, letting out a small moan. Her hair is the color of the fire they're trying to start, and it curls around her forehead in sweaty ringlets. She collapses on her bedroll, using one arm to prop herself up, while hugging the other one to her chest.

"Let me take a look," I say. I haven't redressed her wound since yesterday.

"It's fine," she says, but then grimaces.

Plopping my bag next to her, I squat beside her. As the dedicated "medic" of the group, my pack contains everything I need to change her dressing. After digging through it to find what I need, I spray my hands with an antibacterial solution.

"Remove your shirt, please," I say in my most professional doctor voice. I try not to crack a smile when I say it, but it's hard not to.

She hesitates, but then complies, wincing as she pulls the sweaty shirt over her head.

I keep my eyes focused on the sweat-soaked dressing smudged with dirt, and not on the lace that surrounds her bra. Gingerly, I remove the bandage. The wound is fleshy and raw, but where the skin should be pink, it's turning yellow. *A sign of infection.*

"How's the pain? More than yesterday, or less?" I already know the answer, but I'm trying to play it cool so she doesn't see how worried I am. We're in the middle of nowhere with only a few medical supplies. I don't have antibiotics to give her, which she needs at this point.

"A little more," she admits.

"That's because it's infected."

Her eyes widen. "It is?"

"It isn't bad yet," I reassure her. "But you need antibiotics ASAP." I spray the antibacterial solution on her wound, and she inhales sharply, cursing under her breath.

"That stings."

"Sorry."

I apply a thin layer of triple antibiotic cream on a clean bandage, then cover her wound with it. Once I've secured it with medical tape, I sit back on my heels. "How's that?"

"Better."

My eyes shift to her dirty shirt lying on the ground. "Do you have a clean one you can wear?"

She fumbles around in her own pack for a moment before producing a light green shirt. Holding it up, she says, "They thought of everything."

She's referring to Zenith who she thinks packed these bags for us. What she doesn't know is I packed these bags and picked out the green shirt because I knew it would match her eyes.

"Here, let me help you with that." I take the shirt from her hands. Before she can protest, I've got it over her head, forcing her to poke her arms through the holes. Sienna's face turns beet red as she looks away. I love it when she blushes, making the freckles on her nose and cheeks stand out.

When she finally meets my gaze, I grin at her, my eyes moving to her lips and then back up. The color in her face deepens.

I'm dying to kiss her. I haven't tried since that moment in the AIG, right after she was rescued from Confinement. Right after she found out I remembered everything. I guess I hoped we could forget the past and go back to being us, but too many things transpired while we were apart. Too many things came between us. Namely Rayne and Zane.

I plan to give her time. Time to feel for me what she once did. She once told me she loved me when I was too ignorant and too stupid to understand. I only hope one day she'll feel that way again.

"Trey," Paige calls from where she's set up her own bedroll

a dozen steps away. "Do you have a minute?"

Sienna rolls her eyes at me. "She's very needy, isn't she?"

I chuckle as I rise to my feet. "Be right back."

"Take your time," she says, waving a dismissive hand.

As soon as I'm close to Paige, she grabs my arm and leads me away from the group. She tends to do this a lot lately.

"We need to move. Tonight," she says in an urgent voice, which is really her typical tone. Paige is always urgent—it's who she is.

"I already told you I don't think it's a good idea."

"And you think waiting until daylight to cross this section of the valley is?" Pursing her lips, she glares at me. "I put my neck out for you. I risked the lives of two of my guys as well as my own to rescue your people. The least you could have done was tell me the truth." Her eyes slide to where Sienna sits on her bedroll, fidgeting with a loose string.

"I did tell you the truth."

Her eyes narrow to slits. "You said we were rescuing Fringe members. You didn't say anything about rescuing your *girlfriend*."

I scratch my head. "Why does that matter? She *is* a member of the Fringe."

"You know why, Trey."

"Oh, come on, Paige. After all these years?"

She shrugs. "The heart doesn't forget."

"You're the one who left," I say tersely. Then I force a smile. "Look, I'm sorry if I led you on. Wasn't my intention. But I *am* grateful you helped rescue Sienna and Trina." *But not Jeb. We were too late for him.* I shove those damning thoughts to the back of my mind.

Paige's expression softens. She sighs. "It's just… you and me—we have history."

I think of the scar on my stomach. "Yes, we do."

"And I guess I always thought—" She scoffs, waving her

hands in the air. "Doesn't matter."

"That was a long time ago, Paige."

She tosses her head. "Yeah, I know." Her eyes flit to Sienna, and she lowers her voice. "I owed you for that day. If you hadn't gotten in a fight with my father's men—"

"It's really not a big deal—"

She holds up her hand to stop me. "All I wanted to say is that now we're even." She pivots on her heel and strides away. I watch her for a minute as she checks on Nash and Grey's progress with the fire.

I remember the first time I ever saw Paige, three years ago. We were both eighteen, still naive to the ways of the world. Back then, she was less angry and less edgy, her hair hanging down her back in dark waves. When I entered the underground pool hall with Nash, feeling lost and sorry for myself while still mourning the death of my father, she'd immediately caught my eye. She'd been danger and beauty and fire combined. After whispering something in the ear of the guy she was sitting next to at the bar, she'd sauntered over to me. We'd had a few drinks, then she challenged me to a game of pool and I accepted. When I lost to her, I wasn't sure if it was because I *wanted* to lose to her, or if she was really that good.

I'd been around enough GMs during my life to know the difference between someone who's genetically modified and someone who isn't. And when she beat me, it'd only confirmed it. She played pool like it was something she'd been doing since she was an infant. Granted, I recognized at the time if she were one of the Devil's girls, then she probably spent a lot of time in that pool hall. But this had been different. It had seemed like her brain could calculate every move before it was made.

"You're different," I'd said to her.

To which she coyly replied, "I bet you say that to all the girls."

I smiled. "No, really. You are."

With a wink, she said, "Why don't we get out of here?" She'd grabbed my hand, and about half a dozen pairs of eyes swung our way.

I followed her up the stairs and outside into the alley. We'd started kissing a little. Okay, maybe a lot. She was intoxicating, I'd been trying to drown my sorrow, and I found comfort in her lips. Or maybe it wasn't her lips so much as someone to take my mind off what I'd lost and what I was about to face. I'd never asked to be the leader of the Fringe, but with my father's sudden death, that position had fallen to me. At the time, I hadn't been sure I wanted it.

"Is this really what you want?" I'd finally murmured against her lips.

"What do you think?" she whispered, her back pressed against the brick of the building, a gleam in her eyes.

I'd pulled back a little then. "No, I mean, is this the life you want?"

Her eyes narrowed. "Who are you? Some undercover Enforcer or something? Am I about to get busted?"

I laughed at that. "No."

"Then who are you?"

I'd cleared my throat, hoping it would also clear away some of the fuzziness in my head. "Have you heard of the Fringe?"

"Yeah, so."

I shrugged.

"You're part of the Fringe?"

"Maybe."

She'd tried to take a step back, but she was already against the wall. I watched her swallow. "What do you want?"

"To help you."

Her face had hardened as she propped her hands on her hips. "Look, I don't know why you're here, but you better leave before my dad finds out."

About that time, the door beside us had banged open, and

a string of curses came from the mouths of two greasy guys who had Nash by the neck and were dragging him out. A third man—dark as night and as tall as a tree—stood behind them, taking up the entire doorway.

"Make this memorable," said the man in a voice so deep it sounded as though it was coming from the depths of a barrel. He'd grabbed Paige's arm, forcing her back inside.

The two men shoved Nash to the ground, and I'd noticed his lip was already bleeding. Adrenaline pumped through my veins triple time as the men pulled out boxcutters.

*Fight or flight.*

I chose fight every time.

With every dodge of the silver-handled knife, with every punch I managed to land, I'd thought about the fear in Paige's eyes as the Devil's demon dragged her back inside.

Which is how I ended up with the scar on my stomach and Nash with one on his cheek. I was distracted. And to our credit, two more guys with knives had joined the fight, so we were completely outnumbered.

As Nash and I lay bleeding on the ground, it had been Paige who'd helped us out of that dirty alleyway and to a safer place. It'd been Paige who'd stitched us up because we both knew we couldn't go to a medical center. She'd rescued me and I, in turn, rescued her. I gave her an out from her life with the Devil, who'd taken her in off the streets and become her father figure when she was a small girl.

Paige ran away from him to join us in the Compound. She'd stayed with us a short time, but being underground got to her. Taking at least a dozen rescued GMs with her, she'd set out to find other GM outcasts who had escaped the experimental testing, just like her. It wasn't until almost a year later I heard she'd formed a group called Zenith and they had a camp in the mountains.

So, yeah, to say Paige and I have *history*, is probably an understatement.

# 4

## Sienna

The next day, we stop to rest and make camp next to a crumbling structure. Only three walls remain of what I assume was a small concrete building, but it's enough to create some relief from the sun. There's a plaque giving a name and life to this place, but half is missing. The only word still legible is *ruins*, which I guess is somewhat self-explanatory.

While Trey is talking to Paige—again—I head over to where Asher kneels by a cactus plant. I watch as he takes out a knife, then proceeds to carefully cut off one of the arms. After placing the cactus piece on a bandana spread over the ground, he slices off the spiny outer layer. What's left is a slimy green thing that vaguely resembles a cucumber.

He holds it out to me like he's offering me some. Shaking my head, I settle onto the dirt next to him. He takes a huge bite of the slimy thing, then wipes his mouth with his bare arm.

"Why don't you ever talk?" I finally ask.

He shrugs. "Don't have much to say."

"Aha! So you can talk."

He smiles, his teeth so white against his ebony skin.

"How long have you been living at the Zenith Camp?"

"Couple of years." He chews slowly as if he's savoring every morsel.

"What's it like there?"

He thinks for a moment, his head tilted to the side. "Dusty."

I glance over to where Trey and Paige are still engrossed in an intimate conversation. "Paige is the leader?"

"Yeah. She found me, helped me see who I was. Gave me a home."

"Where were you before?"

His mouth turns down. "Everywhere."

"You didn't have a home?"

He shakes his head, wiping his mouth again.

"How did you not get caught by the Enforcers? I've seen what they do to people on the streets." I recall an image of the guy with the toy truck in his hand, and the smell of burnt flesh from the laser bullets.

"I kept moving, never stayed in one place very long."

I cut my eyes back to Trey and Paige, who are ending their conversation. Trey studies her as she walks away, and I get the distinct impression he's remembering something.

"They knew each other?" I ask, nodding toward them.

"You don't know the story?" Now finished with his cactus meal, Asher wipes his hands on the bandana.

"No. Do you?"

"Yes." He gives me a sidelong glance. "But it's not my place to tell it." Rising to his feet, he says, "Ask Trey. I'm sure he'll tell you."

*Fat chance*, I think as Asher goes over to the cactus and cuts off another arm. I sit there for another minute, admiring the way the sky has turned from blue to orange to hot pink all in a matter of minutes. The air is cooler now, too. With the sun down, my raw, blistered face can finally get a reprieve from the intense heat of the day. I press my hands to my blazing cheeks. They must be the color of a tomato.

Trey drops down beside me. "Here, thought you could use this." He hands me several thick green leaves with toothed edges.

"What is it?"

"An aloe plant. It'll help with the burn."

"What do I do with it?"

Trey takes a leaf, cuts into it with his knife, and squeezes. Clear liquid comes out. He puts it on my finger, and I apply it to my face. The cool gel-like substance soothes my skin, like a refreshing drink on a hot summer day.

"Here, let me get your neck." Trey sweeps my short hair to the side, then applies the gooey liquid to my neck. When I look up, Paige is watching us from afar. She turns away.

"She doesn't like me very much," I say when he's finished.

"Why do you say that?" Collecting the leftover leaves, he stores them in his pack. "She saved your life, remember?"

"I know, but it's the way she looks at me when we're together. It's like—it's like—"

"She's jealous?" he finishes.

"That's not what I was going to say."

Trey smiles. "Then what?"

I twist my hands in front of me, suddenly feeling very self-conscious. *Is this all in my mind? He's right. She* did *save my life.*

"I was going to say wary," I say. "She looks at me like she's wary of me." Taking a deep breath, I plow forward. "Did you guys have a relationship before?"

Trey chuckles, his eyes not quite meeting mine. "Paige and I have… history." Leaning over, he kisses me on the cheek and whispers in my ear, "But it's nothing you need to worry about." He shoots to his feet. Clearly changing the subject, he says, "You hungry? I'm starved. Let's see if we can get some dinner going."

But I don't get up to help him. I'm too busy thinking about this *history* he and Paige share, and the reasons why Asher won't tell me.

Dinner that night is freeze-dried rice and chicken. All we have to do is boil water, add it to the insulated package, stir, and serve. The seven of us sit around the small fire in silence, too busy eating to talk. Grey is the first one done, as evidenced by the giant belch he lets out. Trina giggles, but Paige snaps, "Get some manners, Grey."

"Sorry, Paige," he says, and he really does look contrite. I can't help but notice how his eyes flit to Trina. When she smiles at him, he grins back. That must give him encouragement because he says, "Who's up for a story?"

"I am." Trina raises her hand.

"This is a true story," Grey begins. "It happened a long time ago in a land not too far from here."

Trey nudges my good shoulder with his, giving me a smile. I return it before focusing my attention on Grey again.

"They call it the War of the States. There was much unrest between the people who lived in one nation. No one agreed how things should be run or who should be in charge. The States revolted against one another. Some formed alliances and grouped themselves together based on factors such as geography, political preference, or religious beliefs.

"As these groups struggled to detach themselves from the existing government system, a war broke out. It was a war to end all wars. Streets coated with blood, while bodies piled up and burned in town squares across the country." Grey pauses here. "No one was safe."

"What happened then?" I ask. I'd heard bits and pieces of this story through the years—not that it's taught in our schools or anything—but I've never heard such a detailed account before.

"When there was hardly anything or anyone left, the four Provinces formed. Pacifica, Pride, Atlantica, and Central. Each with their own government and way of doing things."

"When you think about it," Trina pipes up, "our

technological advances would be through the roof if none of this had ever happened."

Trey nods beside me. "Very true. War and the destruction set society back at least a hundred years. Maybe more."

"Because it took so long to rebuild," Grey agrees.

"And some places never got rebuilt," I add, thinking of Legas and the Gateway. Didn't Zane say the government doesn't want that area cleaned up because it's a reminder of what we've lost and who's in control? "I used to believe the government was responsible for the shutdown of all the hotels and casinos on the Gateway."

"That's what they want you to believe," Paige says. "In a way, I guess they were. Some casinos might have been operational after the war, but the government forced them to keep their doors closed. They tried to make it seem like it was about morals, not power, but everyone knew the truth."

"Greed plus power equals corruption," Trey mutters.

"But I don't get it," I say. "Wouldn't they want that revenue? It's my understanding the casinos provided cash—and a lot of it."

Trey shakes his head. "It was something they couldn't control. The government doesn't like things they can't control." His smile is wry. "Trust me."

"But not all governments are like ours," Grey says. "Some are better. More fair."

At first, I think he's making this statement up, but when Paige remains quiet and doesn't correct him, I realize he's telling the truth.

"How do you know this?"

"We've traveled some," Grey says.

"Okay," I say slowly. "But you haven't crossed over into other Provinces, right? I thought the borders are heavily protected."

"We have," Grey confirms.

"But how?"

"It's not as hard as you might think," Paige butts in. "I mean, if you're an amateur, maybe. But we're professionals." I have the distinct feeling the amateur she's referring to is me.

"So what are they like? The other Provinces?" I ask.

"Well, Pride is—" Grey starts, before Paige shoots him a look.

"If you want to know, you'll have to see it yourself," Paige says.

Shrugging, I pretend to scrape the last few bites of rice from my package. If she doesn't want to tell me, that's fine.

Trey clears his throat. "I think what Paige means is the other Provinces are so different from what we know that it would be hard to explain. Right, Paige?" He shoots her a look.

"Yeah, right. Whatever." She gets up from her spot on the ground, tosses her food package into the fire, and lays down on her bedroll, which is several feet away from the group. Her hands go behind her head as she stares at the sky like she's studying the stars. Trina and Grey have moved closer together and now talk in hushed undertones, while Asher sharpens a stick with his pocketknife.

"Ready for bed?" Trey asks me.

Nodding, I stand and toss my own trash into the fire before following Trey to where he's laid out our bedrolls side by side. Trey has done a good job of keeping his distance so far, but when we lay down, he wraps his arms around me and pulls me to his chest, careful to avoid my shoulder wound. It still throbs and pulls a little, but I don't mind.

"Is this okay?" he murmurs in my ear.

A part of me wants to take things slow because we have so much ground to cover and so much lost time to make up for. But his body is warm next to mine. With the cool night air, it feels too good to give up.

Snuggling deeper, I close my eyes. "Better than okay."

# 5

## Zane

"I see you've come to your senses." My father strides toward me, ever the polished businessman in his pressed suit and silk tie. He doesn't visit the Match 360 and Chromo 120 facilities as often as he used to—probably because he now has scientists and doctors who can implement his visions. But that doesn't stop him from dressing the part of the companies' owner and director, even from the comfort of his own home.

I'm headed back to my room after a long swim, a towel draped over my shoulder. Ever since I left Arian's house yesterday, I've been trying to process the decision I made. I thought it would be cathartic, but swimming in my own pool only reminds me of Sienna and Emily, her younger sister. I've never seen a little girl who loved swimming as much as she did.

"Regarding what, may I ask?" I stop in the foyer at the base of the curved staircase.

"Your impending marriage. It's at the end of next week, yes?"

How does he know this? I haven't told anyone yet. "How did you—?"

"The Stratfords contacted me. Seems Arian is excited everything is back on track." When he grins, his face lights up like a Christmas tree. It's been a while since I've seen him this happy.

"Ah, of course. I'd almost forgotten how quickly news travels in your inner circles."

Stepping closer, he places a hand on my shoulder. "I'm proud of you for coming home and making the right decision."

"It wasn't much of a decision to make." That's the truth. Sienna chose Trey. Again. It's not like I was going to stick around to be the third wheel.

"You're a good man, Zane. And you're going to make an even better head of the company someday. With Arian by your side, the two of you will be unstoppable. Every person needs their perfect match. I found mine in your mother. All I want is what's best for you."

His words make me straighten up. Even after all I've learned about him recently, I'm still just that boy who wants to impress his father.

"Thanks... Dad." It's hard to say those words now, especially since they carry a different meaning than they did before. I acknowledge Harlow Ryder is my father, despite the fact we don't share the same genes. But it's hard *not* to think of him differently. He's the man who raised me, yes, but he's not my *real* father. My biological father.

He pats my shoulder, then crosses to the other side of the foyer before turning back. "If you're not busy tomorrow, I'd love to take you to the Match 360 Legas facility. Show you some stuff we've been working on. We hired a new scientist while you were gone."

"Dad, I've been going there since I was three. You don't have to show me around."

"I know, son. But you'll be the head of the company soon—"

My hands shoot up like I can block his response. "Whoa, not too soon, though, right? I mean, you still have a good ten to fifteen years before you'll retire."

Harlow rubs his jaw, suddenly appearing much older than his sixty-something years. "You never know. It may be sooner."

When we enter the Match 360 Legas facility the next day, my first thought is, *How did Sienna break in here?* I know she stole the computer chip, but I can't fathom how she did it. Not only is this place heavily guarded at night *and* during the day, but laser sensors also kick on during the nighttime hours. Even though I don't want to think about her, I can't help but feel a tiny bit of admiration at Sienna's skills. It was a crime, yes, but damn, it's impressive she was able to pull it off.

Harlow leads me to the lab, which is located on the third floor. I know this place well, probably as well as my own home. I spent many hours after school in this lab, creating Re0Gene and a few other products over the years. For instance, I know the metal table closest to the window has a burn the shape of an egg from where I spilled hydrofluoric acid. And I know the glass in the cabinet to my left has a slight crack from when I was frustrated with my lack of progress on the healing serum and slammed it too hard.

Most of the scientists are wearing hazmat suits—a new addition since I was last here—but Harlow walks in like he owns the place. Granted, he does, but still. I'm thinking if they're wearing hazmat suits, there's a pretty good reason for it, and I'd rather be safe than sorry.

"Zane, this is Dr. George," Harlow says, introducing a man encased in a thick suit and see-through hood.

Dr. George extends a gloved hand, his eyes small through the clear part of the hood. It isn't until he removes his mask that I see he's a middle-aged balding man. "Perhaps the two of you would like to wear a suit?"

Harlow waves his hand as if dismissing the idea. "We won't be staying long. Can you show Zane what you've been working on?"

"Of course." Dr. George leads us to a stainless-steel case

the size of a refrigerator. When he opens it, there's a hiss as a substance similar to dry ice pours out. He carefully removes a glass vial.

"What is it?" I ask.

Harlow cradles the vial in his hand as if he's holding a delicate bird. "This is Re0Gene 2.0," he says proudly.

I stare at the vial in his hand. "Re0Gene? As in *my* Re0Gene?"

"Yes, but this is new and improved," Harlow says before handing the small bottle back to Dr. George.

"I don't understand—"

"We took your formula, then used it to create a serum so powerful it can heal the entire body with only a few drops placed under the tongue."

"How is that possible?"

Dr. George pipes in. "Your formula was only lacking a few components, but once I reworked it, it all came together. To my knowledge, this is the most powerful healing agent ever created."

"So if you're working with a healing serum, what's with all the protective gear?"

Dr. George and my father exchange a look.

"What?" I say.

Dr. George is the one to speak. "If the formula is off by even a tiny bit, it can burn your skin right off."

"Okay, wow. I'm not sure how I feel about you using my formula in this way—"

"Zane," Harlow says, "it's for the betterment of society. Don't you care about that? We can't keep this to ourselves."

"Who are you planning to sell it to?" This is what I really want to know. My father has never been a greedy man, but his answer will determine whether I allow this product to go to market. It may not be mine entirely, but the original formula is mine. And I deserve to have a say in who buys it.

"A man by the name of Thomas Walton contacted me a few weeks ago. He works in the Health and Rehabilitation department of the government. I believe he and his colleagues are interested in it."

I stare at my father like he's gone mad. "You want to sell this to them? How could you consider that? After all they've done?"

Harlow sighs, leaning against one of the lab tables. "Now, Zane, I know you're upset by some of the things that happened in Rubex. But I still work very closely with President Shard and various branches of the government. I can't turn my back on them now."

My fists clench, and I have a tough time maintaining control of both my voice and my body. "Yes, you can. It's easy. You tell them you don't have permission to sell this formula. Which is true. I never gave you permission to use my formula to create this Re0Gene 2.0 or whatever it is you're calling it."

Harlow glances nervously at Dr. George, who is watching us with evident confusion.

"I don't understand," Dr. George says. "I thought Zane gave permission—"

Folding my arms, I stare at my father. "Do you have something you'd like to confess?"

"I may have forged the truth a little," Harlow says to Dr. George. "But no worries. I'm sure my son and I will work all of this out. Please, carry on." Grabbing my arm, he steers me toward the door. "We'll get out of your way."

Once we're through the door, I jerk my arm from Harlow's grasp. "You never learn, do you?" I seethe. "When will you stop being so selfish and start thinking about other people? That is my serum and formula. It wasn't meant to be used without my permission. You betrayed my trust." I stride down the hall toward the elevators.

"Zane, wait," Harlow calls.

His pleading tone is all too familiar, and frankly, I'm sick of it. I'm fed up with his lies, his half-truths, his schemes to get people to do what he wants them to do. It reminds me of my brother Steele, who betrayed me in the worst possible way. I'll never forgive Steele for what he did to Sienna.

And right now, my father is no better than he is.

# 6
## Trey

We arrive at the Zenith Camp around noon on the fifth day. It's a good thing, because Sienna and I ate our last granola bar for breakfast and drank our last drop of water an hour before we arrived.

As we near the Camp, Paige does a bird call in what I can only assume is an attempt at letting people know Zenith members have arrived. Dozens of people pour out of tents made from cowhide and other kinds of animal pelts. Paige wasn't joking when she called this a camp. The tents are arranged in neat rows with small fires built all around the open expanse, the smell of burning wood and cooked meat making my stomach growl.

Paige embraces one member after another, many of whom have their hair in cornrows like hers. Some have opted for dreadlocks instead.

Paige is clearly in charge. I know she said something to Sienna about only being in charge of protecting people, but that was a load of bull. She's the leader of this group—there's no doubt about it. Not that I ever did doubt it. Paige has that type of personality. She was born to be a leader, more so than I ever was.

I glance at Sienna beside me. She searches the people surrounding us, her eyes skimming over faces. She's searching for her mom and sister.

Grabbing her hand, I squeeze it. "I'm sure they're here somewhere."

Her eyes focus on my face like she forgot I was beside her. "I'm excited to see them, but I don't know what to say…"

She's referring to her father. She can never tell her mom and sister he'd still been alive in Rubex, that she watched him die, for real this time. It would open a gateway of questions we're not prepared to answer. "You don't have to say anything. The sheer fact you're alive is enough—" Before I can finish my sentence, there's a shout from the other side of Camp.

"Si-Si! You're here!" A little girl with blonde curls and a bright smile comes charging at Sienna. She flings herself into Sienna's arms. She's followed by a red-haired woman who's wringing her hands together, tears filling her eyes. I know I met them while I was in Zane's house and believed I was someone else, but I only remember bits and pieces. Besides, that wasn't me. I want to meet them as Trey, the guy who loves Sienna, not Trey the brainwashed jerk who thought he was in love with some girl from Rubex.

Sienna sobs as the three of them embrace. I'm sure her mother thinks it's because of everything Sienna went through while she was in that prison. And maybe that's partly true. But the truth is it killed her to watch her father die while we were escaping from the AIG building in Rubex. I'm not sure how she's still standing, let alone interacting with other people. I remember what it was like when my father died. It was the worst thing I've ever experienced. I'd wanted to stop living. I'd wanted the pain to stop and the memories to shut down. Sienna had to endure that not once, but twice. Hell, she's stronger than I ever gave her credit for.

Not wanting to interrupt, I slip away and maneuver through the crowd of people who have come out to welcome their Zenith members home. Paige sees me and waves me over.

She's talking with a group of people. I immediately recognize Fringe members interspersed with those from Zenith. Luke, the brown-haired boy I rescued a year ago from experimentation in a Chromo 120 lab, wraps me in a bear hug. He's followed by tiny Riley, a sixteen-year-old GM girl who looks like she's about twelve. Her parents wanted her to be a gymnast, but when her goals didn't align with theirs, she ran away. I found her on the streets of Legas, thankfully, before the Enforcers did. Riley pushes up on her toes to kiss my cheek.

"Great to see you, Boss," she says with a grin.

Mateo is next, his dark dreadlocks a huge contrast to his wide, friendly smile. He is one of the first GMs ever created, and was rescued from the AIG facility when he was a baby.

More and more Fringe members crowd around, giving me hugs and high fives. I try to greet them all, but I can't help but notice the faces that are missing. John, Devon, Kaylee, Tyler... Jeb ... Those are only a few of the kids I'll never see again. Each name is like a punch in the gut.

I let them down. I let them all down.

"Jared," Paige calls to a young man with a comscreen in his hands. I'm about to ask Paige how they get reception all the way out here, when she continues, "How are we doing on manhunt updates? Did we elude the government? Are they on our trail?"

Jared clicks through a few screens. "So far, we're in the clear. They're searching up and down Pacifica's coast right now. Guess they don't think anyone would be crazy enough to cross Death Valley."

Paige grins at this. "Which is the exact reason we did."

Ah, yes. A method to her madness. Paige never does anything without a reason.

"Keep an eye on those government updates," Paige instructs Jared. "I want to be alerted immediately if something changes. Got it?"

Jared nods, his brown hair falling into his eyes. "Of course." He focuses his attention on the comscreen again.

To me, Paige says, "Our comscreens are untraceable, but obviously we don't use Lynks here. If you want an update of what's going on back in Legas or Rubex, see Jared."

"Okay."

Paige calls everyone together by whistling with two fingers. She makes me stand next to her, two groups united, and we are surrounded by at least one hundred and fifty people. A hundred who are members of the Fringe, which leaves fifty members of Zenith. I scan the crowd for Sienna. She's standing in the back, her arms wrapped around both her mother and her sister.

"I wanted to take a moment to officially welcome Trey Winchester and the rest of the Fringe to the Zenith Camp. I know many of you have been here for weeks now, but for those who are new… Welcome." Paige flashes a wide grin, and I get a glimpse of what attracted me to her the first night I met her. "Zenith members, this is Trey Winchester, leader of the Fringe. Trey, this is everyone." Turning, she directs her smile at me. "You'll learn their names over the coming days."

A chorus of *Hi, Trey* comes next. I wave at the crowd of people and all the unfamiliar faces. I've always been good with names, so I know it won't take me long before I learn them all.

I feel like I should say something, so I clear my throat. "Thank you, Zenith, for taking us in when we had nowhere else to go. You are a refuge, and we are forever indebted to you." I nod in Paige's direction. "But please put us to work. I know it's not easy running a Camp like this, so tell us what to do and we'll do it." A few people murmur and clap in agreement. I step back to indicate I'm done speaking.

"I think the first thing we need to do," Paige says, eyeing me but speaking loud enough for the rest of the crowd to hear, "is to set up camp for those who are new. We have supplies and materials in the far tent labeled *Home Construction*. Each home tent is designed to hold up to two people. We do have a Duty Chart with rotating duties around Camp. Check the list daily. It will be nailed to the pole over there." She points to a wooden pole at least seven feet tall that seems to have no other purpose than to display the daily list. "We also have a watchtower, and we take turns manning it." Paige winks at me. "Trey and I will take first shift tonight." Clapping her hands together, she says, "I think that's it for now, but if you have any questions, you can ask me or Asher."

Paige pats me on the shoulder before gliding through the crowd. She may act and look tough, but she also reminds me of a panther—dark, silent, full of stealth and prowess.

I search the Camp until I find a medic station, a crudely constructed wooden building. I've been keeping an eye on Sienna's wound, and though it doesn't look worse, it doesn't look much better, either. She needs antibiotics. Popping my head inside the open door, I'm surprised to see a familiar face. I'd know that shock of blonde hair anywhere. "Laurel!"

"Hi, Trey," she says.

Laurel has been a member of the Fringe for as long as I can remember. We practically grew up together.

"You're in charge of the medic station?" I ask.

"Yep." She grins. "I learned from the best."

On occasion, Laurel would help me in the infirmary in the Compound. That seems like a lifetime ago.

"Do you have any antibiotics? Sienna was shot, and I think it's getting infected."

"Should I take a look at it?" she asks.

"No, I've got it covered. But if you have anything I can give her, I think it'd help."

"Let me see what I have." Laurel goes over to a rolling cart, sorting through the bottles there. Most of them look like they were stolen from someone's medicine cabinet. I don't really want to know. "Here's something." She hands me a brown bottle. Cephalexin.

"This should work." I check the expiration date. The pills expired a few months ago, but I know from experience they'll work. "Thanks, Laurel."

"Don't mention it. Anything for my favorite leader."

As I'm walking out the door, she stops me. "Hey, Trey? It's good to have you back."

"Good to be back."

As soon as I leave the medic station, I spot Sienna entering the Home Construction tent. I duck inside just as the guy sitting at the table surrounded by various pelts asks her, "Which do you prefer? Cowhide, bear skin, or coyote pelt?" He holds up pieces of animal skin. "I even have samples if you'd like to feel."

"That's okay," Sienna says. "Let's go with cowhide."

Leaning over, I whisper in her ear, "Good choice."

Sienna jerks back a little, but when she sees me, she smiles. "Oh, hey."

The guy crosses to the other side of the tent where larger pieces of animal skin lay spread out on the ground. He flips through a few until he finds a brown and white speckled one. When he hands it to Sienna, he winks. "I think I found the best one."

"Is this all I need?" she asks.

"No. Let me grab you some poles, a tarp, and a bedroll."

When the guy tries to hand the stuff to Sienna, I take it instead. "I'll help get her set up and come back later for mine."

As we leave the tent, I say, "Let's find a place to put down your roots."

"I should probably do it myself," she protests, following me to an empty area of camp. She holds the poles while I nail in the stakes.

"Can I do anything?" she asks, kneeling beside me. "I mean, other than hold things and hand them to you?"

I'd almost forgotten about the antibiotics I got from Laurel. I reach into my pocket, then hand Sienna the bottle. "Yes. You can take two of these right now."

"I can't without water."

"Do you still have a water bottle in your pack?"

"Yes, but it's empty."

I nod to the pump a few yards away that draws water from the well. "You can fill it up there."

Sienna fills her bottle and downs the pills. When she returns, she says, "Now what can I do?"

"How are you with a hammer and nails?"

She shrugs, wisps of hair falling from her stub of a ponytail. Her hair grew a lot while she was in Confinement, but not enough to compare to how it used to be. At least she can pull it back now.

"I'm all right."

I hand her the hammer and a few nails. "We need to nail the tarp to these poles. Think you can do that?"

Cocking her head to the side, she says, "I restored an old relic with no instructions and only these—" she wiggles her fingers, "—I think I can handle a few nails and a pole."

Her comment makes me grin. "I never doubted you for a second."

"Good. Now stop distracting me so I can work." She flashes me a smile. If I thought it was hard not kissing her before, it's torturous now.

Twenty minutes later, we step back and admire our handiwork. The cowhide is layered atop the tarp to give the A-frame tent additional protection from the occasional rainstorm.

"What do you think?" I ask her. "Home sweet home?"

She makes a face, and it takes all my willpower not to kiss her. "You mean home sweet tent?" A big sigh is followed by, "Definitely a step up from the last place."

She rarely talks about being in Confinement. I think it's just too hard, especially with Jeb's death still fresh in her mind.

I brush a wisp of hair out of her eyes. "What was it like?"

"What? Confinement?"

"Yeah. But only if you want to talk about it."

Sienna wanders over to a wooden bench made of logs. When she sits, I join her.

"It was hell," she says. "Or at least what I imagine hell to be like. Lonely. Miserable. Blistering hot during the day, freezing cold at night. No way to pass the time. The only thing you have to keep you company are your thoughts of everything you've done wrong in your life. All the mistakes you've made." She pauses, bending down to pick up a small rock at her feet. Using the sharp edge of the rock, she scratches a straight line in the log. Her eyes won't meet mine. "After a while, I started to believe I deserved to be there. I deserved to die."

I take her hands in mine, and the rock falls to the ground. Her hands are so small, her fingernails lined with dirt. She has dark smudges across her cheeks. We could both use a bath right now.

"It's my fault," I say. "You wouldn't have been in Rubex if it wasn't for me. You wouldn't have gone to Radcliffe's home if I hadn't betrayed you."

"That wasn't you, though. You didn't know what you were—"

"I know. But I still feel bad about it. You've sacrificed so much. And you did it for me. Even when I didn't deserve your love. I'm not sure how I'm ever supposed to repay you."

Her face softens and her lips part, and, of course, my eyes are drawn to them. "You don't have to."

Because her lips are practically begging me to kiss her, I lean in, stopping myself right before our lips touch, like I'm asking permission. "Yes." She breathes the word, and it whispers past my lips. My mouth covers hers.

It's the first time we've kissed since the AIG facility after I rescued her from Confinement. In hindsight, that probably wasn't the smartest thing to do. She had just been shot, was still in shock, and trying to process everything.

But hot damn, her lips feel like pillows of fire. They are soft, radiating so much heat I think my head might explode. My hand fits behind her neck, drawing her closer if possible. I would pull her onto my lap, but that may not be appropriate with so many people around. When we do finally pull apart, we're both a little out of breath.

"Sienna?" a motherly voice calls from behind me.

Even before I turn my head, I know who it is. And I have a feeling she saw *everything*. I shoot to my feet while Sienna places her hands to her flaming cheeks.

"Mrs. Preston, it's so nice to finally meet you."

Despite the fact she just caught me making out with her daughter, Mrs. Preston's smile is warm. "Please, call me Vivian. It's so great to see you again. We met in the Ryder's home a while back, but you probably don't remember."

I smile. "Only bits and pieces."

"And there are some pieces," Sienna pipes up, "we both wish we could forget." She's no doubt thinking about Rayne and me.

"How do you like my tent, Mom?" Sienna points to our handiwork a few feet away.

Before Vivian can answer, Emily runs up. When she sees me, she stops and cocks her head to the side. "Trey? Is that you?"

I kneel so I'm at her height. "Hi, Emily. You remember me?"

"Yeah, but you look different. You're really..." She wrinkles her nose. "Dirty."

I laugh along with Sienna and Vivian. Leave it to a kid to tell you the truth. "I hear there's a hot spring around here somewhere. You been yet?"

She shakes her head. "I'm a really good swimmer."

"That's what I've heard."

Her blue eyes study me, no doubt comparing me to Zane whom she spent weeks with. He's like a brother to her now, I'm sure. And I'm just the guy who broke her sister's heart.

Thankfully, she's too young to understand.

"You like to swim?" she finally asks.

"I love to. Just ask Sienna." I wink at Sienna, remembering our time in the Lagoon together. Her cheeks are already pink from being in the sun too long, but now they turn blood red.

Emily crosses her arms over her chest, studying me. Finally, her tone serious, she says, "You may swim with me." She says it like she's bestowing upon me the greatest gift ever given.

This may sound crazy, but I kind of feel like winning her approval is just that—a gift. Her pronouncement, which is especially cute coming from an adorable five-year-old, makes me feel like I've accomplished something huge.

Bowing a little, I say, "Why, thank you for the honor."

As I rise to my feet, Emily slips her hand in Sienna's and whispers loudly to her sister, "Okay, he can stay. I like him because he's cute."

Vivian, Sienna, and I laugh. It isn't until Vivian and Emily walk away to help cook lunch that I notice Sienna discreetly wipe away tears.

"You okay?" I ask.

"I'm fine. Just… memories. They're the worst, you know? Especially because I feel like I'm lying to my mom and sister every time I see them. Every time I don't tell them about my dad."

My hands find her waist. I pull her in until her cheek is pressed against my chest and my chin rests on top of her head. "I know."

I've kept many, many things from those I love. And now

# Fearless

I'm keeping something from her. Something that happened the night the Compound was bombed. Something big.

I'm desperate to shield her from the truth, because I'm not sure how she'll react when she finds out.

# 7

# Zane

The smell of homemade cinnamon buns wafts up the stairs as I throw on a T-shirt and shorts. Clearly Greta has taken up baking this morning, which means she's on the sad side. I can always tell when she is feeling down—she fills our counters and fridges with pies and rolls, cakes and cookies. Baking is cathartic for her. I know she'll never admit it, but the reason she's feeling low is because Vivian and Emily Preston aren't here anymore. Greta got rather attached to them while they stayed in the house.

When I enter the kitchen, I'm surprised to find my father sitting at the counter. Rarely does he come in the kitchen—he prefers his breakfast in the dining room, and can't be bothered by trivial things like dishes and food preparation. He probably thinks the food magically appears in the oven, and then Greta delivers it to the table for him to consume.

"Good morning, Zane," he says in his chipper voice like nothing happened between us yesterday. Then again, my father is extremely good at pretending. He did it for twenty-one years, after all.

I grunt a response, which earns me a stern look from Greta. "Good morning," I mumble.

"I'm glad to see you up. We have a big day planned." He takes a sip from his oversized coffee cup.

"We do?" I look at Greta for help, but she only shrugs and turns away as if she doesn't want to be caught in the middle. I was right, though. There's a large pan of cinnamon rolls on the counter. But when I reach for one, Greta smacks my hand away.

"Get a plate," she chastises.

Following her orders, I take out a plate from the cabinet and a fork from the drawer. Greta dishes up the cinnamon roll, and hands it to me.

"Yes, we do," my father responds. "How do you feel about doing a press conference this morning at eleven o'clock? I think Pacifica needs to know about your impending marriage. It is, after all, less than two weeks away."

"Why, so the paparazzi can crash it? No, thanks."

"Paparazzi means publicity. Publicity equals clients."

"I didn't realize you were lacking in that area," I retort, but then immediately regret it.

"Zane!" Greta says, her mouth agape in horror. It's true, I've never talked to my father with as much disrespect as I have in the past few weeks. Who knew finding out I'm not really his son would set off this angry side in me? I guess he shouldn't be *that* surprised.

"I apologize," I grumble.

My father nods, taking it all in good stride. "It's fine. I think this press conference is necessary, though. I hope you'll be dressed and ready by eleven. If you decide to join me, we'll be in my study." Harlow sets down his coffee mug, gives Greta a nod, and exits the room. His cologne lingers long after he's gone.

As much as I gripe, I'm a fairly obedient son. I'm dressed, ready, and heading down to my father's study at ten minutes to eleven. Camera crews are already setting up their equipment in the wood-paneled room. The oversized study has an aroma of lemon oil and old books, a smell I always loved as a child. Harlow invites me to stand behind his desk with him where a makeshift podium and microphone has been placed.

"Is Arian coming, too?" I ask.

Harlow shakes his head. "No. I thought it was best to have a statement from the head of Match 360 and his son. I hope that's okay."

I shrug. "Fine by me."

At exactly eleven o'clock, bright lights shine on us, cameras point at us, and reporters wait with eager faces.

"Thank you for joining us today," Harlow begins, his face an ever-present display of power and confidence. "It's no secret Match 360 and Chromo 120 are my life. I've spent the better part of my years working alongside some of the most talented scientists that exist today. But today isn't about me. We are holding this press conference because my son, Zane Ryder, the first genetically modified human—" I cringe at his lie, "— has a wonderful announcement he'd like to share with all the Citizens of Pacifica." He gives me an encouraging nod.

Swallowing hard, I plaster a smile on my face as cameras swing in my direction. I've gotten incredibly good at doing this—pretending I'm my father's son, one who is powerful and in control all the time, despite the fact I feel like a phony.

"Many of you know I'm to wed Arian Stratford on November 25th. However, we've decided to push up our wedding to two weeks from now, Saturday, September 30th at the Mosaic Golf and Country Club." Pausing, I clear my throat. "We appreciate all of your well wishes and encouragement, but hope you will respect our desire for this to be a private affair for family and friends only." I nod at the small group. "Thank you all for coming."

One reporter with dark hair raises her hand. "Will you

take questions?"

I glance over at Harlow, who gives a silent nod. "Um, sure," I answer.

"Why the sudden change in a marriage date?" she demands.

Flashing her a winning smile and knowing full well the effect it might have on her, I say, "Arian and I decided we didn't want to wait any longer. We've known we were marrying each other since we were old enough to understand words. Why wait?"

The dark-haired woman falters. Smiling, she takes a step back, opening the way for more questions and raised hands.

"What happened in Rubex?"

"Do you know a woman named Sienna Preston?"

"Is it true you had a relationship with her?"

"What are you and Arian's family plans? Can we expect children soon?"

They hurl questions at me like a firing squad. Holding my hands up in surrender, I say, "I'm happy to answer your questions, but please, let's have them one at a time." I point to a dark-skinned man with glasses. "Why don't you go first?"

"Zane, do you know a girl named Sienna Preston?"

I could easily lie and say I've never met her, never even heard of her. But what good would that do?

"Yes, I do."

"Isn't it true you had a relationship with this girl while you were betrothed to Arian Stratford?"

"I'm not sure what you mean by relationship. We're friends." This doesn't feel like a lie. What we had could never be considered a real relationship. Now, if he'd asked me a few weeks ago if I *wanted* a relationship with a girl named Sienna Preston, that would be a different story. Anything we might have had in Rubex is over now. She made that clear when she chose Trey.

"There are photos of the two of you at the AIG Gala in

Rubex a few weeks ago, before Miss Preston was captured and imprisoned. Isn't it true Miss Preston is a member of the extremist group the Fringe?"

"I honestly wouldn't know the answer. Yes, Miss Preston did attend the Gala with me that night, but only because she was looking for answers."

"What kind of answers, Mr. Ryder?" the reporter presses.

I smile at him before pointing to another reporter. "I think it's someone else's turn to ask a question."

A woman with ochre-colored hair asks where Arian and I plan to live after we're married. I'm not sure what answer I give her—I'm too busy recounting my ambush from that one reporter.

After several more minutes of questions—some a little too personal, such as what mine and Arian's plans for children are, to which I responded something like, "That's something Arian and I will have to discuss,"—Harlow wraps everything up, thanks everyone for coming, and I'm allowed to escape to my room. Ripping off my tie, I shrug off my shirt, feeling peeved by the nosy reporter's questions. I mean, I know my life is one giant fishbowl now that Harlow officially introduced me to society a couple of months ago. But still. There are some things, some people, more specifically, I don't want to talk about.

What Sienna and I had in Rubex was special. It meant something to me.

But it's over now. It's time to move on. Time to be the person I've been groomed since birth to be.

# 8

# Sienna

The Zenith Camp is not at all what I expected. It's more... primitive than I pictured. I'm not complaining, though. It's a million times better than Confinement.

The backdrop of our new home is massive orange cliffs that remind me of the Fire Cliffs back home. But we're a long way from home. That I know for sure.

I'm grateful they're letting a fugitive like me hide out here. Once again, I'm putting everyone who's near me in jeopardy. It sucks.

But mostly, I want to earn my place at this Camp. Make sure Paige knows I'm not just some lazy non-GM girl Trey took a liking to. I'll do whatever it takes to prove myself.

That's why when she assigns me cooking duty, I don't balk. Cooking here is a lot different from in the Fringe Compound. There are no stoves, ovens, or pre-skinned meat. There's a hunting crew who finds and kills the animals, then brings them back to be cleaned by a member of the cooking crew—me.

I'm working on an outdoor tabletop, my hands a bloody mess as I try to skin the rock squirrel that was brought to me earlier. I guess they figured I should start off small. Trey comes up behind me and wraps his arms around my waist, kissing my neck. "You look like a cavewoman," he murmurs in my ear.

"I'd like to see you do this better," I grumble.

Trey gently removes the knife from my hands. "You've mutilated this one. But for future reference," he nods to the basket overflowing with dead squirrels beside me, "here's what you do." He lays the squirrel on its back, then makes a small incision at the tail. "Once you've made your cut on the back, grasp the tail and back skin between the thumb and index finger of one hand, then use the knife to continue skinning a few inches down the back."

When he does it, he makes it look easy. "Now here comes the tricky part," he says. "Lay the squirrel on a rock or log." He places the squirrel on a chopping block beside the table. "Then grasp the squirrel's hind legs and place a foot on top of the tail and back skin. You want to put enough pressure so the skin is held tightly under your shoe." He grasps the hind legs, putting his foot on the tail. "Then slowly pull up on the squirrel's hind legs. You want to work your fingers in there as you gently pull. The squirrel's shirt and pants should come off."

"I'm sorry, did you say shirt and pants?"

Trey chuckles. "Yeah, that's what they call the skin of the squirrel."

The skin of the squirrel slips right off. Now that the squirrel is naked and looks like a hairless rat, Trey puts it back on the table and cuts off the head and legs. He then slices the belly open to remove the entrails. The smell is horrendous, and that's when I about lose my lunch. Gagging, I take a step back.

"Are you freaking kidding me?" I say.

"What?" Trey asks innocently.

"I have to do all of these?" I indicate the pile next to me.

Trey winks at me as he pauses in cutting the squirrel into parts. It looks more like raw meat now instead of a dead animal. "No worries. I'll help you."

A part of me wants to say, *Yes, thank you*! but accepting Trey's help won't earn my place at this Camp or Paige's approval. I know she must think I'm some weakling who always needs to be rescued. And I'm here to prove her wrong.

I'm still curious about her and Trey's relationship, though.

"Can I ask you something?" I say as Trey tosses the squirrel chunks into a bowl before beginning to skin the next one.

"Anything."

I grab a squirrel from the pile, pick up the spare knife, and try to do as Trey showed me, making a cut along the back. The skin is thick and tough, but the knife finally gets through. "So, um, about you and Paige and that history you mentioned…"

"What about it?" Trey's eyes are still focused on the squirrel in front of him.

"It's something Asher said… Never mind. I'm sure I'm overreacting."

Trey is silent for a minute, his forehead furrowed as he works on getting the skin off the squirrel. Finally, he clears his throat.

"Remember the scar on my stomach? And the girl I said I hit on—one of the Devil's girls—that earned me this scar?"

Laying my squirrel down, I turn and face him. "Yeah."

He clears his throat again. "Paige was the girl."

My head is spinning. "What? How? I mean, she's a GM, right? How did she end up with the Devil?"

"He's her father."

"I'm sorry. What?"

"Yeah. He found her on the streets and took her in, adopted her. She had no idea who she was, no memory of being in the AIG facility. I'm the one who recognized her for what she was—a GM."

"So you saw her in this bar, tried to hit on her, and the Devil's men pulled knives on you and Nash?"

"Pretty much."

"And then what happened?"

He glances at me, confusion lining his face. "What do you mean?"

"I mean, how did Paige end up here when the last you saw her she was with the Devil and his men?"

"There's a little more to the story," he hedges.

I cross my arms over my chest, careful to avoid my bloody hands. "I'm waiting."

Sighing, Trey puts down the knife and squirrel. His fingertips press into the table as he turns his head to look at me. "Paige helped Nash and me after we were stabbed. When she found out she's a GM, she decided to leave her father and join us at the Fringe Compound. She stayed with us for a few months but eventually left to find others like herself. Some of the GMs in the Compound went with her. She then started Zenith."

There's something he's not telling me. His eyes shifted when he said she came to stay in the Compound. "Wait. Were you two…" I struggle for the right word. The one that won't make me look and sound like a jealous girlfriend. "Together?"

Trey hesitates, but then nods. "It was a long time ago. History. Paige and I are history."

My throat tightens. "Right. Of course." I busy myself with my dead squirrel. I can feel Trey's eyes on me, so I'm not surprised when he takes the squirrel from my hands and forces me to look at him.

"Sienna, hey. It's over between Paige and me. It was nothing, really."

At first, I don't want to meet his eyes. I'm afraid of what he might see. The doubt, the confusion, the sadness. This isn't about Trey and Paige—it's really not. But it's the final straw. First, I lose my father, then Zane, and now I feel like I'm losing Trey all over again. Except this time, he's in his right mind. Which makes it all the worse.

I'm cleaning my hands in the stream that runs alongside the Camp when Trey finds me.

Something's up. He keeps clearing his throat, his eyes focused on the ground in front of him. "What's wrong?"

"Nothing." His answer comes a little too quickly, so I naturally assume the opposite.

Wiping my hands on my pants, I move toward him. "Trey, what is it?"

His eyes won't meet mine. "There was a press conference this afternoon in Legas. I've been trying to keep up with the news and the Enforcers' hunt for you and Trina. I figured it might help us stay on top of it if we know where they're searching."

My chest squeezes. Have they found us? "What happened?"

"Well, this report wasn't about the escaped convicts. It was about…" Pausing, he clears his throat again. Something he's about to say is making him uncomfortable.

"It's about what, Trey? Tell me."

"Zane. It was about Zane. Apparently, he and Arian have decided to get married sooner than expected."

My heart drops to the ground. "When? Did they say when?"

"Next Saturday."

"Next Saturday? As in eight days from now?"

"Yes." For the first time, he looks directly at me. "I'm sorry, Sienna."

Drawing in a deep breath, I turn away. Zane said he was going back to Arian, but I never imagined this. I'm not sure what I thought would happen, but after everything that transpired between us, how can he marry her? And so soon?

*Because he chose her.*

*Because she's his perfect genetic match.*

*And I'm not.*

Trey interrupts the conversation in my head by laying a

hand on my arm. "You okay?"

I force a smile. "I will be."

"I debated whether I should tell you—"

"No, I'm glad you did."

Trey holds out his hand, inviting me to take it. "Walk you back?"

"Sure." I slip my hand into his.

In silence, we make our way back to Camp, Trey glancing over at me and giving my hand an occasional squeeze. I can tell he wants to say something, but he's not sure how. Or what.

When we reach Camp, Trey is called over to the campfire for an impromptu leadership meeting. Of course, since Paige and Trey are the only leaders here, it's a two-person meeting. And a front for spending more time with Trey. After he kisses my hand, he promises to find me later.

Trey strides over to Paige. I watch as she slips an arm through his, pulling him away and out of earshot. My fists clench.

Before I can do something stupid, an arm wraps around my shoulders and a familiar voice whispers in my ear, "Check that temper, Tiny Spice."

I turn to find Trina grinning at me. "Tiny Spice? Where did that name come from?"

"Grey. He's totally into giving people nicknames. Did you know he has a name for every single person at this Camp? Trey is Macho, because duh. Asher is Stoic because he doesn't say much. I'm Tiger Lily because I'm fierce and beautiful." She smiles widely at this. "Those were his words, not mine." She clicks her tongue. "Hmm, who else? Paige is Dreads because of her hair. Oh! And Nash is Scarface. That one is self-explanatory and not very original. I told him he needs to come up with a better one for him."

"So I'm Tiny Spice, huh?"

"Totally. I mean, don't you think it fits? You're tiny, and

you have this spicy-hot personality. It's perfect."

I laugh at Trina's enthusiasm. This is the happiest I've seen her since—well, since Curly died.

"You really like Grey, don't you?" I say. The two of them have been practically inseparable since we arrived at Camp. There was something stirring in the desert between them, but it's now a full-fledged flame.

"He makes me laugh, and he's constantly telling me I'm beautiful." She shrugs. "What's not to like?"

"Humor and flattery. The two great requisites for any healthy relationship."

Trina laughs, slipping her arm through mine. "Where are you headed? We have a ton of catching up to do."

My mind flits to what Trey told me by the stream. "Do you know?" I ask. "About Zane?"

Trina shakes her head, her forehead crinkling in concern. "Is he okay?"

"Yeah, he's fine." I lead her over to the same homemade bench Trey and I sat on the other day when he asked me about Confinement. It's not the most comfortable thing to sit on, but it'll do. "He's marrying Arian on Saturday."

"Wait. What?"

"Exactly."

Trina shakes her head. "I don't understand. Zane is marrying Arian? On Saturday? As in eight days from now? What the heck happened between the two of you? I thought he called the wedding off."

I twist my hands in my lap. "I couldn't tell him I loved him. And now, it's too late."

"But do you? Love him? What about Trey?"

My head drops into my hands. "I don't know," I moan. I straighten up. "I want to be over Zane. I love Trey, I really do. But then why does it hurt so much when I hear Zane is marrying someone else? I know I can't have both. I should just be happy for Zane, right?"

Trina's hand covers mine. "It's not that easy when you love someone."

"How is it possible to love two people at the same time?"

"I don't know, exactly. I guess our hearts are bigger than we realize."

Heat presses against the backs of my eyes. "What if you don't want to love someone anymore?" I whisper. "How do you move on? How do you get over them?"

Trina takes her hand back, resting it in her lap as she stares down at the ground. "It takes time. That's all. And seeing them happy with someone else." When she looks up, her eyes are watery. "I loved Trey, you know. For a long time. I've seen him with other girls. I watched him choose you. And I won't lie. It hurt." She smiles at me, a genuine one that warms me to the core. "But then I saw something else. I saw how happy he was when he was with you. I saw that you made him better, less rough, less *Trey*. And I knew you were the right one for him. Do I still love him? Sure. I probably always will. But seeing the two of you together doesn't make me sad anymore. It only makes me happy."

Tears fill my eyes and slide down my cheeks. I wrap my arms around her, burying my face in her hair. "Thank you, Trina. Thank you for not hating me. I didn't mean to fall for the guy you loved."

Trina laughs and pulls back, wiping the tears from my eyes. "How could I ever hate you, Tiny Spice? You're the best friend a girl could hope for."

# 9

## Zane

I'm on my way up from the basement after lifting weights when the doorbell rings. Since I'm close, I call to Henry that I'll get it, and then answer the door myself. Two uniform-clad Enforcers stand on the porch. They remove their sunglasses simultaneously as the taller one says, "Zane Ryder?"

"Yes, I'm Zane."

"May we come in? We have a few questions for you concerning a girl named Sienna Preston."

I stare at them a beat too long, my mind whirling through scenarios. Was she caught? Do they know her location? Is she in danger? Trying to play it cool, I invite them in and ask if they'd like something to drink.

"No, thanks," the taller Enforcer says, settling on the couch in our living room. "We don't plan to be here long."

I take a seat across from them in an armchair. "What can I do for you?"

The other Enforcer, the quieter one, leans forward. In a gruff voice, he asks, "What is your relationship with Miss Preston?"

There's no sense denying the truth. I already announced our relationship during the press release when that reporter hounded me. "We're friends."

"Did you help her escape from Confinement?"

Oh, crap. I try to keep my voice steady and my face impassive. "Of course not."

"Do you know who did?"

"No."

"But do you deny you were in Rubex with her before her arrest?"

"We were together, yes. But then I left to come back to Legas to tend to some business here. Sienna stayed, and that's when she was falsely accused of murder."

The two Enforcers exchange a look. "Falsely?"

I quickly realize my mistake. "Sienna would never do such a thing. Of course she was falsely accused."

The taller one asks, "Have you had contact since she escaped Confinement?"

"No."

"Would you inform the authorities if you did?"

I don't like where these questions are leading. They're sniffing me out, waiting for me to stumble so they can attack. Now is probably when I should lawyer up. I rise quickly from my chair. "Look, I wish I could be more helpful, but I haven't spoken to Sienna in several weeks. I do, however, think it's time for you to go."

The Enforcers stand as well. "Just one more question, Mr. Ryder. We've been reviewing your bank statements, and we've noticed several large purchases in the last few weeks. Motel rooms? A boat in Rubex? Girl clothes and sneakers in two different sizes?" The tall one's eyes narrow. "Is there a reason for these purchases?"

Damn that paper trail. I should have known it was traceable. I offer my brightest smile. "Gifts for my future bride. Unfortunately, I'm still learning her size."

"That doesn't explain the motel rooms."

If I act like a cocky jerk, maybe they'll believe me. I am, after all, Zane Ryder. I spread my arms wide. "Guys, I'm on the verge of getting married. Bachelor parties, of course."

The two men exchange a glance before the taller one clears his throat and pulls out his Lynk. He appears to check something on it. "We're sorry to have bothered you, Mr. Ryder. Thanks for your time."

I show them to the door. I'm closing it behind them when the foyer rug shifts, getting caught in the mahogany door. I open the door again to fix the rug, just in time to hear one Enforcer say to the other, "Well, that was a big waste of time. Kid doesn't know anything." I watch as they walk down the sidewalk to their cruiser parked in the driveway.

As I close the door again, I exhale and lean my back against it. Crud. They went through my bank statements. Can they do that?

Probably… if there's cause for suspicion.

What if they come back? What if they dig deeper? They believe me now, but what if they find something that spins around everything I said?

Taking a deep breath, I push away from the door. It's okay. Next time, I'll be prepared.

# 10

## Trey

Tonight, it's my turn to man the watchtower, and I've invited Sienna to join me. Things have been a little off between us ever since she found out Zane is getting married in less than two weeks. I know something happened between her and Zane in Rubex. It's obvious she still has feelings for him. And I know she easily could have chosen him over me.

Sometimes I wonder why she didn't. I don't exactly have much to offer her. And Zane could give her the world.

Before our shift begins, I ask Jared if I can borrow the comscreen. I've been doing this every day since we arrived at the Zenith Camp. I'm sure he's vigilant, but if the government is on to our location, I want to be the first to know. I don't trust anyone else to pass on the information.

With the comscreen in hand, I find a quiet spot, slightly away from Camp and near a cliff overhang. I scroll through news station after news station before doing a more detailed search for any news regarding Sienna Preston or the Fringe. There are a couple of hits. I click on the link, and it takes me to a recorded interview with Madame Neiman, the Assistant President of Pacifica.

"We are using all of our resources to locate Sienna Preston and the remaining Fringe members. It is our top priority.

Our country is not safe until they're locked up behind bars." Madame Neiman averts her eyes from the interviewer and glares right at the camera. "Until they're executed."

My fingers tighten around the comscreen until my knuckles turn white. Madame Neiman and her flair for drama. She's welcome to search for us, but good luck finding us way out here.

I click on another link that references the Fringe. It's a news reporter, holding a microphone in front of the president's home in Rubex. The behemoth gray structure towers behind her like a formidable opponent. "Sources close to the president say they believe the Fringe are hiding out in the desert. No specific location has been given. But if you see these members of the terrorist group, authorities are asking you to contact them immediately."

The screen flashes with headshots of Sienna, Trina, and then myself. The picture they're using for me is from my photo ID for the AIG, when I had a computer chip in my head making me believe I worked for the government and was engaged to a girl named Rayne Williams. I'm wearing a monkey suit, the only time in my life I'd been caught dead wearing one of those. Clothes like that are too formal, too... restricting. It's weird seeing myself dressed that way.

After I turn off the screen, I return it to Jared who sits at a makeshift surveillance station. I say makeshift because all it consists of is a couple comscreens and some walkie talkies. Better than nothing, I guess.

As I walk to Sienna's tent to get her for our shift, my mind replays the news reports. So far, we're in the clear. Sounds like the government is stumped about our location, and they're fumbling in the dark. They think we're hiding in the desert. The desert? Really? It's almost laughable considering the desert covers a good portion of Pacifica. Like unearthing a needle in a haystack.

I find Sienna at a picnic table, playing cards with her mom and sister. She slaps her hand down on top of a pile of cards and cries out, "I win!"

"Nooooo," Emily squeals. "That's no fair. You always win."

Sienna laughs. "That's not true. I let you win the last game."

"But I don't want you to let me win," Emily protests. "I want to win on my own."

"And someday you will, sweetheart," Vivian says in her soothing voice. Sienna's mom has to be one of the nicest people I've ever met. She's an older version of Sienna, and I love seeing how Sienna will age in twenty plus years.

I could stand here and watch Sienna interact with her family all day. When she's with them, her layers are peeled back, exposing who she really is. She's the happiest when they're together.

When Sienna's mom sees me, she gives me a warm smile. "I dare say there's a handsome young man checking you out," she teases, nudging her daughter.

I say hi to Mrs. Preston and Emily as Sienna jumps up from the table. "Sorry, guys, gotta go. Duty calls."

I hate that I'm taking her away from her family. "You can stay here, if you want?"

Sienna rises on her toes and gives me a quick kiss on the cheek, to which Emily giggles and says, "Ooooh, Si-Si has a boyyyfriend."

Sienna rolls her eyes, looping her arm through mine. "No, I want to come. Besides, I promised to keep you company."

"Trey," Emily calls, patting the seat beside her. "Can you play a game with us? Puh-lease?"

"Trey and I have watchtower duty, Em. He can't stay."

Emily's face falls.

We still have a few minutes before our shift. I plop down beside Emily and say, "Sure. What game are we playing?"

"Trey, I thought we—"

I wave away Sienna's concern. "We have some time."

"Do you know how to play Slapjack?" Emily asks.

"Can't say I've played that one before. Will you teach me?"

Emily beams up at me. "Of course. I'm very good at that one."

Chuckling at her hubris, I say, "I guess that gives me an advantage, you know, being trained by the best and all."

Emily folds her arms in front of her and says, "Yes. It does."

Sienna takes a seat across from me and Emily, next to her mother. Emily starts dealing out the cards, but Sienna stops her. "Wait, Em, we have to shuffle them first."

Emily's back straightens like she can't believe her sister dared to correct her. "I know *that*, Si-Si. I was just getting them ready for you." She gathers them up, then hands them to me. "You shuffle."

I can't remember the last time I had a deck of cards in my hands, but it's just like shooting a gun—you remember how to do it even if it's been a while. We used to play cards all the time in the Compound, especially when we were bored as kids. I taught myself a few card tricks, then mastered a few different shuffles. And with Sienna, her mom, and her sister staring at me, I want to show off what I know.

"Do you want an overhand, a riffle, or a pharaoh shuffle?" I ask, my hands flipping and bridging the cards.

Emily's mouth drops open. "Whoa, that's cool."

"Let's see a riffle," Sienna says, her eyes never leaving the deck.

"A riffle it is." I divvy up the deck, dropping half into my hand, then I lever them up and do a bridge shuffle. The cards fall into place like a cascading waterfall.

Sienna gives a low whistle. "Impressive."

"Your father was good at shuffling," Mrs. Preston breaks in. "I never understood how he could do it."

"Let's see the other one," Emily says, her eyes wide.

"Overhand?" I ask. I may be enjoying the attention a little too much, but Zane captured Emily's heart with all the swimming they did together. If I can impress her or her mother, I'm certainly going to try.

Emily giggles. "Yes! That one."

"Okay. You just hold the cards like this, break them, then, using your thumb, you deal off the cards into your other hand like this—" I demonstrate how to do it. "The cool thing is that magicians use this trick to keep certain cards on top. Like this." I show off the top cards, which happen to be an ace of spades, a ten of hearts, and a king of diamonds. I do an overhand shuffle, cutting and breaking in the right places. When I'm finished, I uncover the top cards. "See, same cards from before."

Emily's eyes go round as saucers. "Whoa. That was the coolest trick ever."

I laugh at that. It's a mild trick, but the fact she's impressed means I'm doing something right.

"Now do the other one," Emily says.

Sienna rises to her feet, the darkness now closing in. The sun goes down so fast here. One second, it's sunset and the next, it's full-on darkness. "We have to go, Em."

Reluctantly, I stand also. I'd rather stay here and play with Sienna's family, but responsibilities never wait.

"But we didn't get to play the game," Emily protests.

"How about tomorrow?" I suggest. "Can we take a rain check for tomorrow?"

Emily purses her lips together and sighs. "I guess."

"Will you be safe in that watchtower?" Mrs. Preston asks, her eyes worried.

"Don't worry, Mom," Sienna says, looping her arm through mine. "I'm always safe with Trey."

I clear my throat and stand a little taller, her declaration making me want to prove myself. "I promise I'll keep her safe, Mrs. Preston."

Sienna blows her mom and sister a kiss. "I'll be back before morning."

"Byyeee, Trey. Byyeee, Si-Si," Emily calls out in a singsong voice before turning her attention to the cards on the table. "Hey, Mama, wanna play Find the Fish?"

As we walk away, toward the watchtower, I say to Sienna, "You're pretty lucky, you know."

"How so?"

"You have a great family."

She smiles up at me. "I do, don't I?" Her arm tightens around mine as we pass the campfire and Paige looks up, watching us with narrowed eyes. "You know, Emily really likes you."

This information gives me a serious kick in the chest. I like hearing this. "She's a fun kid."

Sienna clears her throat, one hand rubbing my arm. "She gets… attached to people sometimes."

"Most kids do, right? I mean, that's not a bad thing, is it?"

It takes her a second to respond, and then her words come out measured like she's carefully choosing each one. "Not as long as the object of their affection sticks around."

Ah, I see where this is headed. She's worried I'll leave her again and break not only her heart, but also her sister's as well. How can I prove I'm not going anywhere this time? Not without her.

I tug her to a stop, so I can see her. "She doesn't need to worry. And neither do you."

"But you do realize she's already lost so much. First my father, then Zane—" She stops herself, biting her lip. "I'm sorry. I don't mean to imply you'll leave like Zane did."

A muscle in my jaw clenches. Zane. Zane. It will always be Zane. I will always be compared to the golden boy and his golden attributes. But I can promise her something Zane couldn't.

"I know he hurt you when he chose to go back to Legas. But this is my promise to you—wherever you are, I am." I force a chuckle. "Unless you get sick of me and want me to leave you alone. Then I guess I'd have to respect your wishes."

Sienna grins. "So what you're saying is I'm stuck with you?"

"Yes. Indefinitely."

Sienna loops her arm through mine again, and we resume walking toward the tower. "I think I can handle that."

The watchtower is a wooden platform rising ten feet from the ground on the edge of Camp. Crudely constructed wooden slats form rungs to climb into the tower. Sienna goes first, and I follow. The moon is just bright enough that it allows us to see everything, from one cliff strand to another several miles away.

The platform has one rickety railing that's great for propping a gun, but not really for leaning against. For the first two hours, Sienna and I stand, our eyes scanning the surrounding areas, our rifles ready. At one point, Sienna tips her head back and says, "The stars are beautiful here."

Sienna is a sucker for the stars. I don't know much about them.

"You know," she continues, "I used to believe our world was divided by this thin, sheer *something* that allowed those on the other side to watch us. That those stars were just tiny flashlights of the people on the other side, guiding us, leading us, making it so the night is never so dark we can't see. That even when all feels lost, there's hope."

I like that sentiment. I've never really thought about other worlds or people other than us, but it's kind of cool to think this world is bigger than we realize, maybe even better than we realize.

"Do you think there's hope, Trey? Hope for the Fringe?

Hope for me?"

"What do you mean?"

She turns and faces me, leaning against the railing. When it moves a little, she pushes away from it. "I mean, is there hope for us to have a normal life? Will we always be hiding? Always be running?"

This has been on my mind a lot lately. The Fringe members seem content so far, but what happens when they get restless? Our sole purpose has been to rescue people. To thwart the government's attempts to genetically alter juvenile delinquents. If we're not doing that, then who are we? Why are we hiding?

I answer as truthfully as I can. "I don't know." When Sienna sighs and turns away, my hand encircles her arm, pulling her back. "I don't know what the future will bring. But I do have hope. I have hope that the deaths of Jeb and Garrett and all those in the Compound, even your father's death, were not in vain. Things will get better. They have to."

"I want to believe that," Sienna whispers, looking up at me. "I really do."

"But?"

"But things always get worse before they get better."

I think of the Upheaval and all the devastation and destruction that occurred as a result, years before I was born. I think of everyone I've lost, even those I've never met, like my own mother. All those people I was responsible for in the Compound, and all the people dead because of me. Hell, the girl I love was almost executed because of me.

When I think of everything we've endured, all the people we've lost, I can't imagine it getting much worse than this.

# 11

## Zane

I'm embarrassed to admit I've never taken Arian on a proper date. Sure, we've shopped for china and linens and our future home, but we've never been to dinner together or done any of the usual things couples do. Tonight, I will remedy that.

I arrive at Arian's house as the sun is setting, the sky a day-old bruise. It gets chilly at night, so I'm wearing pants and a long-sleeved button down. That's why when Arian comes to the door in a black sleeveless dress, I'm more than a little surprised. Especially since the night I've planned is mostly outdoors.

"Won't you be chilly?" I murmur, tearing my eyes away from her endless legs.

"Oh, right. Let me grab a jacket." She hurries to the hall closet and pulls out a black coat. "This should do it," she says with a smile.

I follow her out. When we reach my car, I hold her door for her. As she slips inside, her dress hikes up, exposing the length of one silky leg. Embarrassed, I turn away until she's situated.

Once we're on the road, Arian says, "I'm so glad we're finally doing this."

"Me too. I'm sorry it's taken me this long to ask you out properly. I guess I've been... distracted."

"I know." Her voice is soft when she speaks. "But you aren't entirely to blame. Our courtship has been a bit... unconventional. The other GMs have been cavorting with their matches since they were young enough to walk. I wonder why your father felt it necessary to keep us apart?"

There's only one reason I can think of, but I'm not about to mention it to Arian.

His name is Trey.

Maybe my father intended to find Trey and bring him home to take his place as the rightful heir and match to Arian. Maybe he knew our match was a shoddy sham, and he didn't want to flaunt it any more than he had to. Whatever his reason, I don't really want to ask him. "I don't know," I answer.

"Not that I'm complaining," she adds quickly. "Your father is a genius, so I'm sure his reasons were sound."

"Yes. He's a genius."

"The apple doesn't fall far from the tree," she says with a teasing smile. "You're just like him. You know that, right? Someday, you'll take his company to new heights. And I can't wait to be by your side when you do."

My hands tighten on the steering wheel as guilt seizes me. I promised myself no more lies, and here I am, still lying to Arian. She doesn't know Harlow isn't my biological dad, or that I'm not the first genetically modified man, or that I'm not the match created for her. Telling her would destroy her view of everything. Is it wrong I want to protect her innocence by keeping her away from the truth? Once she knows, she can't go back to not knowing.

Reaching across, I squeeze her hand. "Me too. I can't wait for that, too."

We ride in silence until we arrive at the base of a small mountain. The sun has now dipped beyond the horizon, and the sky is getting darker. I park the car, hop out of my seat, and hurry to her side, offering my hand as she climbs out. She takes it, slipping her fingers through mine. I expect to feel an electric pulse, a burst of energy, tingling fingertips. Something. But sadly, there's only clammy skin against clammy skin. I ignore this, focusing instead on her beautiful face. Many married couples lack chemistry and still have a happy, successful marriage. Attraction is great, but it isn't everything.

I let go of her hand long enough to pull a blanket and a basket from the trunk of my car. Hand in hand, we walk toward the mountain, Arian glancing around nervously. "Where are we going?" she asks.

"Only a little way." She clearly doesn't have the right shoes on as she stumbles over the few small rocks on the path. I slow down so it's easier for her.

Once we've made it midway up the hill, we exit the path and find a place to lay the blanket. It's mostly dirt up here, and I'm feeling worse and worse about the execution of this date. Arian looks miserable as she kicks off her shoes and sinks down, ever so gracefully, on the edge of the blanket.

Food always takes my mind off things, so I immediately open the basket and pull out an array of cheese, crackers, and grapes, along with a bottle of wine and two glasses wrapped in a towel. A grin spreads across her face when she sees the bottle. "You thought of everything," she says.

I pour a glass and hand it to her. As she takes a sip, she closes her eyes. Considering I snagged this bottle from my father's wine collection, it's bound to be good. He acquires nothing but the best.

Leaning back on my elbows, I watch as Arian relaxes a little. Her dark hair was pulled up in a fancy twist-thing, but now tendrils hang in messy curls, framing her face. "Tell me something I don't know," I say.

"About?"

"About you. Your family. Whatever you want."

Arian purses her lips, thinking. "I don't really know what

to tell."

Heaven help me, even though I don't want to, I picture Sienna sitting beside me on the Rubex beach, pointing at the sky, sharing her love of the stars and how her father taught her all the constellations. I can still remember how magical that night was, how beautiful she looked in the moonlight, how soft her skin was.

Clearing my throat, I sit up straight, forcing the image of Sienna from my mind. "Come on, there must be something I don't know about you."

Arian studies her hands before glancing at me through her lashes. It's such an un-Arian-like gesture that for a moment, I'm afraid I've misjudged her. Maybe there's a soft spot underneath all those designer clothes and elaborate hairstyles.

"I like to sing," she says shyly.

"Really?" I'm immediately interested in this.

"Yeah. I don't think I'm particularly good. It wasn't a priority of my parents for me to excel in the arts. But I love to sing in the shower or my car—as long as no one is around."

"Can I hear you?"

She vehemently shakes her head. "Too embarrassing."

"Aw, come on."

"No way!" She scoots away as I reach for her.

"What if I don't take no for an answer?" I move beside her, tickling her stomach.

Giggling, she falls back on the blanket and tries to swat my hands away. But I'm too quick; I pin her hands down, hovering over her. Our eyes connect and her smile fades, her breath catching. I lean in and kiss her gently, the taste of wine still sweet on her lips. But kissing her reminds me of kissing Sienna on another night, under another starry sky.

Pulling away, I rock back on my heels before settling on the other side of the blanket. Arian slowly sits up, pinning her hair into place and straightening her dress. Forcing a smile, she says, "I hear you play the piano."

Like a well-bred woman, she's able to switch subjects effortlessly, avoiding the landmine topics, like why I pulled away. For that, I'm grateful. "I've been playing since I was three."

"I think it's great your father has a love of the arts, and wanted you to have a musical talent. I wish my parents had the same vision for me," she says wistfully. She takes another sip of the wine, then sighs.

I feel awful keeping the truth from her. If we're going to be married, shouldn't there be no secrets between us?

Tilting my head back, I stare at the stars, the night sky so close it's like I can reach out and hold a star in my hand. I lay back to get a better view. Arian joins me, her face only inches from mine, her hands resting on her stomach.

"You know the constellations?" I ask.

"Only the basic ones. Big Dipper, Little Dipper—the ones everyone can find."

I point to one constellation in particular. "You see that W shape? That's Cassiopeia. And that one in the shape of a bull? That's Taurus."

When Arian doesn't say anything, I glance over at her. She's squinting at the sky, her forehead lined with concentration, then blows air from her lips in frustration. "Don't see it. Truth is, I've always had a hard time with the constellations." Turning her head toward me, she says, "I didn't realize you were such an expert."

"I'm not. Sienna taught me—" I stop myself. "I'm sorry."

Arian sits up and scoots away, her fingers kneading the edges of the blanket. "You don't have to apologize," she says. "As long as it's in the past, I don't care."

"It is," I assure her as I sit up. "It's all in the past."

Arian goes quiet, chewing on her bottom lip. As the silence lengthens, I pop a couple of grapes in my mouth.

"Would you choose this?" Arian asks suddenly. I stop

chewing, waiting for her to elaborate. "I mean, if this wasn't already your life, would you choose it? This life as a GM?"

I swallow the grapes as I contemplate her question. Would I choose this life? After all I've learned...

Probably not.

"I don't know."

Arian frowns like she doesn't believe me. "I wouldn't," she says.

The shock must be evident on my face. "You—you wouldn't? But I thought this was what you wanted."

"It was. I mean, it is. It's what my parents want, and I don't want to disappoint them. Plus, I know what we can become, and the idea of that excites me. Knowing we were made for each other means something. Don't you think?"

My fingers curl around the blanket, clutching it in a tight fist. I hate keeping this from her. But if she knew—there's no way she'd marry me. "So if it's what you want, then why wouldn't you choose this life? I'm not sure I follow."

Arian gives me a sad smile. "Don't you ever wonder what it would be like to live a normal life? One where you aren't genetically modified or betrothed since birth?"

"You mean like Sienna?"

"Yeah. I guess like Sienna."

I chuckle. "Of course I've wondered. This life is a blessing, but it's also a curse. Our ability to choose has been taken from us."

Arian nods. "Yeah. Exactly."

I know in that moment I have to tell her. She may not want to marry me after what she hears. But I refuse to be the one who takes away that choice.

"Arian, there's something you need to know."

She stares at me, not saying anything, her hands twisting in her lap. She nods once like she's ready for me to speak. But before I can get the words out, she says, "I already know what you're going to say."

"You do?"

"Yeah." Her eyes won't meet mine. "I know you don't love me. And that's okay. I'm okay with it." Her eyes shift, filling with tears. "But maybe you can grow to love me? Someday, maybe you'll feel for me the way you do for *her*. Will you try? Can you promise me you'll try?"

There's a barbell on my chest, pressing against my diaphragm. "Of course I'll try." I take her hands in mine, marveling at how long and slender her fingers are. She has great piano hands. "My goal for the rest of our lives will be to make you happy. Your happiness is the only thing I care about. Now and forever. That's my promise to you."

Arian smiles, and it's a genuine one that warms my insides. Not for the first time am I in awe of her beauty. "That's all I can hope for."

She kisses me then, and thank the constellations above, the only thing I'm thinking about is Arian, her lips, and the family we're about to create.

# 12

## Sienna

The Zenith Camp has a nightly tradition of erecting a bonfire in the center of Camp. It's where people gather to relax and tell stories. Mom and Emily always go to bed early and miss this, but it's one of my favorite things about this place. Tonight, they're playing a game called *In Another Life* where people take turns saying what they would've been if they'd lived a different life.

As I share a rock with Trey, I look through the haze of smoke and dancing embers at Trina. She is positively beaming as she leans against Grey. When she catches me staring, she gives a little smile and wave before snuggling closer to Grey. I wave back.

It's Grey's turn, and he looks at Trina and says, "In another life, I would have been a baseball player."

Trina exclaims, "I didn't know you like baseball!"

"Like it? I love it. Though I've never played on a real team or anything. Only on that patch of dirt over there." He points behind him to the open expanse of desert at the base of the cliffs. He then says to Trina, "Your turn."

Trina purses her lips, thinking. "Hmm, okay, I've got it. In another life, I would've been a doctor. I enjoy helping people, plus blood and stuff doesn't really make me squeamish."

"Great qualities in a doctor," Grey says, smiling.

Trina entwines her arm with his and kisses his cheek. "A doctor and a baseball player? It could work."

"All right, who's next?" Paige calls out. She glances right at me, then away. "Nash? How about you?"

Nash is across from me and to my left. The flames from the fire cast half his face in the dark while the other half glows orange. Nash shrugs and says, "In another life, I'd be married with two-point-five kids and a dog named Harvey."

Everyone goes quiet. The only sound is the crackling of logs. This is so out of character for the *Commander*, the man who lives to blow things up, that I think everyone is surprised, if not downright shocked.

Nash shoots to his feet. "Whatever. This game is dumb." He saunters away.

"Annnnd, that was interesting," Paige says once he's out of earshot.

"And enlightening," someone else pipes up. The crowd around the campfire titters.

"Okay, who's next?" Paige raises an eyebrow in our direction. "Trey?"

Now that all the attention is on him, Trey clears his throat. "Ah, I don't know. I mean, I've never really thought about it. This has always been my life."

"Come on, Trey," Trina yells across the campfire. "Dig deep!"

Trey chuckles. "All right, all right, let's see. I think I would've been—"

"You have to say in another life!" someone calls out.

"Oh, right. Sorry. In another life, I would've been a politician. But not a corrupt one. I like the idea of overseeing the laws that affect our Province. Hell, I'd like to be the one making the laws so they're fair and inclusive."

A few people clap at his answer.

"And now," Trey says, "I'm passing the baton to Sienna."

He pretends to hand me something.

Laughing, I take the pretend baton from him. "Okay, let's see. In another life, I would've been… a spy. I like the idea of taking down the bad guys, and I think I'm fairly good at sneaking into places."

"Very good," Trey agrees.

Paige then chooses someone else to share, and Trey leans over to whisper in my ear. "If I was a politician, I'd hire you in an instant."

"We'd make a pretty good team. You'd make laws, and I'd fight the bad guys. Though we probably wouldn't see much of each other. We'd be so busy. You know, saving the world and all."

Trey chuckles, lacing his fingers through mine. I snuggle closer to him as my eyes rest on Trina. She's giggling at something Grey said.

"Trina looks happy," I say.

"I'm glad she found someone," he says. "And a GM no less."

"Should we check to see if they're a perfect match?" I joke.

Trey chuckles again. "No need. One look and I'd say they are."

I'm not sure what possesses these next words to pop from my mouth. Maybe I'm still testing him, wanting him to prove himself to me. "Maybe it's time you find your own GM match. I mean, now that you *know*… you might as well live up to expectations."

Trey's eyes are serious as he guides my chin so I'm forced to look at him. "There's only one girl for me, and you know it."

My heart melts, but I can't let him see my weakness. Instead, I say the most ridiculous thing ever. "You never know, Paige could be the one for you." As soon as the words leave my mouth, I bite the inside of my cheek. *Stupid girl.*

Trey's face hardens as he lets go of my hand and turns away, his eyes narrowed as he studies the fire. The heat from the flames licks at my already-burning face, the smoke curling toward the sky. My hand suddenly feels cold without the warmth of his.

I try to think of something to say to fix the damage, to erase my words. But that's the thing about words. Once they're out there, they can't be taken back.

*Are you trying to sabotage this new relationship with Trey? Cause if so, you're doing a darn good job.*

I hesitantly rest my hand on his back. He stiffens at my touch. Leaning toward him until my lips are only inches from his ear, I whisper, "I'm sorry, Trey. I shouldn't have said that."

He straightens, his face a mask. "Then why did you?"

"I don't know." That's not entirely true. I'm afraid of being hurt again, afraid of his rejection. It was incredibly painful when he chose Rayne over me. I know he wasn't in his right mind. He'd had his life stolen from him, and that's all he knew. But still. It hurt. I'm scared the same thing will happen with Paige.

I can't admit that to him, though. Telling him how I feel would be like cutting open my chest and giving him full access to my heart.

I don't know if I'm that brave.

"I'm sorry," I say again because it's all I can think to say.

Paige catches Trey's eye, giving him a cunning smile. He nods in her direction, but when he looks away, she smirks at me. My fists clench.

The *In Another Life* game has died down, and one of the Zenith members launches into a story about the time he was attacked by a cougar and killed it with his bare hands. His face is animated as he shoots to his feet and acts out the encounter. As we watch, he pretends to wrestle the beast to the ground.

"I snapped his neck, and he went still," he hollers, his voice carrying across the camp. His whole body goes still as he pretends the fight is over. "And that, my friends, is how you tame a beast." He does a deep bow to a smattering of applause.

"All right, Roderick, have a seat," Paige says. "We all know how you like to embellish."

Roderick plops down beside Paige as everyone snickers.

"Hey, Trey," Paige calls. "Remember when the bathroom in the Compound flooded?"

"Gah, yeah," Trey answers, chuckling. "It took us hours to clean it up."

"You and I stayed up *all night* mopping up water. Remember that?" Paige enunciates *all night*, her eyes flitting to me, wanting to make it clear they spent the entire night together.

"Yeah, I remember," Trey says. "It was awful."

Paige gives him a coy smile. "It wasn't *all* bad, though. Remember?"

Trey clears his throat. "I guess not."

My insides twist at the meaning behind her words. Paige continues. "Remember the time we broke your bed—"

I launch to my feet, refusing to sit here and listen to this.

Trey lays a hand on my arm. "Sienna—"

I stumble away from him. "I-I'm tired. I'm gonna, um, turn in."

His hand drops. As I walk away from the campfire, I'm equal parts relieved and disappointed when he doesn't come after me.

The Camp is small, so it doesn't take me long to reach my tent. Once I'm there, I can still hear the lingering laughter from the campfire. My clothes are saturated with the smoky smell, which only reminds me of Paige and her words and her determination to make me feel small.

Instead of preparing for bed, I grab a change of clothes from my tent, along with a blanket I can use as a towel. After, I head to the stream about a hundred yards away. It's dark and I stumble a few times, but the path is mostly clear. There aren't many trees that grow here, only tall cliffs, sandy dirt, and the occasional weedy plant. The stream is runoff from the mountains, which makes it ice cold. While I've been hacking away at squirrels, Trina's been washing clothes in this stream almost daily, and the shallowest part comes up to her knees. Other than rinsing my hands, I haven't ventured in yet, but it looks deep enough for a quick bathe.

I remove my clothes, except for my bra and underwear, and drop them beside a boulder. When I first arrived at Camp, Laurel gave me some homemade soap she'd made. It smells like the dusting spray my mom used on the furniture back home, but I'm not complaining. Anything is better than the smell of sweat, smoke, and body odor.

Slowly, I make my way to the stream. An animal screams in the night, causing a shiver to travel through me. The moon is a crescent in the sky, its reflection rippling in the water. If this whole bathing at night thing wasn't so creepy, it would be downright beautiful.

Gingerly, I put my toe in the water. It's freezing. I shiver again, bracing myself as I step in. The bottom is rocky, but not rough, the water having smoothed out the sharp edges over time. I suck in a deep breath as the water laps at my shins, then my thighs, only stopping when the water is up to my waist. As quickly as possible, I scrub my body with the soap. I try to wash my hair as best as I can, but with only a bar of soap, it's not that easy. No wonder Paige has cornrows. My stomach tightens just thinking her name.

I'm almost finished rinsing when there's a rustling beside the stream. I stop and look around. It's too dark to see anything, the moon now behind a cloud.

My knees shake from the cold, and my teeth chatter. I rinse the last of the soap away, then start to make my way to the bank. I've only taken a handful of steps when there's a splash a few feet away. My heart is a jackhammer as I bite back a scream, convincing myself it was only a jumping fish.

Something knocks me across the head, and then I'm

floundering. I fall back into the water, my entire body submerged, the cold seeping into every inch of my skin and traveling straight to my bones. As I struggle to regain my footing, my head emerges only long enough for me to gasp a quick breath before strong hands force me back under.

I thrash wildly, my arms flailing, my legs kicking. My shoulder throbs from the struggle. Five seconds pass. Ten seconds pass. Twenty seconds pass. White dots appear behind my closed eyelids. My body is an ice cube.

I can't hold my breath much longer.

There's a muffled shout, another loud splash, and then the pressure releases.

I regain my footing and burst from the water, dragging in a spastic breath. My lungs have closed off due to the cold, and no matter how hard I try, I can't get enough air. Wheezing, I practically crawl back to the shore. Someone tries to help me, but I jerk away.

"Don't touch me," I hiss. It isn't until I'm on the bank that I roll over and see it's Trey, a truckload of concern dumped on his face. Paige stands behind him, dripping wet, her entire body shaking from rage or cold, I'm not sure which. Trey hurries and gets the blanket I brought, wrapping it around my shoulders. I shrug him away.

"It was you!" I scream, rising to my feet and pointing a shaking finger at Paige.

"What the hell were you doing?" Trey demands, centering himself between us like he can protect me if Paige launches herself in my direction.

"If I had known who you were, I would have let you rot in that cell," Paige yells at me.

Please tell me this is not over some guy, because if it is, this chick is certifiably crazy. "I never pegged you for the psycho-jealous type, Paige," I say. "Isn't this a little beneath you?"

"My dad is dead because of you." She inches closer.

I have no idea what the hell she's talking about, and frankly, I'm a little too angry to care. What kind of person goes around drowning someone right after they saved them? A nutso, that's who.

Trey raises his arms, warding her off. "Paige, you have this all wrong. I'm the one who killed your father, not Sienna."

*What is Trey talking about?*

Paige's eyes swing to him. "I'm not an idiot, Trey. You don't think I know that? But the only reason you killed him is because of *her*."

"The Devil's men attacked us first. They stole our goods and our truck."

"You didn't have to kill him," she hisses. "After all we've been through, Trey. Why? Why would you?"

Trey's head droops. "You're right. I was scared. I thought if I let him live, he'd come after Sienna."

Paige reaches for something on the boulder and raises a gun, one she must have left there before she tried to drown me in the river. Trey pushes me behind him as Paige trains the gun on him.

"You and your guys killed my father and my brothers. And then you lied to me! You knew I was trying to find his killer, and you lied!"

"Paige, put the gun down, please. Let's talk about this. Just you and me."

"One of my guys just informed me. He's been tracking my father's killer for weeks. He arrived back at Camp only moments ago, and he told me what he'd found. That the trail led right to you and the bombed-out Compound. I couldn't believe it when he said it was you. You and the Fringe. Did you think I wouldn't find out?"

"Paige. Please. We can work through this. Let's talk—"

"I don't wanna hear any more of your lies, Trey Winchester!" she screams. "You lied when you told me you loved me. You lied about my father's death. You lied about Sienna. Lies, lies, lies!"

I'm frozen to the spot, both because my limbs have stopped working and because of the cold.

"Paige, you don't want to do this," Trey warns.

"I think I do, Trey. Justice for my father and all." The gun shifts a little. Trey may be in front of her, but she's really aiming it at me.

"Paige, remember when you pulled a gun on me in the Compound?" Trey forces a chuckle. "Remember how that turned out?"

"It wasn't supposed to go off!" Paige's expression softens. "I hadn't even realized it was loaded."

"The bullet pinged a concrete wall and then hit you in the leg." Trey laughs. "Serves you right."

Paige is laughing now. "I still have that scar." She lowers the gun to show us, and Trey springs into action, knocking the piece from her hands and wrapping his arms around her torso, pinning her arms to her sides.

"It's over, Paige," he says. His eyes connect with mine. "Go back to your tent, Sienna," he orders. When I just stand there staring at him, he says, "Please."

Only because he said please. I slip my feet in my shoes and start to trudge back to my tent. But then I change my mind. Stopping among the weedy underbrush, I listen. Paige and Trey clearly need to work through some issues, but I'll be damned if I'm gonna leave the two of them alone.

I hear Trey snap at her. "What the hell were you thinking, Paige? You can't go around attacking people."

"I wasn't really going to kill her. I only wanted to send her a warning."

"I'm almost afraid to ask. What warning was that?"

"I may have saved her in Rubex, but I don't like her, nor will we ever be friends."

"She's done nothing to you."

*Damn right I've done nothing.*

Paige goes quiet. "You lied to me, Trey. When you came here asking for my help, you said you needed to rescue some of your Fringe members."

"Which was true. Sienna's a member of the Fringe."

"But you neglected to mention she used to work for my father. And more importantly, she's your girlfriend."

"At the time, I didn't know what we were. I didn't know if she'd want to be with me. Not after everything that happened."

"You lied in the Compound. You told me you loved me."

I don't want to hear this. I really don't. But it's like watching a train wreck—I simply can't walk away.

Trey's tone is cold when he speaks again. "And you left me." He clears his throat. "I didn't lie. I loved you then, but when you left, you broke my heart. That was a long time ago. I moved on."

"And her? Do you love her?" There's no mistaking the bitterness in Paige's voice.

"I do," Trey says firmly. "More than anything or anyone."

My heart swells at his declaration. Trey told me once that he loved me—in the AIG building after I'd just been shot—but it was too soon. After all we'd been through, I wasn't ready to hear it. I know those words don't roll off his tongue easily, so to hear him tell Paige how he feels about me means everything.

It takes a moment for me to realize it's completely silent except for an owl hooting in the distance. I creep closer so I can see what's happening. My eyes are fairly well-adjusted to the dark by now, and I see Paige rest her hands on Trey's chest. "That's a pretty bold statement," she says, her voice soft, almost seductive. "Especially considering you used to feel that way about me."

"That was a long time ago, Paige." Trey gently removes her hands. "I'm sorry about your father. And I'm sorry I lied to you about his death. You and I both know the kind of man he was."

"He didn't deserve to die," she says, sounding broken.

"He shouldn't have attacked our men."

"You shouldn't have gone to their lair!"

Paige moves to strike Trey, but he's too quick. Grabbing her wrists, he holds them tightly between their two bodies. She struggles, but it's futile. Paige may be strong, but she's no match for Trey.

"Listen up, Paige. This is the world we live in. We have to protect what's ours. He started a war, and I finished it. I'm sorry I hurt you, but that's the way things are done." Trey drops her arms, then takes a step back. "If you ever touch Sienna again, you'll have me to deal with. Are we clear?"

Since I don't want Trey to find me eavesdropping on their conversation, it's time to go. As silently as possible, I make my way back to my tent, the blanket wrapped tightly around my shoulders. It isn't until I'm a few steps away from the entrance I realize I left my clothes by the stream. Too cold and tired to trek back, I promise myself I'll get them in the morning.

Once inside my tent, I pull on a T-shirt and sweats before climbing under my blankets, shivering as my body tries to adjust its temperature. My hair is still wet and ice cold so I bury myself completely under the covers, taking advantage of the toasty trapped air.

As I struggle to warm myself, my mind scrolls through Trey's conversation with Paige. When he came back to the Compound that night covered in blood, I'd wondered how many he killed. I'd even wondered if the Devil was among those he'd "taken care of". Not that I feel sorry for the Devil. But a life is a life is a life. It's understandable why Paige is so upset. I'm not sure why she blames me, though. I didn't even know he was dead.

There's a rustling outside my tent, so I poke my head out of my blanket fort. The flap opens, and Trey squats, peering inside. "Hey, you left these at the stream." In his hands are my clothes, the ones I was wearing tonight and the clean outfit I'd brought with me. He sets them inside and nods to the spot beside me. "May I come in?"

I nod and sit up, tugging the blanket up to my chest. Trey settles himself across from me, his legs pulled up, his arms resting on his knees.

"Why didn't you tell me you killed the Devil that night?" I ask.

Trey sighs. "I didn't want you to be disappointed in me. I remembered how much you hated me killing that soldier outside of the bunker, and I couldn't bear to disappoint you again."

"So why did you? Why did you kill him?"

"To protect you. Your debt hadn't been paid yet. He would have kept looking for you. Or worse."

"You did it to protect me? That's the only reason?"

"Of course. What other reason is there?"

I think for a moment. "I don't know. To get back at him for what his men did to you and Nash? To seek revenge for him having control over Paige and never telling her who she really was—"

"He might not have even known Paige was a GM," Trey interjects.

"This is the Devil we're talking about. Of course he knew who Paige was and where she came from. And when you came strutting into that pool hall years ago, he knew he couldn't keep control of her any longer."

Trey shakes his head. "What happened with the Devil? It was never about Paige. It was about you and only you. I knew I needed to protect you from that snake and his organization, and the only way to do it was to chop off its head."

Shivering, I try to hide my trembling hands.

"Are you okay?" he asks.

"I'm fine. Just a little cold."

Trey moves to my side and rubs my arms, the touch of his hands instantly warming my skin. "I'm so sorry about Paige. I don't know why she took this out on you. This is between me and her. She shouldn't have involved you."

"Because she still loves you, Trey. Love makes people do crazy things."

"Nah. That was a long time ago."

"You aren't exactly easy to get over," I say. "Trust me, I've tried."

Trey stops rubbing my arms and shifts his body until he's facing me. "Why were you there anyway? You shouldn't be swimming by yourself at night."

"I wasn't swimming."

"Then what were you doing?"

I shrug. "I wanted to get the campfire smell out of my hair."

"You were bathing?"

"Yeah."

"And Paige snuck up on you and held you under?"

I cut my eyes away from him. When he says it, it makes me sound weak. I should have been strong enough to fight her off.

*Reality check, Sienna. She's a GM, and you're not.*

"Pretty much," I say finally. "How did you know where to find me?"

"I followed Paige. Some guy came and whispered something in her ear, then she left the campfire. She looked pissed, so I knew she was up to something."

"I don't know how she knew I was there."

"She must have spotted you heading in that direction."

I tilt my chin higher. "I could have taken care of myself. I just needed to get my footing, and I—I could have taken her."

Trey struggles to hide a smile. "I'm sure you could have. I

just figured the water was probably cold. No sense leaving you under any longer than you needed to be."

I glare at him, and he chuckles.

"But honestly," he says, "are you sure you're okay?" Before I can stop him, he pulls back the blankets and grabs my feet. "Wouldn't want you to lose one of these." He checks my toes, one foot and then the other. "Coloring looks good."

"Thank you, *Dr. Winchester*," I say, "but I think I'm fine. Can I have my toes back now?"

Trey covers me with the blanket, tucking it snugly around my feet. I love how he takes painstaking care to make sure I'm warm. When he's done, he clears his throat—the obvious tell that he's nervous. "I should probably go."

I want to ask him to stay. To lay with me and keep me warm, but all I do is nod.

Trey rises to his feet, ducking his head because he's too tall for my tent. He's halfway through the opening when he stops and turns. "We're good, right?"

I hesitate, wanting to tell him that my heart is breaking. That knowing about him and Paige is tearing me apart. Obviously, I know he's had other girls before me, but it's killing me to know he used to love Paige—Paige with her cornrows and rough edges; Paige who's stronger and faster than me.

Paige who tried to kill me.

Plastering a smile on my face, I say, "Yeah, of course."

Trey smiles, his right dimple on display. I suddenly have the urge to poke my finger in it. "Goodnight."

He's gone before I have time to respond.

The tent flap opens, waking me from a fitful sleep. My heart thunders in my chest, my first thought that Trey is sneaking in. But then a small figure appears at the end of my bedroll.

"Si-Si?" a little voice whispers.

"Emily?"

"I'm having trouble sleeping. Can I stay with you?"

"Sure." I pat beside me, scooting over to make room for her.

She snuggles up next to me like a cat. Her curls tickle my nose as I wrap one arm around her frail body. The last time I held her like this, back in our home in Legas, she was soft and pudgy with a healthy layer of baby fat. Now, she's all bones and thin skin, and I wonder when that happened. So much has changed for us both since the last time we were together.

There's a sort of comfort that comes with having the warmth of her body next to mine. Maybe for once I won't dream of Curly, his body being tossed over the cliff to the angry ocean below, or about my father, open-mouthed, his body torn apart by bullets.

I swallow back tears, pressing my lips together to keep from crying aloud. My shoulders shake as I pull Emily closer. I try to be strong for everyone—I really do. But I'm still just a girl who's lost and scared. A girl who lost her dad and has to grieve alone.

# 13
## Zane

I've been wearing tuxedos since I was old enough to attend one of my father's fancy parties or galas. But as I stare at myself in the mirror, it's like I'm looking at myself in a tux for the very first time. Probably because this is the one I'll be wearing when I marry Arian tomorrow.

There's a knock on my bedroom door, and then Greta calls out, "Are you dressed? I have fresh laundry."

"Come in."

The door swings open, showing Greta with a pile of clothes in her arms. I move quickly to help her, unburdening her arms of the heavy load. "I've told you before I can do my own laundry," I protest.

"I know, I know," she says, shaking her head. "But I don't mind." When she sees what I'm wearing, she goes still. "Tomorrow's the big day, huh?"

"Yeah. Feeling a little nervous, but I guess that's to be expected the day before I get married."

"I think that's why they call them wedding jitters."

"Right."

Greta twists her hands in front of her. She stares at the carpet for so long I turn to see what she might be looking at. "Greta? Is everything okay?"

She purses her lips together. "Of course."

"Greta…" Something's clearly bothering her. I've known her too long not to recognize that.

Her words come out in a rush. "I know it's not my place to say anything, but why are you doing this, Zane?"

"Why am I marrying Arian?"

"Exactly. You don't love her. Is this really what you want?"

Love. There's that word I'm beginning to despise. Sure, it would be great to marry someone I love. But if I can't have that, then marrying my fake genetic match is the next best thing.

"It's what I need," I answer.

"Oh, Zane. I don't know what happened between you and Sienna in Rubex. But I do know this. You deserve to be with someone you love. And someone who loves you back. It's what your mother would have wanted for you."

Greta is only trying to help, but she doesn't understand the position I'm in. I don't really have a choice.

The muscles in my neck tighten. "Please don't bring her into this," I say through clenched teeth.

Greta looks confused. "Who? Your mother? Or Sienna?"

"Both." I turn away and remove the jacket, hanging it carefully on the hanger to avoid wrinkles.

"I'm sorry, Zane," Greta says in a small voice. "I just—I want you to be happy." I hear her footsteps hurry from the room, the door closing softly behind her.

Yeah, I want that, too. But it's not in the cards.

I have a tough time sleeping that night. Getting out of bed at two AM, I splash cool water on my face. There are circles under my eyes, and my normally copper skin appears grayish.

*This is what you want. It's the right thing.*

I repeat this over and over, trying to convince myself.

After filling a glass with tap water and downing half, I

climb back in bed and stare at the ceiling. Unwittingly, an image of Sienna, with her fiery hair and freckled nose, floats into my mind. I try to push it away, but it hovers there, teasing me.

When she stayed here, she had horrible nightmares. I would hear her cry out during the night, and I would rush to her room to comfort her. I always ended up staying the rest of the night with her, sleeping in a chair similar to the one sitting in the corner of my own. And as I lay here, I can't help but wonder, *Does she still have them? Are they worse now after what she's been through? Is anyone there to comfort her?*

I could have been that guy. The one who stays by her side through the night. Who puts her well-being before his own. I was ready to *be* that guy.

But it wasn't enough.

# 14

## Sienna

The only thing I've ever hunted are snipes, which are these fictitious animals in the desert. But when Trey vouches I'm a good shot, Paige relents and lets me be a part of the hunting crew. Which is perfect because it means I get to spend more time with Trey.

Paige has been less beast-like lately, mostly avoiding me completely. I keep waiting for an apology or something, but it has yet to come. I'm not holding my breath.

We set out early on Saturday morning as the sun is barely peeking over the horizon. It's a crew of six of us. Asher is the head of the hunters and is the only other person I know in the group besides Trey. There's one other girl, but she scares me a little. Her muscles are so big she reminds me of a professional weight lifter. And she has a perpetual scowl on her face. I've decided I don't want to get on her bad side.

We end up hiking along a trail that follows the stream. Trey keeps step with me, our weapons slung across our backs. Occasionally, he reaches out and runs a finger down my arm, sending a tremor through me.

"So you gonna teach me how to shoot a bow and arrow?" I ask him. We've left a little distance between ourselves and the others.

"You want to learn?"

Trey opted for a good old-fashioned bow and arrow instead of a gun, saying he wanted to work on his bow skills.

"Um, *yeah.*"

Trey shrugs, and my eyes are drawn to his round bicep peeking from his shirt. "Yeah, I can teach you," he says.

Asher calls out from up ahead. "This is a good area for hunting. Spread out, but stick with your partner."

Trey slings an arm around my shoulders, careful to avoid my wound that's healing nicely thanks to the antibiotics he gave me. "All right, partner, which way should we go?"

Shielding my eyes from the rising sun, I spot a perfect set of cliffs. It would be an excellent location for bighorn sheep or mountain lions. I point to where I'm thinking.

"Good call," Trey says. He motions for me to go first. "After you."

We both know what today is, but neither of us have spoken about it. Not since Trey first told me about Zane's press release over a week ago. I think this is why he wanted me on the hunting crew—to get my mind off the fact Zane is getting married today.

Just thinking those words causes my chest to squeeze.

To erase any thoughts of Zane, I tug Trey to a stop and kiss him.

"Whoa, what was that for?" he asks when we pull apart.

"Nothing," I say. I readjust my gun and keep walking.

A moment later, a hawk flies overhead and a small rabbit darts behind some low bushes.

"Did you see that?" I whisper.

Trey nods, lifting his bow and pulling an arrow from his quiver. He creeps forward, his arrow ready to let loose. "Toss a rock at those bushes," he says.

After I find a pebble on the ground, I throw it. The bunny comes running out, but he's quick. The first arrow misses him. Cursing, Trey tries again. The second arrow hits him square on.

Trey retrieves his arrows and his spoils, holding the rabbit up by the ears.

"My first kill," he says. "We should be able to eat off him for days."

I laugh at his exaggeration. "We're only getting started."

Trey puts the rabbit in the pack slung across his shoulders. "Let's go catch us a mountain lion."

The cliffs don't yield a mountain lion, but instead, at the base, we spot a mule deer.

"This one's yours," Trey whispers, crouching.

"Trey, I don't think I can. I don't have much experience—"

"This one's yours," he repeats.

I love that he has that kind of confidence in me. But this isn't just a fun shooting session like our Compound target practices. This is our livelihood. Other Fringe and Zenith members are counting on us to bring home game.

"If I fire the gun now," I say, "it will scare off any other potential game."

"So? This would be a huge kill. And if you miss, we'll find a spot further away."

Knowing he won't back down, I sigh and bring the gun to my shoulder. I line up the deer in my crosshairs. Almost as if it senses its imminent death, it stops eating and lifts its head, its nose pointed in the air, its eyes darting.

"Breathe," Trey instructs.

I let out a deep breath and pull the trigger.

The deer crumples to the ground, the bullet hitting her square in the neck.

"Damn," Trey says. "That was incredible, Sienna."

My insides warm from his compliment. I don't know why, but getting a compliment from Trey is like basking in the sun's rays. It really means something when I impress him or make him proud. Maybe because Trey is good at everything? And my own skills are few and far between.

Shouldering the gun, I make my way toward the deer. I'm really hoping the bullet killed her instantly. I don't want to have to put her out of her misery.

I'm only a few steps away from the downed deer when I hear a low, guttural sound, like a growl. At first, I think Trey is teasing me, but when I hear him urgently whisper my name, I stop. Less than twenty feet away, on the other side of the deer, is a coyote. And it's clear from the way he's eyeing me he thinks the animal is his.

"Hell no," I mutter. "This is *my* kill." I slowly raise my gun.

"Sienna!" Trey hisses.

Another coyote joins his friend, then another. The three coyotes surround the deer, edging me out.

I glance back at Trey. He motions for me to stay still. My first instinct is to run because with three coyotes we're completely outnumbered.

"If you run," he whispers like he read my mind, "they'll think you're prey."

"How many arrows do you have?"

"Sienna, don't be rash," he warns. "Let them have the deer."

"No," I say stubbornly. "She's mine."

The coyotes have lost interest in me because I appear to pose no threat, but they think the deer is up for the taking. And I hadn't realized it before, but she's still alive.

"We can do this, Trey," I whisper. "We fire at the same time. Then we only have one to deal with."

Trey is quiet for a moment. "Okay," he relents. "But leave the third one to me."

I nod and slowly load the next bullet into place, never taking my eyes off the coyotes. They're circling the deer now. Once the gun is loaded, I take aim. It's harder now because my target keeps moving.

"On my count," Trey says. "One, two—"

I fire before he gets to three. My bullet barely grazes one coyote, but Trey's shot is clean. His goes down with a whimper.

But now, both coyotes have turned on us. My fingers are shaking as I try to load the next bullet into place. Thankfully, Trey is quicker at stringing his bow and another arrow flies past, taking out the second coyote. I can't let him show me up, so I get myself under control, load the gun, and take aim at the exact time he sends another arrow flying. I'm not sure what kills the coyote, my bullet or his arrow, but the wild dog falls to the ground.

"I had him," I huff, turning to Trey.

He shrugs. "I wasn't willing to take that chance." He moves toward me.

"You mean, you didn't think I could do it."

His hands find my arms. "That's not what I said."

"But that's what you meant," I retort.

Trey chuckles, his one cheek dimple on display. When he speaks, his voice is gruff. "I was more concerned about *you*."

*Oh.* As quickly as it came, my anger subsides.

Trey continues. "I will always do what I think is best when it comes to protecting you."

I cross my arms over my chest. "Maybe I don't need you to protect me."

Smiling, Trey kisses my forehead. "No, I'm sure you don't. But I'd like to feel useful every once in a while." He then walks away to gather his arrows and our spoils.

When our hunting crew arrives back at Camp with three coyotes, one mule deer, two cottontails, four rock squirrels, one gray fox, one kangaroo rat, and a rattlesnake, I think Paige is impressed.

She sidles over to Trey and me as we lay the deer onto the prep table. "We've been tracking that mule deer for weeks now," she says directly to Trey, ignoring me. "Well done."

With a grin, Trey nods at me. "That was Sienna's kill."

Paige's eyebrows shoot up as she turns to me. "You don't say." I can see it's killing her to acknowledge my part in it, but she grits her teeth and says, "Well, then. Nice work, Sienna," before sauntering away to inspect some of the other animals.

And crazily enough, I feel as though I've accomplished a small victory simply because I got a compliment from Paige.

# 15
# Zane

The ceremony is at noon today, which means I should arrive at the church by eleven. I need to make sure the rings were delivered and are there waiting for us. I certainly don't want to botch up my *one* responsibility.

Since this is history in the making—my father's words, not mine—the ceremony will be televised. Only close friends and family will be allowed into the cathedral, but it doesn't really matter since all of Pacifica will be watching.

For one brief second, I wonder if Sienna will see it wherever she is. But I quickly shove that thought aside.

Today is about Arian and me. Starting a life together. Starting a family.

Once I'm dressed in my tux, I head downstairs to the kitchen. The counters are overflowing with muffins, pancakes, and sticky buns.

"I didn't know what you'd want to eat on your wedding day—"

"So you made it all," I finish for her.

Greta gives me a sheepish smile. "Sorry. I guess I got a little carried away. I've been in the kitchen since four this morning."

"Couldn't sleep either?"

She nods. "And I'm sorry about yesterday, Zane. I shouldn't have said anything."

Going around the counter, I wrap my arms around the woman who's been the only mother I've ever known. She has flour streaked across her cheek, and she smells like cinnamon and dough.

"It's okay. You're allowed to tell me your opinion. I may not always listen, though."

Pulling back, she smiles. "Look at you. You're getting flour all over yourself." She wets a rag and wipes at the white smudges on my tux. Once she's assured it's clean, she flings the rag in the sink and nods to the spread on the counter. "What'll you have?"

My stomach churns, not with hunger, but nerves. "I don't think I can eat anything."

Greta steps over to the fridge, then pulls out a pitcher of frothy pink liquid. "I had a feeling you might say that. Here, have a smoothie instead. You don't have to chew, only swallow." She pours the liquid into a glass and hands it to me.

"Thanks, Greta." I take a small sip, then force myself to have another because she's watching me like a hawk.

Once I've downed half of it, Greta says, "Now that I'm assured you've had breakfast and won't be getting married on an empty stomach, I can get myself ready." She removes her apron, neatly laying it across the back of a barstool. "Good luck today. You're going to make one handsome groom." As she passes me, she smiles and pats my cheek. She then shuffles out of the kitchen, humming some tune I don't recognize.

Other than the preacher, I'm the first one to arrive at the church. The wedding planner, April Davies, rushes in a few minutes later laden with boxes of flowers.

"Zane! I'm so glad you're here. Can you give me a hand with these?"

I follow her to her car, helping to haul in the rest of the flowers. Once they're set on a pew, April searches through one of the boxes for my boutonnière. April is a highly competent wedding planner, but I think Arian and I threw her for a loop when we decided to up the wedding by two months.

"Ahh, here it is," she says, her voice breathless. The flower she pulls out is a white rose. As she pins it to my lapel, I take a deep breath.

*This is happening. This is really happening.*

"Nervous?" she asks with a grin.

"Is it that obvious?"

"One word of advice? Don't forget to breathe." Now that the boutonnière is affixed to my coat, she steps back and eyes it. "I can't tell you the countless grooms who have fainted during the ceremony because they forgot to breathe."

I inhale a shaky breath. "Good advice."

Laughing, April pats my shoulder. "You'll do great. Now, if you'll excuse me, I have some last-minute flowers I need to attach to pews."

"Need some help?"

She waves off my offer. "No way. This is your wedding. I've got this covered. Besides, my assistant should be here soon." Her Lynk rings, and she flits away to answer it.

I take a seat in the first pew, staring at the stained-glass windows behind the altar. In a few short hours, I'll be married to Arian. We'll be living together, waking up next to each other, sharing our lives and dreams.

I'm in the process of wrapping my mind around this when heavy footsteps approach. I rise quickly, but it's not someone I expect to see here in Legas, especially after all he's done to piss me off.

"You have a lot of nerve showing up here," I say.

"Now, Zane, is that any way to greet your older brother?" When Steele smiles, I want to knock his front teeth out.

"You are not my brother. You never were and never will be."

Steele waves his hand. "It's semantics, really. We're still half-brothers."

My eyes narrow. "Why the hell did you do it, Steele? You sent an innocent girl to rot in prison. A girl I cared about. And you knew that."

"She may not have killed Radcliffe, but she's still a criminal. She and that Trey scum."

"He's your brother," I spit.

"Only by blood," Steele says smoothly.

"So what, you're working for the government now? Are you their errand boy?"

Steele shakes his head, looking bored. In fact, I'm not surprised when he pulls out his Lynk to check the time. "I did what needed to be done. Harlow is sitting on this company like a mother hen who doesn't know when to cut the apron strings. With the backing of the government, we could do so much more. Infinitely more."

"That's not your call to make."

Steele gives a little shrug before picking up one of the boutonnières in the box. "This for me?" His grin is smug. "Probably not."

My hands ball into fists. I would hate to get in a fight in this tux, but the thrill of beating Steele senseless is very tempting. "You need to leave. Now."

"Settle down, little bro. I'm not here to cause trouble. I really am here to offer support on your wedding day. After all, this is the biggest event of the decade." He sneers after that last remark, like he's making fun of something. I believe Harlow used a similar phrase at the Match 360 Extravaganza when Arian and I were first introduced as a betrothed couple.

"I. Don't. Want. You. Here." Grabbing the lapels of his suit, I shove him down the aisle. He tries to dig in his heels, but he can't get traction. I'm too strong, and I don't stop until I've shoved him out the front door of the church.

Unfortunately, Arian, her parents, and her bridesmaids are outside, walking up the steps. They look horrified when they see me pushing Steele out the door with enough force to roll a truck.

Giving me a confused look, Arian says, "Zane, is everything okay?"

Even *I* know it's bad luck to see the bride before the wedding. I try to shield my eyes as I say, "My brother came to wish us well, but can't stay. Thank you, Steele, for stopping by." I then dart inside, hoping Steele knows better than to enter the church again.

I decide to hide out in one of the upstairs church classrooms until it's time for the ceremony. I practice breathing, because I really don't want to forget to do that. I also practice not thinking about Sienna. That's harder than it should be.

Harlow finds me when it's a quarter till twelve. It's time for me to take my place with the other groomsmen, many of whom were handpicked by Arian to "match" her bridesmaids. Those were her words, not mine.

"There you are, son." Clasping his hands on my shoulders, he holds my gaze. "How are you feeling?"

"Fine," I lie.

Harlow chuckles as his hands drop. "I remember the day I married your mother. I was far from fine."

"You were nervous?"

"I was a mess. But the moment I saw her coming down the aisle…" He pauses, shifting his weight so his hip rests against a table. "She was so beautiful. In that moment, I knew I was the luckiest man in the universe."

Arian is beautiful, yes, but I'm not sure I'll ever feel like the luckiest man in the world, let alone the universe.

"I wish your mother could see you," he says, his eyes getting moist. "You are her son. In every way."

I wish she could be here, too. "Thanks, Dad."

His thumb sweeps under each eye. "I've very proud of you, son. I know the past few months haven't been easy. You had me worried there for a moment." He places a hand over his heart. "But it's the right decision. I promise you won't regret it."

We may have had our differences, he may have lied to me for years, but when Harlow tells me how proud he is, I can't help but stand a little taller, a little straighter. My entire life, all I've wanted to do is make my father proud.

With one arm around my shoulder, he leads me from the room. To the untrained eye, we look like father and son, united in an unbreakable bond. I may not always like the things he does, and he may drive me crazy at times, but he's still my dad—blood or not.

It's a long walk down the stairs and to the sanctuary. Or, at least, it feels like it. As we're rounding the corner and the side door to the chapel is in sight, my father's arm slips from my shoulder and he stops, placing a hand to his chest.

"Dad, are you okay?"

He breathes deeply for a moment, his eyes fixed on the wood-planked floor.

"Dad?"

When he looks up, he tries to smile. "I'm fine. Don't worry about me." He straightens, giving me an encouraging nod. "Don't you have somewhere you need to be?"

"I'm not leaving you—"

"Zane." His stern tone makes me stop talking. "I'm fine. Now go. You don't want to be late for your own wedding." He winks. "Trust me, you don't want to start off your marriage that way."

My voice is firm when I say, "I'll walk you to your pew."

Knowing he can't argue with that, Harlow nods. Instead of going through the side entrance to the chapel, we turn and go to the main doors instead. An usher is there handing out teal programs wrapped in yellow ribbons. I remember Arian picking those out.

The chapel is almost full. And despite my wishes, there are several reporters and video cameras. I knew it would be televised, but I thought there would be one crew. Only one.

"What are they doing here?" I hiss at my dad.

He shrugs, but I know full well this is his doing.

"That was low, Father, even for you. Why couldn't you respect my wishes on my wedding day?"

"This isn't only about you, Zane. We're making history!"

Dozens of eyes turn to stare at us as we make our way down the aisle. Even though my teeth are grinding together, I flash a smile at Arian's parents who are seated on the left—the bride's side, or so I'm told. Greta is seated in the second pew on the right, which is where I steer my father. Once he's settled on his seat, and I'm assured he's fine, I take my place next to the preacher's pulpit and my four groomsmen. The closest one is Arian's cousin Ryan, and he clasps a hand on my shoulder like he's saying, *This is it, man.*

As I wait, on full display for the audience, the cameras, and the reporters, I glance around the room. Flowers in white, yellow, and with edges tinged in teal dangle from the ends of pews and drape across the pulpit. Bows in teal and yellow are affixed to almost every standing surface.

I'm not a fan of teal or yellow, but it's what Arian wanted.

As I scan the crowd, Greta catches my eye and gives me a sympathetic smile.

*See, even she knows this is a mistake.*

*No,* I tell myself. *It's not. Falling for Sienna was the mistake.*

With my hands clasped in front of me, I wait, making sure my face doesn't show my conflict—schooling my expression to show nothing but the dutiful groom. I'm the only one who knows the war waging inside my mind.

*As soon as I see Arian walking down that aisle, every doubt*

*I've had will be erased.*

I repeat this to myself, over and over.

As I stare out at the rows of filled pews, I see Steele slip into one of the back ones. I try to catch his eye, but his attention is focused solely on his Lynk.

It isn't until Ryan whispers to me, "Hey, man, you all right?" that I realize my fists are clenched and my eyes narrowed.

Relaxing my hands, I wipe my palms on my suit pants. "I'm fine," I whisper back.

The organist, who's been playing soft prelude, kicks it up a notch and begins a rendition of *Pachelbel's Canon in D*. I've always liked that song. It's one of my favorites to play because I have fun creating my own arrangements.

Four leggy, gorgeous girls appear at the back of the chapel, wearing matching white and teal dresses. They look like supermodels about to take to the runway. And as they glide down the aisle with their bouquets in hand, that's exactly how they act as photographers snap pictures and video cameras roll.

One girl sashays down the aisle, hips swaying. When she gets to the end, instead of taking the spot next to the other bridesmaid, she places a hand on her hip and spins, striking a pose. A few titters rise from the crowd.

"For chrissake," Ryan mutters beside me.

I press my lips together to keep from laughing.

When the last bridesmaid has taken her place, there's a collective shuffle as everyone turns to the doorway. Arian stands there, absolutely stunning from head to toe. Her dark hair is pulled back in an intricate knot, and her off-the-shoulder dress shows off the smooth curves of her skin. The gown is long and flows behind her like a crystal river. She's elegant and beautiful and poised and radiating—all at the same time.

When she sees me, a shy grin blossoms on her face. I can't help but smile back. My heart is now thudding so loudly in my chest I'm sure Ryan can hear it. I take a few shaky breaths.

# Fearless

*This is it. This is the moment I'll know if I'm doing the right thing.*

With her arm in her father's, Arian begins the long walk to me.

# 16
## Sienna

I'm sitting around the campfire, spooning soup into my mouth, when Nash plops down beside me on a rock. I haven't seen him much since we got to Camp. I think he's been on an expedition or two to cut down trees to use to build more tents and structures.

"Hey," he says, his tone abrupt.

"Hey," I respond. "Soup?" I hold out my bowl in an offering.

He waves it away, leaning in close. "I heard what Paige did to you. Want me to take her out?"

I stare at him, trying to decide if he's serious or not. It doesn't seem that long ago he tried to kill me in the Compound. "How did you hear about that? I haven't told anyone."

Nash shrugs. "Trey told me."

"You aren't—" I shake my head a little. "I mean, you're not serious, right?"

"I can be. Just say the word."

There's no humor in his tone. "I'm sorry, Nash. I don't understand. I didn't think you liked me."

Nash's voice is gruff when he speaks again. "I guess you grew on me. Besides, Trey is crazy about you. And after all you did to save him—hell, girl, I admire you. I may even respect you."

A deep flush spreads to my cheeks. I never thought I'd see

the day when I earned Nash's approval. "Nash, that might be the nicest thing you've ever said to me."

"Don't get used to it," he mutters. Rising to his feet, he awkwardly pats me on the shoulder. "I've got your back. If you need anything, let me know."

As he strides away, I turn and watch him. I can't help but remember the first time I met Nash, when I arrived at the Compound and asked to join the Fringe. I never would have guessed the tough Commander had a softness inside.

"Sienna!" Trina is running toward me, a comscreen in hand. "Sienna, you have to see this."

I launch to my feet and hurry toward her. "What is it?" And after all the forgetting I've tried to do, it's then I remember. Backing away from the comscreen in her outstretched hand, I say, "I can't watch that."

"Sienna, please," Trina begs. "You need to."

"Need to what?" Trey asks, joining us.

"Here." Trina shoves the comscreen in my face, and then I'm watching what I know is Zane's wedding. Trey comes to stand behind me, looking over my shoulder. I can hardly breathe as the camera zooms in on Zane's face. He looks scared, nervous, and… vulnerable. He looks vulnerable.

"Is this Zane's wedding?" I hear Trey ask Trina. She must nod because I don't hear a response.

My stomach twists when Arian starts walking down the aisle and Zane breaks into a huge smile. He looks genuinely happy. I start to push the screen away, but Trina won't let me.

"I know this is hard, but you have to see this," she pleads.

I shake my head as tears fill my eyes. How can I watch Zane marry someone else? I mean, I love Trey, I do. But I also love Zane. I wish I didn't. I wish I could forget him, move on, and focus on this new life I've been given. But it's not that easy.

Arian glides toward Zane, and she's beautiful. I've never seen someone so gorgeous before. And when her father hands her off to Zane and she steps up next to him, her hands in his, they look like the perfect couple. The perfect genetically modified couple.

*They are the perfect match.*

The preacher starts talking about how marriage is a commitment between two parties and shouldn't be entered lightly. His is a very traditional approach to marriage, and I only half-listen to what he says. I'm too busy watching the way Zane stares at Arian like he's seeing her for the first time, seeing her in all her stunning beauty, perfection, and glory.

I try to turn away from the screen, but Trina still won't let me. She shoves it back in front of me. "Keep watching. Please." That's all she'll say.

Trey's heavy hands rest on my shoulders, pulling my back against his chest. "I'm right here." He slips his arms around my waist, and I lean into him, his body a solid brick wall holding me up.

I focus on the screen as the preacher finishes speaking. As soon as he asks for the rings, there's a commotion in the second pew. A man stands up, yells something, and then falls into the aisle. It isn't until Zane runs over and the camera zooms in on the man's face that I realize it's Harlow Ryder.

*Oh no. No, no, no.*

"Keep watching," Trina says again.

I watch with my hands pressed to my mouth and my stomach in knots. There's a crowd around Mr. Ryder now, which makes it hard for the person capturing the video to get a clear shot. I see the bent head of someone giving Harlow Ryder chest compressions—oh wait, that's Zane. After a few minutes of no response, he pounds on his father's chest. Over and over. Medics finally arrive, but it's too late. I know because I've been down this road before.

The video goes blank like someone made the person stop filming. I'm too stunned, too dazed to speak.

# Fearless

When I glance up, Trina is staring at me. "Is he…?"

My mouth is suddenly very dry, like we've been trekking through the desert for days. "Yeah. Harlow Ryder's dead."

# 17

## Trey

I wish Sienna would let me in, tell me what she's thinking. She goes to bed early tonight, saying she's tired from the hunt. But I know better. She's already thinking of how she can help Zane. Not exactly sure how. We're hundreds of miles away, and she's a fugitive. She can never return to Legas or Rubex.

Not in the mood to hang out around the campfire with the others, I retire to my tent early. As I lay on my bedroll, the one thought I've had since I saw Harlow Ryder collapse at Zane's wedding comes into my mind again.

*My father is dead.*

My biological father, that is.

I know I should feel something. Anything. But I don't. I'm numb to it all. Harlow was never a father to me. I stayed in his house for weeks recuperating, and he never once came to see me. Why should I care that the man who created me to be his perfect poster child is no longer living? Why should I care when he never once cared about me?

I don't.

Then why the hell do I feel so guilty?

Sighing, I roll over onto my side.

I wish Sienna were here beside me. I tend to sleep better when she is. Something about her warm body and steady breathing creates an environment conducive to sleep. It relaxes me. *She* relaxes me.

I'm about to drift off and dream of Sienna when I hear the flaps of my tent opening. Sienna must have had trouble sleeping, too.

I'm ready to welcome her into my open arms when Paige crawls in, her Lynk lighting the inside of the tent. I sit up. "What are you doing?"

She gives me a seductive smile. "I thought you could use some company."

I hold out my hand to stop her from coming any further. "Paige, I'm with Sienna now. You know that."

Paige laughs. "Oh, calm down, Trey. I only came to apologize for what happened the other night between me and Sienna."

"You mean the night you tried to drown my girlfriend?"

"Stop being so dramatic," Paige says flippantly. "I wasn't actually gonna drown her."

"Sure looked like it."

"Anyway, I came to apologize, but if you're gonna be a stiff about it—"

"Thanks for the apology, Paige. Now I think it's time for you to go."

"No goodbye kiss?" Her smile is teasing, and I don't like it.

"Like I said, I'm with Sienna now."

"So? She doesn't have to know." She inches closer.

"Paige," I warn. "Whatever we had in the Compound years ago is over. It ended the moment you walked out."

"You're the one who reached out to *me* for help," she snaps, her eyes turning cold. "If it wasn't for me, your precious Sienna wouldn't be here."

"I know. And I appreciate what you did. But this—" I motion to the two of us, "—this can't happen."

"Trey, you awake?" Sienna flips open the tent flap, and I

jump about ten feet. Technically, I'm doing nothing wrong, but the whole scene looks bad. Paige in my tent in the middle of the night? There's really no way to swing that one.

When Sienna sees Paige, her face falls. "I see you're busy." The flap closes.

I push past Paige and stumble out of the tent, pulling on a shirt. Sienna is practically sprinting, moving faster than I've ever seen her go except when we're running for our lives. I hurry to catch up to her, my bare feet snagging on some rocks.

"Sienna, wait," I grab her arm, but she yanks it away. Thankfully, she stops. "Nothing happened."

Rolling her eyes, she crosses her arms over her chest. "Whatever."

"Seriously, Sienna? You think I would hook up with Paige when you're sleeping less than ten feet away? What kind of guy do you think I am?"

She shrugs. "Let's face it, Trey. You and I barely know each other. Sure, we may be really good at kissing. We may make a great hunting team, but do you know what my favorite color is? My favorite breakfast?"

I wrack my brain trying to remember if she ever told me these things. I don't think so...

"How am I supposed to know if you never open up to me?" I finally say.

She throws her hands up. "I shouldn't have to tell you. You should want to know."

What the hell? This isn't making any sense...

"I'm sorry, Sienna. What do you want me to say? I *want* to get to know you better. I *want* to know everything about you and then some. I *want* there to be no secrets between us."

When she doesn't say anything for a minute, I venture, "Is that what you want, too?"

"I don't know," she says, her voice soft.

Sighing, I tilt my head to look up at the sky. "I know a lot of things about you. More than most people know."

"Like what?" she challenges.

I bring my head back down to hold her gaze. "I know you can pick almost any lock. That your Harley is your pride and joy, but she tends to veer to the left. That your best friend's name is Chaz. That your father faked his death and changed his name—twice. That you're scared of snakes but tough as nails. That you'll do anything for someone you love—"

Sienna holds up a hand to stop me. "That's enough. I get it."

"Get what?" I ask innocently.

"What you're trying to do."

I take a step closer to her. "And what is it I'm trying to do?"

Heaving out a half-amused half-exasperated breath, she rolls her eyes heavenward. "You're trying to prove you *do* know me by spouting off random facts."

I chuckle. "I'm only trying to prove a point."

"And distract me from the fact Paige was in your tent a few moments ago?"

"I'm not trying to distract you. Nothing happened. Honest." I cross my finger over my heart like that might prove something.

Sienna cocks her head to the side. "Well, you seem to know me so well. Is there anything I should know about *you*?"

"Yes," I say. "There is one very important thing I haven't told you."

"What's that?"

I gently ease her closer before bending to whisper in her ear. "That I'm hopelessly, madly, and completely in love with you."

# 18

# Zane

My father loved sports cars. And he loved to drive fast. When I was a small boy, my favorite thing to do with my father was ride in his convertible to the Match 360 facility and watch him work in his lab. I know it doesn't sound like very exciting stuff, but I would sit there for hours, watching him mix chemicals and come up with formulas, all while trying to achieve something greater. Something better. On those days, he bought me a smorgasbord of snacks from the vending machines and made me feel like I was the only person in the world who mattered to him.

I liked observing my father in his natural habitat. He would mumble to himself, make notes on bits of scrap paper, and lose his pencil. I often had to hold in the laughter as he searched diligently for it. The whole time, I could see the pencil sticking out from behind his ear. He had expensive computer equipment at his fingertips, yet nothing was better than some lead and paper. He was a simple man with complex ideas.

He used to tell me I was his muse. The one who got his creative juices flowing merely by being in the same room with him. As a kid, I thought he was calling me his "moose". I often wondered why he was comparing me to an animal, until I was old enough to understand the differences in the words.

But now, he's not here. I'm not his muse or his moose or

even his son anymore. He's gone. And I'm parentless.

This drive is a tribute to my father. As I curve around the winding road that leads to the dam, in my own sports car nonetheless, I think of him. He liked to drive fast; therefore, I'm driving fast. Okay, maybe reckless is more like it. But as awful as I feel, I'll do anything for a thrill.

The car screeches to a stop in the gravel parking lot, then I hop out and stride over to the water. The last time I was here, I was with Sienna. I curse under my breath as an image of her fills my mind. If I could, I would remove every memory of her and throw them into this lake. I'd watch them bob and sink, never to resurface again. That's what I need. A complete brain wipe.

The idea is tempting…

I don't want to picture her freckled skin, her green eyes, or the copper curls at the base of her neck. Thoughts of her are driving me mad.

It was a simple plan. Return to Legas, marry Arian, and forget about Sienna, Rubex, and that night on the beach. But somewhere, everything went terribly wrong.

My thoughts turn to my father. It was a heart attack. The way he clutched his chest and had trouble breathing before the ceremony—I should have known. If I'd done something—anything other than send him to sit in a pew—he would still be alive. I've been so angry at him lately, but now that he's gone, all I feel is guilt. I could have been a better son. There are so many things I could have said or done differently.

Steele has been surprisingly helpful these last couple of days. He met with the funeral director this morning. I couldn't do it. I couldn't go to the funeral home to talk about the cremation and pick out an urn. It's too soon. It's all too fast and too soon.

My father was supposed to have years.

Now this company is mine, and I sure as hell don't know

what to do. I'm not ready for this.

I used to think I knew everything about the inner workings of Match 360 and Chromo 120, but without my father, I feel lost. This was his baby, his company. He built it from the ground up. No one can ever take his place.

And I certainly don't want to be the one who has to try.

# 19

## Sienna

Trey thinks I'm crazy, but I think it's a great plan. I'm convinced he needs to pay his respects to his father, and I need to find a way to warn Zane. They're ruling his father's death a heart attack. But it's a lie. I know all about poison that stops the heart. After all, Radcliffe tried to blackmail me into killing Mr. Ryder with a poison that would do just that. I couldn't go through with it, of course, but the poison exists.

Harlow Ryder was murdered. I'm sure of it. And I'm scared Zane might be next.

"Do you realize how insane this sounds?" Trey asks as he quarters a skinned jack rabbit. He and I opted for cleaning and prepping the animals instead of hunting today. Though he has taken me on several outings to teach me how to use a bow and arrow, I still need lots of practice.

"Of course. But what should we do? Hide out here forever? There are boys and girls being stolen from their parents in Rubex and sent to the basement of the AIG where someone is experimenting on them; there's your biological father who was murdered, and now they're trying to cover it up by saying it was a heart attack; then there's Zane, your own brother, I might add, whose life may be in danger. And you want to sit here and do nothing?"

Trey stops long enough to stare at me. "No, I want to

do what will keep you safe. We are not—I repeat—we are *not* going back to Legas. They would have both our heads if they found us."

I latch onto his arm, ready to go into full-on pout mode. "But they won't. We'll have disguises. We'll only travel at night—"

Trey's voice is firm when he cuts in. "The answer is no. Please don't ask me again." He busies himself with removing the skin from the next animal, a squirrel.

It's clear I'm getting nowhere with him, so I search out Trina instead. I find her in the stream washing clothes with two other girls I've yet to learn their names. When Trina sees me, she excuses herself, lays the article of clothing she's scrubbing out on a rock—I think it's a shirt—and makes her way over to me.

"Is everything okay?" she asks.

"What do *you* think I should do?"

"About?"

"About Zane. His father was murdered, Trina, I know it. I need to warn him. He could be in danger."

Trina raises an eyebrow. "Are you sure there's not another reason you want to contact Zane?"

"I'd like to make sure he's okay, if that's what you're getting at. He's been there for me, so yeah, I want to be there for him."

"You can't," Trina says.

"Why not?"

"It's too risky. Too dangerous."

"I'll be careful—"

With an exasperated sigh, Trina says, "Seriously, Sienna? Do you even hear yourself? You're wanted for MUR-DER. You and I barely escaped execution—" She stops and swallows hard, no doubt remembering Curly who didn't. "It's a ridiculous idea." With that, she grabs her shirt from the rock, splashes in to the creek, and resumes her scrubbing.

# Fearless

I suddenly feel like a small child who's been scolded. Of course, Trina is right. I don't know what I was thinking. It would be suicide to leave this camp to try to get to Zane. I've convinced myself he needs me, but I'm sure he's doing fine without me. The truth is, he's probably already forgotten me.

# 20

## Trey

"What did that poor rabbit do to you?" Paige asks, one eyebrow raised as she stares at the game on the table. It isn't until she says something I realize I've practically pulverized the creature in front of me.

"Nothing." I drop the knife.

Paige takes a deep breath. "Look, Trey, I'm really sorry about the other night. I hope I didn't mess things up between you and Sienna. I only wanted to apologize."

Since that was the last of my game to prep, I start cleaning my station. "No worries," I say. "It's already forgotten." I wipe up the dried blood with a rag, then pour bleach on the table to get rid of the germs. Some of the bleach splashes on my shorts.

She runs a hand over her cornrows. "Well, hey, thanks for being so cool about it."

I'm not sure why she decided to do her hair like that. She used to have silky black hair I loved running my fingers through. But that was a long time ago.

"And again," she continues, "I'm sorry about trying to drown your girlfriend."

Paige doesn't apologize. Ever. So she must be feeling horrible about what happened. But to hear her say *drown your girlfriend* sounds insane. Actually, the whole thing was pretty insane.

"I don't know what I was thinking," Paige says. "That wasn't me. Honest. I'm not that person. Not anymore."

"I appreciate your apology, but I'm not the one who needs it."

Paige toes the dirt with her boot. "Yeah, I know. I'm headed to see her next."

"Do I need to monitor the two of you?" I'm half-teasing and half-not.

"Nah, I promise I'll behave." Paige looks like she wants to say something else, but when someone calls her name, she says, "I better run." As she starts to walk away, she suddenly turns and says, "Look, I know it's none of my business, but I overheard you and Sienna talking." Her gaze falls to the ground, and she kicks at a rock. "If you want to go to Legas or whatever, I have a vehicle. It'll be tricky, but you could do it." She shrugs. "Think about it."

Paige walks away, leaving her offer hanging in the air.

Gritting my teeth, I pound my open palm on the table. The leftover bleach stings my skin and my nostrils. I thought when we left Rubex, Sienna and I were putting all of that behind us, including Zane. I have no desire to say good-bye to my crazy-ass father. No desire to see my perfect brother. No desire to *ever* return to Legas.

*But this is what Sienna wants,* I remind myself. And recent events have shown that Sienna is as stubborn as a mule and will do whatever she wants regardless of what I say or think. If I don't get on board with this idea, I have a feeling Sienna will do it on her own.

# 21

## Sienna

"You are gonna look so beautiful when I'm finished," I say to Emily. We're sitting in my tent, braiding her hair. Mom begged me to do something with it. It's too hard to wash it daily in the river, so this is the next best thing.

"As pretty as you?" Emily asks, her bright blue eyes looking up at me.

"Even prettier."

Emily giggles at this, then starts to hum a tune.

"Hold still, please," I say.

Emily sits up straighter, trying to look serious. Her once-beautiful ringlets are now wavy and matted. I pull the brush through her hair to get the knots out.

"Ow!" she exclaims.

"I'm sorry. This side is such a mess."

A deep but feminine voice calls from the other side of the tent, "Knock, knock." Before I can answer, the flap opens and Paige sticks her head in.

Instinctively, my body shifts like I'm shielding my sister from a predator.

Paige watches my attempt at doing Emily's hair before saying, "Need any help in here?"

"We're good," I say.

But at the same time Emily shouts, "Yes!"

Paige chuckles and ducks in, settling herself across from us on my bedroll. It's a tight squeeze, and with Paige in here now, it feels like she's taking up the entire tent with her presence. I swallow hard to calm my racing heart.

"I can always tell when there's a cry of distress," Paige says.

Naturally, after she tried to drown me, I'm a little wary of being alone with Paige. Is she stable? Is she safe around my sister? If she ever hurt someone I love, I'd slap her so hard her head would spin for days.

Emily points to Paige. "I want my hair to look like yours. Si-Si, can you do that?"

I eye Paige's hair. There are at least a dozen cornrows tightly braided to her head. There's no way I'd ever be able to do anything like that. I can barely do a single French braid.

"Well," I hedge, "I think this one braid will look fine."

"But I want hers." Emily goes into full-on pout mode.

"Hey, uh, I don't mind braiding the kid's hair," Paige says, seeming a little unsure of herself—not typical for Paige. "I mean, if she wants me to."

"The *kid* has a name," I seethe. "It's Emily."

Paige runs a hand over her cornrows. "Right. Sorry." Directing her attention to Emily, she says, "Emily, do you want me to braid your hair like mine?"

"We don't need your help," I protest, but nobody's listening to me.

"Does it take a long time?" Emily asks.

Smiling, Paige shakes her head. "Not too long. And you know the best part about these braids?"

Emily's eyes go round. "What?"

"You don't have to wash your hair as much."

"That. Sounds. Awesome," Emily says. "Will you do it on me? Puh-lease?"

"Absolutely." Paige's eyes flit to me. "I mean, as long as your sister doesn't mind?" Her head tilts in my direction like she's waiting for permission.

When I let go of Emily's hair, the braid begins to unravel. "Fine. Whatever." Scooting out of the way, I allow Paige to take my place behind Emily. I sit close, though, because if Paige so much as looks at Emily wrong, I'm taking her out.

She combs her fingers through Emily's hair, gently untangling it. As she begins to braid, it's like her fingers multiply. There are pieces of hair everywhere, and she somehow keeps up with all of them without mixing them together.

"I never had a mother or sister growing up," Paige says. She's speaking to Emily, but I have a feeling her words are also directed toward me. "But my father had lots of girlfriends." She forces a laugh. "Lots."

It's weird to hear her talk about her father, knowing she's talking about the Devil. I can't picture that man showing an ounce of compassion. What would it be like to be raised by him?

"One of them—Isabella—was the closest I ever came to having a mother. When I was little, she would braid my hair and sing me songs. Once I was older, she taught me how to braid." As a side note, she adds, "She also taught me how to pick up men, but that's another story." Glancing at me, she points to Emily and mouths, *Young ears.*

I want to say, *Did she teach you how to hit on other girls' boyfriends as well? Cause you sure are good at it.* But I don't. I bite the inside of my cheek to stop myself from saying something I'll regret.

Paige now has one row done, easily moving on to the next. "My father was loving, but he could also be cruel. And jealous. He didn't like it when I talked to guys. And he certainly didn't like it when I left him for the Fringe."

Hanging on to every word, Emily pipes in. "I don't like boys. They're stupid."

Laughing, Paige pats her head. "Keep thinking that,

girlfriend. Keep thinking that."

"Why did you leave?" The words pop out before I realize I asked a question.

Paige shrugs, her eyes focused on Emily's hair. "Because of him. Because of Trey."

"You loved him." It's a statement, not a question.

"Not at first. I was only eighteen, but he opened my eyes to what I was. What I could become. My father never gave me that opportunity. I was more of a prize to show off, rather than a daughter. He practically kept me in a display case for his men to ogle, but never to touch." Paige leans toward me, her hands still entangled in Emily's hair. "Not that it stopped some of the men," she whispered. "This one guy and I got a little too close, if you know what I mean, and my father's right-hand man gutted him like a fish."

"Did you say something about fish?" Emily chirps. "Ew, I hate fish."

"Yeah, me too, small stuff," Paige says, then winks at me.

I turn away. I'd hate for her to think we're anything but enemies. She can braid my sister's hair and tell stories until the cows come home, but it's never gonna change what happened between us.

When Paige finishes several minutes later, Emily's hair is perfectly braided in half a dozen cornrows. We don't have a mirror for her to look into, so she runs her fingers over her head, feeling the tight braids.

"I love it," she exclaims. "Thank you, Paige." Emily flings her arms around Paige's neck, and I cringe. It's not Emily's fault. She doesn't know Paige is a snake.

Paige's eyebrows raise in surprise before her arms tighten around Emily's back. "I'm glad you like it. Now, when it's time to wash it, in about ten days or so, come to me and I'll give you some pointers. Okay?"

"Okay." Emily bounds out of the tent, shouting something

about showing Mom her new hair.

"She's fun," Paige says, smiling.

I start to rise to my feet, intent on getting out of here and away from Paige as quickly as possible, but her hand latches on to my arm, stopping me. I give her a scathing look, and her hand slides off.

"Look," Paige says. "I'm really sorry about the other night. When Dalton returned to Camp and informed me that Trey killed my father, I snapped. I was angry with Trey, and I took it out on you. And I shouldn't have."

I shift my body until I'm facing her. "What do you want me to say? Thank you? I forgive you? Sorry, Paige, not gonna happen. You freakin' tried to drown me. And then a gun? I mean, seriously? If Trey hadn't come…" I let the thought hang like a vulture ready to swoop down on us.

"I wasn't trying to hurt you. I was about to let you up when Trey came. And the gun? It wasn't even loaded. It was just me being dramatic." She rests her hand on my knee. "I'm sorry. But if you don't want to forgive me, that's your choice."

She launches to her feet and ducks out of the tent.

It takes me a minute to recover from having her so close. Kind of like finding a rattlesnake in the bed and watching it slither away—grateful it didn't bite, but shocked by the narrow miss.

How dare she put this back on me. I have every right to be angry with her. And if she gets too close to my family, I will strike.

# 22
# Zane

I've only met my father's lawyer a handful of times, but when I see the plaque on the mahogany door, I immediately recognize the name. Porter Steadman.

Steele and I are meeting with him today to go over my father's will and assets. When the door opens, we are greeted by a middle-aged man with distinguished gray running through his dark hair. His smile is warm but sympathetic.

"Please, come in." After he invites us to sit in leather upholstered chairs facing an ornate oak desk, he takes a seat behind it, clasping his hands in front of him. "I'm so sorry about your father. He was an exceptional man."

I shift awkwardly in my seat. I'm not ready to sit and talk about what kind of man Harlow was. Not here. Not right now. Not with a man I barely know. So I nod and say, "Yes, he was."

Beside me, Steele crosses his legs. "I believe you have some documents for us?" Leave it to Steele, always the businessman. No time for chitchat or pleasantries.

"Oh, yes, of course." Mr. Steadman pulls out a leather pouch from his desk, then unzips it. Out comes a small handheld device and a computer chip. After sliding on his reading glasses, Mr. Steadman inserts the computer chip in the slot on the side of the device and powers up the machine. Silence fills the room as he scans the digital documents in front of him. "Well, this is odd," he murmurs, mainly to himself.

"What?" I ask, leaning forward in my seat.

The lawyer shoots a glance at us. "If you'll just give me a minute." He hurries from the room with the machine clutched in his hands.

"What is going on?" I mutter, slumping back in my seat.

Steele shrugs but doesn't say anything, only pulls out his Lynk and starts typing away. When Mr. Steadman enters the room a moment later, he apologizes and takes his seat.

"It appears your father changed his will two days before his death. I was out of town last week, so I was completely unaware of this change. He met with my colleague Jin Lee."

"Changed his will?" I question, easing to the edge of my seat. "Changed it how?"

Mr. Steadman fixes his gaze on me. "Zane, your father named Steele as the one to inherit the company and most of the assets."

Steele sucks in a sharp breath, his Lynk momentarily forgotten.

"I don't understand," I say. "My father was very clear I was to be the one to run the company—"

"I'm sorry." Mr. Steadman's voice is firm. "He did, however, leave you the safe house." He glances at the screen. "It doesn't indicate an address for the safe house, but I assume you know where it is?"

I'm in too much shock to nod or say anything. Mr. Steadman turns his attention to Steele. "Your father left you Match 360, Chromo 120, his condo in Rubex, and all other assets." Then addressing us both, he says, "The house on Hamstead Hill is to be sold and split equally."

Mr. Steadman drones on and on about signing legal documents and a bunch of other stuff, but I've tuned out. I can't believe it. I've lost everything. Everything. How could my father do this to me? I thought we'd worked it out.

Maybe, in the end, he wanted to keep the company in the family. Have it go to someone who shares the same DNA.

What will I tell Arian? I have no job, no income, only a safe house in the mountains that's been compromised. I'm as good as broke.

I rise quickly from my chair, scooting it back several inches in the process. Mr. Steadman looks at me in alarm. "I—need some air. Excuse me."

Once I'm in the parking lot, I pace back and forth. This isn't how it's supposed to be. My life has been mapped for me since birth. First Sienna threw everything off course, made me doubt what I knew I was born to do. And just when I thought I was back on track, life throws me another curveball. What am I supposed to do now? Everything I've known, everything I've worked toward, is gone. A single document has erased my future.

*I wish Sienna were here.*

I push the unwanted thought away. But I can't deny the truth. If Sienna were here, she'd know exactly what to say to calm me down. Her emerald eyes would offer sympathy and support. Her soft hands would offer comfort. Her measured words would offer perspective. Maybe even hope.

I try not to think about it. If Sienna were here, all of those things would be wonderful. But in truth, it would be her lips, and the feel of them against mine, that would offer the power to help me forget.

# 23

# Zane

"How did it go with the lawyer?" Greta asks when I return home. She's in the kitchen, rolling out dough. "Not well," I say, leaning against the counter. "I was completely blindsided."

Greta stops rolling and wipes her hands on her apron. "Oh no, what happened?"

I shrug, letting my hands fall to my sides in frustration. "I don't know. My father changed his will a couple of days before his death, and he left both companies to Steele. We're to sell the house and split it equally."

"There must be a mistake," Greta says. "Your father would never do that. He's been talking about leaving the companies to you since the day you were born."

"I guess he changed his mind."

Greta shakes her head, moving to the fridge. "That doesn't sound at all like Harlow."

"It's an official document with his signature. He changed it, and he signed it."

Greta pulls out a stick of butter. "There must have been a reason."

"I already know the reason. He decided to keep the company in the family."

Greta drops the butter on the counter, moving to place

her hand on my cheek. "Oh, sweetie. You *were* his family. He loved you very, very much. I've never seen a man so proud of a son before. You may not have had his DNA, but you've always had his heart."

I swallow back the tightness in my throat, wrapping my arms around Greta. "Thank you," I whisper.

When I pull back, her eyelashes are coated with tears. "I miss him," she says, wiping her eyes.

"Me too." I pinch the bridge of my nose to keep my own tears at bay. "He was a better man than I gave him credit for, especially recently." I start to leave the room, but Greta's voice stops me.

"Zane?"

I turn around.

"You don't need a company to do great things. You only need to be you."

Her words resound in my ears as I trudge down the hall, my footsteps heavy. I pause outside my father's office. The door is closed. I haven't been in there since before he died. It's like a tomb that houses his memory. This office *was* my father. The wood-paneled walls, the leather-bound books, the mahogany desk—those things embody his spirit.

I turn the knob, applying a little pressure, and the door swings open. It takes me four hesitant steps until I'm completely inside, then I shut the door behind me. Everything is as he left it. Papers on his desk, the wastebasket tipped over like he was searching for something he'd thrown away, his bar cart still covered in decanters of liquor.

The office smells like him. Expensive cologne, imported leather, and aged brandy.

His leather chair sits lonely behind his desk, growing cold from lack of use. If I try hard enough, I can picture him there, his glasses perched on the bridge of his nose, tiny papers littering his desk as one idea after another pops in his head.

I circle the room, running my hands over the engraved volumes of his thousands of books until I make it to his desk. Taking a seat in his chair, I close my eyes, letting a decade's worth of memories take over my mind. My tenth birthday party when my father hired an entire circus to come and perform. I was addicted to acrobats for a month after that. Or the first time my father took me to the ocean and taught me to sail.

But there are bad memories, too. The year he forgot my birthday and missed my party because he was busy launching a new product. Or the time he broke my lacrosse stick because he thought it was too dangerous for me to play. After all, he wouldn't want me to mess up my perfect face. Or the time he lied to me about my biological father and how my mother died.

Harlow wasn't a perfect father, but he was mine.

I sit up in the chair, opening my eyes. Absentmindedly, I pick up one of the scraps of paper from his desk, then another. They are torn like they are all a part of a bigger piece of paper. It becomes a kind of game as I try to puzzle them back together. There's a few missing, so I search the floor for them, thinking they may have fallen off the desk. When I don't see them there, I look in the overturned waste basket. Bingo. Two scraps of paper lay at the bottom of the otherwise-empty can.

I add the final pieces to the paper puzzle, squinting at the words. The writing is practically illegible, the cursive scrawled like someone wrote it in a hurry. But I know what it says. My heart pounds as I read a final message from my father.

*I'm sorry, Zane.*

Once the shock of seeing a message to me from beyond the grave wears off, I notice the series of numbers and letters at the bottom of the page.

10-NO-155

Is this some sort of code or something? Are these numbers supposed to have significance? Ten. What is significant about the number ten? There are ten bedrooms in this house? There are ten Match 360 or Chromo 120 facilities around the Province? There are ten reasons why he left the company to Steele instead of me?

And what's with the word *no*? No, he didn't think I should be the heir? No, he didn't mean to hurt me, but it's business, not personal? No, I shouldn't be reading this?

The number 155 is the most confusing of all. It's such a large number I have no idea what it could represent. I lean back in the seat, my hands pressed together, forming a triangle. This was my dad's signature stance, one he did when he was mulling things over. I guess I hope to absorb some of his thought process by pretending to be him for a second.

My eyes wander around the room, searching for a clue to what he was thinking. He clearly left this message for me, but why?

And then I see it. I rise slowly from the chair and make my way to the wall of bookcases. My fingers trail the spines of one of my father's most-prized possessions—a collection of antique encyclopedias. He bought them off the black market because such a collection hasn't been available in over fifty years, not since before the Upheaval.

NO doesn't stand for the word *no*, but for letters in the alphabet. And the number ten doesn't have any special significance other than the number on an encyclopedia. Sure enough, my fingertips rest on an encyclopedia in the middle of the bunch. It's number ten and it encompasses N-O topics.

The book is in pristine condition, but even so, I delicately remove it from the bookcase. An item this old must be handled with care. It's what my father would have wanted. I flip to page 155, and there it is. A piece of paper folded and folded until it's only a small rectangle. I take it out and carefully replace the book.

Before opening the paper, I take a deep breath. It feels like there's a strange significance to this moment, that somewhere, Harlow is applauding me from beyond the grave.

It's a typed letter, and as I read further, I realize it's not a letter at all, but a death threat.

*Mr. Ryder,*

*You have a very lovely son. If you'd like him to live a long, full life, you'll do exactly what I say. Zane Ryder must not inherit your company. The company and the entirety of its assets should be bequeathed to your eldest son, Steele Ryder. Change your will before your son's wedding, or he'll never live to see his wedding night.*

*Best,*

*A Concerned Citizen*

"What are you doing in here?"

I jump at the sound of Steele's voice. He's standing in the doorway, taking up most of it with his bulky frame. I've never realized how scary my brother looks until this moment.

I quickly fold the paper, hurriedly shoving it into my back pocket. "Just reminiscing."

"This is my office now," Steele says. "You shouldn't be in here."

"Technically, I own half this house. And since we haven't decided who owns which half, I think it's fair to say this office *could* be mine."

Steele glowers.

I straighten up to my full height. "Do you even miss him, Steele? Or was his life and legacy some sort of prize to be won?" Without waiting for an answer, I shove past him, my heart about to explode with rage, my hands clenched.

It isn't until I've made it out the front door, down the

steps, and slid into the front seat of my car that I let what I read finally sink in.

My father didn't change his will because he didn't love me. He changed it to protect me.

And the fact he died two days later is more than a coincidence.

My father was murdered. And I will find the person responsible.

# 24

## Sienna

P aige hasn't sent me with the hunting crew since Trey and I came back with the mule deer and three coyotes. I was impressed with our kills, but I guess she wasn't. I'm kind of sick of being in competition with her. She's clearly smarter, faster, stronger, and a much better shot. Why can't she let me have my small successes?

Don't have to think too hard about that one. It's because she wants what she can't have. Trey. My boyfriend.

Even though she came by and apologized for trying to drown me—*psycho!*—she's now making my life a living hell by putting me on outhouse duty. I guess because I didn't accept her apology? Who knows.

It seems as if I should be used to the smell of feces after living with my own for a month, but nothing can prepare me for this. I gag as soon as I lift the tarp—a ghetto version of a door. I'm wearing gloves, but I think a hazmat suit would be more appropriate for this job. With my supplies, I get to work.

I'm in the process of removing the third outhouse— wooden boards nailed together to form a seat with a real toilet seat attached—to a different location, when Trey finds me.

He eyes the toilets. "What are you doing?"

"I'm moving the outhouses, as instructed. Apparently, the poop containers are full."

Chuckling, Trey looks around. "So you have to do what exactly?"

"Well," I say in my official outhouse-spokesperson voice. "First, you remove this carefully constructed structure—" I roll my eyes as I point to the makeshift potty. "Then I cover the full hole with dirt." I point to my pile of dirt. "Then—oh, and this is the best part—I dig a hole for the new poop. Fantastic and fun. I couldn't *ask* for a better job." I give him a sarcastic smile.

Trey laughs, throwing his head back. "At least you haven't lost your spirit."

"Nope, Paige can't take that away," I say through gritted teeth.

Moving closer, he rubs my arms with his hands. "How about a break?" he murmurs, his eyes already focused on my lips. "I think my little poop scooper needs one."

"Ah, but I'm not scooping, only covering." I hold up my gloved hands. "You might want to take a rain check on that… um, break. You don't want to know where these hands have been."

Ignoring my warning, Trey leans in, kissing the skin right below my ear, which, of course, sparks a flare-like response. Like I've just shot a firework into the sky, something that reads, *Yes, I want this. No, don't stop.*

But then I catch a whiff of the outhouse, the one I haven't moved yet. I push Trey away with my elbows. "Um, yeah, not here. Not happening."

Trey grabs my arm, leading me a safe distance away from the stench. "You know what we need?" he says, his voice low.

I cock my head to the side to indicate I'm listening.

"We need some time. Just the two of us. What do you say? You up for finding those hot springs tonight?" He tweaks an eyebrow as one side of his mouth turns up in a crooked grin.

My stomach tightens at the thought of being alone with Trey. It's been so long… "Maybe."

Trey's mouth moves into a full grin, dimple and all. "I'll take that as a yes." He kisses my cheek, his lips brushing my ear as he says, "Meet me outside your tent tonight once everyone is asleep." His words are low, rumbling into my ear.

"Okay," I whisper back.

I'm expecting him to leave and go back to whatever it is he was doing before he found me, but instead, he stays put. "Great. Now, put me to work."

"You're offering to help?"

"Of course."

"Okay. Do you wanna dig the hole for the next outhouse?" I point to the designated spot.

"Sure." He grabs the shovel from the ground, getting right to work.

I find myself staring at his hunched-over form, at the hair at the base of his neck curling from sweat. I admire the way the shirt clings to his strong back and shoulders, showing off the lines of corded muscles. The biceps in his arms grow and flex with each scoop of dirt.

I'm toast. I'm so into him it's not even funny. He has my heart sitting right in the palm of his hand.

I only hope he's careful with it.

Once the rest of Camp is quiet, I steal out of my tent. Trey is already outside by the smoldering campfire, waiting for me. He holds a finger to his lips, reaching to take my hand in his. We sneak through Camp until we reach the stream. That's when he finally speaks. "I think if we follow this, it will lead us to a trail that takes us to the hot springs."

I grip his hand tighter. Without any fires going, it's pitch black at night. The air is tinged with the smell of smoke and burning wood. Once we're far enough away the light won't bother the other Fringe and Zenith members, Trey clicks on a flashlight, shining it on the ground in front of us.

"How far is it?" I ask after we've walked in silence for a few minutes.

"Not more than a mile," Trey responds.

A coyote howls in the distance, and I jump. He chuckles and draws me closer so I'm now hanging on to his arm instead of holding his hand. I think he likes the whole damsel-in-distress routine. Probably makes him feel like a big, powerful man.

Now that the sun is long gone, the air has turned cool. I shiver, trying to draw warmth from Trey. He's like a bear coming out of hibernation—his body is always warm.

"I've never been in a hot spring before," I say to fill the silence. "Have you?"

"Yeah. Once. There're some not far from Legas."

I bite my tongue to keep from asking if it was with Paige. I'd prefer not to know. Also, the last thing I want is him thinking about her while he's with me.

"You know," Trey says, "I wouldn't have blamed you for choosing Zane."

Well, that came out of nowhere. I tug him to a stop. "What do you mean?"

"I mean, Zane was there for you when I wasn't. I know you have strong feelings for him. Hell, you may even love him. If you had chosen him, I would've understood."

"Is-is that what you wanted? For me to choose Zane?"

"No! God, no, Sienna. I'm just saying I hope you're here with me because you love me, and not because you feel guilty."

I try to swallow back the lump climbing up my throat. My voice is soft, almost hoarse when I speak. "I do love you, Trey."

In the moonlight, his eyes are warm as he tucks a stray piece of hair behind my ear, his hand lingering next to my cheek. "That's all I need to hear."

He takes my hand in his again, and we walk in silence the rest of the way. But something has changed between us. And it's a good thing. The air is charged with electricity, and when his thumb glides along the back of my hand, my stomach flips. There's nothing keeping us from being together. Zane is gone. He chose Arian. And I'm choosing Trey.

We have to climb over a few rocks and shimmy through a few tight spaces to reach the hot springs. Once we're there, we undress in silence. I have a tank top under my shirt, which I leave on with my panties. Bathing suits are somewhat of a luxury for fugitives on the run. Trey removes everything except for his boxer shorts. This is starting to feel all too familiar...

I can't see the colors and intricate detail of his phoenix tattoo until the moonlight slants across his skin. Unconsciously, I reach out and trace the outline of the giant bird and its wings. Trey's back muscles tighten beneath my fingertips.

"When I thought you were dead," I say, "I had this weird dream."

Trey turns to face me, his eyes searching my face.

"I dreamed we were swimming in the Lagoon and then you... disappeared. There was this bird. A phoenix. Watching me, studying me. Then I heard this voice—your voice—telling me not to give up. It was like you were... there."

Trey closes his eyes for a second. When he opens them, they glisten with tears. "When you talk about me dying, it's like you're talking about someone else. It's a little surreal. I don't remember anything from that night."

"Do you remember going after the Devil and his men the night the Compound was bombed?"

"Yes." He smiles. "And I remember holding you in my arms. But then it's...blank."

I figured as much. I'm not sure how much he knows or if he even wants to know, but I feel like I have to tell him. "I got up to use the bathroom. And that's when the bombs hit.

Curly—" Tears fill my eyes at his name. "Curly and I are the ones who found you. When I refused to leave without you, he carried you out. Carried you the whole way."

Trey swipes at his eyes. "I owe him my life—" His voice breaks. "And yet, I couldn't save him."

I'm openly sobbing now. "Neither could I."

Trey wraps me in his arms, our bodies shaking with grief. His tears bathe my shoulder while mine run down his chest. "I'm sorry," he murmurs over and over. He holds me until my tears run dry.

When I tilt my head back, he kisses me, the remnants of our salty tears mingling as he parts my lips with his tongue. My head is spinning, my body aflame, as his hands caress my arms, sparking heat in this otherwise-chilly night air.

He only stops kissing me long enough to pick me up in his arms and carry me to the hot springs. I wrap my arms around his neck, burying my face in his skin. He smells of campfire, cedar, and a hint of sweat. I cling to him because he's the only solid thing I can count on right now.

The water is the temperature of a hot tub, and after the cool night air, I welcome it against my skin. Trey settles on a rock or something submerged in the water, then pulls me onto his lap. Our scenery tattoos glow, a reflection against the water—his a tree of strength and mine a butterfly of change.

His fingers trace my Fringe tattoo, then trail down my arm until I'm shivering. I use my fingers to memorize his face, outlining his lips, his nose, the dimple in the center of his chin. When I move down his neck to the soft spot between his collarbone, he closes his eyes and tilts his chin back, an almost-imperceptible groan escaping from the back of his throat. I don't stop there. My hands have a mind of their own, and all they want to do is explore the solidness of him. They run over his shoulders, tracing the muscles, gliding over smooth skin, then move down to his biceps and the corded muscles there.

When I reach his hands and intertwine them with my own, he opens his eyes. Those are the eyes of the man who's stolen my heart.

For a long time, we stare at each other. I focus on the deep blue outer ring of his irises and the thick, dark lashes framing his eyes. Any girl would kill for his eyes, and on him, they're incredible.

I blink slowly, not wanting to tear my gaze from his, not wanting to ruin the moment. He does the same, his lashes catching on each other. We stay like this for minutes, possibly hours. My heart thunders in my chest, and I know he can feel my pulse through my fingertips. Every inch of me is *alive*. So alive and aching for his love.

When his eyes do shift, they flit from my eyes to my mouth to my cheeks like he's taking me all in, memorizing each detail. Under his gaze, I feel beautiful, wanted, loved. But these are only words. There's no way to truly describe how he makes me feel. It's an otherworldly sensation that leaves me floating above my body, like I'm watching a red-haired girl and a dark-haired boy surrounded by darkness, but only aware of each other.

When Trey finally does speak, his voice is deep, husky, almost hoarse. "Sienna, I love you."

"I love you, too," I whisper.

His lips find mine and he kisses me, urgently this time. Like he can't get enough and is afraid I might disappear. My heart trips over itself as it steadily gains speed. It's going so hard I fear it may burst from my chest. When his hands entangle themselves in my hair, I can't breathe.

After several minutes of kissing, Trey pulls back and asks, "Is this okay?"

"More than okay," I murmur, drawing him back to me. I want to be as close to him as I can. I want to feel his warmth, his solidness, his hands. "I don't want this night to end."

## Fearless

"It doesn't have to," Trey says, tugging on my bottom lip with his teeth.

And that's the way we stay—in a hot spring, in the moonlight, in a place where we're the only two people who exist.

# 25
## Zane

I haven't seen Arian since my father's cremation. I'm not sure what she's thinking or what's in store for us. Still trying to process my father's sudden death, I haven't had much time to think about my future with Arian or if there *is* a future with Arian.

When I arrive at her house, I find her lounging out back by her pool. She rises from the chaise, then kisses me on the cheek. It's hard to read her emotions because her eyes are covered by giant sunglasses.

"How are you?" she asks, her mouth lined with worry. She pulls her sunglasses off; her eyes are worried, too.

"I've been better." I ease onto the chair next to her.

"I'm so sorry, Zane. I can't imagine what you're going through—"

"My father left everything to Steele," I blurt out.

Arian stops mid-sentence, one hand still in the air, because I think she was about to rest it on my leg. Her hand drops to her lap. "What?"

"We met with the lawyer the other day. My father left Steele everything—the company, the condo, all of his money. Everything."

Arian shakes her head. "I don't understand. Harlow has raved about you, about us, since the time we were born. We didn't have normal childhoods because of it. I mean, he always said he was protecting us so one day we could be the poster children for his company, for your company when you took over after his death." Arian stands and paces in front of me. "Something's not right."

Do I tell her the truth? Would doing so put her in danger? No, she needs to know.

"My father received a death threat only days before he died. I don't think he had a choice."

Arian's mouth drops open. "Someone threatened to kill your father? Who would do that?"

"The note wasn't about my father." I pause. "It was about me."

"Who would want to kill you? You're Zane Ryder."

This is something I should have told her before I allowed her to walk down the aisle toward me. If Harlow hadn't had a heart attack, she and I would be married right now—on our honeymoon even—and I still haven't told her the truth about who I am.

Leaning my head against the back of the angled chair, I heave a huge sigh. "Arian, there's something I need to tell you. Can you take a seat, please?"

Once she's sitting gingerly on the edge of her lounger, I launch into the story of my mother, the genetically modified embryos, and the baby switcheroo. The whole time I'm talking, she stares at me like she's waiting for me to tell her this is all a big joke. When I never do, she leans back, places her head in her hands, and says in a small voice, "So you and I were never supposed to be together?"

Closing my eyes, I try to figure out the best way to answer her. I remember how I felt when I learned all this for the first time. I was angry, hurt, confused—but Sienna had been there to help pick up the pieces.

That's what I need to do for Arian right now—pick up the

pieces. And give her some hope everything will work out as it should.

When I open my eyes, Arian is staring at me, her beautiful face so broken and confused. "No, we weren't. You were made to be a perfect genetic match for my brother, Trey Winchester, who is now the leader of the Fringe."

Arian gasps at this revelation. Tears fill her eyes. Slide down her cheeks. "I don't know who I am anymore."

I take her hands in mine. "You're still you. You're still the intelligent, gorgeous, genetically modified Arian Stratford, who is destined to do remarkable things. But your worth doesn't need to be tied to me or any guy. You can do or be anything you want."

"Anything?"

I nod firmly. "Absolutely anything."

Arian gives me a shy smile. "I'd like to study music, see if I can make a career of it."

"See! You're finding yourself already."

"Thank you, Zane. I feel like you've given me a purpose."

With a smile, I kiss her hand. "You've always had a purpose. Now you're free to live it."

"Thank you," she whispers. She sits a little straighter. "What will you do now?"

I study her face, memorizing each detail. This may be the last time I see her. "It's time for me to find my own purpose."

# 26

# Zane

Someone's tailing me. I first noticed the black SUV a few miles back. They've maintained a safe distance, never passing me, never coming closer, but they've made every turn I've made and sped up when I've sped up. I change lanes to be sure, and they change lanes also.

The windows are tinted, making it too dark to see inside the vehicle. I can't go home. Greta is there. And if they wish to do me harm, I won't lead them to her.

I picture the note with the death threat. My father changed his will to protect me, but what if it wasn't enough? Maybe these guys want to make good on their promise.

I make a turn, heading away from the suburbs and toward the Gateway. Of course, they do the same. When I'm almost to the Gateway, I check my rearview mirror again. There aren't any other cars around now, and they've gotten bolder. They're right on my tail, their vehicle urging mine to go faster. I look for a license plate, but there isn't one on the front of the car. I press the accelerator hard, the engine purring in response as my little sports car surges forward, leaving a wider berth.

They speed up also, until they're so close I can make out two figures in the front seat. Their vehicle bumps the back of mine, sending me fishtailing a little. Once I regain control, I take off. I turn the corner so fast I'm fairly confident I almost skied the car on two wheels. The SUV does the same. For the first time ever, I push my car to the limit. I know she's faster than the SUV behind me, and being lower to the ground, she can take the turns at a higher speed, too.

The speedometer climbs as I grip the steering wheel hard, my knuckles turning white. The distance between us increases. Without slowing down, I turn onto the Gateway, the car fishtailing again. I have to find somewhere to hide.

That's when I spot the MGM Grand, or what's left of it. It certainly doesn't look so "grand" anymore. Half the building is missing like its insides were gutted. I turn fast onto the street that will take me to the old parking garage. I'm not sure if it's still safe, but it's the only option I have at the moment.

My wheels screech as I tear through the parking garage, climbing higher and higher with each turn. I'm sincerely hoping they didn't see me come in here.

I park behind a pillar where I have a perfect vantage point of any cars that might come up the ramp. Rolling down my window, I listen for the sound of tire treads. So far, there's only silence.

When several minutes have passed, I inch the car out of its hiding spot and drive slowly down the ramp. Before exiting the garage, I stop and look both ways—the road is clear, no sign of the SUV. Once I reach the main road in the Gateway, I stop and do the same. The road is empty. I turn and floor it, not slowing down until the Gateway is but a speck in my rearview mirror. My hands relax on the steering wheel as I decelerate to a more reasonable speed.

As I near the suburbs and more traffic, I glance behind me again. Thankfully, the SUV is nowhere in sight.

I breathe deep as the momentum of what just happened hits me. Someone tried to kill me. Again.

There was the time at the Match 360 Extravaganza when I was almost beheaded by a bullet. But that was different. Back then, I was the face of the company; I represented what the company stood for. But now, I'm nothing. I don't own the company, and my father is dead. Why would anyone want to kill me?

Not for the first time do I wish Sienna were here. She would know what to do. Or, at least, we would be able to figure something out together. Trey, too. He and I worked together like a well-oiled machine to come up with a plan to rescue Sienna, Trina, and Curly from Confinement.

But Sienna can never return to Legas, not until she's exonerated of her crimes. Even then, Madame Neiman won't stop hunting for her and the rest of the Fringe. Which means I'll never see her again. Unless…

A thought forms.

I don't know if it'll work or if she'll see it, but I have to try.

# 27

## Trey

Today is Sienna's birthday. I don't know if she remembers, because it's easy to lose track of time here at the Camp. The only reason I know it's today is because her mom confided in me. I want to do something special for her, and I've been wracking my brain to think of something.

I finally decide the best gift is something simple. Sienna is a no-frills kind of girl—and I'm not exactly known for my romantic capabilities.

I catch up to her after breakfast where she's brushing her teeth at the communal trough. Laurel made this kind of disgusting homemade toothpaste, but it's supposed to help our teeth so they don't fall out before we're thirty. When Sienna smiles at me, her teeth are coated in the thick beige paste. I wait until she rinses before getting close enough to kiss her cheek.

"Hey," I say, "do you want to take off? Go somewhere?"

She shakes the excess water from her toothbrush, rubbing her other hand across her mouth. "What about hunting? I thought a group was going today."

"They don't need us. Paige said we can take the day off." Truth is, I think Paige still feels guilty for what she did to Sienna. Maybe this is her way of making it up to her.

"The entire day? What about other chores?"

She has no clue. Smiling, I say, "Do you have any idea what today is?"

At that moment, Emily bounces between us, jumping up and down. "Si-Si! Happy birthday! Happy birthday!"

Vivian hurries over and wraps her arms around Sienna. "Happy birthday, my beautiful girl. I can't believe you're eighteen."

"Wait," Sienna says. "Today's not my birthday." Her eyes swing between us. "My birthday is—"

"October 6th," Vivian finishes for her. "And that's today. Just ask Asher. He's the one keeping track of the calendar."

Sienna's gaze follows Vivian's finger to where Asher is making marks on a wooden board. When Asher looks over and sees Sienna, he smiles and gives her a thumbs-up.

"We need to do something fun," Emily says, twirling one of her braids.

Vivian glances at me, and I nod. I've already told her my plan. "Well, hun, Trey and I already have that covered."

"You do?" Emily and Sienna say at the same time.

"Um, yeah," I say. "How would you guys like to go for a hike?"

Sienna raises an eyebrow. "Okay."

"Yes!" Emily squeals. "I wanna go!"

"And then tonight, we can celebrate," Vivian suggests. "I'll cook dinner. Maybe some rabbit stew? It'll be like old times."

Sienna smiles at her mom. "Yeah. I'd like that."

Vivian hugs her daughter again. "Happy birthday, sweetie." Then to me, she says, "What time, Trey?"

"Let's leave in an hour. We can get an early start. That way, we can be back in plenty of time to get dinner going."

Vivian agrees. "Sounds good."

Excited, Emily runs away, with Vivian following close behind as she calls after her daughter to come and brush her teeth. At first, Emily dodges her mom's attempts to catch her before giggling and falling into her arms. Chuckling, I turn back to Sienna. Like her older sister, Emily is quickly grabbing a hold of my heart.

"So we're going hiking?" Sienna asks, closing one eye as she gazes up at me.

I grip her arms, adjusting her body until she's out of the sun. Leaning over, I kiss the side of her mouth. "First of all, happy birthday. You're eighteen now, which means you're technically an adult. Since I'm twenty-one, I get to welcome you to the land of adulthood. Feel any different?"

Sienna shrugs, a grin playing at the corners of her mouth. "I don't know. Should I?"

"Not really. Age is just a number."

"Okay, so what's the second thing?"

"Well, second, I don't have anything elaborate planned, but I thought it would be fun to spend time with you and your family. Does that work for you?"

It's now a full-fledged grin. "Can't think of anything better."

"Meet you outside your tent in an hour?"

"I'll be there."

My arms slip around her waist as I pull her in for a quick kiss. "See you soon," I whisper.

Hand in hand, Sienna and I walk down the trail, away from Camp while Vivian and Emily follow. I have a pack full of food and water and a beautiful girl by my side—life can't get better than this.

Emily breaks away from her mother and runs ahead of us, twirling with her arms spread wide. She stops and kicks at the dirt, creating a cloud of clay-particles and covering her shoes and shorts in orange silt.

"Emily!" her mother chastises, but Emily only giggles and

runs further ahead. "Emily, slow down. You need to stay with us!"

Emily glances back and laughs, but keeps going. She's pretty far ahead now.

"It's okay, Vivian," I say, "I'll run ahead and catch up to her."

Sienna gives me a grateful look.

"Thank you, Trey," Vivian says.

I start jogging, but when Emily sees me catching up to her, she squeals and runs faster. Chuckling, I increase my speed. Her little legs are no match for mine, but I act like she's so fast I'm having trouble catching her. "Slow... down... Emily," I pretend pant. "I... can't... keep... up."

She giggles and keeps running. It's amazing how much endurance little kids have.

When I reach her, I scoop her up in my arms, spinning until I'm almost dizzy. She laughs, her arms clutching my neck. As soon as I set her on the ground, she says, "Let's do it again."

I chuckle at her fortitude. She reminds me so much of Sienna sometimes. When I check to see where Sienna and her mother are, they're a speck in the distance. Guess I didn't realize how far we ran.

"How about this?" I suggest. "How about I race you back to your mom and sister? If you win, I'll let you ride on my shoulders for a while."

Beaming up at me, she nods. "Ready-set-GO!" She takes off running before I realize we're starting.

I sprint after her, always staying a couple of steps behind, making sure she wins. "You're too fast," I call.

She giggles uncontrollably and hollers back, "You're too slow."

When her legs become sluggish, I can tell she's getting tired. I turn my run into a slow-motion jog as I pull up beside her. "You're not gonna let me pass you, are you?"

Sweaty curls stick to her forehead, and she's breathing hard. "No way!"

With one last burst of energy, she propels herself forward, falling into her mother's arms. "I did it," she pants. "I win!"

I slow to a stop. "You know what that means." I swing Emily onto my shoulders and she wraps her arms around my head, covering my eyes. "Wait, I can't see," I joke. "Where did everything go?" My hands go out in front of me as I pretend to feel the air around us.

Emily laughs and uncovers my eyes, her weight shifting as she does.

"I bet someone's tired after all that running," Sienna says, peering up at Emily.

"Yeah, I'm pretty beat," I joke. Sienna snorts and slaps my arm. "Oh, you mean Emily? Yeah, I think I wore her out."

"Did not," Emily says. "Wanna race again?"

Vivian lays a hand on Emily's thigh. "Settle down, sweetheart. You don't want to wear yourself out before we get to the canyon."

"Fine," Emily says. She relaxes on my shoulders, bending down to whisper in my ear. "I love you, Trey. You're the bestest in the whole world."

Sienna overhears and raises an eyebrow at me.

"Looks like you have some competition," I tease.

Sienna laughs, the happiest I think I've ever seen her. "Looks like I do."

We've been hiking for about an hour when it's clear Emily is beat. I've been carrying her most of the time, but when I set her down, at her insistence, she whines to her mom. "I'm tired, Mama. Can we go back now?"

"Sure, sweetie." To Sienna she says, "I'm sorry to bail on

your birthday hike, but I think you'll be in good hands." She gives her daughter a wink that doesn't go unnoticed by me. "I should probably get back and start cooking that stew."

"We can walk back with you, Vivian," I offer.

"No need for that," Vivian says. "You kids go and have fun."

"You sure, Mom?"

"Absolutely. Just don't be late for dinner." Vivian kisses Sienna on the cheek.

"Come on, love," Vivian says, pulling Emily close. "Let's get you back to Camp for a nap."

Sienna and I watch them head down the trail toward Camp. The sun is high in the sky now and beats down on my shoulders.

Sienna sighs like she's watching a piece of herself leave, then she turns to me and says, "You're really great with Em."

"So are you."

"Yeah, but I'm her sister. I kind of have to be."

I chuckle at this. "Not true. I'm sure there are some pretty sucky sisters out there. You happen to be a good one." Now that we're alone, I need to touch her. I pull her into my arms and kiss her forehead. "The other day, you said I didn't know you," I murmur. "I want to spend the rest of the day doing that. Getting to know you."

"Trey," she protests, pulling back to look up at me. "I was just upset when I said those things."

"No, you were right. I know a lot about you, but there's still a lot I don't know, too. I want to know everything."

"Even the boring stuff?"

"Especially the boring stuff."

She grins. "Okay, let's see. I suck at math. I love to swim. My favorite color is blue. My favorite breakfast is chocolate oatmeal because my dad used to make it for me and my sister every morning. Hmm, let's see, what else?"

"First boy you ever kissed."

Her face flushes. "Um, why don't we skip that one?"

"Aw, come on. I thought we weren't keeping secrets. Not anymore."

Her eyes won't meet mine. "Well…" she hedges. "I don't want you to be upset."

There's only one reason I would be upset. "Zane? Your first kiss was Zane?"

She nods, biting her lip.

My teeth clench unconsciously, but I try to shrug it off and pretend it doesn't bother me. No matter how hard I try, I will always be in the running with Zane. "No big deal. We all have a past."

"But you were my second," she says in a rush.

"And your last?" I say, my voice hopeful.

She smiles at this. "What about you? Who was your first?"

I have to search the recesses of my mind for this one. It was so long ago. "I'm not exactly sure. I mean, there was the three-year-old girl I planted one on when I was toddler."

Sienna giggles. "That one doesn't count."

"Good. Because I can't remember her name anyway."

Sienna laughs again. "For real. Who was your first kiss?"

An image of me and a blonde, pressed up against the wall in the hallway of the Compound, bursts into my mind. I can still remember how she tasted—like cherry suckers.

"A girl named Jayla. I was twelve and she was fourteen."

"Dang. An older girl," Sienna teases.

"What can I say? Older girls flocked to me back then."

We resume walking. By now, we've reached the base of a slot canyon. "Should we check it out?" I ask Sienna.

"I'm game."

The entrance is narrow, not wider than a person, but once we squeeze ourselves through, it opens a little. We're now surrounded by thousand-foot walls of orange rock that have been smoothed over time by rainwater. They curve and flow for miles. The bottom is nothing more than sand and silt.

"It's beautiful," Sienna says, her head tilted back, her eyes trained upward.

"Let's keep going," I suggest. We move deeper into the slot canyon. At times, it's so narrow we have to scramble over or slip through rock walls.

"You're not claustrophobic, are you?" I ask as we enter one part so narrow, my back and front scrape against the rock as I turn sideways to squeeze through.

"Thankfully, no," is her reply.

When we reach a part that has a small stream running through, we jump over it. Sienna is in front of me, and I reach down and splash the water in her direction. It soaks her back, and I know just from touching the water that it's cold.

Sienna faces me, her shocked expression turning into determination to get me back. "Oh, you're gonna get it."

I scramble backward as she sends a wave of water in my direction. When only a few drops hit my legs, I laugh at her attempt and splash more her way. This blast of water gets her square in the face. She sputters as she pushes her wet hair out of her eyes. Trying to control my laughter, because I really didn't mean to hit her with that much, I jog to her side. "I'm sorry," I say, using the bottom of my shirt to dry her face.

She pushes my hands away and dries her face with her own shirt, exposing a strip of her pale, flat stomach.

"I'm sorry," I say again. "You're not mad at me, are you?"

"Mad? Why should I be mad when there's revenge?" She gives me a wicked grin. Before I realize what she's doing, she kicks the water, splashing it all over the front of my shirt and shorts.

"Wow," I say. "That's cold."

Sienna laughs. "Oh, come on. You were getting a little too hot, Trey. Admit it."

I love seeing her like this. Smiling, laughing… mine.

Grabbing the front of her wet shirt, I pull her close. "You're right. I was getting a little hot. Only because I'm too close to you."

Sienna's cheeks turn pink. I love it when I make her blush.

She responds by pressing her lips against mine. They're soft and warm and still wet from the water. Her tongue runs over my top lip, and I come undone. One hand moves to the back of her neck and the other pulls her body closer. I can feel her heart beating through her chest, like the hooves of a galloping horse. It's hard to think, hard to breathe. I'm engulfed by the taste of her, the smell of her, the feel of her smooth skin and warm hands. I can't get close enough. I've never wanted anyone or anything more in my life.

When we pull apart, mostly to take a breath, Sienna's cheeks are the color of ripe pomegranates. She presses her hands to her flaming cheeks. "Wow."

I chuckle at the shy way she peers up at me through her lashes. "Wow is right."

"You know, you're pretty good at this whole kissing thing," she says.

The next words just slip out. "Better than Zane?"

She hits me on the shoulder. "Trey!"

"Sorry, unfair question. Strike it from the record."

Sienna throws her head back and laughs. I love that she's happy. That she can forget about this crappy life and just live for today. Her smile makes the world seem a little fairer, a little more just.

"But I'm a ten and he's an eight, right?" I tease.

Sienna starts to walk away, smiling as she looks over her shoulder and shrugs. Once she's a good distance from me, she calls, "You're definitely a ten."

I follow her. "And Zane? What about Zane? Is he a ten, too?"

She shrugs again, her smile secretive.

"You're killing me!" I say. Then, because it's too tempting, I scoop her up in my arms and take off running through the creek, kicking up water behind me. It splashes my back and calves as I run. We're both soaked now.

"Put me down," she squeals.

She probably thinks I'm gonna dump her in the deeper part up ahead, but I haven't decided yet. She's fun to tease, but I don't know if I want to be on the receiving end of her anger.

"Put-me-down. Put-me-down. Put-me-down!"

When her pleas don't work, she resorts to kissing my neck. I slow to a stop as her lips move to my earlobe. Damn, it feels good.

"Okay, okay, you win," I say, setting her on her feet. She tips her head back, lips curved mischievously.

"No," she says, "you do."

I do feel like the luckiest SOB alive. Sienna is beautiful, intelligent, and a total badass. And more importantly, she's mine.

I kiss her nose, her forehead, and then her chin before finally allowing my lips to touch hers. She sighs, her arms tightening around my neck. I could easily stand here all day and kiss her. I could kiss her through the night and into the next day, but if we don't hurry through the canyon, she may be late for her birthday dinner.

Reluctantly, I remove her hands from around my neck and kiss her nose one more time. "Should we keep moving?" I murmur. "Could be several more miles before we reach the other side of the canyon."

"Okay," she says. I can tell she's disappointed, but I'll be sure to make it up to her later.

We've been inside the slot canyon for well over an hour

when I hold up my hand to stop Sienna. "Did you hear that?"

"Hear what?"

"That—that sound." I listen again. It's the patter of raindrops against rock.

"It's raining," Sienna says, tilting her head back and opening her mouth to catch some. That's when I feel the first drop.

Oh shit.

"This is bad," I say. "Very, very bad."

"It's just a little rain, Trey," Sienna says, rolling her eyes.

"Babe, you don't understand. That water will fill the slot canyon. This little bit of rain can be extremely dangerous. We have to go. Now." I grab her hand. I have no idea how much further it is in the other direction. It could be a few hundred yards, or it could be a few miles. Our best bet is to go back the way we came.

The rain picks up, the drizzle turning into a steady patter. The rocks are slick with water, and we slip and slide over them as we try to climb.

Sienna trips, banging her knee. "Ow," she cries.

After I help her to her feet, I urge her on. The canyon is filling quickly with water, the small space leaving nowhere for the rain to go. The water is now up to our ankles, and we slosh through it, the space so narrow my shoulders brush both sides of the canyon as we forge on.

When the canyon opens and we reach the small stream from before, where we had our water fight, it's now a raging river we have to cross. "Hold on to me," I say. She clings to my arm, and I start across. The current is strong, the water coming up to my waist. Sienna almost gets swept away, but I grab her arm and don't let go.

In one spot, water pours down the canyon wall, creating a powerful waterfall. I think of the narrow places we still have to squeeze through. This is what makes rain in a slot canyon so dangerous. There's nowhere for the water to go, which means we're trapped. And this is when hikers drown.

I don't tell Sienna this because I don't want to worry her. We keep moving, me keeping one hand on her arm at all times. The rain comes down in sheets.

We reach one of those narrow openings, the water hitting our waist here. Sienna's eyes are wide with fear. "Trey…"

"You go first. I'll be right behind you." Reluctantly, I let go of her arm and watch as she slips through the first opening. I follow her, my back scraping against the rock as the water pushes me through. I catch a glimpse of her fiery hair, almost the same shade as the canyon we're traversing, as she slides between two more rocks and climbs up a makeshift ladder.

When I catch up to her on the other side, her teeth are chattering. As quickly as it started, the rain slows to a stop. We're at a higher level now, and this creek bed is still dry.

"That was scary," Sienna says, breathing hard. I give her a moment to catch her breath before urging her forward. We've just rounded a bend, the rock walls still towering over us, when the wind picks up, whistling through the canyon.

And then I see it. Something much more terrifying than what we just experienced. It looks as though the earth is moving. Dirt, mud, and sticks, rolling over themselves as they travel closer, climbing the canyon walls. It takes a moment for me to realize what it is—a wall of muddy water headed our way.

"It's a flash flood!" I holler at Sienna.

"What?" She turns in the direction I'm pointing.

"We have to get to higher ground." Turning, I frantically scan this part of the canyon that can't be more than twenty feet across. Not too far is a boulder that should be tall enough if we can reach it in time. I grab Sienna around the waist and run, half-dragging her toward the boulder. "I'll give you a boost."

Sienna's eyes are fixed on the quickly approaching water that will soon sweep us away.

"Hurry!" I say. She steps into my hands, and I heave her

onto the rock.

"How are you getting up here?" she says, her face contorted in fear.

Mother nature is a beast, and she's bearing down on us hard. I don't have time to think, only time to act. I pull out some rope from my pack, throw one part of it around a tree branch hanging over a cliff, probably from the last flash flood they had here, and grasp both ends of the rope. I climb, the wall of water now reaching my feet and sweeping away anything in its path. Once I'm parallel to the boulder, I start to swing back and forth, eyeing the branch as I do. It's thick, but not that thick. If it gives way, I'm a goner, lost to the raging water below me. I heave myself back and forth, back and forth, as Sienna looks on in despair, her hands covering her mouth.

If I fail, this will go down in record books as the worst birthday ever. I give one last swing and then let go, flying through the air until my feet hit the boulder. It's slick with rainwater, so my feet start to slide down the side, but Sienna grabs my shirt and holds on tight.

"I've got you," she says, breathless.

I tumble onto the rock, and Sienna falls beside me. For several minutes, I lay on my back, rain coating my face, my chest heaving and my heart thundering.

"Damn, that was close," I say once my heart resumes its normally steady rhythm. I turn my head to look at her. She's lying next to me on the rock. "I can't promise you gold or diamonds or even a roof over your head—" Sienna smiles at this one, "—but I can promise you adventure. With me, it will always be an adventure."

Sienna rolls toward me, leaning over and kissing me as her wet hair dangles in my face. I push it away from her eyes, so I can see her better. "I don't need any of those things," she says. "And I'm fine with a little adventure. In fact, I prefer it."

"And that's why I love you, Sienna Preston." I pause. "That

and a million other reasons."

"Oh, really? Why don't you name one or two... or a hundred?"

Chuckling, I pull her close and kiss her nose. "Where in the world do I even begin?"

For hours, we wait out the flood on the boulder. We eat most of the food I packed, and when Sienna shivers from her cold, wet clothes, I wrap the blanket I brought around her and hold her close. By nightfall, the water still hasn't receded. My rear end hurts from sitting on the hard rock, and I know Sienna feels the same, but she hasn't complained.

"Looks like we'll be spending the night here," I say as shadows fill the canyon. Now that the sun is setting somewhere on the other side of these canyon walls, it'll get dark in here fast. "I'm really sorry you'll miss your birthday dinner."

Sienna groans. "We have to spend the night? Oh no. My mom's gonna kill me."

"We'll just explain what happened. Besides, you're eighteen now. You're an adult." I give her a crooked smile.

Sienna gazes up at me through her eyelashes. "That's true..."

I chuckle and scoot closer. It's no fun having space between us. Cupping her chin in my hands and studying each freckle on her nose, I say, "There have been lots of girls in my life—"

"Puh-lease," she interrupts, pulling away. "I don't need to hear this."

I take her hand in mine. "Just let me finish, okay?"

She grumbles a reply.

"Like I was saying, there's been lots of girls in my life, but none of them compare to you. The way I feel about you? I've never felt this way about anyone."

Sienna looks doubtful. "What about Paige? I overheard you at the stream. It sounded like you felt that way about her once upon a time."

How do I explain the difference between her and Paige? It's like comparing the sun to the moon. One you can't live without, and the other you barely notice.

"What Paige and I had? That was something completely different. Did I love her? Sure. Did I see it being anything more than a fling in the Compound? Maybe. But she left before we could figure out what we were."

I tug her closer until I can see each individual eyelash lining her eyes. "I have this dream," I say. "This beautiful, perfect dream. About us."

"I like dreams." Sienna smiles. "Especially ones with you in them."

"Then you'll love this dream."

"Tell me about it," she murmurs.

"No can do."

"Trey!" she protests.

Chuckling, I kiss her forehead. "Someday," I promise. I kiss her nose, then her chin, finally letting my lips rest on hers. She tastes like apricots, left over from the dried fruit we ate earlier. My hands pull through her hair, then trail down her shoulders. She's too thin, her shoulder bones poking through her shirt. I know she lost weight in Confinement, but I was hoping the past couple of weeks had maybe put more meat on her.

Her stomach grumbles with hunger.

"Here," I say, opening my pack and pulling out the rest of the dried jerky. "Eat this."

She tries to push it away. "I'm not really hungry."

"Tell that to your stomach." I shove the jerky into her hands and watch as she takes a tentative bite.

"This brings back bad memories," she says, swallowing

hard like she's forcing it down.

"You don't like jerky?"

"No, it's just that—" She bites her lip. "Jerky is what they gave us in Confinement. Jerky and bread. That's it."

Good Lord. No wonder she lost so much weight.

"I'm sorry," I say. "You don't have to eat it. I just thought you might be hungry."

"I'm rarely hungry anymore." Even as she says it, her stomach growls, an angry beast inside her.

My eyebrows rise. "Sure about that?"

She shakes her head. "What I mean is, I may be hungry, but I can't eat." After a second, she adds, "Or sleep."

All this time, I thought she was holding it together. Dealing with her grief in her own way. The only time she talks about what happened in Rubex is if I bring it up. But if she's not eating or sleeping, she's not coping. She's hurting and not letting me see. "Your dad?" I say. When she nods, I add, "Jeb?"

"Yeah. All of it. Being in Confinement. Not being able to tell my mom about my dad. Reliving their deaths—Dad and Curly—over and over. I feel so... helpless." Tears cloud her eyes. "So incredibly helpless."

"You don't have to deal with this on your own. You know you can talk to me, right? Anytime. I'm here."

"I know."

It's quiet for a minute, the only sound the rushing water below us. It's completely dark now. As a cloud passes in front of the moon, an owl hoots in the distance, the sound ricocheting off the canyon walls.

"You know," I say, breaking the silence. "That's the way I felt when you were in Confinement. That helplessness? Yeah, I felt it. Once I had the chip removed and remembered everything, all I wanted to do was protect you. But I couldn't. You were locked away in that prison hell, and there was no way for me to get to you. I felt... useless. Helpless."

Sienna runs her fingers over my lips, leaving a tingling trail. "You figured out a way, though. You always do."

"Not always." No doubt both of our minds are filled with images of her father and Jeb.

Sienna's hands fold in her lap, and my lips suddenly miss her touch. "I sometimes wish we'd met under different circumstances," she says. "There's just so much... stuff. Weighing us down."

I know what she means. What would it be like if I wasn't Trey Winchester, son of Bryant Winchester, former leader of the Fringe? If I was a normal guy who met Sienna at a school function or something. If we had been born fifty or a hundred or even a hundred and fifty years ago. Everything would be different. Our lives, our futures, our goals, would all be different.

"If we can get through this, we can get through anything."

"True." She pulls her hair back, holds it there for a moment, and then lets go, the strands swinging into her face. She shifts her body so she's facing me. "Tell me something. Something I don't know. From your childhood."

"Like what?"

"I don't know. Maybe something you liked to do?"

"Okay, well... my father was trained in Jiu Jitsu, so when I was young, he taught me everything he knew. Part of the reason Nash and I used to fight so much."

"But you weren't doing Jiu Jitsu when I saw you fighting in the Compound, right?"

"No, not that day. Nash and I were going through a kickboxing phase."

Sienna shakes her head, like she's remembering something. "You guys were a little out of control. I mean, Nash kicked you in the ribs. Who does that?"

I can recall that day easily. Nash shouldn't have won that fight, but I got distracted. Sienna was watching, and all I'd wanted to do was impress her. "We can be a little intense sometimes."

"Tell me about it," she mutters. "So, other than beating up your cousin, what else did you do for fun in the Compound?"

"When I was a kid, we'd stack the chairs and line the walls of the cafeteria with tables. Then we'd play kickball or soccer or some other sport. It was the only room big enough." I picture me and my friends, all the lights off in the Compound, us sneaking around. "We also played hide-and-seek a lot. Especially when the power went out." There were also clandestine meetings with girls when the generators were down, but I'm not stupid enough to share that with Sienna.

"You had a very unique childhood."

I guess I did. Especially compared to Zane, whose life was filled with dinner parties, tuxes, and schmoozing with the rich. Glad that wasn't me.

Sienna tosses a small pebble over the boulder. It gets lost in the darkness and water below. "You know, I have a hard time picturing you as a little boy. When I try, I picture this kid with massive muscles and a gun in his pants, bossing everyone around."

I laugh, the deep sound bouncing off the canyon walls. "That pretty much sums it up."

She playfully slaps my arm. "Does not. I'm sure you were adorable."

"The cutest."

"Did you have any idea you were a GM? I mean, surely you noticed you were different from the normal kids in the Compound, right?"

I think back to my childhood. Sure, I noticed differences between myself and the other kids, especially Nash. He was a few years older, and I could beat him in every wrestling match or game we ever played. I guess I thought I was either super athletic or just lucky.

"There were times I wondered why I could do things other

kids couldn't. I even asked my dad once if I was genetically enhanced." I chuckle, remembering that conversation. "Which led to an hour-long discussion about why he and my mother would never choose to have one of their children genetically modified. After that, it never crossed my mind I could be a GM. I mean, you don't really expect your father to lie to you, you know?"

"What did you think when you found out? When Zane told you? Did you believe him at first?"

I rub my palm against the rough surface of the boulder. "I'll admit, it was a lot to take in. But then it all kinda made sense."

"I wish I could have been there for that conversation," she says, a small smile playing on her lips.

Because I want to feel her skin, and because I'm tired of denying myself, I tuck some of the hair behind her ear before running my thumb down her jawline, from ear to chin. She closes her eyes and sighs.

This is my invitation to lean in and taste her lips. It's not enough, though. It's never enough. I deepen the kiss, gently laying her back on the rock, her spine arching against the jagged places. I slide my arms under her to protect her from the rough stone. My lips move from her mouth, to her neck, to her collarbone while Sienna's arms tighten around my back, refusing to let me pull away. Not that I want to. Our bodies fit together like a jigsaw puzzle.

Sienna shivers beneath me, murmuring against my mouth, "It's getting colder."

I help her sit up and readjust the blanket that's slipped from her shoulders, wrapping it tight around her. I'd barely noticed the drop in temperature, but she's right. Our clothes are dry now, but we don't have layers to protect us from the cold. I pull her between my legs until she's resting against my chest. Body heat is the only thing that will keep us warm tonight.

"I'm sorry about today," I say. "I hope I didn't ruin your birthday."

"Ruin it?" Sienna tilts her head, appearing contemplative. "Not at all. This was the best birthday ever."

"Even though you almost died?"

Laughing, she snuggles deeper into the cavity created by my arms and legs. "I told you I like adventure."

I chuckle at her answer.

"Besides," she adds, "I'd rather have a million adventures with you than a lifetime of boringness."

"I feel the same," I say.

She stares up at me. "Really?"

Taking her hand and placing it over my heart so she can feel it beat and know it belongs to her, I say, "Really."

Sienna smiles and closes her eyes, burrowing deeper into my arms. When the silence between us turns to soft snores from Sienna, I hug her tight and vow to stay awake all night in order to protect her. From anything or anyone who might try to hurt her, but especially from her dreams—I will do whatever it takes to keep her safe.

# 28

## Zane

When I stride through the automatic doors of the WCBC News Station, the receptionist raises her head, her cheeks turning crimson. "Mr. Ryder, we weren't expecting you today."

The mounted comscreen behind her plays the local news. There's Steele, looking sharp in a three-piece suit. He stands outside the Match 360 facility as he's interviewed by a nameless, faceless person. I can't hear what he's saying, but the headline underneath reveals the subject of his statement.

*After the death of his father, Steele Ryder inherits Chromo 120 and Match 360.*

"I'm not scheduled, but I'd like to issue a statement," I say to the receptionist whose name is Hanna or Hazel, or something like that. I'm normally good with names, but after being chased by an SUV, my head is spinning.

"Right. Of course. Let me see if we have a studio open." She flashes me a bright smile. "Be right back."

When she returns a few minutes later, she motions for me to follow her. "You'll be in Studio Six. Were you planning to take questions as well, or is this a statement only?"

"Statement only," I respond, following her down the brightly lit hall, past doors that read Studio 1, Studio 2, and so on. Each has a red light affixed to the wall to indicate if filming is currently taking place. We pass two lit up red bulbs, but the others are off.

"Here we are," she says, pointing to the door. "Studio Six." She pauses, wringing her hands together. "Do you... need anything else?"

"No, this is great. Thank you."

As I step into the room, she says, "Bronson will be filming you, so if you need anything while you're here, he or I can assist you."

I thank her again and enter the studio. I've been in most of these over the past few months doing interviews and issuing press releases. But I don't think I've been in Studio Six before. This one has a small stage with two upholstered chairs and a small table in between, perfect for one-on-one interviews. Off to my right is a news desk. Bright lights shine down on the pre-constructed scene. Cameras and equipment are at the ready for the next potential victim.

Bronson enters from a different door. He's young, wearing a tight black T-shirt, his hair spiked in about fifty different directions. I've never worked with him before, so I'm guessing he's new.

"Do you have a preference?" he asks, striding toward me with a headset on and a comscreen in hand. "Casual chair or business-like desk?"

"Can we do casual chair but maybe a close-up shot?"

He grins. "Now you're talking. I like a man who knows exactly what he wants." He speaks into the headset. "Can I get Rachel in here for makeup?"

A moment later, a petite blonde enters the room, pushing a cart. "Did someone call for makeup?"

"Let's get him bronzed a little, hmm?" Bronson says, pointing at me.

Rachel motions for me to have a seat in a director's chair, and I hold still while she brushes something called bronzer on my cheeks, chin, and forehead. She then outlines my eyes with some black, inky thing. I've done interviews before, but I've never had this kind of makeup on. I'm about to say something, but stop myself when I see Bronson with his arms crossed over his chest and his head cocked to the side, studying me.

"His nose is too shiny. Fix that," he instructs.

Rachel puts powder on my nose, darkens my eyebrows, then leans back to take in her work. "Perfect." She beams.

With one raised eyebrow, Bronson nods in approval. "I agree." He winks at me.

Rising from the chair, I thank Rachel. To Bronson, I say, "Where do you want me?"

Bronson laughs. "Oh, I can think of a *million* places. But for now, why don't you take a seat in the left chair."

Ignoring his salacious comment, I make my way across the studio and settle myself in the chair.

While Bronson gets the camera ready and Rachel stands off to the side, watching everything, I think about what I'm going to say. The right words Sienna needs to hear.

"Your makeup looks great," Rachel calls.

I give her a thumbs-up, adjust the blazer I'm wearing, and take a few deep breaths to calm my nerves. I'm about to put myself out there in front of everyone. But especially in front of *her*. That's if she sees this.

Bronson signals to me he's ready. I nod, giving him the go ahead. He counts down on his fingers—5...4...3...2... and points at me.

I flash my most endearing smile as the camera begins to roll. "Citizens of Pacifica, thank you for tuning in. I have an important announcement I would like to make. As many of you know, my father, Harlow Ryder, recently passed away and left Match 360 and Chromo 120 to my older brother Steele. While this came as a shock to me, I've decided it is time to find my own purpose."

*Fearless*

"Arian Stratford and I have resolved to end our engagement and part as friends. Many of you are probably wondering if there is someone else. You may have seen pictures of me with a girl in Rubex. Her name is Sienna Preston, and while the government would like you to believe she killed Colonel George Radcliffe and Rayne Williams, she is innocent of both crimes. They are hunting an innocent woman."

Pausing, I steel myself for what I'm about to say next. "Sienna, if you're listening, I still love you, but I know we can never be together. We will always have that one night under the stars. Every time I look at Ursa Major, I will think of you. That is where I'll find you."

# 29

## Sienna

Trey and I make it back to Camp the next morning, once the water recedes and we're able to traverse the canyon safely. Despite the cold, it wasn't all bad spending the night in the canyon with Trey. I'll probably have to do damage control with my mom, but it's worth it.

As soon as we enter Camp, Trina spots us and rushes over. "Where have you guys been? Your mom was worried sick."

"There was a flash flood," Trey says. "We got stuck in the slot canyon."

"Right," Trina says sarcastically, eyeing us. "Flash flood."

"It's true," I protest.

"Whatever," Trina replies. "Anyway, you have to see this." She waves a comscreen at me.

I have half a mind to fling that stupid thing into the creek. I'm done with the outside world, and unless it's a news report stating the government knows our location, I don't want to know what's going on.

"How do you have access to this thing all the time?" Trey asks. "I thought Jared was in charge of the comscreens?"

Trina pokes out her hip, and with a sly smile, she says, "I *may* have an admirer."

"How does Grey feel about that?" Trey teases.

Trina shrugs. "He doesn't have to know everything.

Besides, someone needs to keep tabs on what's going on back in Legas." She pushes the comscreen at me. "You'll want to see this. Apparently, Harlow Ryder left his company to his eldest son, Steele. Zane gets nothing."

"What?" That doesn't make sense. Zane was supposed to inherit everything. Even when he found out Harlow wasn't his biological father, Harlow still wanted him to take over the company someday. What happened to change his mind?

"That's not all." Trina presses play on the comscreen.

An image of Zane fills the screen, and I suddenly feel as though I've been punched in the chest. It's so much easier to pretend I don't have feelings for him if I don't see him. Zane stares right into the camera and tells the Citizens of Pacifica he and Arian have called off their engagement. Then he talks about me, but I'm so flustered, I can barely understand the words. Something about me being innocent.

"This is the best part," Trina whispers with a grin. Trey shoots her a scathing look, but she doesn't notice. She's too focused on the image of Zane.

I tune in to what he's saying, and my heart does a million flip flops.

"Sienna, if you're listening, I still love you, but I know we can never be together. We will always have that one night under the stars. Every time I look at Ursa Major, I will think of you. That is where I'll find you."

The screen clicks off, but I can't stop staring at it. Slowly, I turn to look at Trey. His face is a mask of hurt and anger. "Night under the stars, huh?"

"Nothing happened, Trey," I say quietly.

"Just like nothing happened last night," Trina says with an exaggerated wink.

When I give her a murderous look, Trina places the comscreen in my hand and quickly excuses herself.

"It doesn't sound like nothing," Trey says.

"You're one to talk," I snap. "While I was with Zane that night, you were probably making out with Rayne somewhere." As soon as I say it, I know I've gone too far.

Trey sighs heavily. "No matter what we do or how far I think we've come, we always end up here. Right where we started." He runs a hand through his hair, his bicep flexing. "I want to put all of this behind us."

"Same here. But we might not be able to."

"Zane wants you to know he still loves you. And I think he hopes you still love him."

I think so, too. But what I don't understand is why Zane would air our most intimate night together in front of all of Pacifica. It doesn't seem like him. At all. I mean, first he says he can't come find me, but then he says where he'll find me. Almost like... almost like...

A clue. Or a message.

Clicking the comscreen on, I hit play again.

"I've already seen it once," Trey says, the irritation evident in his voice. "I don't need a reminder."

"Shh. I think I found something."

I watch the press release with critical eyes this time. Apparently, Trey does, too. He leans forward, staring at the screen. "Is he—" He shakes his head. "Is he wearing makeup?"

I shush him again and focus on the last part of the press release, where he tells me in front of all of Pacifica that he loves me. Zane mentions our night together, Ursa Major, and then he talks about finding me there.

When the screen clicks off, I say to Trey, "He's sending us a message. He wants to join us, but doesn't know where we are. We have to go to him."

"Go where?"

"He mentions the stars. Ursa Major. That was in Rubex, but there's no way he'd want me to meet him in Rubex. It's too dangerous. There has to be something I'm missing."

I watch the video one more time. When it's finished, I say, "The stars. The stars are really important. Where else can you go to look at stars?" Then it hits me, like a gosh darn brick in the face. "I've got it. I figured it out."

"What? Where?"

"He wants to meet us at a planetarium."

Trey looks doubtful. "You sure?"

"One hundred percent."

"But how are we supposed to figure out which one?"

I turn the comscreen back on and do a search, typing *Ursa Major* followed by *planetariums*. There's one that pops up. Clicking on the link, I scroll through. The article talks about Henrick Schneider, a wealthy donor who contributed enough money to build the Schneider Planetarium. He was very fond of the Greek myth concerning Ursa Major, that the alignment of the stars is Callisto, a nymph who was turned into a bear by Zeus' jealous wife Hera. The article goes on to say because of this obsession with Ursa Major, a large statue of a bear is displayed in the grand lobby of the planetarium, as a tribute to the stars, the Greek gods, and Callisto.

"This is it," I whisper. "Schneider Planetarium. This is where Zane wants to meet us."

Trey peers over my shoulder. "This place closed down years ago."

Leave it to Zane to think of some place so obvious, yet completely undetected. "Which makes it the perfect place." I take a deep breath, not sure how Trey is going to react. "We have to go, Trey. I don't know how, but we have to. This is your brother. He could be in danger, especially after airing that public statement about me being innocent. If he didn't have a target before, he sure does now."

"Where's it located?"

I scroll down, searching for an address. I click on it, and it takes me to a map. My heart sinks. "It's a couple hundred miles north of Legas."

"Which means, it's at least a hundred miles from us."

"At least." All of my excitement fades away. It would take us days to walk a hundred miles. Zane could be gone by then. I let out of a whoosh of air like a balloon deflating. And that's exactly how I feel—deflated.

Trey rubs his chin, lost in thought. "Can you give me a minute?" he says suddenly, his eyes focused on something behind me. I turn and follow his gaze. It's Paige. "Be right back."

Not really wanting to stand around and watch Trey and Paige together, I search out my mom. I have some major groveling to do. I find her hanging wet laundry on the rope line that runs the length of Camp.

"Hey, Mom," I say.

"Sienna!" She drops the shirt she's hanging, and it lands in a pile on the ground. "Sweetie, where were you? You had me so worried when you didn't come back last night."

"I'm sorry, Mom. Trey and I hiked the slot canyon, and then it rained which produced a flash flood, and then we were stuck there and had to sleep on a rock all night and—"

Mom stops me. "But you're okay? You're not hurt?"

"No, I'm fine. But I'm sorry I missed dinner. I was really looking forward to that rabbit stew."

Mom places her hand on my cheek. "I'm just glad you're okay." She stares at me a beat too long before bending to pick up the now-dirty shirt. Throwing it on a nearby table, she says, "Guess I'll wash this one again."

"Can I help?"

"Sure. There are some clothespins right over there."

I grab a shirt from the bucket, wring it out, and hang it over the line before securing it with two clothespins. Mom watches me for a minute before doing the same. When she clears her throat, I know she wants to say something.

"So," she begins, "you and Trey seem to be getting pretty

serious."

"Yeah, I guess."

"Do you love him?"

My cheeks warm. I'm not used to talking about this kind of stuff with my mom. "Yeah." Then I add, just so it's clear, "A lot."

There's a pause before Mom says, "So last night…"

"Nothing happened, Mom," I say, my cheeks a full-on bonfire. "We got stuck in the canyon. That's all."

Mom nods, but there's no mistaking the relief on her face. Even if something had happened, it's not like I would tell her. Not sure what she's expecting. I'm eighteen now. I don't need her permission.

I drop the wet shirt I was about to wring out into the bucket. "Um, I think I'll change out of these dirty clothes now."

Mom nods, a small smile tugging at her lips.

I'm halfway to my tent when Trey catches up to me. He has a big grin on his face.

"What?"

"I just got us a ride to the planetarium," he says.

"A ride?"

"Yeah. Did you know Paige has a few vehicles for emergency use?"

"Then why the heck did we walk here?"

Trey laughs. "I think to build character or something? Anyway, she says she'll lend us one."

I fling my arms around his neck. "Thank you, thank you, thank you." When I pull back, I kiss him squarely on the lips. It's meant to be a quick kiss, but Trey's hands drag me closer and refuse to let me go. Not that I mind. Kissing Trey is like sitting too close to a campfire. It warms my entire body and leaves me struggling for air. When I'm feeling a little lightheaded, I murmur against his lips, "How soon can we leave?"

"Whenever you want."

"Now?"

Trey groans. "Five more minutes?" His lips move to my forehead, my neck, and then my ear.

My stomach somersaults. After all he's done, I can grant him this.

So I kiss him in reply.

# 30

## Trey

The correct terminology for this vehicle is a Magnum All-Terrain. I don't know if Sienna will be all that impressed we'll be riding through the desert with no shelter from the elements other than the steel frame of this vehicle, but personally, I'm pretty stoked. I've always wanted to drive one of these.

Before we leave, I make Sienna smear some sun cream on her face and shoulders. It was a gift from Laurel when she found out we were leaving. Apparently, she makes the stuff from scratch with coconut oil or something like that.

The Magnums are parked a short walk away, hidden between cliffs. The keys are in the ignition, as Paige said they would be. As I'm waiting for Sienna to say goodbye to her mom and sister, Paige appears with something in her arms. They look like walkie talkies on steroids. They're about four times the size of a normal military-grade one. She's already stocked the back of the vehicle with guns and ammo, so not sure what this is for.

"Here, you may need this," she says, handing me one of the devices. "Obviously, we don't do Lynks around here because they're easily traceable, but we do have these. If you need to get in touch with us, these have a high-powered radio frequency that can transmit from several hundred miles. I'll keep this one near me at all times. If something should happen, alert me immediately. We'll bail you guys out, if needed."

I take the walkie from her and place it on the console. It takes up the entire surface area. "Thanks, Paige. Unless someone's tracking Zane, we should be fine."

"His message was pretty cryptic," she agrees. She rests one arm on the Magnum and leans into it. "How are you doing?" she asks, giving me an all-knowing look.

"What do you mean?"

"With all of this? Zane being here? He and Sienna..." She raises an eyebrow at me.

Clearing my throat, I shuffle my feet through the dirt. This isn't something I want to talk about with Paige. As far as Zane and Sienna are concerned, I've tried not to think about it. He's my brother. I should welcome him with open arms, especially after all the shit he's been through these past few days. But he's also the man in love with my girlfriend. How the hell are we ever supposed to get close with that hanging between us?

To my pleasure, Sienna shows up before I have to answer Paige. She looks so darn cute with the white blotches of sun cream on her cheeks and nose. The cream is so thick no amount of rubbing helped. I move toward her and kiss her forehead since I can't get to her cheeks. She blushes underneath all the white, probably embarrassed about the display of affection in front of Paige. But I don't care. I want the entire world to know how I feel about her.

I can't believe when we were in the Compound I wanted our relationship to be a secret. What a dumbass I was back then. I guess I didn't realize what a good thing I had until it was torn from me. There's no way I'm letting anyone get between us this time.

Paige gives us a tight smile. "Have a safe trip." She whips her braids around and strides away, her ever-present swagger catching my eye. Paige is a great asset if you need rescuing, but she's way too full of herself.

Sienna flashes me a huge smile before climbing into the passenger side of the Magnum. It takes all my willpower not to move to her side of the vehicle and kiss her—her eyes, her nose, her lips, everything. She's too tempting. And I'm too weak.

Once I'm assured Sienna is buckled—because one thing I know about this vehicle is that it can *move*—we leave the overhang of the cliffs behind, bumping over rocks and loose dirt. We won't hit a road for miles. I hope Sienna enjoys this off-road experience as much as I will.

The sun is warm on our faces and bare arms, the wind rushing past our ears as we speed over the desert. I dare a glance at Sienna and see her throw her arms wide, tilting her head back like the sun is her power source and she's in recharge mode. In this open vehicle, her hair swirls around her face. She has the biggest grin, and it makes me smile. I reach over and touch her arm, because with the roar of the wind, it's too hard to get her attention.

Startled, her eyes open. "This is awesome," she hollers over the noise.

I nod in agreement, flashing her a smile. When I reach for her hand, she allows me to take it. Her fingernails are bitten to the quick and she has calluses on her palms, but still, her hands are small and delicate.

Although, she'd probably smack me if I ever told her that.

I'm seriously in my element as I drive over rocks, small plants, and mounds of dirt. I realize this is supposed to be a sort of rescue mission and all, but I'm having way too much fun to consider this work. With Sienna here beside me, laughing her tail off, I feel like the luckiest guy in the world.

So I focus on this moment. On us. And try not to think about what it will be like when she and Zane are reunited. I can't go there. Just can't.

# 31

## Sienna

It's so easy to lose track of time. But when Trey and I pull into the overgrown parking lot of the planetarium, it feels like it's been days since we left Camp, not merely a couple hours.

We are the only car in the parking lot, and my heart sinks a little. Trey and I look at the abandoned building and then at each other. I'm the first to say what we're both thinking. "Is this a trap?"

Trey climbs out of the car. I'm about to follow when he holds up his hand to stop me. "Please. Let me check it out first, and I'll let you know if it's clear."

I hesitate and then nod. One of us should stay behind in case Zane comes. Trey strides to the building, tests the door, which is locked, and then peers into the dusty glass. He catches my attention, holds up a finger like he's saying *hang on*, and then darts to the back of the building.

My heart picks up to twice its normal speed. I suddenly feel very alone and very exposed. The hair raises on the back of my neck and I twist my head, scanning my surroundings. There's no one here. Only us.

I turn back to the building, studying it. There's a ton of glass, and the dome-like structure on top is the shape of a planet. With the ring of mirrored windows running around the entire building, it looks like Saturn—or one of those planets with rings—crashed here.

I've never been in a real planetarium before. I've heard about them, of course. But all the ones I know about are in the same shape of disrepair as this one. The leaders of Pacifica have always said, *Why look to the stars when we have everything right here.* Such a shame.

Trey opens the front door from the inside, then motions for me to come.

I hurry up the sidewalk and through the door he's holding open for me. "Is Zane—"

"Not yet. But he would have had a longer drive than us. We'll find a place to wait."

As soon as we enter the grand lobby, I see the giant statue of the bear the article boasted about. He's missing a few claws and there's a chunk out of his leg, but other than that, he's fairly intact. There he stands, a tribute to Callisto and Ursa Major.

Turning to Trey, I say, "Can we check out the planetarium? I've always wanted to see one."

"Absolutely. It's up these stairs. I found it during my search-for-Zane tour."

I follow him up a winding staircase and into a large, auditorium-like room. Except this auditorium has a dome ceiling and is pitch black.

"Hang on," Trey says. "I got this." He disappears for a minute. Suddenly, a million stars light up the sky, aka dome, above me.

"Holy… It's beautiful," I breathe, my head tilted all the way back so I can see every star, every constellation. I feel Trey beside me before I see him.

"It is," he admits. "I don't really know much about the stars. It wasn't part of my formal education. You know, being underground and all."

"How did you—?"

"They still have a generator back there. Crazy, huh?"

Without even trying, I can picture my father pointing at the sky, naming the constellations one by one. His deep voice thrums in my head. He was my educator, my inspirer, and my mentor. He's the one who triggered my desire to learn about the stars, though we were never taught about them in school.

I fumble for the nearest chair and take a seat, leaning back and propping my feet on the seat in front of me. Trey settles beside me as I start pointing out constellations. "There's Ursa Major, the one shaped like a bear. Then there's Canis Major. You see how it looks like the stick figure of a dog? It contains the brightest star, Sirius. And if you look over here, you can see Leo, which takes the shape of a lion." I'm about to name more when I feel Trey staring at me. Sure enough, when I turn to him, he isn't looking up at the stars at all, but directly at me. "What?" I say.

"It's nothing."

"No, really," I press, sitting up and placing my feet on the floor. "What?"

"It's just... I like seeing you like this."

"Like what?"

Trey squirms in his seat beside me. "I don't know. Happy?"

I run my hand over the cracks in the plastic armrest. "Being here reminds me of my dad. I feel closer to him."

"He taught you, didn't he? The constellations?"

"Yeah."

Trey reaches for my hand, pulling me closer. "I'm glad I got to meet him."

My eyes suddenly feel like I've been standing next to a smoky campfire for too long. It takes all my willpower to keep the tears at bay. "Me too."

We sit there for a few minutes in silence until Trey clears his throat. "Can you show me more?"

With a smile, I point out the next constellation, the voice of my father still ringing in my head.

# 32
# Zane

It takes a few hours to reach Schneider Planetarium, so it's dark by the time I pull into the parking lot. I'm wishing upon every star and every constellation Sienna pointed out to me that night in Rubex that she somehow saw the press statement and will be here, waiting. It was risky to air that message. I know it's dangerous, so if she doesn't come, I can't really blame her. For all I know, she's thousands of miles away, maybe in another Province by now. But a guy can hope.

I park my car beside what looks to be an all-terrain vehicle, complete with a roll bar. Is this Sienna's, or is there someone squatting here? I guess I'll find out soon enough.

Careful not to trip over out-of-control roots and fallen branches, I make my way to the front of the planetarium. The door is unlocked, so I cautiously walk inside. I don't have to guess where she might be, if she's here. With my Lynk light on, I follow the cracked signs that point toward the planetarium. There's a musty, moldy smell in here like a wet towel sat in the washer too long. I'm almost to the stairs when there's a rustle to my right. I turn my Lynk light just in time to see an oversized rat scurry away.

I climb the stairs two at a time until I've reached the top. I'm not trying to be the picture of stealth, but something about the pitch dark makes me move slowly and quietly. The planetarium is lit up with all the stars and constellations overhead. It looks similar, if not a good deal brighter, to the sky I witnessed on the beach of Rubex with Sienna. I'll never forget that night.

I shine my Lynk around the domed space. Then I see her, cuddled up against Trey as they lounge in the stadium seats. Their eyes are closed as if they're sleeping.

As I inch closer, Sienna must sense my presence because her eyes fly open. My light is trained on the ground so I don't blind her, but the light bounces off the floor and makes her face glow. Slowly, she smiles and rises from the seat, careful not to wake Trey. The seat creaks in protest like it doesn't want her to leave. I understand that feeling completely.

She makes her way over to me, slipping between the seats, but stops a few feet away like she's unsure how close she should come. "Hey," she says, her voice soft, hoarse.

"I guess you got my message."

Her smile could rival the sun. "It took me a few tries, but then it clicked."

I glance upward. "It's a great view."

"The best." An awkward silence falls between us before she blurts out, "I'm really sorry about your dad."

"Thanks."

Sienna takes a few steps closer, hesitates, and then slips her arms around me. "I'm sorry," she whispers.

It takes a moment for it to click she's finally in my arms again—I've dreamt about this moment since the day I walked away from her in the desert. My hands encircle her back, pulling her closer. "For what?" I murmur into her hair. It smells like lemons and campfire.

She pulls back. "For everything. For how things went down in the desert. I should have told you then how I felt, but I just… couldn't."

I want to ask her why, but there's a more important

question forcing its way out. "Are you guys... together now?"

Sienna glances back to where Trey is still asleep several rows behind us. "We're working to get back to where we were before all of this happened."

"I see." My arms drop as I take a step back. It hurts too much to be this close to her, knowing I can't have her.

"I'm sorry," she says again, wrapping her arms around herself like she's trying to get warm.

As angry as I want to be, I can't. Not when she seems so completely broken. Her clothes sag, indicating how much weight she lost in Confinement. Her cheeks are hollow and her eyes haunted. She looks so different from the defiant girl I met on top of the Megasphere months ago. After everything she's been through, it's finally caught up to her.

I hate seeing her like this.

"You don't need to apologize. It is what it is." My voice comes out gruffer than I mean it to.

Sienna nods and rocks back and forth a little, her arms still cradling her ribs. After a moment, she says, "You don't really think it was a heart attack, do you?"

It takes me a second to realize she's changed the subject. "No, I don't."

"He was murdered."

"I think so, too. I found this hidden in his office." I pull out the death threat, unfold it, and hand it to her. "He died two days later."

Sienna reads the note, her lips forming silent words. "That isn't a coincidence," she says, handing the note back to me. "Do you know who sent it?"

"Not yet. I need your help figuring it out. And earlier—" I stop, not sure if I should tell her about the SUV that followed me.

"What?"

"It's nothing."

"Come on, Zane. You know you can trust me. If you want my help, you have to tell me everything."

Of course, she's right. Why hold anything back now? "There was a black SUV following me earlier today."

Sienna chews her bottom lip. "What did you do?"

"I tried to lose them. They bumped my car, and I almost lost control. But when I reached the Gateway, I hid in an abandoned parking deck."

"It was a black SUV, you say?"

"Yes. I think there were at least two people inside."

"Did you get a license plate or anything?"

"No. It didn't have one in the front."

Sienna leans against one of the stadium seats, quietly thinking. "Do you have any idea who might want you dead?"

"Honestly? No. I'm not the owner of the company, nor do I have a lot of money."

Sienna crosses her arms. "My bet is on Steele."

I suck in a sharp breath. The thought has crossed my mind, but I've always quickly dismissed it. I rub my temple. "You think Steele's responsible?"

"It just seems a little too convenient your father receives a death threat, is murdered, and then Steele inherits his company, especially since he's a government pawn. Right?"

"I don't know. Steele may be driven, but I can't imagine him hurting his own father." Even as I say it, I'm not really sure it's true.

"We both know what Steele's capable of…" She trails off, the thought hanging like a dust particle in the air.

I don't really want to believe my brother could do something so horrendous, but after what he did to Sienna and her friends, nothing is off the table. And to be truthful, he didn't look that surprised when Mr. Steadman, the lawyer, read the will and named him heir to our father's companies. No, he wasn't surprised at all. In fact, it was as though he were *waiting* for the announcement.

I slam my fist against the wall, making Sienna jump. "That son of a—"

"Don't worry," Sienna says, placing her hand on my arm. "We'll make him pay."

"Who pay?" Trey's deep voice booms like a bear coming out of slumber.

I flinch away from Sienna's touch, her hand dropping as I prepare myself to see my brother again.

"Hello, Trey," I say, taking in the way Trey's arms never quite touch his sides. How do his arms get that big? As much lifting as I do, I'm not even that ripped.

Another reason to hate my brother. He has the girl and the muscles.

"Hello, Zane."

We stand there, facing off like two roosters in a cock fight. I'm trying to read Trey's expression when he says, "Good to see you, brother. I'm sorry about Harlow."

Trey is the one who crosses the gap. He pulls me into a hug. I don't really want to hug him, but I allow it. Out of the corner of my eye, I see Sienna wipe her eyes.

"Looks like we're even," I say, the words rising out of me like a bursting volcano.

Trey steps back, cocking his head. "How so?"

"I've been stripped of everything. No father. No mother. Just like you. We're more similar than we've ever been." Unfortunately, I can't stop the bitterness that creeps into my voice. "We both have nothing."

Trey's eyes rove to Sienna. "I wouldn't say nothing exactly."

I slap my hand against my thigh. It makes a nice crack that echoes throughout the domed space. "That's right. You do have more than me. You always will."

"Zane—" Sienna says, taking a step toward me.

I hold up a hand to stop her. "It's fine. I wasn't expecting anything else."

An awkward silence follows, until Trey breaks it by saying, "We're glad you contacted us. The whole reference to the beach in Rubex was a little over the top," he grins at Sienna, "but we caught on. Eventually."

"It was meant for Sienna," I say. "But thanks for making sure she arrived safely."

Trey shrugs. "Hey, I take care of those I love. I always do."

My fists clench. "Are you saying I don't love her?"

"If you did, you wouldn't have left her in the desert."

His words are a weight to the chest. "Seems like you'd be grateful I did."

I watch as Trey slings his arm over Sienna's shoulders. "I'm *very* grateful. Haven't I thanked you yet?"

Sienna slips out from under Trey's arm, a scowl on her pretty face, and plants herself between us. "Boys!" she snaps. "That's enough. You both need to grow up a little."

Trey chuckles, but I'm sufficiently chastised. "You're right. I'm sorry I've been acting like such a whiny baby about all of this."

"Perhaps we should kiss and make up," Trey says with a smirk.

Sienna rolls her eyes. "If you think it'll help, go for it. But I refuse to be the cause of your contention anymore."

Looking contrite, Trey holds out his hand to me. "Truce, brother?"

I stare at his hand far too long, a part of me wanting to slap it away even though Trey's done nothing except be *him*. Finally shaking his hand, I say, "Truce."

Sienna smiles as our hands drop and we step away. "Good. Now we can focus on what's really important. Figuring out who killed Harlow and wants Zane dead." She then tells Trey about the black SUV.

I didn't think it was possible, but Trey actually looks

concerned about my safety.

"You have to come with us to the Zenith Camp," he says. "It's the only way to protect you."

"I can't. Not until I know Greta is safe."

Trey's brow furrows. "Who's Greta?"

"She's our housekeeper. But she's like a mother to me. She practically raised me when my—I mean, *our*—mother died."

"You think she'd want to come to the Camp with us?" Sienna asks. "My mom and sister are there. I know they'd be happy to see her."

"I don't know," I say. "But I have to make sure she has a place to stay before Steele sells off the house."

"She's welcome to come, too," Trey offers. "Where is she?"

"At home."

Trey pushes his hands through his hair, probably to show off his biceps and how they flex when he does. *Geez.* "Why don't we crash at your house tonight, so long as that's okay? We can leave in the morning. Head back to Camp."

"It's a four-hour drive," I warn him.

Shrugging, Trey says, "It's not like we have anywhere else to be. Right, Sienna?"

"Exactly," Sienna pipes up. "Our number one priority is making sure you're safe. That's why we came."

"It's the *only* reason we came," Trey hints.

"Really? I could have sworn you guys came because you missed me." I cut my eyes to Sienna when I say it, half-teasing and half-not.

"Don't flatter yourself," Trey says, his tone sardonic.

I'm still staring at Sienna. Although she won't meet my eyes, I have a sudden feeling I'm not so far off from the truth. Trey may have come to offer protection, but Sienna's reasonings are more complicated.

I guess I'll have to find out for myself.

# 33

## Sienna

Being back in Zane's home dredges up many memories, some good and others not so good. And as we walk down the hallway of bedrooms, Trey's hand resting lightly on my back in a protective gesture, it feels strange. The last time I was here, Trey wanted nothing to do with me, and now—

It's amazing how quickly things change.

Zane stops outside the room that was mine when I stayed here before. I can already picture the cream duvet and silk drapes. "Here you go, Sienna. I figure you'll be the most comfortable in your old room."

For some reason, I like how he calls it my "old room". And sure enough, when I go inside, it's exactly as I remember it, exactly as I left it, even though it's been over two months since I was here last.

Trey and Zane continue down the hall, and I can hear Zane showing Trey to the room my mother stayed in. I stand at the door, listening. Once I hear Trey thank Zane and his door shut, I open mine. There are so many thoughts running through my mind, so many things I need to say to Zane. This may be my only opportunity. As Zane passes my room, I grab his arm, pulling him inside and closing the door behind him.

"Sienna," he says, startled. "Is everything okay?"

If I don't hurry and say what I need to, I may lose my

nerve. "I liked your press conference."

"Which one?" he responds with a wry smile. "I've given so many lately."

"Your last one."

"Ah, the one where I made a fool of myself." He rests his hand on the bedpost, his fingernail scraping against a small piece of peeling wood. He won't meet my eyes.

"No," I say, "the one where you told me you still loved me. I—" I stop, not sure how much to say. "I didn't know what to expect, after everything that happened between us. You decided to marry Arian. I mean, you would be married right now if..."

"I know," he says. "But I'm not." He takes a step toward me, his fingers moving to my chin, bringing my focus to him. His hands are warm and familiar and comforting.

"What I wanted to say is that I liked your press conference—" My lips barely move because I'm afraid if I move, it will end this moment. And heaven help me, but I can't stop staring at his lips. "I liked your press conference, but we both have to move on."

"Is that really what you want?" He blinks slowly, his eyes dragging me in.

I shift my gaze away from his. Trey is the one for me. It will always be Trey.

"Yes," I say, but even as I do, I can't look at him. I can't allow his chocolate and buttercream eyes to sway me. Or his familiar hands to move me. I've made up my mind—now it's time to stick to it. Leaning up on my tiptoes, I solidify my decision by placing a kiss next to his ear and whispering, "I'll always love you. But I just... can't."

Zane's fingers tighten under my chin, our mouths only inches apart. "You can't," he whispers, "or you won't?" His eyes rove over my face, settling on my lips. "I haven't given up on us. As long as my heart beats, I never will."

My breath catches. His lips are so close I can practically

taste them. All I'd have to do is lean in an inch or two—

"Goodnight, Sienna," Zane whispers. He places a kiss to the side of my mouth, leaving my cheek tingling. Then he moves to the door and is gone.

I stand frozen in the middle of the room, my heart pounding, my knees quivering. When my heart rate returns to normal, I flop down, fully clothed, onto the king bed. Once I crawl under the covers, I sink into the cushiony down. I haven't slept in a bed this comfortable in months. The cot in Confinement was horrendous, and the bedroll at Camp wasn't much better. When the only thing separating you from the hard ground is half an inch of cushion, you're not exactly in for a restful night's sleep.

I'm positive I'll be asleep in an instant, but as I lay cocooned in that soft bed, I can't stop thinking about what Zane said. He isn't giving up on us. Which is so wrong. He needs to move on, find someone who can love him as much as he deserves to be loved. I want him to have what Trey and I have.

And yet, the thought of Zane with someone else sends a tremor through me. He deserves to be happy, though. As much as it pains me to let go, I have to. For his sake.

After several minutes of tossing and turning, I hop out of bed. Maybe a glass of water will help me sleep.

I pad down the hall, the antique clock ticking in time to my footsteps. When I reach the stairs, I flip on the lights, the ones perfectly positioned on the baseboard to illuminate the steps so I don't trip. The kitchen is dark, the only lights coming from under the cabinets.

I go right to the cupboard that houses the glasses, hoping Greta hadn't decided to rearrange the kitchen once I left. Thankfully, everything is where I remember. The dispenser on the fridge has cold water, so I use it to fill my cup.

I'm standing at the counter, gulping the water, when I hear a noise. "Zane?" I whisper. Maybe he couldn't sleep either.

I set the glass on the island and creep down the hallway, toward the living room and front door. The noise sounds again, like floorboards squeaking in protest as someone tries to move stealthily through a room. I'm about to call his name again when a dark shadow crosses the foyer. I shove my fist in my mouth to stifle a scream. This person is too short to be Zane or Trey.

Someone is in here, someone who's not supposed to be.

Heart pumping against my ribs, like an out of sync bass drum, I slide along the wall until I reach the back stairs. Taking them two at a time, I sprint down the hall to Trey's room. As quiet as possible, I slip inside. Trey's breathing is soft and heavy which means he's sound asleep.

"Trey, wake up." I gently shake his arm. It only takes a couple of tries before he sits up fast, his hand instinctively reaching for his gun on the nightstand. "Someone's in the house."

Trey is out of bed and pulling on his jeans faster than I can turn around and give him privacy. He trains his gun in front of him as we creep to the door. When we reach the threshold, Trey says to me, "Where?"

"Downstairs," I whisper. "I saw him in the foyer. He could be anywhere now."

"We have to get to Zane." Before we enter the hallway, Trey scans his gun both ways, making sure it's clear. "Stay behind me," he whispers.

We sneak down the hall to Zane's room, but he's not there. The covers are pulled back on his bed, but his bed is empty. When Trey turns to me, his face is doubtful. "Maybe Zane's the one you saw."

I shake my head, hard. "No way. The build was all wrong."

"Guys, is everything okay?" It's Zane, standing in the doorway, his hair ruffled.

"Were you just downstairs?" I ask.

Zane rubs sleep from his eyes. "No. I got an alert on my Lynk letting me know a door downstairs is open. I was on my way down when I heard the two of you. What's going on?"

He takes two steps into the room, which is when I see a dark shadow in the hallway behind him and the glint of a knife.

"Watch out!" I scream.

It's a good thing Trey has remarkable aim because he takes the guy down with one shot.

Clearly dazed, Zane turns and stares at the figure in the hall. He flicks on his bedroom light, and the room is immediately bathed in a glow too bright and too harsh. I blink my eyes rapidly.

Moving closer, I check out the man on the floor. Dressed all in black with a twelve-inch knife only inches from his fingertips, he writhes in pain. Blood oozes from the wound in his right shoulder. He's trying to cover it with his hand, but it isn't doing much good. Trey's shot wasn't a kill shot, only meant to incapacitate him.

Trey kneels, getting right in his face. "Who are you?" he demands.

The guy only smirks.

"Okay, let's try an easier one," Trey says. "Who sent you?" Trey presses his thumb into the wound in the man's shoulder. He sucks in a sharp breath, his body shaking in pain, but he still won't yield.

"Trey," I say hesitantly, "what's he doing?" The man looks like he's chewing the inside of his cheek.

"Oh no," Trey says. "No, you don't." He slaps the man's cheeks, but he only bares his teeth into a twisted smile, blood coating his teeth. A moment later, the man's entire body convulses, his eyes rolling back into his head as he froths at the mouth.

Stifling a sob, I take a step back. The man's body goes still. He's dead. "What just happened?" I cry out.

"Cyanide pill," Trey says.

"Who was this guy?" Zane says. "And how did he get in my house?"

"An assassin," says Trey. "Sent to kill you. It's a good thing Sienna and I were here."

Zane's eyes swing back and forth between us. "How did you—"

"Know? Sienna was downstairs, and she saw someone sneaking around the foyer."

"I couldn't sleep," I offer in a small voice. "I went downstairs to get some water."

Zane's eyes widen. "Greta." He hurries out of the room, stepping over the body and then running down the hall. Trey and I follow him. Turns out, Greta's bedroom is on the first floor. When we reach her room, Zane places one hand on the door and listens. "I think I hear her snoring," he says, "but I want to make sure she's okay." He quietly pushes open the door, the hallway light carving a path into the room and illuminating the figure in the bed.

Sure enough, Greta sleeps soundly, her chest rising and falling with each breath. I can't believe the gunshot didn't wake her, but maybe it's for the best. The less who know about the death threats, the better. No sense worrying her.

Zane locks her door from the inside, then closes it tightly on our way out.

We stop by the laundry room to grab some cleaning supplies before trudging back upstairs. Trey and Zane set to work moving the body to the backyard where they dig a shallow grave, while I work on scrubbing the blood out of the walls and carpet. Turns out blood is not the easiest thing to wipe clean. No matter how much I scrub, the stains are still there. I opt for letting the cleaning solution soak for a time.

When the boys return, sweaty and covered in dirt, we take turns showering in my bathroom, one person always on the lookout. It's now two o'clock in the morning, but I'm wired. Having an assassin almost murder you in your sleep will do that to a person.

The boys are adamant I'm not sleeping alone tonight. As Trey put it, "What if they send someone else to finish the job?" We all decide to sleep in the same room, with the door locked and a chair propped under the door.

I settle in the bed, and Trey and Zane take the floor with nothing more than a blanket and a pillow. I should be grateful for these two cute bodyguards. But as my head hits the pillow, the thing I'm most thankful for is a body that couldn't fall asleep and a mind that wouldn't shut down.

Most of all, I'm thankful no one I care about died tonight.

# 34
## Trey

It isn't hard to convince Zane to do another press statement the next morning. As we buried the body the night before, he and I both agreed we needed to send the bastards who tried to kill him a message.

Sienna and I wait at the house, keeping Greta company, while Zane drives to the news station. And as we sit at the counter, watching Greta make biscuits, I can't help but feel a little jealous. Greta was supposed to be *my* replacement mother. *I* was supposed to enjoy her cooking for the past twenty-one years. If Zane and I hadn't been switched at birth, everything would have been different. My life would have been different. Not necessarily better, but different.

Every now and then, Greta glances at me and smiles. After doing this several times, she finally apologizes. "I'm sorry, Trey. You just look so much like your mother. She's been gone for so long, but being around you—" She pauses, wiping her eyes. "Well, being around you keeps her memory alive."

"You know?" Sienna says. "About Zane and Trey being switched at birth?"

Greta nods. "Zane told me. He thought I should know the truth."

"Were you close with Penelope—I mean, my mother?" I ask.

With tears in her eyes, Greta says, "We were best friends for years. It's like I told Sienna a while back, when Penelope died, I offered to help take care of Zane. I knew Harlow had a lot on his plate, and he didn't really know how to raise a child. I've loved Zane as if he were my own." Reaching out, she grabs my hand. "But I didn't know about you. Oh, how I wish I'd known about you, Trey."

I'm feeling a little uncomfortable, and I even consider faking a cough to remove my hand, but I don't want to be rude. Instead, I sit and wait for her to release me.

"Would you like to see a picture of your mother?" Greta asks.

"Yeah, sure."

Sienna and I follow Greta into the hallway where there's a row of pictures on the wall. "That's her," Greta says, pointing to an attractive raven-haired woman.

I lean closer to get a better look. Her eyes are blue and striking, her skin a golden bronze. And it's true. I do look a lot like her.

I'd wondered once or twice why I looked nothing like my parents. My father was blond, and my mother had mousy brown hair. Both had much paler skin than mine, but I always thought it was because they'd spent so much time underground.

But seeing Penelope, my real mother, I feel like there's a part of me I've never truly tapped into. I never had a relationship with my real father—never even knew him as anything other than the genetically altering swine I thought he was. And now it's too late. My chest tightens as the loss of knowing my real parents hits me.

I mumble something incoherent, then stride away from the hall of pictures. I can hear Greta asking Sienna about the stain in the upstairs hallway to which Sienna lies, sheepishly replying she spilled grape juice last night. Greta laughs and says not to worry; she has a special solution for grape juice stains.

I don't remember much about my time in the Ryder home before I went to Rubex. But as I wander into a large room with an oversized black piano, I see a comscreen sitting on the table. I pick it up, scrolling until I find the news station where Zane should have done a statement this morning. Sinking down on the couch, I find the latest news. Sure enough, Zane's press statement aired a few minutes ago. I tune into it.

Zane starts off by thanking everyone for their support as he navigates his new lifestyle and finds a purpose. He then says, "And I'd like to thank whoever tried to kill me in my sleep last night. It was a commendable attempt. But as you can see, your assassin failed."

The camera clicks off. I smile at the comscreen. *Well done, Zane. Well done.*

Sienna drops down on the couch beside me. I hadn't realized she'd come into the room. Her eyebrows are knit together in concern. "Will Zane be okay on the way home from the studio?"

I'm worried about that, too, but I try not to let it show. "He should be fine, as long as he comes straight home. The people who tried to kill him won't know the assassin didn't succeed until the statement airs, which was only a few minutes ago. Since it's a recording and not live, he has a small window to make it home."

"Have you heard from him?"

"Not yet."

Sienna stands and begins pacing the floor, glancing at the wall clock every few minutes. When Zane bursts through the door ten minutes later, she throws her arms around him. But I'm not paying much attention. A new press release has caught my attention. It's a news article. I skim it quickly, my heart sinking.

I didn't think it was possible for the government to stoop any lower, but they've just proved me wrong.

Rising to my feet, I hold out the comscreen to Zane and Sienna. "Guys, you have to see this."

Sienna stares at the comscreen in my hands. "What is it?"

I take a deep breath before saying the words that will change the course of our history forever. Just like the Upheaval, just like the day the city went dark, just like all those times in history that can't be erased.

"The government issued a decree."

"What kind of decree?" Zane asks.

"A decree to wipe out everyone who isn't genetically modified."

# 35

## Sienna

I stare at the comscreen in Trey's hands, my eyes skimming the words of the decree.

### OFFICIAL DECREE OF THE COMMONWEALTH OF PACIFICA

*As stated on this 8th day of October, Two thousand, one hundred and fifty-two, all Citizens of the Commonwealth of Pacifica must report to their local hospital or government facility to receive a Statement Card. All Citizens must complete a series of tests to determine eligibility. Those who are genetically altered will receive tax credits, government stipends, and better job positions. Those who are not genetically altered will receive the option of doing so, paid in full by the government.*

*Progress is our future, and perfection is our goal. In order to perfect our society, we must perfect the individuals in it. It is our goal to inspire the Citizens of Pacifica to want to better themselves.*

*Any of those who do not comply with this order to report for testing will be punished as seen fit by the law of the Commonwealth of Pacifica. Citizens of Pacifica have until midnight on Thursday to comply with this order.*

"This can't be happening," I mutter.

"This is bullsh—" Trey starts to say before I interrupt him. "Chaz," I say.

Both Trey and Zane look at me. "We need to get to Chaz. Have to convince him to come back to Camp with us. He's not safe here."

"And neither are you," Trey says. "We need to secure Chaz, then get back to the Zenith Camp as soon as possible."

"So what's the plan?" Zane asks. "We get Chaz and go to this Zenith camp you've been hiding out at? What about the decree?"

"Once Sienna's safe, I can worry about this stupid decree and what it means for non-GMs."

"You don't need to worry about me—" I start to protest, but Trey holds up a hand to stop me.

"We'll move tonight under the cover of darkness," Trey says, his face hard, his hands on his hips. "We'll grab Chaz and be back at the Zenith Camp before morning. Sienna, call Chaz and tell him our plan. Zane, if Greta is coming with us, prepare her. This is a primitive camp. She needs to understand that."

This is one of the things I love the most about Trey. He is a natural-born leader. Even when there's nothing to lead, he takes charge, making decisions, assigning tasks. And he does it so effortlessly.

I give him a ten-four salute. "Got it, Boss."

That response must soften him because he chuckles, looking a little embarrassed. "Sorry. It's just habit. Don't mean to sound so bossy."

Rising on my toes, I give him a quick kiss on his cheek. "I wouldn't have it any other way," I say.

I've tried to call Chaz all day, but there's been no answer.

Considering he rarely leaves his house and always has his Lynk close by, it's odd he's not answering. I think it raises some red flags for Trey, because that night, when it's time to get Chaz, he asks me to remain at the house with Greta. He tries to play it like she may need my protection, but I know the truth—he's being overly protective.

I balk at the idea of staying. "Chaz is my friend, and I'm going. Now let's get a move on. We're wasting time."

I'm marching down the sidewalk to Zane's car when Trey's hand stops me.

"Sienna. I think you should stay here."

"The hell I am." I shake his hand off and climb into the front seat of Zane's Aria.

"It's a losing battle, man," I hear Zane say before I close the door. Folding my arms over my chest, I wait.

*How right he is.*

Trey will have to pry my body out of this car if he doesn't want me to go.

Trey heaves a huge disappointed sigh as he slides into the backseat. He places his large hands on my shoulders and leans forward, whispering in my ear. "I'm constantly thinking of a thousand ways to protect you, but you won't let me."

I turn in the seat to look at him. His eyes are earnest, worried even. I fumble for his hand, giving it a squeeze. "That's because I don't need protecting. But when I do, you'll be the first person I'll rely on." Letting go of his hand, I face forward as Zane settles in the driver's seat.

"I talked to Greta," Zane says as we drive toward the sketchier area of town. "She's not coming with us."

"Why not?" I ask. "Did you scare her off with the primitive camping part?"

Zane smiles, his hands resting loosely on the steering wheel. "No. She doesn't want to leave the city. Has a friend or someone she can stay with on the other side of town."

"Are you—okay leaving her?" I ask.

"Of course. I'll miss her, but I think she'll be happier here."

"You think she'll be safe?" Trey asks from the back.

Zane nods. "If I'm out of the picture, I can't imagine anyone trying to hurt her."

We pull onto the street where Chaz's apartment is located. Several streetlights are busted, creating eerie shadows on the pavement. Windows are broken, and some are barred.

"I still don't understand why Chaz lives here," Zane mutters. "As smart as he is…"

Chaz's apartment building is as rundown as it always is. We have to avoid piles of trash on the sidewalk leading up to the building, and the concrete steps are slick with algae or some other dark, creeping fungus. Like Zane, I don't know why Chaz doesn't live with his parents in the suburbs. Something about wanting to be independent. I guess this is what independence buys when you don't have a large trust fund knocking at the door when you turn eighteen.

When we reach his apartment, the door is slightly ajar. Every rational thought flees my mind. I kick the door open, even though both Trey and Zane, ever the protectors, try to shove me behind them so they can go first and check it out. The door bangs against the adjacent wall, sounding like a gunshot.

"Chaz!" I call as I search each room. Trey is right behind me, his gun out and trained on the dark spaces and corners. "Chaz!"

There are chip bags littering the coffee table and dirty dishes in the sink, piles of clothes on the floor of his bedroom—a room that smells like sweaty socks—and toothpaste streaks on the counter in the bathroom. But no Chaz.

"He's not here," I say after we've completed our search and are back in the living room, looking around. I spot his Lynk on the coffee table, underneath a chip bag, which is strange.

"He left his Lynk," I say, picking up the black device. It's password protected, so I can't get in. "He'd never leave home without it, unless he thought he was being tracked."

"Where would he go?" Trey asks.

"And leave his door open?" Zane adds.

I glance around the apartment. "I don't know, but something's not right," I say. "Chaz rarely leaves his house, unless he's out of chips or something. And even then, he'd take his Lynk."

"Maybe he went to stay with his parents for a few days?" Zane suggests, fingering an old, wool blanket draped across the sofa-back. That's the blanket Chaz uses to hide the hole in the back of the couch, the one leaking stuffing. This was the couch in his parent's house until they decided to upgrade shortly before Chaz graduated and got his own apartment. But that hole has been there forever. When we were younger, Chaz and I would write each other secret messages and hide them there.

I'm going off a prayer when I remove the scratchy blanket and stick my hand into the hole, the white stuffing from the couch tickling my palm.

"What are you doing?" Trey asks.

"Looking for a clue," I say, still feeling around inside the couch as far as my arm will allow. I come up empty-handed. "Darn. There's nothing there."

"You think he may have left you a message?" Zane says.

I go to the kitchen, check each cabinet, and then look in the cookie jar that's shaped like a pineapple. No hidden note or coded message. Only cookie crumbs and one half-eaten cookie. "I don't know," I say. "It's just so unlike him to leave his door open and not have his Lynk with him. Maybe we should search again to see if he left a note or something telling his whereabouts."

"I'll check his bedroom," Trey says, already disappearing down the hall.

"I'll check the bathroom again," Zane says.

I make my way back to the living room and place my hands on my hips, studying the room. The inside of the couch was a no-go. What about underneath? The couch *is* Chaz's favorite spot in the entire world.

Getting down on my hands and knees, I search under the couch, first with my hands and then by peering underneath. There's nothing there except stray socks.

"Yes! Jackpot," Trey cries out from the bedroom.

I jump to my feet, then hurry to the back room. Zane gets there right as I do. "Did you find something?"

Trey stands in Chaz's messy bedroom, holding up a string of firecrackers and matches. His smile is apologetic when he sees me. "Uh, no, sorry. I guess I got a little excited. You never know when these might come in handy." Pocketing the firecrackers and matches, he resumes his search of the room.

Chaz's array of computer equipment and comscreens take up one entire wall of his room. Everything seems to be here, so wherever he went, he obviously didn't plan to stay long.

"Could this be it?" Trey asks, holding up a crumpled piece of paper.

I take the paper from his outstretched hand and read the words scrawled in Chaz's handwriting:

*We never belonged there, but all I want to do is go back.*

"Where did you find this?" I ask.

"In the trash," he answers.

I read the words two more times as Zane looks over my shoulder. "It's very cryptic, isn't it?" he says.

Maybe for some, but not for me. "I know exactly where he is." I fold the piece of paper and tuck it into my pocket. "Let's go."

Trey and Zane follow me to the door. "Wait. Where are we going?" Zane asks, making sure the door is closed properly once we leave the apartment.

"GIGA," I say.

"Giga?" Trey questions.

"The Genetically and Intellectually Gifted Academy. It's where Chaz and I went to school before he graduated and I dropped out."

"Why would he go there?" Trey says, making a face. "Most people don't want to go back to school once they leave."

"Oh, and you know a lot about school, do you?" I joke.

Trey shrugs. "Enough to know it's not someplace I'd like to have a one-person sleepover."

Once we're in the car, I give Zane directions to GIGA. He's heard of it, of course, most GMs have, but he went to a different gender-segregated school.

"Remind me how it is that Chaz was able to attend an all-girls school," Zane says with a grin. "I would have given my right arm when I was in upper grade."

Trey chuckles in the back. "Me too."

Rolling my eyes, I say, "His father is a professor there, which gave Chaz an opportunity to attend. I think the fact he's not a GM made it easy to overlook the fact he's a boy."

"Meaning they didn't think GM girls would fall for a guy who's not a GM?" Trey laughs. "Trust me when I say GM girls don't always care about that."

"You talking from experience?" I say drily, turning in my seat to glare at him. "I don't see how. You are a GM, after all."

Trey's smile is sheepish. "It was before I knew."

Now it's Zane's turn to laugh. "I have to agree with Trey on this one. My father did his best to keep me and Arian apart all of these years, but he didn't once stop to think there may be *other* girls I'd meet. Girls who weren't genetically modified."

My cheeks flame. I know instantly he's talking about me.

Trey leans forward between the two front seats. "Yeah, I've been wondering about that. How exactly did the two of you meet? Was it a dinner party?"

Zane shakes his head, a smile bubbling at his lips. "We met before that."

"That's funny," Trey says, glancing at me. "I could have sworn Sienna said you two met at a dinner party where she was pretending to be a reporter or something to get close to Harlow."

Zane nods. "She was there that night, yes. But we'd already met twice before."

"Oh, really? That's interesting." Trey leans back in his seat, but there's no mistaking the change in his tone. *He knows I lied to him.*

"It was nothing—" I start to say.

But at the exact same moment, Zane says, "I saved her twice."

Trey pops back up between us. "Saved her? Twice?"

"You didn't save me," I retort. "I didn't need saving."

"This sounds like a great story," Trey says, rubbing his hands together. He's trying to pretend this doesn't bother him, but I can tell it does by the way his eyes won't quite meet mine.

Zane launches into the story about discovering me at the top of the Megasphere and how he thought I was a jumper.

"The Megasphere, huh?" Trey says, finally meeting my gaze. There are so many questions in his eyes. He's no doubt remembering how upset I was when he decided to bomb it with the other Fringe members.

I need to explain. Or at least try to. I don't want Trey to think the reason I was upset he bombed the Megasphere is because it's where I met Zane. "I used to go there a lot," I explain. "It was my haven. After my dad died, it was the one place I could go to get away and get some perspective. Something about being up there made me feel like I was on top of the world. Like I was looking down at all the other people and their problems." I shrug. "Mine didn't seem so bad when

I was up there."

"And then I went and bombed it," Trey says and curses. "I'm really sorry. If I'd known—"

"It's okay," I interrupt. "What's done is done."

Trey goes quiet for a moment, then says to Zane, "You said twice. What was the other thing? The other time you rescued her?"

Closing my eyes, I pray Zane doesn't give all the details on this one. Like how I was wearing nothing more than my bra and panties when he pulled me from the bottom of the lake. That will not go over well with Trey.

Zane's face splits into a grin. "The dam. She cliff-jumped but didn't surface, and I had to go in after her."

Trey clears his throat, his knuckles turning white from his grip on the seat backs. "You guys went swimming at the dam together?"

"No," I interject. "I was by myself, or so I thought. Zane saw me jump off the cliff. When I didn't surface, he came in after me."

"Why did you jump off a cliff?" he asks, his eyes narrowed. I shrug. "Why not?"

"Okay," Trey says slowly, "so you jumped off the cliff for fun, but didn't surface. Did something happen? Did you hit your head?"

"Nooo," I reply, drawing the word out. "I was… thinking."

"At the bottom of the lake?" Trey's tone is incredulous.

I cross my arms over my chest, turning away from him. "You wouldn't understand."

"Apparently not," Trey mutters as he leans back against his own seat.

As we pull into the parking lot of GIGA, Zane catches my eye and mouths, *Sorry.*

I shrug it off.

The school itself is secluded, set back from the road in a

posh area of town. When we climb out of the car, I hear a car horn several streets away and the buzz of the electrical current as it powers the streetlight, but other than that, the night is quiet.

The outside of the glass building is lit up enough so we're not stumbling around in the dark. I've never noticed the sidewalk pavers before, the way they light up right before our feet touch them like there's an underground sensor or something. I guess I've never really had a reason to be here in the middle of the night.

It isn't until we're walking up the sidewalk that Trey leans in and says, "I can see why you decided to leave those encounters out of your history-with-Zane-information-session at the Lagoon." His voice is a loud whisper, and I know Zane can hear him. He's only a few feet ahead of us.

"It was nothing," I say with a sigh. "They didn't warrant a mention."

We've reached the building now. The smell of dirt and mulch is thick over here. The landscapers must have replanted this week.

One tug on the front doors confirms what I already suspected—the doors are locked.

"We'll have to find another way in," I say. "The janitor sometimes leaves the bathroom window to the girls' restroom unlocked."

"And you know that how?" Trey asks. He's clearly feeling pissy. *Ugh. Guys and their moods.*

"My dad worked here for years. I know the ins and outs."

Trey softens a little at this. I guess he realizes he can't be too mad at the girl who lost her father—for the second time.

We traipse to the back of the building. It takes a few minutes for me to find the right window because they all look the same. Sure enough, the one to the bathroom is unlocked and slides right open. Unfortunately, I'm too short to reach it even though it's ground level. *Story of my life.*

"Here, I'll give you a boost," Trey says.

His boost turns out to be him lifting me up by the waist and setting me on the ledge.

"Thanks for making me do all the work," I joke, trying to get things back on track between us. But Trey's smile is forced. Looks like it's going to take more than witty banter to make up for lying to him.

I swing my legs to the other side, then jump down into the bathroom. The room is dark, but the moonlight from the open window glints off the porcelain sinks. It smells like cleaner and disinfectant in here. As I move toward the door, I hear Trey and Zane's feet hit the ground with a soft thud, one right after the other.

"Where do you think he might be?" Zane asks once we're in the hallway. "I came to this school for a decathlon in eleventh grade and I remember how big it is."

"You were on the decathlon team?" I say. "No, wait. Of course you were. Don't know why I'm surprised." I stop and look up and down the hall, trying to picture which way Chaz might have gone. Zane's light shines on the hallway to the right. It lights up a sign near the ceiling that says Computer Lab with an arrow pointing down another hallway. "Bingo," I say. "Where else would a computer nerd want to hang out?"

As we walk down the halls of my former school, I can't help but feel nostalgic. I see the place where Chaz waited for me after class, my old locker, and, of course, the Stairs from Hell, aka the Stairway to Heaven. And I know if I go up those stairs and turn the corner, I'll find my dad's old office.

Things were so simple back then. Sure, school was tough and I wasn't making the grades I wanted, but at least my life was solid. I had a father and a mother who loved me, who provided for and protected Emily and me. There was no running from the government, no murder charges, no blood on my hands. I was innocent.

What I wouldn't give to be that girl again.

But is that true? Would I really want to be that Sienna again? She was weak, helpless, naive. When I think of all I've learned, how much I've grown, I'm not really sure I'd trade that Sienna for this one.

The door to the computer lab is closed. We ease it open, Zane shining his Lynk light on the floor in front of us. We're greeted by dozens upon dozens of computers and comscreens. But something red and blue peeks out from the floor between two rows of computers. We move toward it, and, sure enough, it's a sleeping bag with a person in it.

"Chaz?" I say, kneeling by the bag.

Zane shines his light on the face of the sleeping person. Chaz's eyes slowly open, then he shields them like he's being blinded by high beams. He struggles to sit up as I fling my arms around him.

"Sienna?" he says, his voice groggy. "You found me? I knew you would."

I ease my body next to Chaz's as he notices Trey and Zane standing behind me.

"Hey, man," Trey says, kneeling to give Chaz's shoulder a firm squeeze. "You doin' okay?"

"Yeah. Sorry to send you guys on a treasure hunt, but as soon as I heard that decree, I got scared. Didn't know what to do."

"So you came here? To our old academy?" I question.

"I figured they'd never look for a non-GM here. It *is* a school for the genetically gifted."

"But how did you know we'd come?" I ask. "We were hiding out, three hundred miles away. What made you think we'd return to Legas?"

"I saw Zane's press statement about finding you under the stars or something like that. I figured you'd be coming back for him, and when the decree released, I knew you wouldn't forget about me."

Grinning, I tap Chaz on the forehead. "I always knew you were a genius, but this just confirms it."

Chaz looks at Zane then. "And I'm sorry about your dad. That really sucks."

Zane nods. "Thanks. I appreciate it."

Trey rises to his feet. "We're planning to take you back to the Zenith Camp. You'll be safe there. But we should probably get going. We wanna travel at night."

"Wait." Chaz holds out a hand to stop us. "Did you see the dogs?"

Trey leans against a computer desk, his arms crossed over his chest. "What dogs?"

Rubbing his eyes as if trying to get rid of an image of something, Chaz says, "They have these genetically enhanced canines. They've been sniffing around my apartment ever since the decree released. I think they're trained to find those who aren't GMs."

"Who's they?" Zane asks

"How can they find a GM?" I say at the same time.

"The government is the one behind this. As for how they can do it, I'm not really sure—"

"It's fear," Zane says. "Dogs can sense fear. If you're a non-GM, your body produces a hormonal surge when you're scared. Otherwise known as fear."

"And yours doesn't?" I ask.

"Typically, no."

"I don't care how they can do it," Chaz says. "I just want to make sure they stay away from me. I mean, I know I'm a tempting snack and all—" he pats his belly, "—but still. I'd like to keep all my parts intact."

"Are they aggressive?" Trey asks, pushing away from the computer desk.

"Yeessss," Chaz draws out. "And big and muscular. We're talking about one scary dog."

"It's the MSTN gene," Zane says. All eyes swing to him. "It's the gene that makes the protein myostatin. Myostatin restricts muscle growth. They've removed the myostatin protein to make the dogs more muscular."

I'm the first one to voice what we're all thinking. "Can they do that to humans?"

Zane nods. "Absolutely. My father's scientists do it all the time. It's part of creating the perfect genome. Any parent who wants their child to have a larger muscle mass and excel in sports chooses to have the myostatin protein edited out. For all we know, Harlow did that to Trey."

"You do have a lot of muscles," Chaz agrees.

Gah, I love Trey's muscles. Every dip, curve, and bulge. "Yes, he does."

Trey scoffs at this. "I have a normal amount of muscles. I mean, I don't look disproportionate or anything, right?"

"No way," I say. "You're perfect."

Trey chuckles at this. "Well, I learned something new." He pats Zane on the back. "I think we'll keep you around, brother. You have a wealth of knowledge in that perfectly shaped head of yours. Not to mention insider secrets."

I'm glad Zane's approval rating has risen on Trey's personal scale, but my mind is swimming with all of this information.

"Steele's probably already sold all of Chromo 120's formulas and secrets to the AIG," I say.

The room goes quiet.

"They know everything?" Chaz's eyes are wide as they swing from me to Trey and then to Zane for confirmation.

"I wish I had more faith in my brother," Zane says, "but the truth is, Sienna's probably right. I imagine Steele was selling to the government everything my father built before his body was barely cold." It's easy to hear the bitterness etched in his voice.

*Fearless*

And I don't blame him. What would it be like to discover the last of your family betrayed you in the worst conceivable way? Thank the stars he still has Trey.

# 36

# Trey

I promised Sienna's mother I would keep her daughter safe. And I don't intend to renege on that promise. My number one goal is to get Sienna out of Legas as quickly as possible. Sure, I'm concerned about Chaz also, but he's a dude and he's not the one I'm in love with, so his safety takes a back burner to Sienna's.

That's why as we walk down the dark hallway of Sienna's old school, I make sure I know where Sienna is at all times. She probably wouldn't appreciate this conscious effort—but what she doesn't know is likely for the best.

"Wait, guys," Chaz says suddenly, holding out his arm to stop us. "Do you hear that?"

We stop and listen. There's a low guttural sound coming from another corridor.

"Please tell me that's not what I think it is?" Chaz says in a loud whisper, slowly backing up.

"How did they find us?" Sienna asks.

"The bathroom window?" Zane guesses.

"They wouldn't be able to make that jump," I say. "It's probably nothing."

Zane holds up a finger. "Actually, they *would* be able to make that jump. If they're enhanced the way I think they are, based on Chaz's description, these dogs are smart *and* strong.

There's really nothing that could stop them."

"Oh lordy, please tell me you're joking," Chaz whispers, clutching his backpack. "I think I'd like to go back to my sleeping bag now."

I clamp my hand on Zane's shoulder. "Zane and I will check it out." I give Sienna a stern look. "You stay here." When she opens her mouth like she's about to argue, I add, "With Chaz," and she nods.

Since I'm the one with the gun, Zane gestures for me to take the lead. Not that I need his permission. And not sure why he doesn't carry a gun. After a death threat and an assassin, he still doesn't think it prudent to carry a weapon? That's what makes me a better partner for Sienna—I'm willing to do whatever it takes to keep her safe. Zane can't even protect himself.

As we creep down the hallway toward the sounds, a tiny unwanted thought enters my mind. *He kept her safe in Rubex. Safe while you were playing house with Rayne.*

I push the thought aside. We've reached the end of the corridor. I hold up a hand to stop Zane. With my gun trained in front of me, I peer around the corner. Sure enough, at the end of the hallway are two of the biggest dogs I've ever seen. With their noses to the ground, they track a scent, but then stop next to a locker, intent on whatever's inside. Muscles bulge along the length of their body, making them appear distorted and otherworldly. Cords of muscle run down their legs, and their necks are so thick they'd put a steroid-using weight lifter to shame.

They are scary as hell.

I duck back. "They're unbelievable," I whisper. "But there are only two of them." I hold up my gun, because even though the gunshot will be loud, it's the only option we have.

"What if you miss?" Zane whispers back.

Seriously? He's questioning my shot? After I saved his life?

"I won't," I mutter.

Repositioning my gun, I poke my head around the corner and take aim. Almost as if he sniffs us out, one bestial dog raises his massive head, beady eyes directly on me. His lips bare in a ferocious snarl, and he takes off running. Toward us. Muscles quivering, he covers a great distance with each stride.

"Holy hell," I say before firing the first shot. Moving targets are always harder to shoot, so I'm not entirely surprised when the first bullet misses him. I fire again and again, but the bullets only ricochet off the beast, like his body is a suit of armor. The second dog is now close on his heels.

"Run!" I holler. Zane and I sprint down the corridor, toward Sienna and Chaz at the end of the very long hallway. "Run!" I yell. "Get outside now!" For once, Sienna doesn't question me; she grabs Chaz's arm and yanks him into motion.

The dogs' paws thump against the concrete floor behind us as Zane and I sprint, our speed matching stride for stride. I ignore the snarls and growls of the beasts, focusing instead on the red EXIT sign at the end of the corridor.

In these types of situations, my mind is always ten steps ahead. I already know our best option for escape is to get out of the school and to Zane's car. If we run into a classroom and lock the door, we'll be trapped. We can't hide here. When the Agency comes to collect their tracker dogs, they'll find us. And Sienna will go back to prison and—

Stop. I refuse to taint my mind with those images. If Sienna is ever caught by the Agency or any government official, there will be no leniency. That's why it's my job to make sure she gets back to Camp safely.

Sienna and Chaz have reached the door now, and they shove it open. An alarm sounds, a noise so loud it reverberates all the way to my toes. Surely the dogs must be in pain with their overly sensitive ears and all, but when I glance behind me, I realize the sound hasn't slowed them down. They are right on our heels, teeth snapping and saliva dripping.

We've almost reached the door when Sienna screams from outside. I move faster than I've ever moved before, not sure what I'll find when I get there. I kick the door open and Zane follows me, slamming it closed and trapping the dogs inside. Their bodies hit the metal door with such force they dent it outward, leaving a dog-sized imprint. Whimpers mixed with snarls come from behind the closed door.

But when I turn, scanning the dark school grounds for Sienna, Chaz, and the culprit of Sienna's scream, I realize the snarls aren't coming from behind the door, but from the four hulking beasts in front of us. The ones that have Sienna and Chaz frozen in place ten feet away.

Sienna's stance is defiant; I only hope she doesn't do something to get herself killed.

I gauge the distance from here to Zane's vehicle. We could try to outrun them, but Sienna and Chaz aren't as fast as Zane and me.

Then I remember the firecrackers tucked in my pants pocket, and a plan forms. While maintaining eye contact with the largest of the four canines, I slowly pull the firecrackers and the matches out. His growls become more intense, and his muscles ripple like he's getting ready to spring.

"Don't move," I hiss as Sienna shifts her weight from one foot to the other. I'm not sure what she's about to do, but I do notice the way her fists raise to protect her face. *That girl.* I couldn't love her any more if I tried. She thinks she's going to *fight* the genetically enhanced dogs.

"We're gonna try for Zane's car," I say through gritted teeth, not wanting to startle the dogs, but hoping everyone can hear me. "When I say run, *run.*"

Sienna gives an imperceptible nod while Chaz shakes his head and whispers, "No-no-no-no-no."

"You can do this," I say.

In one swift motion, I strike a match, light the strand, and fling the firecrackers at the ground in front of the beasts. The night air is immediately filled with an ear-splitting *pop, pop* as the firecrackers let loose, one after the other. Smoke curls around the dogs, and for a second, they're stunned, retreating a few steps. But it won't last long.

"Run!" I shout. Instead of beelining toward the car, I sprint toward Sienna, grab her hand, and pull her with me.

The beasts shake their heads and growl, coming out of their stupor. As the four of us run toward Zane's vehicle twenty yards away, two of the dogs in the front lurch forward, ferocious growls surging from the depths of their thick necks.

I run as fast as my legs will propel me, keeping a tight hold on Sienna's hand. She screams at the exact moment I feel something sharp cut into my calves. One of the dogs has latched onto my leg. I pause only long enough to kick it off before resuming my pace.

We're almost there.

Ten feet.

Five feet.

I jerk on the handle and throw Sienna inside the vehicle, then slam the door shut. Zane and Chaz are fighting a dog a few feet away.

Knowing they need help, I scramble on top of the car, slipping and sliding as I do, and pull out my gun. Every animal has a weakness, an Achilles heel. I just have to find it.

I take aim at the dog that is now clamped on Chaz's shirt, searching for the shot. The canine's back trembles with strength, and his sides bulge with muscles. But when he tips his head back, I see it. The one soft spot at his neck that's not protected. I fire the shot and the dog squeals in pain before crumbling to the ground, ripping part of Chaz's shirt as he falls.

Chaz lets out a holler and runs toward the car, sliding inside. Now that Chaz is safe, I focus on the dog Zane is battling. When the dog gets close, Zane kicks it and sends it a few feet, but it keeps coming back for more. I can't get a clear shot.

"Zane! Grab his jaws and expose his neck," I call.

The next time the dog tries to attack him, Zane slips to the right and grabs him in the coolest wrestling move I've ever seen. The dog's tail whips and his teeth gnash at the air, but Zane has him in a powerful headlock so he's clear of the extra pointy canine teeth. Zane tilts the beast's head back so his neck is exposed. He must really trust me not to miss. I fire the shot right into the dog's neck, and he goes down in a heap.

But there are more now. The two from inside have joined their comrades and now circle Zane.

"Come on!" I shout at him. He can make it up here on the hood; I know he can.

He hesitates only a moment before he sprints to the car, the beasts nipping at his heels. I scramble to the very top of the roof where the dogs can't reach us. When Zane's only a couple of feet away, I lean over and hold out my hand. He grabs it, and I pull him up.

"Thanks," he says, wiping blood from his arm. Not sure if it's a claw mark or a bite mark, but there's a deep gouge in his forearm.

"That looks like it hurts," I say.

"No worse than yours," he replies, looking pointedly at my left calf.

I haven't given any thought to my calf, but now I see the chunk of flesh missing and the blood oozing from the wound. It isn't until I see it that the pain hits.

"It's fine," I lie.

The car is now surrounded by the four remaining beasts. They try to scramble on top of the hood but keep sliding off. I'm the only one with the gun so I'm the only one who can end this. I've fired at least half a dozen shots, which means I should have half a dozen more. I can't miss.

I aim at the largest one, the one I had a staring contest with, but I can't find his soft spot—he never leaves it exposed long enough to get a shot fired off. I try for a different beast, and he goes down. I aim and fire at the next one, but it takes two shots before I hit the right place. The third one makes it on top of the hood, snarling and gnashing his teeth at us.

In an attempt to help, Zane slides down the windshield and grabs this dog in the same wrestling-style move. But the hood is so slick he and the dog end up sliding right off onto the ground on the opposite side of the car from where the biggest beast of a dog prowls.

It takes only a second to realize the greatest danger is the big beast, who now slinks to the side where Zane fights the other dog.

"Hey!" I shout, trying to get his attention. "Hey, over here!" I wave my arms. He looks up at me and snarls but stops his trek. I need something to distract him, anything that might leave his soft spot exposed. I reach into my pocket, and my hand closes around one lone firecracker that must have come off the string. I hurl it straight into the air, which causes the beast to briefly raise his head. I take aim and fire, getting him right in the underside of his jaw. He staggers, then falls to the ground in a ginormous heap, his muscles still quivering.

I hear Zane groan and then a snap. *Oh no.* I scramble off the car, but Zane is rising to his feet, wiping his palms on his pants.

"You okay?" I ask, my voice coming out gruff. It tends to do that when I get a little emotional, though I'd never admit it to Sienna.

He glances down at the dog at his feet. "I am now."

"How'd you—?"

"Snapped his neck."

I lean back against the car, the events of the night and the pain in my leg making me a little lightheaded. Now that there's no danger, Sienna bursts from the car and throws her arms around me. I bury my face in her hair. Such a simple act, yet it helps clear my head.

After a moment, she pulls away and goes to check on Zane. She doesn't hug him like she did me, but she does touch his arm and wince. I take it she hasn't seen my leg yet.

I lean in the car to check on Chaz. "Hey, buddy, you doing okay?"

"Oh, lordy. I think I'm having heart palpitations," he wheezes. "That was some scary crap." He leans over, his face almost touching his knees.

Chuckling, I pat him on the back. "You'll be fine. Take deep breaths."

I straighten slowly, scanning the parking lot of GIGA. It's littered with the bodies of the beasts, their blood darkening and staining the concrete. I'm sure it will look worse in the morning.

Someone sent those genetically enhanced beasts after us, which means someone knows we're here.

# 37
## Zane

Trey is always in charge. He was born to be a leader. Or rather, he was born to be *me*. The me I never was. The me my father wanted for his company.

I keep my eyes focused on the steering wheel as I wait for someone to tell me where to drive. We're ten miles outside of Legas now, parked on the side of the road.

"What are they going to come up with next?" Chaz moans. "I mean genetically enhanced dogs. Really?"

Now might be a good time to tell them about Re0gene 2.0.

"I have an idea what's coming next," I say. "Not that it's necessarily a bad thing. It could be good for our military."

"What is it?" Trey demands.

"It's something called Re0Gene 2.0."

"Is it similar to the Re0Gene you created?" Sienna asks, staring at me through the rearview mirror. She's sitting in the back next to Trey.

"It's better," I say. "A few drops under the tongue can heal the body completely."

Chaz whistles under his breath. "I'd like to get my hands on some of that."

"Wouldn't we all?" Trey mutters. I notice how he glances down at his leg when he says it. His leg has a t-shirt bandage wrapped around it, as does my arm. Sienna insisted she take care of both wounds—mine and his.

That's when I remember what's in my glove box. Reaching over, I open the box and pull out the purple serum I carry with me everywhere. I seem to need this stuff all the time lately.

I toss it to Trey first. "Dab a little on your leg."

"Thanks, man." When he's lathered some of the serum on his calf and the skin is beginning to heal, he hands it back to me. "Your turn."

Without using any of the serum, I put it back in the glove box.

"What's wrong?" Sienna asks. Nothing ever gets past her. "Why aren't you using it?

"Because I would rather test Re0Gene 2.0 and see how well it works."

"You have some?" Chaz looks around the car like I've hidden it somewhere.

"No. But I know where I can find it." When I turn the car on, the AC blasts me in the face. I swipe the temperature to low. I'm tired of sitting here doing nothing. It's time to act.

Trey catches on immediately. "Can you still get in the Match 360 Legas facility?"

"No. I'm sure Steele has already changed all the codes. But I know someone who can." I nod at Sienna in the rearview mirror. She responds with a smug grin.

Trey shakes his head quickly. "I don't think that's a good idea. You'll have to do it on your own."

"I can only do it with Sienna's help. We all know she's the best at breaking in."

Trey rubs the back of his neck. I know he's worried about her. He always is.

"I'll take good care of her," I say as a last attempt to get his approval.

"Fine," Trey growls. "But if something happens, it's on

your head."

I throw the car in gear, pressing the accelerator all the way to the floor. We careen down the dark road like a shooting star cruising through the night sky.

Let's hope nothing happens. I don't know if I'm prepared to feel Trey's wrath.

After we stop at Chaz's house to get some equipment, we arrive at the Match 360 facility. A dull glow spreads across the horizon, which means it should be light within the hour. We don't have much time.

We've decided Sienna and I will go, since I know my way around and Sienna knows how to get inside. Before we exit my Aria, we each fit a tiny earbud in one ear and Chaz tests it. When I can hear him clearly, I give him a thumbs-up. Trey is in the back seat practically chewing his fingernails off.

"If anything happens," he keeps saying, followed by, "just holler and I'll come running."

Sienna kisses him on the cheek. "We'll be fine. Promise."

Sienna has her own gun, but Trey leans into the front seat and forces his into my hand. "Take it. And remember—" he glances at Sienna who's climbing out of the car, "you do whatever it takes to keep her safe. Got it?"

"Of course." I exit the car and tuck the gun into the waistband of my pants.

Sienna takes a deep breath, her chest expanding and contracting, then says, "You ready?"

"Let's do it."

We jog to the back entrance of the facility and crouch behind a grouping of plastic barrels. Not sure what they're used for.

"There are two guards this time," Sienna whispers. Sure

enough, two armed guards roam around the back courtyard of the facility.

"Steele must have upped his security."

Sienna frowns, and, of course, my eyes are drawn to her mouth. I shake my head a little to clear my thoughts. "This may still work." Her hands search the ground around us before reemerging with a fistful of rocks. She drops one in my palm. "Do you think you can hit that water tank over there?"

I follow her pointing finger. There's a tank about twenty yards away. When I see the distance, I'm almost insulted she had to ask. "Most definitely."

"Okay, when I count to three, throw your rock."

"Got it."

"One… two… three."

I let loose the rock and watch as it hurtles through the air before striking the tank with a resounding *ping*. A second later there's a smaller, softer thud like a rock hitting the side of the building. The two guards stop roaming and stare at each other before one silently points in the direction of my rock ping. They split up, one going one way and one going the other to check out the noises. We're clear as long as they don't turn around.

Sienna and I sprint to the back entrance of the facility—a metal door that has no handle. Honestly, I've never been in this entrance before, so I have no idea what to expect. But Sienna acts like this is her second home.

"Okay, Chaz, we're here."

A second later, Chaz says, "You're in," as the door clicks open.

Once we're inside, Sienna puts her hand on my chest to stop me from moving forward. Instinctively, I flex my pecs. Her eyebrow raises as her mouth tweaks at the corner. "Sorry," I whisper.

She looks like she's trying not to laugh as she pulls baby

powder from the pack she's carrying on her back.

"Tell me again why Chaz has baby powder in his apartment?" I muse.

This time, a short laugh bursts out. "I think it's to help with chaffing."

I watch as she throws the powder on the floor in front of her. At first, I'm wondering what the heck she's doing until I see the lines of lasers that have appeared from the dusting of powder.

"So that's why you wanted the baby powder from his apartment," I muse.

She smiles and nods but doesn't say anything. I should probably be quiet, too. Sienna closes her eyes, taking a deep breath. When she opens them again, she has this determined expression I've never seen before. "Hold this, please," she says, handing me her pack.

I shoulder it as Sienna rises on her toes a few times. Stretching. She's stretching.

She's about to take a step forward, toward the lasers, when I grab her hand. She stops and turns, surprised.

"Please be careful," I whisper.

Her face softens as she leans up on her toes to kiss my cheek. "I've got this," she says next to my ear.

I know she's taken, but that doesn't stop me from wanting her. Wanting to hold her, to touch her. My hands have a mind of their own. They tuck a piece of loose hair behind her ear, caressing her cheek as they do. "I still worry about you."

"Between you and Trey, it's a wonder I haven't been confined to a bubble," she teases. Then she grows serious. "But I've got this. Really. You have to let me do what I know I'm good at." With that, she turns away, ending the discussion.

I take a step back to give her room to maneuver. She crosses over the first two lasers. For the next ones, she moves like a gymnast, bending and twisting through the beams. Her back is practically brushing against the floor as she manipulates her body under one particularly difficult one. She's limber and graceful, and as I watch her, I'm mesmerized. I had no idea her body could move like that.

When she reaches the other side, she gives me a triumphant smile before hurrying to a control panel on the wall. "Okay, Chaz. How do I override the lasers?"

Chaz's voice comes through my headset, too. He explains how she needs to cut the blue wires, but she's not to touch the red or black ones. After a moment, the lasers disappear and Sienna closes the control panel.

"You're clear," she says.

I stride across the floor to join her in the stairwell.

"Which floor?" she asks.

"Third."

We take the stairs two at a time. When we reach the third level, I tug the door open and inspect the hallway. There shouldn't be anyone here except for one or two night guards roaming the halls, but you never know. "Clear."

Sienna follows me to the lab on the left, the one my father brought me to a few short weeks ago. The lights are still on like someone worked through the night, but it's empty. I go straight to the stainless-steel case that looks like a medium-sized refrigerator. When I open it, mist seeps out. I search for the glass vial with Re0Gene 2.0 imprinted on it. There are five of them, so I take them all, wrapping them in an old T-shirt and placing them in Sienna's pack.

"We need to find the formula they used to create this," I say, scanning the room. I focus on the nearest computer. It would be too easy to keep the formula on something as simple and as hackable as a computer. And knowing my father and his paranoia, he probably has it locked up in a safe somewhere.

But after the last break-in, it won't be in his office, that's for sure. He'd choose someplace else, someplace less conspicuous.

"I'll be right back," I say to Sienna. "Stay here." I hurry into the hallway before she can protest. When I was a small child, I noticed a gray metallic box on the wall next to the water fountain. I remember asking my father about it one day and he said it was a treasure box, a place to hide things that were important. At the time, I'd been reading a lot of Robinson Crusoe, so I was positive he meant it had gold and jewels inside.

But as I stare at it now, I'm not sure what I'll find. It requires a key, which I obviously do not have.

"Stand aside," Sienna says, coming up behind me. "I've got this."

So much for her staying in the lab. I should have known she wouldn't listen to me.

She removes something from her hair—perhaps a hair clip?–and inserts it into the tiny keyhole. Concentration lines her face as she bites her lip and fiddles with the lock. "Al... most...there!" she exclaims as the metal door pops open.

"Nicely done," I say, beyond impressed. I've heard about her skills, of course, but seeing her in action is something completely different. She's risk, danger, and impossibility rolled into one tiny, beautiful package. Though she'd probably smack me if I referred to her as *tiny*.

"Not to get off topic, but how did you learn to do all of these things? I have a feeling your parents didn't enroll you in an after-school spy program."

Sienna laughs. "Not exactly. After my dad died, I dropped out of school and found employment with the Devil. His minions, one in particular named Victor, trained me." She shrugs. "Apparently, I was a natural. Or as Victor used to say, his prodigy."

We peer inside the metal box only to find it empty. "I should have known," I say. "That would've been too easy."

"Hang on," Sienna says, pressing against the back wall of the lock box. The wall shifts under her fingers. We exchange a glance. "That's either one crappy box or—"

"Something's back there," I finish for her. "Let me try."

Sienna moves aside so I have full access. My pulse is normally like a ticking clock, steady and predictable, but it quickens slightly at the idea something could be back there.

I push against the back, but it's pointless. "I need something sharp, like a knife or something."

Sienna reaches in her pocket, then hands me a pocketknife. "I stole it from Trey," she says.

The knife has a blue handle with the words, *"Our choices define us"* engraved on the hilt, along with the initials BGW. I know immediately it's from Trey's father—my father.

Using the tip of the knife, I pry away the back wall of the metal box. It pops out of place and dislodges itself. And there, sitting behind the wall, is a computer chip in a protective sleeve.

"There it is," I say. "How did you know?"

"If there's one thing I've learned about your father," she answers, taking the knife from me and storing it in her pocket again, "he loved a good Trojan horse."

"He did, didn't he? And this would be considered a double Trojan horse. The outside *and* the inside is deceptive."

"Probably his most calculated move yet."

Not entirely. His most calculated move was naming Steele as heir in order to protect me, then leaving me a clue so I'd know what happened.

It hits me then. He's really gone. And I'll never see him again. Not in this life anyway. For years, he was my idol, the man I wanted to become. He molded and shaped me to be this… this person he believed I could be. He knew the truth—I wasn't the one with the characteristics he chose—yet he still treated me like a son and groomed me to be his successor.

Until Steele stole everything from me.

My neck muscles tighten.

"You okay?" Sienna asks, tiny lines wrinkling her forehead.

"Yeah, I'm fine." I pull my Lynk from my pocket. Trey says I have to dump it before we leave Legas, because it's easily traceable. But for now, it's coming in handy. "Let me make sure this is the right chip." I insert the computer chip into the bottom of my Lynk. It takes a moment for the file to upload. When it does, it's a series of code, but I recognize a lot of it from the Re0Gene I created not too long ago. "This is it." I remove the chip, then pocket both it and my Lynk. "We better get out of here before someone sees us."

After fixing the box as best we can—there's no way we can get that panel back the way it was, not without spending a good deal of time and effort—we head to the stairwell. When we reach the first floor, Sienna keeps going.

"I need to see something," is all she says.

I follow her down to the basement. I haven't been down here in years, not since my father installed a special security system that stopped my access. Although now I know all I do, I believe it was Steele who did that, not my father.

When we reach the basement, we come face to face with a metal door that has a series of security devices attached to the wall.

"This is more intense than the AIG facility," Sienna says, studying the devices. "Looks like a fingerprint, retina, and—" She stops at the last. "What the heck is this one?"

I examine it. It has a tiny needle embedded in the top of the scanner. "Finger prick. It tests your blood."

Sienna's eyes widen. "Seriously?" She shakes her head at the thought. Then to Chaz, who is still waiting for instruction, she says, "Can you get this open for me?"

"Tell me where you are and what you see," Chaz responds.

I hear Trey in the background say, "What are they doing? They should be done by now. Tell them to hurry. I'm not liking this."

Sienna rolls her eyes at me, then tells Chaz everything he

needs to know.

"This may take a minute," Chaz warns.

Sienna leans back, propping her foot on the wall behind her. "That's okay. We have time."

I hear Trey curse through the headset. He must be breathing down Chaz's neck about right now.

It takes Chaz two and half minutes to bypass the fingerprint and retina security devices. Then he says, "One of you is going to have to do the finger prick and I'll alter the results from here."

"Why can't you bypass it?" Sienna asks, eyeing the device.

"It won't let me. But I think I'll be able to adjust it once the blood is in the system. So, who wants to get pricked?"

"I'll do it," I volunteer. I place my pointer finger in the finger-shaped slot. The needle is quick and pierces my skin with a sharp prick, leaving a bright red dot of blood. I suck on my finger until the blood stops.

"Did it work?" I hear Trey ask Chaz.

Chaz's tone is indignant when he responds. "Of course it worked." Then to Sienna and me, he says, "And… you're in."

The lock clicks, and Sienna tugs hard on the heavy metal door. As we cross the threshold into this restricted basement area, the first thing I'm aware of is how much cooler it is in here. Sienna rubs her arms like she notices the same thing.

I glance around the dimly lit room. We're in a small lab complete with work tables, chemical drums, and hazard signs. "Nothing special about this place," I say.

Sienna doesn't respond because she's already halfway across the room where there's a wall of curtains. She rips them back to peer through. Not sure why she's interested in checking out what's going on outside. Trey and Chaz will surely let us know if we need to make a quick getaway.

Moving like she's on a mission, Sienna strides to a door adjacent to the wall of windows. She tries the handle, and it turns easily. When she disappears through the entrance, I hurry after her. Apparently, the wall of windows doesn't look outside, but into another room. A larger room.

I exhale slowly, trying to make sense of what I see. There are rows upon rows of white hospital-style beds with a single stand and IV bag hanging beside each one.

"There must be at least fifty beds in here," I say, my eyes doing a quick sweep of the room.

"At least." Sienna moves toward one of the beds, reaching to finger an IV bag. "There were people here, Zane. This IV bag is only half-full. And there are drops of blood on these sheets, like someone bled out as the IV was inserted."

"Where did they go?"

Sienna shakes her head. "I don't know. But this is exactly what I found in the basement of the AIG facility, except those beds had bodies in them. People who looked like they were sleeping."

With her words ringing in my ears, because I suddenly have a horrible thought, I check each IV bag. Sure enough, they are all half-empty, some more than others. Past the beds is something that looks like a small training facility with mats and weights and a boxing bag. A comscreen hanging on the wall catches my eye, and I move toward it. I take the device off its hook and swipe at the screen. The government logo—the triskelion—flashes across the screen followed by the motto: *Progress is our future.*

"What is it?" Sienna asks, coming up behind me.

"This is a government-issued comscreen. Our comscreens have the Match 360 logo." I tilt the screen so Sienna can see.

"Which goes with our theory Steele has been working with the government for years. Also gives a motive for why he would want your father dead."

"If Steele thought my father was standing in the way of his relationship with the Agency, he would need to remove him from power." I think back to conversations I've overheard between my father and Steele over the years. There was definitely some contention there. Steele always wanted the company to be more. He wanted to share the genetic codex formula with the AIG years ago, but my father refused. This was his company, and he wanted to retain control of it. My father's belligerence may have cost him his life.

"And it also makes sense why he would want you out of the picture as well," Sienna says. "Steele knew you would never go along with his plan to align with the government."

"So he sent the death threat, forcing my father to change his will, granting himself full access to all of Dad's assets and placing himself in the decision-making position once my dad was dead."

"Exactly."

I glance down at the comscreen in my hands. "You think Chaz would be able to get in this? It's password encrypted."

At the sound of his name, Chaz breaks in, his voice echoing through my ear bud. "I'm sorry, but did someone just question my ability to hack into something? I know you didn't."

I'm about to apologize when a lock clicks, and there are voices in the outer lab.

"Quick! We need to hide," I hiss. There aren't many places. As I scan the room, I mentally calculate the size of the object that will hide us the best. When I see the large exercise balls in the corner of the room, I realize that's our only option.

We sprint to the corner and crouch behind the balls, our heads pressed into our knees. Sienna's breathing is rapid, but as the door opens and the voices move into the large room with the beds, she quickly quiets her breaths. I'm still holding the comscreen, and I sincerely hope they don't notice it's missing.

The first voice is easily recognizable. My hands tighten around the screen, the sharp edges cutting into my skin.

Steele.

The person he's talking to has a deep no-nonsense voice.

"We shipped off the first batch yesterday," Steele says. "And we are prepared to receive another shipment of individuals today."

"How long until the transformation is complete?" the man asks.

"Two days tops."

"But then there's testing?"

"Yes." Steele's voice moves closer to where we're hiding. I feel Sienna stiffen beside me. Even she knows how precarious our situation is right now. If she's caught—

I try not to think about it.

Out of the corner of my eye, I see Sienna reach for her gun. Giving a slight shake of my head, I lay my hand across hers. The warmth and smoothness of her skin is distracting. Despite the buzz of electricity zipping through my brain from the nearness of her, I try to focus on what Steele is saying.

"Yes," Steele continues. "We test them for strength, agility, courage, and obedience. We have to make sure they're ready before we send them to Rubex."

"Does everyone pass the tests?"

"Not everyone. Those who don't go under for more… adjustments."

It sounds like the man claps Steele on the back. "Well done. This is shaping up nicely. I'm sure Madame Neiman will be pleased."

"Thank you, sir. All I've done is model this facility after the one in the AIG. You guys are the brains behind this whole operation."

Disgusting. I can't bear to hear Steele sucking up to this government inbred.

"Thank you for your time, Mr. Ryder. I'll be in touch."

The lights turn off and the door closes behind them, the voices fading away. Sienna and I wait an extra minute, just to be safe. Her knees crack as she straightens.

"I'm going to take this comscreen with us. Maybe we can get some useful information from it," I say as I zip open Sienna's backpack and place the screen inside. But Sienna isn't listening. She crosses the room to one of the beds, then sinks down on it. I stride to her side. "What's wrong?"

When she turns to me, she says, "Didn't you hear them?"

"Of course I did, but—"

"Zane, they're altering the DNA of non-GMs and shipping them off to the Capital. Why? Why would they do that?"

I sit next to her. "They want to form a perfect society?"

She shakes her head, hard. "No. No, it's something… more."

I tap her bag. "Maybe we'll be able to figure it out once we access what's on that comscreen."

Lost in thought, Sienna doesn't respond immediately. I touch her arm. "What? Oh, yeah. You're probably right." She launches to her feet and grabs the bag from my hand, throwing it over her shoulder.

As I follow her out the door, I can't stop thinking about what Steele said.

*We test them for strength, agility, courage, and obedience.*

Why those traits specifically?

Clearly, something is going on in Rubex. And before we go to the Zenith Camp, we have to find out.

# 38

## Sienna

As we drive away from the Match 360 facility, my mind is still reeling from what I overheard in the basement. *We test them for strength, agility, courage, and obedience. We have to make sure they're submissive and ready to follow commands.*

Is this what they were doing to the people in the basement of the AIG? Steele did say he modeled their basement facility after the government's.

While I stare out the window at the hot pink sky of the breaking dawn, Zane relays the conversation we overheard between Steele and that Agency man.

When he's finished, Trey shakes his head and says, "Those bastards. I bet they think just because they destroyed and drove out the Fringe we won't do anything to stop them. We may be gone from Legas, but that doesn't mean we'll roll over and let this happen."

"What can we do?" Chaz asks. "They have manpower, guns, ammo."

"We have people," Trey says. "And guns. Maybe not as many as they do, but we're not afraid to fight."

"Me neither," Zane says. "Especially if it means I might get my father's company back."

"We need to get Sienna and Chaz back to the Zenith Camp

and recruit some help."

I've remained silent throughout this whole exchange, so I'm not surprised when Trey places his hand on my knee and says, "Hey, you okay? You're awfully quiet."

I turn away from the window. "Did I tell you about the boy named Ren I met in Rubex?"

Trey shakes his head.

"He was nice to me. He let me borrow a bike. Then government soldiers invaded the poorer part of the city and dragged children away from their families. Ren was one of them."

"Sienna, I'm sorry—" Trey starts to say, reaching for my hand.

I shift away from him. "I saw him again. In the basement of the AIG. He was one of those people in the beds. And I didn't do anything to help him. I was so worried about saving my own skin."

"You were wanted for murder." Trey tries to reassure me. "It's understandable."

"No, it's not," I say fiercely. "First, I left Kaylee to die in the Compound, then I left Ren and a hundred others in the hands of those government scum."

The car brakes suddenly as Zane pulls over onto the side of the road. He puts the car in park and turns quickly in his seat, his eyes finding mine. "If this is anyone's fault, it's mine. I left you alone in Rubex."

"And I'm the one who sent you there in the first place," Trey says, his voice quiet. He reaches for my hand again. This time, I let him take it. "We've all made mistakes. But we must move forward and not look back. Understand?"

My chest constricts. That's what I've been trying to do since the moment I knew my father was dead. "I'm trying," I say. "But one thing I know is I don't want to hide anymore. I want to fight."

"Sienna," Trey warns.

"Sienna's right," Chaz breaks in. At that moment, I could kiss him. "She and I aren't fragile dolls that need to be protected. We want to help. Besides, you need us."

Trey's eyes are worried. "But if you're caught…"

"I know the risks," I say. "Just like I knew the risks when I went to Rubex. Just like I knew the risks when we came to Legas to get Zane and Chaz." I then add, "I'm not afraid to take risks."

Trey rubs his jaw, considering our words. "So what's the plan?"

"Uh… guys," Chaz says slowly, staring at the comscreen he's been trying to hack for the last fifteen minutes. "We have a problem."

Trey reaches to the front seat and takes the screen from Chaz. After a few seconds, he raises his head, his face pale. "What is this?"

Chaz's eyes are round. "It's their plan. It's why the Agency is altering the DNA of non-GMs."

"Why?" I ask, my tone riddled with impatience. "Tell us, please."

"They aren't creating perfect individuals," Chaz says. "They're creating a perfect army."

The car goes silent.

"Unbelievable," Trey mutters, one hand rubbing his forehead.

"A perfect army?" I say. "For what? To fight? Fight who?"

"Who knows," Trey says. "Maybe to stop anyone who tries to go against them?"

"We have to stop them," I say. "If they're trying to create an army, we have to stop them."

"It sounds like it's too late," Zane says. "You heard them. They've been sending batches of modified soldiers to the Capital."

"Exactly. Which means we don't have time to waste."

Trey's eyebrows rise. "You want to go back to the Capital?"

"I think we have to."

"No. No way." Trey is adamant as he shakes his head. "I may be a pushover when it comes to you, but there's no way in hell I'm escorting you back to your death sentence. We need numbers. We need an army of our own."

I think of the men and women who've had their children stolen from them. How angry and hurt they must be. They surely hate the government as much as we do. But they're untrained. And compared to genetically altered soldiers, they wouldn't stand a chance. "We have to go back to Camp. We have to prepare ourselves to fight."

Trey nods in agreement. "And this time, we have the upper hand because we know what their plan is."

"But we don't know where they're planning to attack," Chaz interjects.

"Or when," Zane adds.

Trey lays a hand on Chaz's shoulder. "That's where you come in, my man. We need you to put those hacker skills to good use. Think you can uncover more stuff on this device?"

"I'm on it." Chaz gets to work, his fingers flying over the screen.

"Which reminds me," Zane says, carefully removing one of the Re0Gene 2.0 vials from my pack, "it's time to test this stuff." As we watch, he puts a few drops under his tongue. He holds out his arm so we can observe the serum at work. Within a matter of seconds, the skin on his arm fuses together, leaving a smooth surface behind.

"Well, I'll be damned," Chaz mutters, staring at Zane's wound-free arm.

"That stuff will come in handy during training," Trey says. "Okay, Zane. Before we drive to the planetarium, I want to swing by the hospital and check out this Statement Card crap.

They want all Citizens to report to a local hospital, so I think we should see what's going on so we can make a plan on how to proceed."

"Got it, Boss," Zane says, and if Trey notices the sarcasm in his voice, he doesn't say anything.

The hospital is overflowing with people. Lines of men, women, and children snake down the sidewalk and into the parking lot. Trey rolls his window down a bit to assess the scene.

Babies are crying, children are tugging on the hems of their weary mother's shirts, and the men have day-old stubble. Dozens of Enforcers with automatic rifles keep the Citizens in line, herding them like cattle at an auction.

"This is insane," Zane says, his fingers gripping the steering wheel harder.

"We need to leave. Now," Chaz mutters from the front seat.

"We can't just leave," Trey says. "These people need our help."

At that moment, a man half-runs, half-stumbles up to an Enforcer standing guard outside of the hospital. We hear the man shout, "Where is she? Where is my wife? I want to see my wife!"

The Enforcer appears to be trying to calm the man down, but with little success. The man keeps saying, "Where is my wife? I know she's here. What have you done to her?"

"Sir, I need you to calm down and come with me."

Several more Enforcers surround the man, and some don't seem as calm as the first one.

"Get him to shut up, would you?" one snarls, raising his gun.

"No violence," another says.

By now, the crowds of people in line have turned their

attention to the scene in front of the hospital. Mothers shield their children—I assume to protect them in case things get violent.

"What is going on?" I whisper to the others.

"I don't know, but it doesn't look good," Chaz says. A second later, he adds, "Um, Zane, we might want to keep driving."

An Enforcer has noticed we've stopped to view the confrontation, and he now marches over to our car.

"Go," Trey hisses. "Drive!"

We start to move forward, but the Enforcer steps into our path and puts his hand up, indicating for Zane to stop.

"Oh crap," Chaz says, placing his hand over his heart.

"Act natural," Trey says through clenched teeth. He's sitting beside me in the backseat.

My heart hammers triple speed, but when Trey pulls me close like we're a couple on the verge of making out, I sink into him, burying my face in his shoulder. Our names and pictures have been all over the Bulletins in Rubex and the news in Legas. It will be a miracle if the Enforcer doesn't recognize us.

"Good morning, Officer. What can I do for you?" Zane asks, his melodic voice even more musical and sweet. I peek over Trey's shoulder. Too bad it's not a female Enforcer—Zane's charms are a force to be reckoned with.

"We're checking all Citizens, for Statement Card purposes, and confirming who's a GM and who's not. Do you mind?" The Enforcer pulls out a handheld device. "It's a quick finger prick."

Zane inserts his finger into the device, a different finger than the one pricked earlier at the Match 360 facility, and there's a small poof, like air being blown into a tube. Zane removes his finger. As he waits for the results, the Enforcer stares at the screen in his hands. From this angle, I can barely make out a picture of Zane and some words beneath.

"Zane Ryder?" the Enforcer asks, squinting at the picture and then at Zane.

"Yes, sir."

The Enforcer peers into the car. "Do you have any non-GMs traveling with you today?"

Zane shakes his head. "No, sir."

"We need to issue you and your friends a Statement Card. If you would step out of the car, I can make sure you receive expedited service."

"We actually have a private appointment to receive our cards tomorrow. But I appreciate your concern."

The Enforcer pockets the device, then takes a step back from the car. "I'm sorry to bother you, sir. Please have a good day."

"Thank you, Officer."

As soon as Zane rolls up his window, there's a collective whoosh as we all exhale. I pull away from Trey and breathe deeply, trying to calm my racing heart.

"That was close," Trey mutters. "Too close."

"Tell me about it," Chaz exclaims. "I almost crapped my pants!"

"It's a good thing the Ryder name still carries weight," I add.

Zane's eyes find mine in the rearview mirror. "It is. Until it becomes too much of a burden."

As we drive away, I turn and watch out the rear window. The disgruntled man is still too upset to be reasoned with. An Enforcer pulls out a syringe, sticks him in the neck, and the man crumbles to the ground. I watch as they carry his body into the hospital, and he disappears. Gone forever.

# 39

## Trey

We're a few miles from the hospital when I lean forward in my seat and say, "Turn the car around. We need to go back."

Something's going on at that hospital, and we're the only ones able to do anything about it.

"Are you serious?" Chaz asks, his voice incredulous and his eyes wide. "We barely made it out as we did."

That man's wife is missing. She reported to the hospital as she was instructed to do, and then disappeared. And I have a sick feeling this government decree is a front for something much more sinister.

Are the two connected? The government decree and the creation of a perfect army? I wouldn't put it past those government bastards to do something so sick.

Sienna grabs my hand, squeezing it. "He's right. Something's happening to those people, and it isn't simple testing."

Without saying anything, Zane turns the car around, the tires squealing in protest. The centrifugal force sends Sienna sliding across the seat, bumping into me. Her cheeks turn a rosy hue as she mumbles a quick *Sorry.*

Chuckling, I bring her close and whisper in her ear. "You have to promise me something."

She blinks slowly, her nose wrinkling in curiosity.

"Promise me when I ask you to stay put you won't question my decision."

She starts to argue, but I stop her lips with mine. I'm expecting her to push me away, because she's good at that, but surprisingly, she leans into the kiss, her body relaxing beneath my hands.

Zane clear his throat. As Sienna and I pull away from each other, he catches my eye in the rearview mirror and frowns. Holy hell. I didn't mean to rub it in, but it's hard not to touch her when she's so close.

I rest my forehead against hers and say, "Promise me."

She smiles. Why do her smiles turn my insides to scrambled eggs? I'm supposed to be tougher than that. Stronger than that.

"Okay, fine," she says. "I promise. But only so long as I agree with the stipulation."

"You know how to make this hard on me, don't you?"

Zane interrupts us by saying, "Where are we going exactly?"

"To the backside of the hospital," I answer. A plan is slowly forming. This is why I want Sienna to listen when I ask her to stay behind. I can't have her in unnecessary danger.

"What are we doing exactly?" Zane asks.

"Finding out what's going on in that hospital. It's clearly more than genetic testing."

Zane takes a few side roads to get us to the back of the hospital. I instruct him to stop the car before we reach the building.

"I can take it from here." I climb out of the vehicle. When Sienna starts to follow me, I hold up a hand to stop her. "This is when I need you to stay behind."

"I'm not letting you do this yourself," she says, her stubborn streak coming through.

"I'm not asking for your permission. But I would like for you to honor your promise. Zane, make sure she stays here."

I jog away, glancing over my shoulder only once to confirm Sienna isn't following me. Thankfully, she stayed behind and is now safely back in the car. Leave it to Zane to be able to reason with her. He really is better at it than I am.

Once I reach the rear of the hospital, I crouch behind a large bush and scan the area. One solitary Enforcer patrols the grounds. I rustle the leaves of the bushes to get his attention, then duck behind another bush. When he comes over to check out the sound, I sneak up behind him and tap him on the shoulder. As he turns, I punch him in the face, knocking him out. His face must have a lot of sharp angles because my hand throbs after the impact.

I drag his body behind the nearest bushes and quickly undress him. The only way into that building is if I look like I belong.

Once I have on the Enforcer's uniform, which happens to be a little big in the waist, I tuck my gun in the back of my pants and pick up his M-16. I walk out like I belong here.

The Enforcer has a key card attached to his shirt, which I use to gain entry into the building, using a side door. When I enter, I'm in a sterile hallway, all white and bright, smelling of disinfectant and antiseptic.

"Hey, buddy, where ya been?" a voice calls out from down the hall. An Enforcer with an identical uniform stands at the end of the corridor, his gun slung over his back. "They're ready for us to load."

Load? I decide to play along. I stride down the hallway toward him.

"Sorry. Had to take a leak."

The guard clasps me on the back, steering me down another hall. "Are you new to the force? Don't think I've seen you around before."

Ah, hell. He's suspicious.

I try to play it cool. "Yeah, um, I've been on nightly

roundup for a while, but was just transferred to this facility. Still learning the ropes."

"I thought the streets were pretty clear lately. They still doing the nightly roundup?"

I shrug, the weight of his arm an uncomfortable reminder of how close I am to the enemy. If he had any idea who he had in his grasp right now… "Not as much. Probably why they reassigned me."

His hand tightens on my shoulder. "Ah, well, welcome to the cleanup crew. You stick with me, and I'll show you how things are done around here." He smiles, showing off a set of crooked teeth. "I'm Officer Kimball."

I think fast. "Officer Turner. My friends call me Ty."

When we reach a set of swinging metal doors, his arm slides off my shoulder. "You done a cleanup yet?"

"Not yet." I glance up and down the long hall. Doors line this hallway, and at least half a dozen Enforcers enter and exit rooms.

"Each person who comes in is tested, then placed into one of three categories: Usable, Modifiable, or Disposable."

"What's the difference?" I ask, eyeing two Enforcers who carry an older woman down the hall. She looks like she's been drugged.

"Usables are those we can modify to use in the military. Modifiables are those who can better society after being modified. Disposables are, well—" he grins, "well, they're disposable. That's where our cleanup skills come into play."

"Cleanup skills?"

He's about to answer me when a severe-looking Enforcer hollers down the hall. "Hey, cleanup boys! We have a pile of Disposables in Room 154."

Kimball's face is disturbingly gleeful as he smiles in my direction. "Duty calls."

As we near Room 154, I brace myself. I'm not sure what

I'll see, and I've seen some horrific things in the past. Nothing prepares me for the pile of bodies stacked on an oversized rolling cart. Limbs hang over the edges of the cart—limbs of men, women, and small children.

Breathing slowly to remain in control, I try to keep myself from hitting something or someone. I can't blow my cover. Not yet. Not while I'm deep behind enemy lines.

"Hey, man, you okay?" Kimball watches me closely. He must notice something's up.

I clear my throat and look him straight in the eyes. "Of course. No problem here."

He stares at me a second longer before grabbing a hold of the cart, indicating I'm to do the same. I could easily push this cart myself, but I pretend it's heavy as we drive it down the hallway.

I try to keep my eyes focused forward, but I still catch glimpses of the people—of the bodies. Dark skin, light skin, old people, young people. There is no rhyme or reason to these "disposables". I have so many questions, but I don't want to raise his suspicions. Maybe one question wouldn't hurt.

"What makes these Disposables?" I ask as we turn a corner.

Officer Kimball shrugs. "Not sure exactly. Maybe they have a disease or something that can't be helped by altering their genes?" He lowers his voice, glancing around. "*They* only want to keep those who can benefit our society in some way."

Anger explodes inside me. What right do *they* have to determine who gets to live or die? That's not for anyone to decide.

My hands grip the cart so hard my knuckles turn white. We reach a set of doors leading outside. They whoosh open, their sensors embedded somewhere in the ground beneath our feet.

A utility truck is there, waiting for us, its back open. We roll the cart up the ramp as the driver, another Enforcer, exits the vehicle and comes around back to help us. I follow their lead, lifting bodies off the cart and placing them on the floor of the truck. I move and place them as carefully as I can. With each one, I try not to think about how they were someone's daughter or mother or father or friend.

Kimball and the other Enforcer move mechanically, like this is just another day on the job. They've seen enough death to last them a lifetime, and now they're immune. Either that or they're just following orders. Doesn't do them any good to care.

When the last body has been placed, my partner in crime clasps me on the back. "This one is all yours. Time for you to learn the ropes."

"Where are we going?" I ask.

Kimball grins, and I can't help but stare at his overlapping teeth. "To finish the cleanup." He rolls down the metal grate, then pats the back of the truck. "Officer Topeka, why don't you show our new recruit the scenic route?" he says to the other Enforcer. "Yes?"

I could take them. I could take them right here and now. But if I do, I'll have no idea where they're disposing of these bodies. I decide to play along a little longer.

"Let's go," Officer Topeka says.

Kimball heads back into the building as I climb into the passenger side of the truck.

"You're new, aren't you?" he asks as he puts the truck in gear.

I give him the same story I told Kimball. As we're driving away from the back of the hospital, I see Zane's car parked down the street. I roll down the window and pretend to hock a loogie, trying to get their attention. They won't be on the lookout for me inside of a government truck.

Zane or someone must see me, because they inch forward. I keep watch in the rearview mirror. Yes. They saw me and are following at a safe distance.

When Topeka turns onto the road that leads to the lake

and the dam, I ask, "Where are we taking these dead bodies?"

"Dead bodies?" He seems to find my question amusing, letting out a little laugh before casually saying, "Oh, they're not dead. Not yet. I mean, they will be soon enough."

"They're not dead? But they were so... still."

"They're drugged." He glances at me. "You really are new, aren't you? Didn't they teach you anything in orientation?"

"Only the basics of what I'd be doing. Guess they forgot to mention this part." As I shrug, I can only hope the rage I'm feeling doesn't show through. As we curve around one bend and then another, I think of all the ways I'd like to kill this guy. With my bare hands. Like to kill all the Enforcers in that building, especially Kimball with his crooked teeth and snide remarks.

I check the side mirror again. Zane is smart enough not to follow directly behind us, so I don't see him for a while, not until we reach a straighter stretch of road. His little silver sports car crests the hill, the sun glinting off the hood. We're closer to the dam now, and it doesn't take a rocket scientist to know that's where we're headed.

Are they dumping these unconscious people in the lake?

Can I save them?

I turn several ideas over in my mind, all the while keeping tabs on Zane.

We drive partway across the dam before Topeka stops the truck. "Time to unload," he says, already climbing out. I hang back as he unlocks and lifts the metal door, one hand on the gun shoved in the back of my pants.

"Help me get this one," he says, pointing to a middle-aged blonde woman.

I avert my eyes so I won't see her face and the wedding ring on her left hand. Is this the wife of the man from earlier?

I curl my arms under her armpits, lifting her as Topeka grasps her legs. We carry her down the ramp to the wall that separates us from the arched concrete chasm below.

I've heard stories about this place. About the many people who died while building this dam. How their bodies were never recovered, and concrete was poured over them as they continued to build the massive structure. How those workers now lay in a concrete graveyard, forever preserved in rock and stone.

And as we hold her next to the wall, I have a sick feeling in my stomach. I now know what they do with the Disposables. And why no one ever finds their bodies. Encased in stone, they just… disappear. Forever.

"Up and over, on the count of three," Topeka says. "One, two—"

"Don't even think about it," a familiar voice says, and it's the one time I'm glad she didn't listen and decided instead to use her own instincts for this situation.

As Topeka turns to Sienna, I loop one arm around the woman's body to keep her from falling and seize the gun from my pants. I point it right in his face. "Step away slowly," I tell him as Sienna joins me.

Topeka growls, slowly lifting his hands. "I knew something funny was going on. No recruit is that clueless."

"And yet, you still brought me here," I comment. "Sienna, grab his gun, please." Sienna gets his gun, pats him down, and then returns to my side. "Keep an eye on this guy," I say. After lifting the woman in my arms, I carry her back to the truck and place her carefully next to a man in suspenders. Now that I know they aren't dead, I check for signs of life. Sure enough, her chest rises and falls ever so slightly. How had I not noticed that before?

I rejoin Sienna where she still has her gun trained on the Enforcer.

"What are we gonna do with this guy?" she asks.

Peering over the wall of the dam to the concrete ledge over

seven hundred feet below, I say, "Perhaps he should join those he's already sent over? Seems fitting."

Sienna nods in agreement.

I study the bottom of the dam, searching for signs of broken bodies. My theory must be correct. At the base of the dam, several cement trucks rest. They must dump the people, then add another layer of concrete. Clean and easy.

Training my own gun on Topeka, I say to Sienna, "Check the glovebox for some rope or something."

She strides over to the truck, climbs inside, and then returns a moment later with rope.

"Walk," I say to Topeka, shoving the gun into his back. I steer him to a shiny gold door that seems out of place on top of the dam. It's locked, but I'm able to kick it open. Surprisingly, it's a bathroom. Not sure why they need a bathroom up here, but whatever. Serves my purpose well. "Have a seat," I order.

Topeka slumps against the wall, grumbling the whole time while I tie his hands and feet.

"They're gonna find out," Topeka sneers. "And when they do, you're both good as dead. They don't like loose ends."

"Who are the *they* you keep referring to?" I ask.

"The people in charge. They'll find you. I can promise that."

Smiling, I pat his cheek. "And that's why I'll be long gone before they come looking. Me and that truck full of people. That truck full of *Disposables*." I practically spit out the last word.

"There's more," he sneers. "There's always more. You can't save them all."

I look him full in the eyes, because I don't want him to forget my face. "Who says I can't?"

With my hand on her back, I lead Sienna from the room, closing the door behind us.

As we head back to the truck, Sienna laces her fingers through mine. "What's the plan now?"

"We'll drive the truck back to Camp. These people can heal and regroup under our watch and care."

Sienna tugs me to a stop and rises on her tiptoes, kissing me full on. "Have I told you lately how amazing you are?"

I can't help but chuckle at her earnest expression. "I was thinking the same thing about you."

"You could've killed him. But you didn't."

"I knew you wouldn't want me to."

She turns thoughtful. "We make a good team, don't we?"

Pulling her close, I kiss her forehead. "The best."

# 40

## Sienna

We are a caravan of misfits.

There's no way Zane's Aria can make the trip to Camp, so he parks it at the planetarium, and he and Chaz follow us in the ATV. When I look in the side mirror, I can see Chaz's face and his smile so wide I'm afraid he may get bugs in his teeth if he doesn't close his mouth. Someone's enjoying their off-road experience.

The government truck Trey and I are in bounces over the underbrush and small rocks. So far so good. These trucks are made to handle all types of terrain, so hopefully, it will sustain our trip to Camp.

I find myself nodding off, only to be jolted awake a few minutes later. Trey taps his hands against the steering wheel like he's drumming to an invisible beat. He doesn't know I'm awake, so it gives me a chance to study him. The muscles in his arms flex to his drumming beats, and even his leg taps out a rhythm. I wish I could dive into his head to listen in on the song that's playing through his mind.

Of all the things I love about Trey, I love his hands the most. They are large and solid, his fingernails cut short, the calluses slowly returning on his palms, and the middle finger on his right hand slightly crooked from when he broke it "fighting" with Nash before I arrived at the Compound.

I love his eyes, too. Oh, and his lips. His lips are definitely the best. And those shoulders—a girl could get lost in his embrace...

Trey catches me ogling him and winks. "Awake so soon?"

"It's impossible to sleep in this truck." I scoot closer until I'm sitting right beside him. "Plus, your off-roading skills could use some work. Way too bumpy."

Trey laughs, lifting his hands from the steering wheel. "Would you like to drive?"

We hit a rock, and I literally fly a few feet into the air. "Trey! Don't forget we have *people* in the back of this thing."

Trey grips the steering wheel, his face sheepish. "You're right. I'll try to do better."

Leaning my head on his shoulder, I wrap my arm around his arm. His shoulder is all muscly, but it's still comfortable. A much better pillow than the side of this truck.

"Do you ever dream of what your life might be like when all of this is over?" I murmur, staring out the windshield. "I mean, when we're not hiding and fighting."

Trey snickers. "Is there really such a life? If there is, I can't imagine it. This is all I've ever known."

I lift my head to look at him. "You deserve to have a normal life. One where you live in a house, go to work—" I pause because the next thing I'm about to say seems so intimate, "and come home to a woman who loves you."

Trey's eyes connect with mine. "Sounds nice."

"It can be. I mean, my parents were together for almost eighteen years before my dad died. For the first time, I mean." The familiar pang of emptiness drums against my chest.

"Is that what you want? To get married? Have a family?"

I notice the way he asks, like he's afraid of the answer. Is he scared of this type of thing? Commitment? Marriage? The idea of a family? Obviously, I'm still young, but it's something I want. Someday.

I don't want to scare him off, though. "I don't know. Maybe?" I pause. "What about you? Is it what you want?"

He shrugs, his eyes refusing to meet mine. "I don't know. Maybe?"

I'm about to call him out on his cop-out of an answer—he can't just duplicate mine—when I decide to let it go. This is clearly something he's not comfortable talking about.

But as I sit there, my answer gnaws at me, the lack of truthfulness in it. When I can't stand it a moment longer, the words burst out. "Okay, I lied."

Trey raises an eyebrow. "About?"

"I lied about wanting to get married. I do want to get married someday. I want to have a family and children. I mean, I'm not talking about tomorrow or anything, because hello, I'm only eighteen, but it's everything I've ever wanted. Before all of this crap went down," I add.

Trey's face lights up like I've electrocuted him. "I lied, too."

"You did?"

"Yeah. I totally want to get married. I want kids, a family, a wife. I want the whole package." His eyes bore into mine. "More specifically, I want *you*."

My breath catches. For a moment, I allow myself to go there. To transport myself to the future where there are no worries other than the fit of my wedding dress. I picture myself, walking down an aisle, preparing to start a life with someone I love. And when I reach the end and look up, Trey's the one standing there, waiting. It *is* Trey. It's always been Trey.

My fingers nestle themselves in the curls at the base of his neck. "I want you, too," I whisper.

Trey smiles as he stares at the road. "Are we saying what I think we're saying?"

"I think so." Every inch of me is abuzz.

"You'll marry me? Someday?"

I grin so wide my cheeks hurt. "Yes. Yes!"

With one hand on the steering wheel, Trey reaches for my hand, pulling it up to his lips and kissing it with such tenderness it makes my insides ache in all the right places. "You have no idea how happy you've made me."

"I love you."

"Not as much as I love you."

I settle back against the seat and smile at him. "We'll have to agree to disagree on that one."

Once we're less than an hour from Camp, Trey radios Paige to let her know we're coming and not to be alarmed by the government vehicle. Paige's voice comes through staticky, but it's clear she heard and understood us. She says something about preparing the Camp for the new arrivals.

When we arrive, we park the truck between the two cliffs. Zane and Chaz park the ATV beside us. The three of us stand to the side as Trey unlatches the lock, then rolls open the back of the truck.

The sight is devastating. Barefoot men, women, and children huddle together, their eyes round with fear. There are at least thirty of them. The women whimper and clutch the children tighter.

My stomach rolls as I think of each one of them being thrown over the side of the dam to the chasm below, their bodies breaking against the concrete. I tighten my hands into fists, digging my nails into my palms to regain control.

Trey holds up his hands and inches forward. "It's okay. I'm not going to hurt you. You're safe now." When no one moves, Trey tries again. "We rescued you from the hospital, and you're now at a place called the Zenith Camp. We'll take care of you. I promise."

An older gentleman rises to his feet and unsteadily steps

forward, out of the truck. He takes Trey's face in his hands, gratefully kisses each cheek. "Thank you, son. Thank you." The others follow the old man's lead, rising to their feet and shuffling out of the truck. Some grasp Trey's hand, others kiss his cheek or hug him, the small children wrapping their arms around his legs.

Trey leads the group up the path on the short trek to Camp. I slip between the others until I'm beside him, taking his hand in mine and giving it a quick squeeze. "You're a hero," I whisper, beaming up at him.

"No more than you are."

When we arrive at Camp, we're greeted by all the Zenith and Fringe members, my mother and sister among them. I pull them in for a tight hug before Mom is off helping some of the women get settled. Emily is ecstatic when she sees Zane. He picks her up, swinging her around while she giggles.

Once she's firmly back on the ground, Emily attaches herself to the children, no doubt excited to have playmates. Paige shows the group a table set up with an assortment of meat and veggies. I hate to admit it, but I'm impressed she was able to pull all of this together in such a short time.

Once everyone is fed and somewhat settled, Trey calls an emergency meeting around the campfire. He invites a small group of people—Paige, Trina, Nash, Grey, Chaz, Asher, Zane, and me to join him. He starts off by talking about the decree—which the ones who stayed at Camp already know about. Jared and Trina did a good job of informing everyone when the press release hit. Trey then describes what he witnessed in the hospital.

"So," Paige says, "if you hadn't hijacked that vehicle, all of these people would be dead?"

"Yeah. And there are hundreds more."

"We have to do something," Grey pipes up.

"I'm glad you feel that way," Trey says. "I think we should

put together a small group to go back to Legas. We need to put an end to this."

Paige crosses her arms over her chest. "How do you propose we do that?"

Zane is the one who answers. "By destroying the hospital and the main Match 360 building. Once we've ensured they're empty, of course."

"Zane," I break in, "are you sure you want to do that? What about everything your father created?"

"If he knew how his genetic codex was being used, he'd be angry," Zane says. "He'd want me to do this."

"I'm game," Nash says.

"Me too," Trina adds.

"If she's going, you can definitely count me in," says Grey. Trina blows him a kiss.

"Paige?" Trey says, addressing her directly.

"Someone needs to stay here to help with the new arrivals. Asher and I can stay."

"Good idea." Trey turns his attention to me. "You'll stay here, too."

"No, I'm coming." There's no way he's leaving me here.

Trey's eyebrows rise. "Fine. But you'll do as I say."

It's moments like this Trey falls into the role of leader, not boyfriend. Cause there's no way I'd let my boyfriend talk to me this way. "Fine."

Trey turns to Chaz. "I'll stay here," Chaz says. "I don't mind."

"Sorry, buddy. We're gonna need you out there. You're the only one with exceptional hacker skills."

Chaz's face falls. "Can I remain in the car most of the time?"

"Sure." Trey pats Chaz's shoulder. To the rest of us, he says, "Try to get some rest. Let's plan to leave first thing in the morning."

When the crowd disperses, I wander off to find my mom and Emily. Mom is helping an auburn-haired woman set up her tent. "Sienna," Mom says when she sees me, "this is Zoe."

Zoe smiles at me. "You were one of those who helped rescue us, right? I never got to thank you properly." She takes my hand in hers and shakes it, a very loose handshake. "Thank you."

"No problem. I'm glad we were there."

"Me too." Zoe resumes stretching out the animal skin for her tarp.

"Zoe," I say, "can I ask you something?"

Zoe straightens. "Sure."

"There was a man outside the hospital saying he'd lost his wife. Do you have any idea who that might've been? I mean, do you have family you've been separated from?"

Zoe's lips twist, her grief evident. "We all do, hun. The most we can hope for is they somehow escaped, too."

"Tell me who. I'll find them. We're headed back in the morning."

Tears fill Zoe's eyes. "My husband and daughter. She's ten."

"What are their names?"

"Ezra and Annie."

"How did you get separated?"

Zoe exhales, her chin quivering. "When we first arrived at the hospital, we were given a form to fill out. I've always had health problems, so once they saw my form, they took me back immediately."

"And your husband?"

"Ezra and Annie were asked to wait in the waiting room. They were told their form was still being processed."

"Then what happened?"

"They led me to this big room with lots of beds, said I would go through some painless testing. They gave me a shot of something, and that's the last I remember. Woke up in that truck with all those people you guys rescued." Tears slide down her cheeks. "They were going to kill us, weren't they?"

When I nod, her hands fly to her mouth. "Oh, God. Annie. I have to get to Annie."

I lay a hand on her shoulder. "Don't worry. I promise I'll find them."

For the next two hours, I do the same thing. I go through Camp and ask each person we rescued from the hospital if they have someone they need to find. By the time I'm finished, I have a long list of names I've typed out in the comscreen we snagged from the basement of Match 360. I keep promising I'll do everything I can to find their loved ones, but as the list grows, I'm not so sure.

What if I can't find them? Or what if it's too late?

I hope I didn't offer misplaced hope.

# 41

## Trey

With a truck full of guns, ammo, and dynamite, we arrive in Legas by midmorning. Too pumped about this mission, I didn't sleep at all last night. Actually, I haven't had a proper night's sleep in days, but it doesn't matter. I'm fueled by adrenaline.

We park several blocks from the hospital to go over the plan one more time. Our first mission is to rescue Disposables and clear the hospital. Once it's clear, we'll blow it up. Though if there are any Enforcers still in there when it blows... I won't worry over those losses.

"Everyone knows their job, right?" I ask, eyeing my trusted group of cohorts. Zane, Trina, Grey, Chaz, Nash, and Sienna stare back at me, nodding. "Once we're in there, we won't be able to communicate, which means you have to stick to the plan." I pointedly focus right on Sienna as I say that. She rolls her eyes, giving me an exasperated look. I can't help but chuckle.

"Don't forget, Chaz," I continue, "you stay here in the truck and be ready to offer hacker assistance if needed. Got it?"

Chaz nods, his face filled with uncertainty.

Clasping him on the back, I say, "It'll be fine. Everyone, just stick to the plan."

We disperse then. I watch as Trina and Grey start down the road headed to the front entrance of the hospital where they'll "convince" those in line to come back another day. They may have to take out some Enforcers in the process, but they're prepared for that. I'm glad Grey is with Trina; I know he won't let anything bad happen to her.

Nash heads to the backside of the building where he'll work on setting up explosives. Zane, Sienna, and I cross the street, slip through the bushes, and steal onto the hospital property. We conceal ourselves behind some bushes, our eyes focused on the truck at the back entrance to the hospital. There's one Enforcer in the driver's seat, waiting on his next shipment of "Disposables."

I motion to Zane and Sienna to wait. Then I walk right up to the driver's side and knock on the window. When the door is cracked, I shove it all the way open and grab the man, forcing him to the ground. "Keys," I demand, pressing my gun to his temple. He fumbles in his pocket, then throws the keys on the ground.

Zane hurries over, picks them up, and pockets them. "Thanks."

"You'll never get away with this," the Enforcer sneers.

I punch him with just enough force to knock him out. Then I remove his clothes and climb into the back of the truck to change. When I'm done, I pocket the rag I'll use in just a moment and throw Zane some rope I found in the back. "Tie him up and put him in the back of the truck." To Sienna, I say, "I'll be back in a jiffy."

She kisses my cheek. "See you soon."

I stride through the automatic doors with more confidence than last time. That's because I know where I'm going and what I'm doing. I spot a nurse down the hallway. She's dressed in a white uniform, complete with a white bonnet-looking thing. I smile when I think of Sienna wearing that.

Catching the nurse's eye, I wave and give her my most endearing smile. Zane would probably have been better for this part since he's great at wooing the ladies. But he wouldn't have been able to stomach what I have to do next.

She smiles back, waiting for me to catch up to her. "Do you have a rag and bucket I can use? One of the *patients*—" I put special emphasis on the word patients, "—woke up and vomited all over the back of the truck. I need something to clean it up."

"Oh, sure," she says. I follow her down the hall to a storage closet. When she goes inside, I do, too, checking first to make sure no one saw me. The hallway is clear.

"Oh!" she exclaims in surprise when she sees me. I close the door tightly behind us. Her eyes flit to the closed door.

I flash her another smile. "I'm sorry. I lied to you. I don't need a bucket or a rag." I take a step toward her. "I just wanted a moment alone with you."

The woman's cheeks turn pink, her face changing from uncertainty to pleasure. "Oh—okay."

One hand reaches behind her neck, tilting it back until the entire soft spot of her neck is exposed. She sucks in a sharp breath, the vein in her neck pulsing in time to her quickened heartbeat. Pulling the rag from my pocket, I press it firmly over her mouth and nose. Her eyes widen as she inhales the chloroform. "I'm sorry," I whisper. A moment later, her eyes roll back into her head and she slumps into my arms. I cradle her, gently lowering her to the ground.

Pocketing the rag, I leave the woman in the closet and hurry outside to where Sienna waits.

"You ready, love?" I say.

Sienna nods, excitement in her eyes. I swear, that girl lives for danger.

I scoop Sienna up into my arms and she goes limp, like one of the people in the hospital who have been shot up with something to make her sleep. I carry her through the automatic doors to the storage closet. Another Enforcer is coming down the hall toward us. "Everything okay, Officer?" he asks, eyeing Sienna.

"Uh, yes, sir. This one woke up a little, so I was bringing her back inside for more medication before we do a Disposables run."

"You want me to take her? I'm on my way to the Treatment Room."

I tighten my grip on Sienna. "Oh, no thanks. I got it."

The Enforcer shrugs and continues down the hall, but before turning the corner, he stops and glances back at me. I continue down the hall, probably in the wrong direction of the Treatment Room. But when I chance a peek back, he's thankfully gone.

I double back to the closet, then slip inside. Sienna opens her eyes as I set her on the ground.

"How'd I do?" she asks.

"You were the perfect unconscious person."

Sienna's eyes flit to the nurse on the floor and her uniform. "Seriously?" she says. "I have to wear that?"

I grin. "Do you want me to help you undress her?"

Sienna gives me a murderous look. "You stay on that side of the closet. I've got this."

I turn around, giving Sienna and the passed-out nurse some privacy. Each minute that ticks by bring us one moment closer to this whole building going up in flames. I can hear Sienna grunting as she works to remove the nurse's uniform.

"Everything okay over there?" I ask.

"Fine," she says through gritted teeth. "Oh!"

"What?" I almost turn around, but Sienna's hand on my back stops me.

"Nothing. This nurse is heavier than she looks."

A few minutes later, Sienna takes a deep breath. "Okay, I'm done."

I turn to find her straightening herself. The white uniform

hits her just below the knee, and she's pinned her hair back to fit under the cap-thing. "Well, dang," I say, then give a low whistle.

"What?" she says, her face turning red.

"You look cute is all. Darn cute."

She smoothes invisible wrinkles in the front, refusing to meet my eyes. "Well… thanks. I guess."

"You ready?"

She nods, and I open the door. "Remember," I say, "if someone recognizes you, get the hell out of here. Yes?"

"Okay."

Sienna and I exit the storage closet at the same time. Too late, we realize we forgot to check if the hallway was clear. There's an Enforcer coming down the hall toward us. I'm sure we're done for. But all he does is raise his eyebrows, giving me a thumbs-up. Apparently, I'm not the only one who takes nurses into storage closets. With a grin, I return the gesture.

When the hallway comes to a T, Sienna goes one way and I go the other. "Be careful," I whisper. Her back straightens and she walks tall down the hallway, no doubt trying to prove she can do this. As an Enforcer passes her going the opposite direction, I watch as she reaches out and snatches his Lynk from his back pocket. But when that same Enforcer turns and checks her out, whistling crudely as he appreciates her rear, I almost strangle him. I take a deep breath, unclench my fists, then turn and go the other way.

I have to trust her.

# 42

## Sienna

I'm not prepared for what I see. The Treatment Room is located on the second floor and is essentially not a room at all. There are people and beds in every nook and cranny—beside the nurses' stations, taking over the waiting rooms, filling the hallways. This must be where people come, thinking they're going to be tested, but where they receive medication, knocking them out instead.

The very thought leaves me feeling sick to my stomach. I slip in between the beds and start questioning the patients, especially any who fit the descriptions I was given. On the four-hour drive back to Legas, I memorized the list. I spot an aging man with a bald spot and hurry over to him.

"Hi," I say. "Can you tell me your name, please?"

He eyes me warily, then answers, "Timothy."

Bingo! We have a match. "Well, Timothy, I know your wife, and you need to come with me so you can meet up with her."

"I haven't received my Statement Card yet," he protests.

"No worries. I'll have it made for you," I lie.

I grab his arm, help him off the bed, and lead him to a spot in the corner of the room, behind some tall potted plants. "Wait for me here, please. There are a few others I need to grab."

As I continue my search, a nurse comes up to me, frowning.

"What are you doing with that older gentleman? He's supposed to remain on his bed."

"I'm sorry, but I have strict instructions from downstairs. They want me to bring some of the individuals down. I have a list."

The lady's forehead crinkles. "That's odd. I haven't received any information about that."

"You can call down if you like?" Sweat beads under my armpits. *Please don't let her call and ruin my bluff.*

She shrugs, seeming to buy it. "No, I'm sure it's fine. Carry on."

I continue my search, but I can feel her eyes boring into my back. I find someone's teenage son, someone's wife, someone's mother, and someone's father, but no Ezra or Annie. There are other family members missing, too, but I try not to think about the reason I can't find them. Instead, I focus on the ones I *can* save.

I've just about given up on finding Ezra and Annie, because my time is limited, when I spot them. They are huddled on chairs in the waiting room; I guess they ran out of beds. I practically sprint over to them.

"Is your name Ezra?" I ask, out of breath.

He nods.

"And you're Annie?" I say, turning to the blonde girl. She nods, her eyes round.

The man named Ezra grabs my hand. "Can you tell us what's going on? We've been here since yesterday. My wife was with us, but we got separated. Do you know how long this will take?"

"Come with me," I whisper. "Your wife asked me to bring you to her."

"You know Zoe?" the man asks.

"I met her."

"Is she safe?"

"Yes. And you will be, too, as soon as I get you guys out of here."

"Ezra Simmons?" a loud voice calls out. "Annie Simmons?"

I hold up a finger to my lips. "We have to go. Now."

We start toward the group of people I've gathered.

"Ezra and Annie Simmons? Are you here?"

It's the same nurse I talked with earlier. She spots me across the room, her eyes narrowing when she sees I've collected a man and girl with the same descriptions as the two on her paper. The two next to be given their sleepy juice.

"Nurse? Nurse!" she calls, determinedly marching toward us.

"To the stairs. Quick," I say to my small group. "There's a man named Zane with a truck waiting in the back. Go now!" I shove them through the door to the stairwell. Then I turn to confront the nosy nurse.

"Was that Ezra and Annie Simmons?" the nurse asks as she draws closer. "They're next on my list."

I shake my head and wrinkle my brow, trying to look confused. "No, ma'am. That was John and Susie Davis. They're on *my* list."

The woman straightens, her mouth turning down like she ate something sour. "May I see this list?"

"Sure. Let me just…" I whip out the Lynk I stole earlier, "pull it up for you." I pretend to search the Lynk. "Ah, here it is." I turn the Lynk to show her the blank screen. When she leans forward to get a better look, I slam the device into her nose. She cries out and stumbles backward.

I take off for the stairwell, but not before I hear her radio for help. When I reach the first level, I burst through the door. My small group of stowaways are shuffling down the hall toward the back entrance. I've almost caught up to them when an Enforcer turns the corner, headed right for us. His eyes rove over the mismatched crew, but I give him a bright smile.

# *Fearless*

"Where are you taking these folks, nurse?" he asks.

"They were marked Disposables, but they're actually Usables and Modifiables. I'm taking them to the correct locations."

The Enforcer eyes the older gentleman with the bald spot. I know what he's thinking—how could this old man be useful—so I lean in and whisper in his ear. "He's ex-military."

The Enforcer nods like that would explain it. He motions for us to carry on.

I lead the group around the corner, like I'm taking them to another room. Once we're out of eyesight, I hold up a hand to stop my ragtag group. I tiptoe back to peer around the corner. The Enforcer is gone.

"Let's go," I say, motioning for them to follow. We backtrack, crossing through the corridor to the other side where the exit is. Zane jumps down from the truck when he sees us, opening the back and ushering the people inside. We've already stocked the truck with blankets, food, and water so the people will be comfortable on our journey to the Zenith Camp.

"I'll be right back," I say to Zane.

I hurry through the automatic doors, then stride down the hall to the red box on the wall. I can't forget to do this part of the plan.

"There she is!" It's the nurse from upstairs. An Enforcer follows close behind.

*Crap.*

I pull the fire alarm and the ear-splitting screech fills the air, growing louder with each whine. Red lights near the ceiling flash, warning people to exit the building.

"Grab her!" the Enforcer yells, already taking off toward me.

I start to run, away from the exit—because it's blocked by the Enforcer—and deeper into the maze of the hospital. Turning one corner, then another, I almost collide with another Enforcer. "Sorry," I mumble, not looking up. I step around him and start to walk away when he grabs my arm.

"Sienna," he hisses.

It's Trey. Oh, thank heavens, it's Trey.

"I've been made," I whisper, glancing behind me. The alarm continues to shriek, my ears throbbing from the irritating sound.

"It's okay," he says. "I got this." He firmly grasps my arm, escorting me down the hallway. When we turn the corner, there are several Enforcers, their guns drawn.

"I've got her," Trey calls over the blaring alarm. "The little nit tried to slip past me, but I stopped her."

"Well done, soldier," an Enforcer with graying hair says. His black uniform is a little different with four lines indicating his rank instead of the triskelion on the shoulder. He must be the one in charge of this operation. "Put her in the interrogation room. We'll find out who she is and what she's doing here."

Trey's hand on my arm stiffens. "Copy that." He gives a soldier's salute, impressing me with the rigidity of his stance and response. He half-walks, half-drags me down the hall, his fingernails digging into my arm. The fire alarm stops, the silence almost eerie after the deafening noise.

When we're out of earshot, Trey says, "You okay?"

"Can you loosen your grip some?" I say through clenched teeth.

"Right." His fingers loosen. "Sorry. Just trying to make it look realistic."

Trey glances over his shoulder as we near a corner.

"Are they still watching us?" I ask.

"Some are, and some aren't. Sorry, but I have to make it convincing."

I sigh, already knowing what's coming. "Do what you have to do."

Trey jerks my arm hard, sending me flying into the side of his body. Pain shoots from my wrist to my shoulder. Thankfully, it's opposite of the one with the bullet wound. "I said walk," he yells in my face. I plant my feet, refusing to budge. Trey picks me up, slinging my body over his shoulder like a sack of potatoes. "If you won't walk, I guess I'll have to carry you."

Several of the Enforcers laugh and clap at Trey's harshness. A part of me wishes Trey would put me down so I could run over and kick them all in the kneecaps.

We turn the corner and Trey asks me again, "Are you okay?"

"I'll probably have a bruise on my arm, but other than that..." My arms slap against his back as he carries me, the blood rushing to my head from being upside down.

"I'm sorry," he says again.

"Trey, it's okay. I know you'd never hurt me on purpose." I give him one quick pat on the back.

"We need to grab one more load of Disposables. We may have to improvise, though."

"Count me in."

When we arrive at the room where the Disposables are piled on an oversized rolling cart, Trey gently sets me on top of some man's legs and tells me to pretend I'm drugged. As exhausted as I am, it's not hard to imagine laying perfectly still on the cart. The tricky part will be laying on top of other people.

Making a face, I gingerly settle onto the pile, someone's belt buckle poking into my back. I even take someone else's arm and drape it over myself, shoving my foot under the crook of another woman's bent knee so I appear just as haphazardly piled as they are. Letting my arms fall to the side, I relax my face, going limp. I swear, I deserve an award for all of these acting moments.

We don't leave immediately. I think Trey is waiting, hoping the hallway will be clear by the time we reach it.

"Okay, let's go," Trey says. The cart starts to move. Even though I want to open my eyes to see where we are, I keep them closed. But not too tightly. I don't want it to look like I'm trying to close them.

The cart turns, and if my sense of direction is correct, we're nearing the spot where we met the group of Enforcers. "Here we go," Trey mutters, and I have a feeling some, if not all, are still there.

"Hey, soldier, I thought you were taking that broad to interrogation."

"No need for interrogation. They decided she's a Disposable." The cart continues to move.

"Such a shame," one Enforcer says. "I would've liked to take her home with me tonight."

I'm expecting Trey to remain silent and continue moving toward the exit and the waiting truck, but instead, he says, "You couldn't have handled her."

My mouth wants to smile so, so bad, but I maintain control, thankfully.

Some of the Enforcers laugh, and one says, "Dodge, you got schooled."

The guy I assume is Dodge says, "Fair enough."

The cart continues moving. The next thing I hear is that Dodge guy next to the cart, saying, "Hey, why don't I help you with these? You shouldn't have to do this by yourself."

"Thanks, man, but I got it. Really."

"Nah, I insist."

I try to keep my breathing steady, though my heart is pounding triple speed. It takes a lot of work. I'm not sure what Trey is going to do when we get outside and this Dodge dude sees all the non-drugged people sitting cozy in the back of the truck.

I only hope he has a plan.

The sound of automatic doors opening lets me know we're almost there. The cart stops, and I hear the metal door of the truck shuffling open.

"What the—?"

I open my eyes in time to see Trey punch Dodge in the neck, Dodge crumbling to the ground in a heap. Trey quickly drags his body to the side and leaves him in the bushes.

"Quick, let's load these people," Trey says to Zane. I hop off the cart while he and Zane carefully load each person into the back where they're placed on blankets and pads.

"What's wrong with them?" Annie asks, her eyes wide.

"They had some medication that makes them sleepy," I tell her. "They should be awake soon."

My knees quiver as I climb into the front of the truck and pull out the Lynk I stole. Hopefully, it still works after bashing it against that nurse's head. It does.

The Lynk is locked, but I can still make an emergency call. I dial emergency services, putting the second part of our plan into place.

"There's a bomb set to go off at County Hospital in less than ten minutes. They need to evacuate everyone."

I click the Lynk off. Since I previously pulled the fire alarm, rescue services should already be on their way. They'll be too late to find the bomb, but at least they'll be here if anyone is injured during the blast. Though, if they take this threat seriously, no one should be.

Trey and Zane hop in the front, Zane in the driver seat. I'm sandwiched between the two of them, like Meat Crap Delite between two slices of delicious bread. Trey squeezes my knee. "Well done in there."

I smile, basking in the glow of his praise. Trey doesn't give out praise often, but when he does, it *means* something.

Zane drives the truck to the spot where Chaz, Trina, Grey, and the other truck are parked. We then switch trucks, Trina and Grey climbing into this one because they are taking these people back to the Zenith Camp.

"Don't forget," Trey says to Grey, who's driving. "You need to secure Greta and Chaz's parents before leaving the city.

They're expecting you, so they should be ready to roll."

Grey gives a nod, clasping Trey's hands. "We'll see you soon. Be careful, man."

Trina and Grey drive away, their van loaded with the two dozen people we rescued.

As if on cue, a large explosion sends a wave of heat our way, the ground trembling beneath our feet. "Looks like Nash did his part," Trey says. "He should be here any moment."

Soon, we see Nash stride down the road toward us, the sky a fireball behind him. I swear there's a swagger to his steps. He enjoys his blow-up assignments a little too much.

Nash and Chaz climb into the back of the empty truck Zane is now driving. Rescuing these people and blowing up this hospital was only the beginning.

We have more work to do.

# 43

## Zane

The Match 360 Legas facility represents everything my father was—stalwart, intelligent, and ground-breaking. It seems almost fitting this building should go down with the man who created it.

When we reach the facility, Trey and Nash unload the weapons and dynamite, while I go inside to make sure everyone clears out. This time, though, I don't sneak through the back like a fugitive, but stroll right through the main door. Vanessa, the secretary, is sitting at the front desk. Clearly not expecting me, she greets me with a confused smile. "Zane, what are you doing here?"

"I came to say goodbye."

"Are you—going somewhere?" she asks hesitatingly.

"You could say that." I start toward the elevator bank, but halfway there, I stop and address her. "You may want to exit the premises. I have it on good authority a bomb is going off in ten minutes."

Eyes wide, Vanessa rises from her chair while simultaneously pressing a button underneath her desk, triggering the fire alarm system. The alarm blares. I stick some earplugs in my ears, because the sound is piercing, and stride to the stairwell. So much for using the elevators.

I take the stairs two at a time, not stopping until I reach

my father's old office. The door is ajar, indicating someone left in a hurry. Steele.

Pushing the door open, I enter the room. It's exactly as my father left it. I look around, memorizing every piece of artwork and every piece of furniture. I sat on the couch right there, doing homework. Learned to play chess on that table in the corner. Like his office at home, this room houses many memories of him.

Just as quickly as it started, the fire alarm clicks off. No doubt the authorities have been alerted, though. I remove my earplugs and throw them in the trash can. I don't have much time.

"I'm surprised to see you here, Zane," Steele says as he enters the room and shuts the door.

"I'm sure you are, Steele. Especially considering you hired a hitman."

Steele smirks. "I don't know what you're talking about. If you're still upset about Father leaving everything to me, then—"

"Don't play dumb, Steele. I can see right through your act. I guess I missed all the clues before. But now I know the truth."

Steele takes a few steps toward me. "And what's this truth you claim to know?"

"That I was never more than a thorn in your side. That you poisoned our father after you sent him a note, threatening my life if he didn't change his will and name you the heir. That you hired an assassin to kill me the other night."

Steele smiles. "If that were true, you wouldn't be standing here, would you?"

"Let's just say I had help. Didn't you see my press conference?"

Steele strolls over to the liquor cart, then pours himself a drink. He offers me one, but I'm not stupid enough to take anything from him. "Zane, the stories that fill your head are astounding. You really think I would do these things? Frankly,

I'm hurt by your accusations."

I laugh at his words. He won't fool me this time. "Frankly, I'm hurt you want me dead."

Steele takes a swig of his drink. "Sounds like we're at a crossroads."

I turn away from him, glancing out the window at the parking lot below. If I try hard enough, I can picture my father's sports car parked in that first spot, the one closest to the building.

"Do you remember the Christmas I was five?" I don't wait for him to answer. "You were twenty-five then, and I got this really cool remote-control car. I think it did flips or tricks or something, and it could roll on water. I was so excited. But do you remember what you did?" I turn around to face him. Steele stares at me, expressionless. "You took it and hid it. I searched for that toy for days, so upset. I found you playing with it outside, and I couldn't understand why you would take my toy. Why an *adult* would want to play with my toy. Then, while I watched, you smashed it on the ground until it lay scattered in a million pieces. You said it was a stupid toy, and I didn't deserve it. Do you remember that?"

When he doesn't answer, I continue. "Or how about the summer I was ten? You came from Rubex to visit, and found me in your old room playing with your telescope. You hadn't touched that thing in years, not since you left the house. But Dad kept your room like a shrine. You were so angry you went to my room, took my microscope, and said it was now yours. That I was never allowed to touch your stuff again. You remember that?"

Steele's expression doesn't change.

"I gotta say, Steele, you weren't the best big brother. But it's taken me almost twenty-two years to realize that."

My right hand reaches into the back of my pants, gripping the gun that's there. Trey is the one who convinced me I needed this, and now that I'm face to face with Steele, I think he may have been right.

I pull it out, training it on Steele. "Which means there's only one way to end this."

With his drink still in his hand, Steele holds out his arms, looking amused and unconcerned. "Go ahead. I dare you. But frankly, I don't think you have the guts to do it. You always were a coward. Even Father thought so. I imagine his real son Trey isn't, though, am I right?"

My fingers tighten on the trigger. He's only trying to goad me, but right now, I'd like nothing more than to put a bullet between his eyes.

"I will let you live. On one condition."

Steele shrugs. "Let's hear it."

"You leave me and my friends alone. No more assassins, no more trying to find me. We cut ties, and we end it now."

"End what?"

"This." I motion to the two of us. "We forget we were ever brothers."

Steele edges toward the desk. "I'm afraid I can't agree to those terms, Zane."

"Why not?"

"Because I won't be happy until you give back what you stole from me." Steele reaches into a desk drawer, whipping out a gun faster than I can respond. He points it at me and moves closer. "Like I said, we're at a crossroads."

My stomach tightens. There does not appear a way out of this. Either he shoots me or I shoot him. Only one of us will leave here alive.

"How about we both put down our gun on the count of three?" I suggest. "I may not want you to be my family, Steele, but I don't want to kill you."

"That's a shame, because I don't mind killing you." The gun clicks as he chambers a bullet. "I want the serum and the formula you stole."

"It's not yours," I hiss.

"Father left the company to me, which means it is." Steele inches closer. So far, neither of us is wavering, and I'm not sure how this will end. "I have a multi-million pac deal riding on this. I *need* that formula."

I hid the serum and the formula at the Zenith Camp. "I don't have it."

"Well, where is it?"

"Someplace safe."

Steele cocks his head to the side, studying me. "My patience is wearing thin—"

The door behind me bursts open, and a gun goes off. At first, I think I've been hit. But it's Trey who shot—firing a bullet into Steele's shoulder. He now stands over Steele, ready to finish him off.

"I wouldn't... do that... if I were you," Steele gasps. Air hisses between his teeth as he sucks in a breath followed by a low moan.

"Oh, stop being a baby," Trey says. "It's only a flesh wound."

"Enforcers... are... on their way..."

"Yeah. And we'll be long gone by the time they arrive." Trey smirks. He holds out the gun to me. "You wanna do the honors?"

I shake my head. "No, let's just leave him."

Trey trains his gun on Steele again. "I can't. Not after all he's done."

"Trey. Please." Pausing, he looks at me. "Let's go."

Trey's finger quivers on the trigger as he considers my request. Slowly, his hand lowers. "I hope you bleed out," he says to Steele. "Though you deserve to be tortured." To me, he says, "We better get going, brother. That bomb threat is *real.*" He then winks at me.

"Bomb?" Steele cries. "You're seriously going to blow up

Father's company?"

Trey slings his arm over my shoulder as we exit the office.

"I want my formula!" Steele hollers. "Zane!"

We close the door behind us, Steele's screams now muffled behind the glass. "Thanks for being there, *brother*," I say to Trey.

Grinning, Trey replies, "I always will."

I may have lost one brother, but I've gained a better one.

# 44

## Trey

The explosion of the Match 360 building is like a beautiful firework in the sky. I think it's our best explosion to date. We stand at the bottom of a hill, on a higher spot of desert not far from the building, and watch the bombs rip through and gut the inside. The ground shakes with each blast. I think Nash may have overdone it on the explosives, but who am I to criticize? As long as he gets the job done, I'm good with it.

I'm surprised Zane agreed to go along with this plan— Match 360 being his father's legacy and all. But he hasn't complained. I did see him wipe his eyes once or twice as the building went up in flames, but that could have been because of the proximity to the smoke.

Sienna slides one arm through Zane's and leans against him like she's providing support. I wait a moment and join them on Zane's other side, placing my arm around his shoulders. "You have a new family now, brother."

Zane nods. "I feel like I'm watching my entire childhood go up in smoke."

I squeeze his shoulder. "It's time to start a new life. Are you ready?"

Zane stares at the burning building and the rescue trucks that are now arriving. "Yeah," he says finally. "I think I am."

On our way back to the Zenith Camp, we radio Paige to let her know we're coming. But there's silence on her end. Sienna keeps trying, every ten minutes or so, but the only thing that comes through is static.

"Maybe they're hunting and she left the radio back at Camp?" Sienna offers. But she and I both know that would never happen. Jared or someone would be in charge of the radio, especially since they know we're still out on this mission. My hands grip the steering wheel harder as I urge the truck faster.

Zane is the first to spot the smoke when we're a few miles out. "Is that normal?" he asks. Smoke rises in the distance, like an invisible hand reaching for the sky.

"No. It's not," I mutter. The way the smoke creates a haze, making the whole sky gray—it's more than a simple campfire.

Besides, neither the Zenith nor the Fringe members would allow a fire to burn so high and so bright. Our goal is to keep a low profile—a smoke screen rising into the sky, viewable for miles, is anything but.

The amount of smoke intensifies as we get closer to Camp. Through the air conditioning vents, the smell of burnt grass and charred wood seeps in. Sienna coughs at the strong smell.

The truck is silent as I park in between the two cliffs and jump down. The truck Trina and Grey drove back to Camp—that's assuming they *made* it back to Camp—is missing, along with the other ATV. Every inch of my body courses with adrenaline as I jog over the desert quicksand and up the path to Camp. I can hear Sienna trailing behind me, her breathing heavy and stuttered.

The smoke is a lot stronger now; it stings my nose and makes my eyes water.

As I burst into the open, I see it. Or what's left of it. Fires consume our small tent homes, blasted by bombs. Bodies lay strewn from one end of the camp to the other. It's a war zone, the most horrific thing I've ever seen.

*No. Nonononono.*

Sienna cries out beside me, an animalistic howl that tears through the sky. She sinks to her knees, tears bathing her cheeks as she clutches her chest, like her heart is failing her. I try to comfort her, but she shrugs me off. She's retreated to a place I'm not allowed to come.

"Holy crap," Chaz says as he, Zane, and Nash join us. His eyes are round as he takes in the scene. "This can't be happening; this can't be happening," he mutters over and over. "What about my parents? This can't be happening."

Someone lets out a long string of cuss words. I turn in time to see Nash kick over scorched tables and fallen tents. He picks up a large rock and heaves it fifteen feet. "I will kill them!" he screams. "I will kill every last one of them!" He snatches a melted gun from the ground, cocks a bullet into place, and strides away. "I need to shoot something," he mutters, his voice choked with emotion.

The bodies are burned so bad they're not recognizable. But still I look. I have to know how many men and women I lost. Trina and Grey? Paige and Asher? Are they among the dead?

My hands clench and unclench as I walk past smoldering fires and charred animal skins. The stench of burnt flesh makes me gag.

I reach the spot where Sienna and her family had their tents. Remnants of animal skin hang from burnt poles. Then I see something that makes me stop moving, stop thinking.

A shock of red hair next to charred blonde curls.

*No. Please, God, no.*

I inch closer. A smaller body next to a larger one. Lying facedown.

I turn and retch a few feet away. I can't let Sienna see this.

When I look up, I see her stumbling toward me, her eyes fixed on the tent and the two bodies at my feet. I reach her in time to catch her as she falls to the ground, her cry digging a hole in my heart.

I hold her tight, pulling her close as I say, "I'm here. It's okay. I'm right here."

She sobs in my arms. "They're gone, Trey. They're gone."

Clearing my throat to get rid of the knot that's lodged there, I push the hair away from her forehead. "I know, baby. I'm so sorry. I promise I'll make this right."

She jerks away from me. "You can't make this right!" she screams. "Don't you understand? They're dead!" Her arms sweep the area. "They're all dead!"

I stare at her, my eyes stinging. She needs someone to lash out at. I can be that person if she needs me to be.

Sienna hits me in the chest, using my body as an outlet for her anger. I stand there and take it. She does it again and again, crying out, "My mom… Emily… I'll never see them again. I can't—I can't—"

I wrap my arms around her to stop the flailing, but she fights a little longer, until she can't anymore. Whimpering, she finally relaxes in my arms. With her face pressed against my chest, I stroke her hair and try to whisper soothing words, even though words and intentions are meaningless right now. "I'm here. I'm right here. And I'm not going anywhere. I promise."

With my arm around her shoulders, I lead her away from the burned bodies of her mother and sister. She doesn't need to see them, to remember them like that.

A low-pitched whirring sound starts in my brain, growing steadily louder as we reach the open area of Camp. The wind picks up, swirling the smoke around my head. The sound isn't coming from inside my head, but from the sky above. I cough and look up, my eyes stinging from the smoke.

It's a hovercraft.

My first instinct is to run, but there's no point. There's nowhere to hide. Letting go of Sienna, I push her behind me, like that will somehow protect her. Then I stand there, my eyes firmly fixed on the vehicle as it lands on the ground.

The hatch opens, and out steps Steele. I immediately reach for my gun and train it on him.

"I see you found my surprise," he says. He smirks as he strides closer.

"I should've killed you in the Match 360 building," I growl.

Zane appears beside me. Not sure where he came from. "You're responsible for this?" he says. "Steele, how could you?"

Four Enforcers jump down from the hovercraft, their automatic rifles pointed directly at our chests. "Drop the gun. Now."

We're outnumbered. One gun against four isn't exactly good odds. Our best chance for survival is to do as they say.

Slowly, I bend down and place my gun on the ground. As I stand, I lift my hands in the air. "What do you want, Steele?"

Steele shrugs, wincing as his shoulder pulls from where I shot him only a few hours ago. "It was a simple request, really. All I wanted was the serum and formula that's rightfully mine. I gave Zane a chance to give it to me, but he wouldn't comply."

"So you blew up our Camp... and killed all these people?"

"I was angry," Steele says like a petulant child.

Rage builds inside me, but before I can say or do anything, I hear an inhuman scream as something rushes past me, streaking like a bullet toward Steele. It takes a moment to realize it's Sienna, her red hair streaming behind her as she charges toward him. "Sienna!" I holler. "No!"

I don't know what she's going to do—she isn't even armed. As her hand rears back to strike him, he grabs her arm, twisting it and her until her back is locked against his chest. I'm about to spring forward to stop him when Steele pulls out a .22 and presses it against her temple. The Enforcers look like they're just itching to pull the trigger, so I stand my ground.

"All right, Steele, you've made your point," Zane says, his voice choked with anger. "Let Sienna go, and I'll give you the formula."

Steele cocks his head like he's considering this request. "I'll make a deal with you. If you bring me the formula *and* the serum, I'll let you and your gang of screwups scurry out of here alive. As long as you promise to get the hell out of Pacifica and never return."

"I'm not promising that," I scoff.

Steele shrugs. "That's fine. Madame Neiman is expecting me to kill all of you, so..." The gun against Sienna's head shifts. Normally, Sienna would fight back in this kind of situation, but her whole body is slumped against Steele like she's given up. Her eyes are squeezed shut, and her shoulders shake like she's crying. For all I know, she rushed Steele *hoping* she'd get shot by an Enforcer.

"Fine," I say. "But I swear, if you go back on your word, I will personally put a bullet between your eyes."

Steele gives me a patronizing smile. "Now, Trey, is that any way to talk to your brother? It's such a shame you were raised like a heathen when you were created for so much more."

It takes all my willpower not to pick up my gun and shoot Steele right then. I know I wouldn't miss, but with Sienna so close and the Enforcers a little too trigger happy for my comfort, I don't want another bloodbath on this soil.

"I'll get your formula," Zane says. "I buried it near the outhouse."

Steele gestures to one of the Enforcers, "Go with him."

With a gun pressed against his back, Zane leads the Enforcer to the backside of Camp where the outhouses are located—or what's left of them. A few minutes later, Zane emerges with the formula and vials of serum in hand. It pains me to see us losing this one bit of leverage we had over the Agency. But if giving it up will save Sienna's life, then, of course, there's no question.

Zane holds up the vial and computer chip in its protective sleeve. "Let her go, Steele," Zane says. "This is what you want, so let her go."

Still keeping a tight grip on Sienna, Steele puts his gun away and holds out his hand for the serum and formula. All of my muscles tighten, ready to spring into action if Steele goes against his word. As soon as Zane places the items in Steele's hand, Steele lets go of Sienna and shoves her in my direction. Because she's so weak and disoriented, she falls to the ground.

"You may collect your trash," Steele says to me with a quick look of disdain toward Sienna.

My teeth clench as I help her stand and lead her away from Steele and his henchman. If I ever have the displeasure of meeting Steele again, I will first make him apologize for killing all these people I care about; and second, I'll make him grovel at Sienna's feet for saying that about her; and third, I'll make him eat a bullet. In some ways, I look forward to that reunion.

Steele strides back to the hovercraft, the four Enforcers keeping their guns trained on us. As Steele climbs into the vehicle, he calls, "Kill them. Kill them all."

As the hovercraft door closes, I shout, "We had a deal! You lying sack of shit. We had a deal!"

The craft takes off, the wind swirling dust and smoke around as the vehicle hovers ten feet off the ground. I suppose Steele thinks he can watch our destruction from the safety of his escape vehicle. The muscles in my neck and along my back tighten as I spring forward, grabbing my gun. Shots begin firing from the Enforcers as I drag Sienna behind what's left of the crude building used to house supplies. I don't know where everyone else is, but I hope they're okay. Bullets ping against the metal trough, sizzling past the destroyed clothes line.

"Oh, hell, no." I hear Nash before I see him. He runs into

Camp, gun blazing as he lets off round after round. Now that I have backup, I inch out from our hiding spot and fire at the first Enforcer. He goes down. Nash hits the second and third, and I pick off the fourth. It isn't until Nash gets closer and says, "Dude, you're bleeding," that I realize I've been shot.

It's just a flesh wound, but it got me right in the thigh.

Nash opens fire on the hovercraft. The bullets ping off the side, the craft quivering above us. I'm sure Steele has reinforced glass, so it's not surprising the bullets ricochet instead of penetrate. But Nash continues to fire until the craft disappears on the other side of a cliff.

I breathe deeply, the pain in my leg finally hitting me. "Where the hell were you?" I say to Nash.

"Sorry, man. I went for a walk. I was up near the canyon when I heard that hovercraft."

I clasp him on the back. "I'm glad you made it back when you did."

"Me too," Chaz pipes from a few feet away as he pops up from behind the aluminum trough. I had no idea he was hiding back there. No wonder they were aggressively attacking it.

"Zane," I say. "Where's Zane?"

"I'm right here," Zane calls. He rises to his feet, wiping the dirt from his pants. "As soon as they started firing, I hit the ground. I think they thought they'd shot me." After a second, he adds, "How's Sienna?"

Sienna. Shit. I forgot to check on her.

I find her where I left her, behind the supplies building. She's curled into a ball, her arms wrapped around her legs, her head pressed into her knees. When she hears me, she raises a bleak, tear-streaked face. My heart clenches at the sight.

"Everyone okay?" she asks tiredly. But then she notices my thigh. "Trey, you're bleeding. Were you shot?"

I kneel beside her, pain shooting through my wound. "I'm okay. They're okay."

"But your leg—"

"I'll be fine."

She nods and hides her face again.

I scoop her up, her head nestled under my chin, and carry her back to the truck. She doesn't need to see this. She doesn't need to see any of this. The least I can do is remove her from the scene.

When I place her in the front seat, she grabs my arm, refusing to let me go. I cup her face in my hands, bending to kiss her cheeks. "I'll be back in a little while. I have some things I need to take care of."

"Please. Don't. Leave. Me," she sobs, her eyes swollen, her face wet with tears.

I'm about to climb into the truck beside her because I won't leave her when she needs me, when a voice behind me says, "I'll stay with her."

I turn to find Zane, his shoulders slumped, his eyes red. The reality of what happened back at Camp must finally be catching up. Nodding, I switch places with him. Sienna grabs onto him and buries her face in his neck as his arms encircle her. Now that I know she's in good hands, I limp back to Camp.

Nash and Chaz are moving among the bodies. Chaz stops, leaning over to vomit before resuming his search. He's looking for his parents, and Nash—well, he's just looking.

I head to the medic tent, or what's left of it, knowing I need to stop the bleeding and make sure there are no bullet fragments in my leg. The medic tent is destroyed, first aid equipment strewn all over the ground. I find a roll of gauze that isn't too dirty, and a bottle of alcohol I'm not sure whether it'd been used for cleaning or drinking purposes. Don't really care.

It's a little trickier to find a needle and thread, but I paw around enough that one eventually surfaces in the rubble. An overturned drawer from a blackened medicine cabinet is hiding some floss and a couple of needles.

Taking a seat on a log, I remove my pants and check the wound. The bullet only grazed my thigh, thank God.

The alcohol burns as I pour it over the wound, the liquid washing away the blood. After a minute, I sew the wound shut as best as I can. I've never sewn my own skin before, so I have to stop and take deep breaths when I start to feel lightheaded. When I'm finished, I wrap the gauze around it to keep it from getting infected. It'll be sore for a while, but the pain is nothing I can't handle.

I rise to my feet, then re-button my pants. As I gaze around the bombed-out campsite, I have to know. How many did we actually lose? How many did that bastard murder in cold blood? The bodies on the ground don't match the number of people who inhabited the Zenith Camp. Did some escape?

I navigate among the burned bodies, trying to identify the dead, until it's too much to take. There's no way I can tell who's gone and who might've survived. Closing my eyes, I vow that Steele and Madame Neiman will pay.

An arm slings around my back. I open my eyes to find Nash there, holding me up. I didn't realize how weak my knees had become until he stepped in. "Thanks, man," I say. "Just… thanks."

Nash nods, tears streaming down his cheeks. In all the time I've known Nash, I've never seen him cry. Not even when his parents died.

Holding on to each other, we trudge to the metal barrel next to the charred wooden building used to house food and supplies. I pull out shovels, wordlessly handing one to Nash.

For the next two hours, we dig. We dig until our backs ache, our hands bleed, and we're drenched with sweat. We stop only long enough to pump and drink water from the well that was luckily untouched during the attack. We make one large communal grave, because it's too much to dig individual ones.

# Fearless

When the last body has been placed in the massive grave, we fill it back up. The sun is low in the sky by the time we finish.

# 45
## Zane

S ienna cries herself to sleep in my arms. I sit in the truck, holding her, afraid to move and wake her. Her hair tickles my chin.

Such a tragic, senseless act. All of those people. Dead.

Emily and Vivian. Gone.

And Greta? I have no idea if the truck carrying her and the dozens of people we rescued made it here, if she was one of the burned bodies. I want to believe the woman who is like a mother to me is still alive. That she's okay.

I close my eyes, pinching the bridge of my nose. Sienna shifts in my arms, and I hold my breath. As long as she sleeps, she can escape this nightmare. I know the moment she wakes up, it will hit her like a concrete wall. If I can save her from pain, even only for a short while, I'll do whatever I can.

Oh! I almost forgot. I pat my pocket, making sure the one vial of serum I smuggled is still there. Steele may think he got all of them, but I actually kept one for myself. As soon as I see Trey, I'll give it to him to use. He needs it right now more than I do.

When Sienna finally does wake, her eyes are swollen and bloodshot. I watch her face, ready to comfort her. I can see the moment she remembers, the second it hits her. She starts to smile at me, but then stops, tears filling her eyes as she whimpers. "I thought it was a horrible dream," she whispers.

"I'm sorry."

She straightens, roughly running a palm over her face. "I want to see them."

"I don't think that's a good idea."

"I need to say goodbye."

I can understand that need, that desire to say goodbye to the ones you love. I never had the chance to say goodbye to my own mother because she died the day I was born. I wish I'd had that opportunity.

"Okay," I say. "I'll take you back."

When I help her down from the truck, she's a little unsteady on her feet. Taking her hand in mine, I lead her back to the remains of the Camp. On the way there, we pass a tiny patch of wildflowers. Sienna tugs me to a stop, then bends over to pick a handful until she has a small bouquet. She takes my hand again, and we continue the rest of the way in silence.

When we get to Camp, she stops and sucks in a breath, her hand trembling in mine. I think she's about to fall apart, but she surprises me. She closes her eyes for a moment, composing herself, and then walks over to where Trey and Nash are piling dirt on the buried bodies.

She looks so small, so pale, and so vulnerable as she says, "Can I say a few words?" She holds the scraggly bouquet of wildflowers, and it reminds me of when she stayed at my house while Trey was healing and I kept finding her in the garden. That was when I showed her forget-me-nots. I know she was thinking of Trey when I told her about them, but I was thinking of her. I'm always thinking of her.

"I think that's a great idea," I say.

Trey nods and lays down his shovel, limping to her side and placing one large hand on her back. It engulfs her, from shoulder blade to base of her spine.

Sienna sniffles and lays the wildflowers on the edge of

the oversized grave, her hands shaking as she does. "My mom loved flowers, daisies especially, but my dad always had a hard time finding them. Mom was all the goodness of the world wrapped up in one person—" She stops and breathes deeply, tears streaming down her cheeks. "She was everything to me. And I can't believe she's gone."

She closes her eyes for a moment, and when she reopens them, something inside me shatters. They are dull and full of despair. She's completely broken—even her body looks like it might crumble under this crushing sorrow.

I step beside her and take her hand so Trey is on one side, holding her up, and I'm on the other, steadying her. This is hard for her, so the least I can do is offer my own condolences. "Emily," I say, "was a force to be reckoned with. She was smart as a whip and knew how to get what she wanted." I squeeze Sienna's hand. "Very much like her sister." Sienna gives a half-hearted smile through her tears. "I've never met anyone who loved to swim as much as she did." I hold up my free hand. "My fingers are still pruney." Sienna lets out a sound that's half-cry half-whimper. "And ice cream? She loved ice cream."

"With sprinkles," Sienna adds softly.

"With sprinkles," I confirm.

Sienna straightens a little like some of her strength has returned. "Emily had so much love inside of her. Even when I wasn't the sister I should've been, she still loved me. Unconditionally. I should have—" She stops as a sob escapes, but then tries again, "I should have—" She can't finish. Letting go of my hand, she turns to Trey, her shoulders shaking. Trey engulfs her in his arms, and she's swallowed up by him and his love for her.

When her crying subsides, Trey asks Chaz to take her back to the truck. The two of them cling to each other as they stumble down the path, away from the devastation of the Camp.

Now that the memorial is finished, Trey and Nash clean

up the shovels. I grab the one on the ground nearest me, then carry it over to the metal barrel. When I get there, Trey is kneeling by it, holding a piece of wood in his hands.

"What's that?" I ask, depositing the shovel in the bin.

Trey tilts it so I can see. The wood is smooth and flat like someone took time to sand it down. Carved on the surface are the following words: *If you want to fight and win, you need PRIDE. PS*

I repeat the words aloud. "If you want to fight and win, you need pride. That's a very inspirational quote."

"I think it's Zenith's contingency plan," Trey says.

"Contingency plan?"

Trey rises to his feet with a soft groan, the bandage around his thigh dirty and showing spots of blood. "Yeah. This must have been Paige's plan all along. That if they were ever attacked, they'd run. Any members left behind would know where to go."

"Some of the crew escaped?" I ask.

Nash comes up behind us, reading the message over Trey's shoulder. "They went to Pride."

"Yeah," Trey says. "I think so."

"Pride?" I ask. "As in the other Province?"

"Do you know of another Pride?" Nash says with a smirk.

"No. I'm surprised is all. I didn't think we could cross the border." The entrances are walled and heavily guarded. From what I've heard, people are shot on sight if they're caught trying to cross.

"Paige must have figured out a way," Trey says. "She must have realized it was their only option. And ours." Trey turns the wood over. "Look here. These must be coordinates."

I peer over Trey's shoulder. Sure enough, numbers are carved into the wood.

"So that's the plan?" Nash says. "We follow them to Pride in the hopes some of them made it there alive? Sounds like suicide."

"I'm all out of options, Nash," Trey says. "If you can think of something better, please tell me. Tell me now."

"It could be a trap," Nash adds.

"I'm fully aware of that. And still willing to take the chance." After a long pause, Trey adds, "Are you?"

Nash toes the dirt with his boot. "I guess. You know I'll follow you anywhere."

"Okay, then," Trey says. "Let's gather any supplies that weren't destroyed in the fire. Weapons, ammo, food, clothing, anything."

"On it," Nash says, already opening the wooden shed.

Trey's about to walk away, but I stop him with my hand on his arm. "Trey."

He turns to face me. "What is it, Zane?"

I reach into my pocket and pull out the vial of ReOGene 2.0. "Figured you may want this."

Trey stares at the serum in my hand. "Is that what I think it is?"

"Yeah. I didn't give all of it to Steele."

"Is this the only one you have?"

"Yes, which is why you need to use it."

Trey shakes his head, taking a step back. "You should save it. For someone who really needs it."

I don't know why he has to be so stubborn. I'm trying to help him. I see how he's hobbling around, clearly in pain. Why won't he just take the darn serum?

"Trey," I say, "there's more than one dose in here. Even if you have some, there will be more for someone else."

Trey looks doubtful, but at my insistence, he takes the vial. He unscrews the cap, then dribbles a few drops under his tongue. After replacing the cap, he hands it back to me. Less than thirty-seconds later, Trey rubs his thigh. "God, that tingles."

"That means it's working."

"Where were you a few hours ago when I was stitching up my leg?" he jokes. "I could have used this earlier."

"Sorry about that," I apologize. "I didn't remember I had it until I was with Sienna, and I didn't want to leave her—"

"It's okay, man," Trey says, clasping me on the shoulder. "I'm just messing with you." He looks me square in the eyes and says, "Thank you. Seriously, thank you."

Trey turns away, heading to gather supplies for our trip to Pride.

I take one more long look at the destroyed campsite, my only hope that Greta was among those who escaped.

# 46
## Trey

The fires smolder down to nothing but coals as we gather supplies and load the truck. By the time we're finished, it's dark and our stomachs grumble with hunger. It *has* been a while since any of us thought about food.

As we eat a quick meal of dried fruit and jerky, we decide on driving arrangements, Sienna and me in the truck, Zane and Chaz in the ATV. Technically, everyone could fit in the back of the utility truck, but Zane and Chaz aren't too keen on that idea. Something about Chaz getting carsick. However, Nash volunteers to crash in the back. I think he wants to be alone, not that I blame him.

My leg is completely healed thanks to Zane's miracle serum. I didn't know Zane could be so devious—keeping one vial as he handed the rest off—but I'm kind of grateful for my genius brother.

Before we leave, Sienna visits the mass grave one more time, her tears watering the soil. I let her have a few minutes by herself. I know how hard it is to say goodbye to someone you love.

When she's wept until her shoulders sag, I take her hand and lead her to the truck. Coyotes howl in the distance, sending a shiver through her. The air is cooler at night, so I pull her close and rub her arms, trying to warm her. But she doesn't seem to notice the change in temperature, just like she doesn't notice my hands on her arms. Before she climbs in the truck, I turn her to face me.

"I know this is hard," I say. "But I promise I will do everything I can to make you smile again."

"I don't think you can," she says, her voice small, her lips quivering.

"Someday," I promise. "Someday the pain will lessen."

She nods as tears roll down her cheeks. I kiss her gently because I don't want to overstep. She's mourning and fragile, and I don't want to take advantage of the situation. I just want her to know how much I love her. That I'm here. I'll always be here.

When I pull back, I say, "We should probably get on the road before it gets too late." I help her climb in the truck, then close her door.

Once I'm in the driver's seat, I signal to Zane to make sure he's ready. His hand pops out the window in a thumbs-up. The truck rumbles to life. I maneuver the vehicle around weedy bushes and rock formations. We have to do a little off-roading to get to the main road that will take us to the wall. We're looking at a day's travel at most.

As we pull away from our spot between two cliffs, Sienna presses her hand and forehead to the glass. I imagine her saying goodbye in her own way. When she's finished, she settles back in the seat and closes her eyes.

For the past few hours, I've been on autopilot. I haven't had time to stop and think or mourn those we've lost. So many Zenith and Fringe members, people I've known and loved for years. But now that I have a moment, face after face of the people I knew flash through my mind. I don't know who's dead and who's alive, and that's the most troubling part of all.

The longer we drive, the quicker the landscape changes, from red rock cliffs to mountainous terrains. I'm on the lookout for Enforcer checkpoints, but so far, we're in the clear. I try to stick to back roads instead of interstate, mostly because much of the roadways and infrastructure were bombed during the Upheaval, but also because I think Enforcers are more likely to troll those areas.

Sienna fell asleep a while ago, and now snores softly like she hasn't slept in a year. It isn't all peaceful, though. It's punctuated by the occasional whimper or clenching of her fists. When that happens, I grab her hand and hold it tight in my own. After a moment, her body relaxes.

I'm not sure what we'll find when we reach the border separating Pacifica from Pride. I still haven't decided if we should find a weak spot along the wall, or if we should take our chances going directly to the gate. I don't know if they'll even let us in.

When I'm so tired I can barely keep my eyes open, I motion to Zane to stop. We pull off the road, maneuvering the vehicles behind a strand of trees as out of sight as possible, and sleep for a few hours until the sun comes up.

When we're only an hour from the border, based on the coordinates Paige carved into the wood, the landscape changes again, the open, flat land now allowing visual for miles. This area looks like a war zone. Overturned tanks and bombed-out shelters mark a military graveyard.

Leaning over, I gently shake Sienna awake. It takes her a moment to get her bearings, but once she's rubbed the sleep from her eyes, she stares out the window.

"What is this place?" she asks quietly, almost reverently.

"I have a feeling this is where one of the battles occurred during the Upheaval."

I slow the truck as we pass convoy after convoy half-buried in the desert sand. Some are turned over, and what's left looks more like scrap metal than wreckage; whereas some are almost fully intact, like the driver abandoned the vehicle and tried to make a run for it. Not sure where they would run, though. There's nothing for miles.

"Trey, look at that," Sienna says suddenly. She points to something fifty yards away resembling a giant boulder with wings.

"I think it's a helicopter," I say. Wanting to check it out myself, I pull over on the shoulder and climb out of the truck. Sienna follows me as Zane and Chaz park the ATV. Chaz gets out sputtering.

"I swear," Chaz mutters, "if I have to endure one more bug slapping me in the face, I'm gonna scream." He coughs, spitting on the ground a few feet away. "Sienna, it's your turn to ride in that thing."

"That's what the helmet is for, Chaz," Zane reminds him as he removes his own helmet. Is it wrong that I get a great amount of satisfaction seeing Zane's perfectly styled hair going a million different directions? He doesn't look so perfect anymore.

We cross the open expanse to the wreckage.

"Holy, motherload," Chaz says, whistling softly. "That's a Sikorsky UH-60 Black Hawk. Those things were used in combat for decades. I mean, before the Upheaval."

"How do you know this?" Nash asks.

Chaz shrugs. "A quick search of the government database for military helicopters." He shrugs again when we all look at him. "Hey, what can I say, I was bored one day."

"But how did you access it?" I ask. "The database for the former United States? I thought all of those files were locked."

Chaz stares at me like I've offended him. "I know you didn't just ask me that," he mutters, turning away to inspect what looks like a rusted propeller.

"Must have been some pretty heavy artillery to be able to take down this beast," Zane says, skirting around the edge of the wreckage. The cockpit is buried in the sand so only the tail end and part of a broken propeller is visible.

"I still don't understand why or how this happened," Sienna says, her voice hoarse from so much crying. "Why did one nation split into four Provinces?"

"There's a lot about that war we'll probably never know or understand," I say. "At least not from Pacifica's government. They've always been so secretive about what happened back then."

Zane stands erect, pulling his face back like he's giving himself a serious face lift. "We, the Commonwealth of Pacifica, believe in looking forward, not backward. Progress is our future!" His voice is nasally as he imitates President Shard.

Nash snorts at Zane's impression and wanders off.

Sienna speaks up. "You sound just like him. And ew, gross, you look like him, too."

Relaxing his face, Zane says. "The only impression I'm good at. Though my father was never a huge fan of it—" Zane suddenly stops speaking and swallows hard.

I rummage around the wreckage for anything we can salvage, but my search is in vain. One of the seats must have been ripped from the helicopter. Whatever was under there was taken long ago. "Looters must have recovered anything worth saving," I comment.

"What about this?" Zane asks, lifting a rusted metal box the color of the forest. He sets it on the ground and pops open the latch. "Looks like first aid supplies."

"Bring it," I say. "Can never have too many of those."

Once we're done searching and admiring the bones of the beast, we head back to our parked vehicles.

Chaz runs ahead, holding his pants up as he goes. Chaz isn't a big runner, so the sight of him half-running and half-waddling provides some much-needed comic relief. "I call shotgun in the truck!" he hollers as he runs.

Sienna's hand slips through mine. "I'll ride with Zane. I

don't mind."

I'm about to protest and insist she ride in the truck, but she's already walking toward the ATV. With a sigh, I climb in the truck and glare at Chaz. "Seriously? You had to send Sienna to ride with Zane? You couldn't handle it for one more hour?"

"Sorry, man, but I needed to talk to you in private." He pulls out the comscreen Zane stole from Match 360. "I haven't had a chance to tell you because of... everything that happened."

"What is it?"

"I figured out where Pacifica is planning to attack."

"Where?"

"Believe it or not, it's Pride."

"Makes sense," I say. "Pride is a threat to them. They're just over the border, which means they're too close for comfort. Plus, they're larger, stronger, with a more powerful government." I clasp him firmly on the shoulder. "Well done, Chaz."

"Now aren't you glad I'm riding with you?"

My hands grip the steering wheel as I start the truck and pull back onto the road. "Sure, Chaz." As we drive, I keep glancing in my rearview mirror so I can catch a glimpse of her. Her red hair whips in the wind, but there's no smile. Not this time. She's gone through too much.

We've only traveled a few miles when a loud blast rocks the truck, causing me to swerve off the road. "What the hell?" I say as I regain control. Another blast hits a few yards away, striking the windshield with dirt and rocks. A third hits a moment later, off to the right, the explosion resembling a volcano of dirt and smoke.

"Oh Lord, have mercy," Chaz mutters, crossing himself.

I swerve to avoid colliding with a massive fireball. "Someone's not too happy we're here."

Chaz grips the door handle, pressing his back against the seat. "Are they warning us or trying to hit us?"

"Not sure," I say, my teeth clenched. I glance again in the

rearview mirror to make sure Sienna and Zane are okay. At that moment, another blast erupts from the ground right beside their vehicle. As I watch in horror, the ATV is thrown to the side and rolls several times.

"Oh no. No, no." Throwing the truck in park, I jump out before it's barely stopped moving. I can't get to the ATV fast enough. Another blast erupts a few yards away, knocking me off balance. These aren't normal landmines. They seem to erupt without provocation, like someone is setting them off.

My heart pounds in my throat as I reach the vehicle. It rolled several times, landing upside down. Kneeling on the ground, I peer through the frame. Sienna's eyes are closed, a series of cuts lashing her face. But the thing that gives me the most cause for concern is her legs. They're pinned, the rolling of the vehicle crushing the dashboard and bolting her in place.

Zane is conscious, but dazed. He groans from his seat. "Is she okay?"

I move to the other side and help him maneuver through the window. Once he's free, he limps in place, a deep gash above his knee.

"I'm gonna need your help," I say, slightly out of breath, not from exertion, but from fear. If given the right circumstance, apparently, even a GM will experience a healthy dose of it. "Think you can help?"

Zane nods, even though he's unsteady on his feet. He has a cut on his forehead I hadn't noticed before, a trickle of blood running down the left side of his face. He hobbles to the other side of the vehicle.

"We have to try to push this piece of metal off her legs. On the count of three. One… two… three!" We heave and shove until the crushed part of the ATV moves a few inches. "Again. One… two… three." We push again, a loud grunt escaping my lips. I focus on the rise and fall of Sienna's chest and not on the lacerations to my own hands from pushing the dented metal off her. As long as she's breathing, she's okay.

When there's enough room to get her out, I unbuckle her and carefully ease her through the opening. Once she's free, I scoop her up in my arms. Her body is limp, her head hanging at an awkward angle over my arm. I've only taken a few steps toward the truck when another landmine goes off, this one a little too close for comfort. Cursing, I shift Sienna's weight. Zane grabs my shirt, holding me back as he reaches into his pocket. He produces a white handkerchief, which he proceeds to wave over his head.

"What the hell are you doing?" I hiss.

"A white handkerchief. A sign of peace. Or surrender." He continues to wave it over his head, wincing as he does. Lowering his arm, he clutches his side. In addition to his hurt leg, he probably broke a few ribs.

It's too smoky to see anything past twenty feet, but when I hear a sound like a vehicle approaching from a distance, my instincts tell me to run. I'm almost to the truck when I realize it isn't one vehicle but several, at least half a dozen. Which means we're way outnumbered.

A loud voice speaks over an intercom system. "Hands where we can see them." The convoys move closer through a dusty, hazy cloud, stopping only a few feet away. Zane raises his arms in surrender, and Chaz gets out of the truck, doing the same. Obviously, I'm not about to set Sienna on the ground so I stand where I am, not moving, not blinking. I have an injured girl in my arms, not an AK-47. Though, to be honest, I kind of wish I had my hands on one of those about right now.

"She's injured," I call out. "Thanks to your landmines. Can we get some help?"

Through the haze, a young man wearing a cowboy hat and boots steps out of one of the convoys, an M-16 strapped to his back and a piece of straw dangling from his lips. "Those were meant to be a warning."

"They did a little more than warn," I retort.

He chews slowly on the straw. "May I ask what business you have in this part?"

Nash is still in the back of the truck. I only hope he's not planning some kamikaze stunt. I don't want him to try to be the hero and end up doing something stupid that will get him or us killed.

Zane steps in, ever the diplomat. "We were coming to seek refuge within the walls of Pride."

The man looks us up and down. "Why do you want refuge in Pride?"

"The government of Pacifica murdered almost everyone we care about," I growl. "And we'll be next if we don't leave." I shift Sienna's weight. "Besides, we have some information your leaders may find useful."

Removing the piece of straw, the man smirks. "I had a young woman say the same thing less than twenty-four hours ago. She had a scraggly group with her."

Paige. It has to be Paige. So some of the group did escape and make it here safely. That knowledge brings me great relief. I still don't know who made it out alive, but it's better than thinking I lost all of my people. At least now, there's a sliver of hope.

"That must be Paige. She's part of our group."

Underneath the brim of his hat, the man's eyes narrow. "How do we know y'all ain't spies?"

Exasperation surges through me, making my tone sharp. "Guess you're just gonna have to trust us."

Zane steps forward. "I'm Zane Ryder, sir. You may have heard of me or maybe my father, Harlow Ryder? Trust me, I'm not a spy."

The young man resumes chewing the straw as he eyes Zane. He then leans over to confer with a bald dark-skinned guy who is a little more liberal with his gun, keeping it constantly trained on us. After a moment, the dark-skinned man nods and steps forward. "Hand over your weapons. Now."

I nod to Zane, and he removes the gun from the back of my pants and hands it over. I have more in the truck, but I'm not about to volunteer that information. Especially since Nash is in there.

"Now open the back of the truck," the leader says smoothly.

I clear my throat and say, "I may have forgotten to mention we have one more with us."

The back of the truck opens. Nash comes out, a gun in his hand as he eyes the group before us. "Which one of you should I kill first?" he growls. "You woke me from my nap."

The leader with the cowboy hat steps forward. "Thank you, sir. I'll take that." He holds out his hand like he expects Nash to give him the gun.

"Go ahead, Nash," I urge. My arms are growing tired from carrying Sienna. I'd like to think I'm stronger than this, but digging a mass grave took everything out of me.

"Fine," Nash grumbles, handing it over.

Now that we're unarmed, a young man with glasses rushes forward. My body tenses as he heads straight toward Sienna and me, but there's no sign of a gun or any weaponry for that matter.

"I'm a medic," he says. "Come. Let's get her stable." He leads me to the back of one of the convoys, which turns out to be a medic truck. I climb in with a grunt, the added weight making it difficult but not impossible. When he nods to a hospital bed, I gently lay her down. She's still breathing, but it's ragged.

The man begins working on her. A mask that pumps air is placed over her nose, and an IV is inserted into the crook of her arm.

"Is she genetically modified?" he asks as he hangs a bag of liquid above the bed.

"No, she's—" I'm about to say normal, but then I stop myself. Sienna is far from normal. She's extraordinary. My breathing hitches as my eyes swell. I clear my throat, not used to this kind of emotion. No one has made me feel this weak or this helpless or this... exposed before. "Please tell me she's gonna be okay."

The man gives me a tentative smile. "We'll know more once we get her back to the base."

"The base?"

"Yeah, you guys will have to go through detox and questioning before we can let you into Pride."

"What about the group who came before us? Where are they now?"

The medic shrugs. "Not sure. You'll have to ask Colt."

"Who's Colt?"

The medic was fiddling with Sienna's IV, but he now looks straight at me. "He's the one who let you live."

# 47
## Zane

Once Sienna and Trey disappear into the back of one of the trucks, a petite woman approaches me. "Hi, I'm Sarah. Let's get you cleaned up."

"Wait," I say. "I have to get something. Something important."

Sarah eyes the wreckage behind us. "I don't think anything survived that."

"Please," I plead, "I have to try." If Sienna needs medical attention, I have the thing that could save her. I just need to get to my pack...

"Fine." Sarah grips my arm, then leads me to the overturned ATV.

Flattening myself on the ground, my ribs screaming in protest, I wedge myself through the window and search for the pack. It's not there.

"Is this what you're looking for?" Sarah asks, the brown canvas bag dangling from her fingertips. It's ripped open and looks as though it's been run over a few times.

"Yes." Limping, I hurry over to her. "Where did you find it?"

She points to a spot twenty yards away. "It must have been thrown from the vehicle when you rolled."

"Was there anything in it?"

"No, just the bag."

I hobble over to the area she found it and hunt around. If the pack flung that far, maybe the vial is here somewhere.

Something glints from the sandy, weedy ground. Shards of glass. The vial is broken in a million pieces, the serum now sprinkling the desert. *Son of a—*

"Find anything?" Sarah calls.

All of that effort to get the serum… and it was all for naught. It's hard not to feel despair when my entire contribution was useless. Gone is the chip with the formula and the vials of serum. The only way to have access to the healing properties of the serum is to recreate the formula, which, given the circumstances, is next to impossible.

Straightening up, I limp over to where Sarah waits. "Nothing."

I follow behind her to a truck, which looks like a rolling hospital, complete with a bed, heart monitor, and oxygen masks. "Sorry about the landmines," she says. "They're only a precaution."

"From what?"

"People entering our country without our permission." She nods at the hospital bed, and I take a seat on it.

For the next few minutes, she works in silence, stitching the wound above my knee, cleaning the cut above my eye, wiping the blood, wrapping my torso—apparently, I have a few broken ribs. No wonder it hurts like the dickens. Broken ribs are the worst; time is the only thing that heals them.

When she's done cleaning me up, she escorts me to the back of a beige military truck.

As I climb in, my stitches pull tight against my swollen knee. Inside, it's dark and smells of rusted metal. It takes a moment for my eyes to adjust. There's a long row of crude metal benches lining both walls of the truck. Chaz and Nash are seated on one side. There's also a guard, dressed in fatigues with a rifle resting on his lap. I take a seat across from them, the pain in my ribs like molten lava beneath my skin. Weirdly enough, I suddenly feel the need to introduce myself.

"Hi," I say, nodding to the guard. "I'm Zane." He only smirks in response.

"Shut up, Ryder," Nash mutters, his head down.

From outside the truck, someone yells, "Let's move out." A moment later, the truck rumbles to a start and begins a slow crawl away from the scene of the accident. I can't see anything from here because the back flap of the truck blocks out any light or view.

Chaz focuses on me, his eyes worried. "Is she going to be okay?" I know instantly he's talking about Sienna.

I'm wondering the same thing. But before I can offer some optimistic response, the guard pulls out a walkie talkie and speaks directly into it, "Elijah, can you give me a status update on the girl?"

Static crackles through, and the man named Elijah answers. "She's stable. I'll know more when we get back to the base."

The guard moves the walkie talkie away from his mouth. "You guys hear that?"

Chaz nods and mutters a thanks.

The knot in my chest loosens slightly. As long as Sienna is okay, I can handle anything else. I only wish I had the serum, so I could heal her instantaneously.

"What is this base Elijah mentioned?" I ask the guard.

He raises an eyebrow, shifting his gun. "You sure are a chatty one."

"Just curious."

"Shut up, Ryder," Nash says again, this time glaring directly at me. Chaz also gives me a warning look that says *shut your mouth.* I ignore both. No one ever got information by staying quiet, that's for sure.

"So the base?" I press.

The guard snorts. "It's our interrogation center."

I can hear Chaz gulp all the way from where I sit across from him. "Interrogation? Why? You don't believe us?"

The guard grins, showing off several missing teeth. "Doesn't matter whether I believe you. I'm not the one you need to convince." He leans forward with a smirk. "Let's just say you better get your story straight." Chuckling, he pulls out a pocketknife and proceeds to clean his nails with it.

Is this an intimidation tactic? I haven't been around enough bad guys to know. Apparently, his methods seem to be working on Chaz who looks like he's about to piss his pants.

"We—we told you the truth," Chaz stutters.

The guard laughs. "Yeah. You'll be the first to crack. I can already tell."

Chaz's shoulders hunch forward as he turns away.

"I'd like to see you crack me," Nash says, staring the guard down.

The guard cracks his knuckles. "I'm already looking forward to it."

"Hey," I say to the man. "You don't have to be so callous. We came to you for help."

The guard's laugh is cruel. "Are you trying to give me a lesson on etiquette? Seriously, Mr. High and Mighty? I mean, I understand where you come from you shit gold, but still—"

"Wait," Chaz says. "You've heard of Zane?"

The man answers in a high falsetto. "Zane Ryder, the Prince of Man. The first genetically modified human and heir to Harlow Ryder's company." The guard holds up a finger, then continues in a normal voice, "That is, until he wasn't."

"How much—" Chaz's voice cracks, so he stops and starts again. "How much do you know about where we come from?"

"Too much," is his answer. The guard settles back, closing his eyes. "Now, if you don't mind, we've been monitoring your approach for hours, so I'm exhausted." He stretches out his feet and crosses his arms over his chest, his gun dangling off his lap. "Promise me you'll be good. No funny business."

Chaz nods in reply, but, of course, the guard can't see him. Only moments later, soft snores echo from that side of the truck.

I shake my head in disbelief. "Seriously? He trusts us?"

"We should snap his neck," Nash says. "Just get it over with."

I shake my head because that's *not* a plan I can get behind.

"Well," Chaz says, "Nash is crazy scary, but you and me? We're like the icing on top of a cake. Good-looking and sweet. We can't hurt nobody."

I think about my confrontation with Steele in our father's office. I had the chance to kill him, and I didn't take it. I stopped Trey from finishing him off. If we had ended his life then, would all the Fringe and Zenith members still be alive? Or would Madame Neiman have sent a different henchman to do the job?

I guess Chaz is right. I'm too nice to hurt anyone. I'd always thought my niceness was an asset, but turns out it's my downfall.

My hands swipe across the dust-covered seat. "I'm going to pretend you didn't just insult me."

Chaz chuckles. "No offense, man. But your pricey suits and perfectly gelled hair can only get you so far in this world. Right now, you and me? We are way out of our league."

I shrug at his comment. I know I'm out of place—Zane Ryder doesn't belong in this world. But I don't belong in the Chromo 120 world either. Steele made sure of it. But who's to say I can't become part of this one? People change, mostly when they have to adapt to a new situation. And I'm perfectly capable of adapting.

"But you're a hacker," I say. "I thought you'd be comfortable anywhere as long as you have a computer at your fingertips."

Chaz stares at me like I'm the dumbest person on the planet. "No way, man. I prefer to remain behind the scenes. More specifically, I prefer to remain in my own home." He purses his lips together. "Except when my apartment is compromised, and I have to run from genetically enhanced super beasts."

"That was… unfortunate," I say.

"Unfortunate?" Chaz repeats. "Um, no. That was hella crazy."

Chaz's expressiveness produces a smile from me. "Yes. That too."

"What are you two bozos talking about?" Nash interjects.

Chaz launches into the story about the genetically enhanced canines and how we fought them off. Nash nods, impressed.

"Wish I would've been there," he says.

We sit in silence for a moment, the only sound the soft wheeze of the guard's breathing. Chaz leans forward, resting his elbows on his knees. "Can I ask you something?" he says to me.

When I nod, he says, "What's up with you and Sienna? The tension between the two of you could power an entire city block."

"And that's my cue to leave the conversation," Nash mutters. He slumps down on the bench and closes his eyes.

"What's up with us?" I repeat, stalling as I search for an answer. "We're friends. Really, really good friends."

Chaz's eyes narrow as he studies me. "Man, stop lying. What happened in Rubex?"

I'm suddenly very interested in the lines on my palms. "What can I say? I love her. When we were in Rubex, I fell more in love with her." I raise my head. "I thought she felt the same. There was this moment, this brief point in time, when I thought it could be me."

"You thought she would choose you over Trey?"

"Yeah. I mean, it's not like I was planning it to happen.

But I was there and she was there, and it—" I pause and exhale slowly, like doing so can erase some of the memories. "It was perfect."

"But?"

"Then Trey betrayed us. And everything got screwed up."

Chaz rubs his upper lip in contemplation. "Have you talked to Sienna since everything went down?"

"No," I say, shaking my head. "There wasn't time. Besides, she knows how I feel. It's never been about me."

"You sure?"

"Ninety-nine percent."

Chaz leans back, placing his hands on his thighs. "As someone who deals with codes and numbers, I can tell you there's a significant difference between ninety-nine and one hundred percent." He gives me a knowing smile. "That one percentage point can make a *big* difference."

I shift my weight on the metal bench, thinking about Chaz's words. "So you're saying I should talk to her?"

"Before you give up completely? Um, yeah. I'd say that's a good idea." Chaz shakes his head. "Man, to be so smart, you sure are dumb."

My eyebrows rise in response.

"Uh, I mean when it comes to girls," he backpedals.

I chuckle. "What I don't understand is why you care? I'd think as Trey's minion, you'd want me to stay away from Sienna."

At my words, Chaz guffaws. "Trey's minion? His *minion*? Seriously?" He shakes his head in disbelief. "I can't believe you went there."

"Well, you *do* work for him."

Chaz waves away my statement. "The point is I care about Sienna. She's my best friend, and I only want to see her happy. If that's you, great. If it's Trey, wonderful. If it's neither of you, even better." He makes a face like he tasted something sour.

"All of this love triangle stuff makes me nauseous."

The sleeping guard grunt-snorts as he sits up straight, shaking his head. "Wait, what—? Who's nauseous? Don't go hurling in the back of my truck."

Chaz and I exchange a glance as Chaz struggles to suppress a grin. "I'm fine. No hurling, I promise."

When we arrive at this so-called base, the guard who finally told us his name is Zeke leads us out of the truck. I see a white building in the perfect shape of a rectangle before a hood is placed over my head. It's warm and stuffy inside, and it smells vaguely of moldy burlap. Footsteps approach, and I can only assume we've been joined by more of Zeke's men. Possibly the ones from the front of the truck.

"The less you know, the better," Zeke says, latching onto my arm. I picture his men doing the same to Chaz and Nash.

We are lead over gravel, then pavement. Doors whoosh open, and I'm hit with cool air as we step inside. These floors are smoother, my shoes gliding over the polished surface.

"Riley, take Chubs to Cleansing Room One," Zeke orders.

"It's Chaz," Chaz says through gritted teeth.

"Whatever," Zeke mutters. "And Leon, take Big Shot to Cleansing Room Three. The blast is a little more powerful in that one. Might knock him down a peg or two."

"Am I Big Shot?" Nash asks. "You can just call me Commander."

Zeke chuckles. "Riiight. And you can call me God."

"Where am I going?" I ask.

"Pretty Boy, you're with me. You'll be in Cleansing Room Two."

Zeke grabs my arm again, then leads me a short distance. When we stop, he removes the hood and pushes me into a chamber the size of my shower stall back home. It's made of glass block which means it's somewhat see through. Zeke is nothing more than a blurred image on the other side of the wall.

"Remove your clothes," he says. "It's time for detox."

"All of my clothes?" I ask.

"Yes, sir," Zeke replies. I see him turn around, giving me some semblance of privacy.

I do my best to remove my clothes, though my aching ribs and throbbing knee slow me down. I shiver as the cool air rushes past my skin.

Without turning around, Zeke says, "Place your clothes in the incinerator to your right."

Sure enough, there's a rectangular box, flush with the wall, that says *Trash*. I pull the metal handle, then throw my clothes inside. A whirring sound comes from beyond the door like I've activated a slumbering beast.

Zeke turns around now, reaching to press a red button on the wall beside him. "Hold on. It's about to get a little breezy in there." He chuckles at his own joke.

A burst of warm air strikes me, knocking me back a few inches and sending a shooting pain through my internal organs. I grab a hold of the metal handles conveniently placed inside the chamber. The air is followed by a blast of hot water, akin to a fire hose on full force. It stings my skin as it hits, the throbbing in my ribs intensifying. More air comes like I'm stuck inside a wind tunnel, followed by more water. The final blast of air lasts for so long I feel as though I'm about to lift off the ground.

The entire process reminds me of a human car wash, and it's one I'd like to not repeat any time soon.

As the machine shuts down, approximately ten minutes after it started, Zeke throws me a towel and a bundle of something white.

"What's this?"

"Your new clothes," he says with a smirk.

After toweling off, I pull on the baggy shirt and pants that look—and smell—suspiciously like doctor scrubs. Now that I'm dressed completely in white, Zeke leads me out of the room and down the hallway.

A petite brunette with skin the color of caramel meets us partway down the hall. "Mr. Ryder, I'm Cassandra. If you'll follow me, I'll take you to your room."

"Please, call me Zane." Cassandra leads me to a sterile hospital room. The walls are white, the floor tiles are white, even the bed and bedsheets are stark white.

Cassandra instructs me to lay on the bed, which I do. She busies herself around me as I admire her slender hands moving deftly from one machine to another. She's clearly skilled and at ease in this type of environment.

"You'll feel a slight pinch," she says as she finds a good vein in the crook of my arm.

"Is this really necessary?" I ask. "I thought IVs were needed only when the patient isn't eating or drinking. But as you can see, I'm perfectly fine. A little banged up, but fine."

She shrugs, her eyes not meeting mine. "I'm only following orders."

Sighing, I motion for her to continue. There's a prick and a stinging sensation as the fluid enters my system.

"You may feel a little burning," she says as she readjusts the IV bag above me.

"Yes, I already do." As I say it, my tongue feels too big for my mouth. My eyelids are heavy now, too. I fight to keep them open.

Cassandra lays a hand on my shoulder. "Don't fight it. Just give in."

"Wha—" I stop, realization dawning, and start again. "What did you give me?"

# Fearless

"Something to help you rest," she whispers, only inches from my ear. There's no malice in her voice, yet I still feel as though I've been tricked.

This IV isn't to help with pain; it's to incapacitate me.

And I was naive and stupid enough to let it happen.

# 48

## Trey

My butt hits the chair hard, and the hood is removed from my head. I'm in an interrogation room, which means I'm about to be questioned. I look around for the tray of metal tools that often accompanies spaces such as these, but those are absent from this one. Maybe these bozos aren't as tough as they act.

As soon as the guy with the cowboy hat and straw in his mouth, Colt, enters the room, I say, "Where's Sienna?" When we reached the compound or whatever this place is, they separated us. They wheeled her away while I went through detox and got these weird white clothes. They then put a hood back over my head. Not sure why. I've already seen the inside of their operation.

He takes a seat across from me. "You mean the hot little redhead currently under my care?"

"Watch your mouth, soldier," I growl.

He chuckles. "You're a fierce one. I like that."

"Where. Is. She?"

"She's well taken care of. That's all you need to know." Colt smirks, crossing his leg at the knee. "Now tell me about this information you have for me."

"I'd love to share it with you. But I need some guarantees first."

"What kind of guarantees?"

"None of my people are harmed. Not the ones with me, nor the ones who came before."

"I never said the others in your group were here—"

"I'm not finished," I say, interrupting him.

His eyes narrow. "You'll do well to remember you're on my soil now. And I don't like terrorists."

I have to laugh at that one. "I'm not a terrorist."

"You sure do know how to make demands."

I lean forward in my chair. "No. I know how to keep my people safe."

We stare at each other for several moments, neither of us blinking, a battle of wills or wit or whatever. Colt finally waves his hand in the air. "Carry on, then."

Settling back against my seat, I say, "Like I was saying, I need your guarantee none of my people will be harmed and that we can find refuge within your country for as long as we need." I pause, exhaling softly. "In return, I give you everything I know about Pacifica and their plans."

"Their plans?"

"Their plans for war."

Colt stares at me for a long moment before removing his hat and placing it on his lap. "Well, Mr. Winchester, I'd say things just got real interesting. You have yourself a deal." He holds out a calloused hand, but I don't take it. Not yet.

"One last thing," I say.

His hand drops. "What's that?"

"The redhead you referred to earlier is named Sienna. And she *will* receive the best care possible." At Colt's continued smirk, I clarify. "That's not up for negotiation."

"If I didn't know better, I'd say you have a thing for this Sienna. Am I right?"

Colt's laugh brings a tightness between my shoulder blades. *Keep it close to your chest, Trey. Don't give anything away. A man in love is a weak man. Especially if he's a leader.*

"I don't have time for that nonsense," I say, my tone hard. Guilt fills me at the denial of our relationship. But I have to deny it. In order to protect Sienna, I can't let on that she means anything to me. She's my Achilles heel, and if the enemy knows that, they'll use it against me. Against us.

"Smart boy. Women are nothin' but trouble."

"I couldn't agree more."

Colt chuckles, reaffixing his cowboy hat. "I'm taking a liking to you, Trey Winchester." He holds out his hand. "I agree to your terms."

I shake his hand then. "Thank you."

"Now about that information…"

For the next two hours, I give Colt a detailed account of everything I know. How the government is creating super soldiers with the intent of taking over Pride and possibly other Provinces. I describe what Sienna saw in Rubex in the basement of the AIG, the dozens of men and women stolen and changed, as well as the men and women in the basement of the Match 360 facility in Legas. I also tell him about the group of people we rescued from the hospital after the government issued their decree.

"What are these super soldiers like?" Colt asks.

"I haven't encountered one yet. But we did meet their genetically enhanced canines. If the soldiers are half as powerful as those beasts, Pride and the other Provinces have much to fear. Speed, strength, agility, courage—anything that makes a good soldier will be enhanced. Picture the perfect army."

Colt rubs his sideburns as he contemplates this. "How do you propose we stop them?"

"By creating our own army, of course."

Colt shakes his head. "We're not equipped to go against an entire army of super soldiers."

"You have us. Me and Zane, Nash, and any of those who

made it out of the Zenith Camp alive. We may not all be genetically modified and may not be super soldiers, but we do know how to fight."

"Are you?"

"Am I what?"

"A GM?"

"Yeah."

Colt smiles at this. "I figured you were."

"So where's the rest of my crew?"

"You mean the ones who came before you?"

"Yeah. Where are they?"

"Oh, they're not here."

The muscles in my neck tighten. "I'm sorry?"

"They were sent to Old Richmond, the capitol of Pride."

"Why?" I demand, my blood pressure rising.

"That's where I send all new arrivals." He says this like it's an everyday occurrence for people to show up at their doorstep.

"Where is this Old Richmond place?"

Colt spreads his hands wide. "Far from here."

"Are they okay?"

He shrugs. "I assume so."

I'm almost afraid to ask. "How many... arrived?"

"I didn't really count, but maybe fifteen or so?" He leans back in his chair. "There was the leader with the cornrows—"

"Paige."

Colt snaps his fingers. "Right, Paige. She's a tough one."

I smile. "Yes, she is."

"Let's see. There was the dark fella—"

"Asher," I say. "Was his name Asher?"

"Honestly, I don't remember his name. He didn't talk much, that's for sure."

Definitely sounds like Asher. "Okay, who else."

"There was the red-haired woman and that young girl."

My heart rate spikes. "I'm sorry, did you say there was a

redhead and a young girl? Was the girl blonde, maybe about five or so?"

Colt shakes his head. "I don't know."

I'd love to believe it's Sienna's mom and sister, but I saw their burned bodies. Buried their burned bodies. This other red-haired woman and girl must be the ones we rescued from the hospital.

But still, there's that small bit of hope. Maybe there's a higher power watching over us after all.

"So what now?" I ask. "Can I see Sienna?" I try not to sound too eager, but I have a feeling I failed by the way Colt's mouth turns up at the corners in a sly smile.

"Sure. I think I can arrange that." Rising from his chair, he leads me from the room—without the hood this time. I follow him down a bright, narrow hallway. We pass several closed doors with a rectangle of glass inserted in each slab of wood, allowing a quick view of the room behind the door.

Sienna's room is the furthest away. As I enter, I swear we're in the afterlife. Everything is white.

Sienna lays motionless in the bed, her pale skin blending into her surroundings—white sheets and white pillows. Her hair is like fire against a backdrop of snow.

I take a seat by her side, dying to touch her. Restraining myself, I wait until Colt leaves the room and the door clicks closed behind him before I reach for her hand.

I rub a finger up and down her arm, connecting her freckles one by one. Leaning over, I brush the hair off her forehead, my fingers lingering next to her warm skin. I press my forehead against hers, inhaling and then exhaling, like maybe if I breathe for her, she'll have enough strength to open her eyes.

There are so many things I want to say, but I feel silly talking to her when I have no idea if she can hear me or not.

Is this what it was like when Sienna sat by my bedside after the explosion in the Satellite Government Facility? Did she wait? Did she worry?

A nurse dressed in pale blue scrubs enters the room. She's such a contrast to the surrounding whiteness that it takes a moment for it to click that she belongs here. I sit up straight.

"Why hasn't she woken up yet?" I ask.

"Her body is still healing from the trauma of the accident." She checks the IV, then fiddles with a machine keeping track of Sienna's heart rate.

"What's wrong with her?" I ask.

"Her spinal cord was severely damaged. It might take weeks to heal. And even then, there's no guarantee." Her tone is clinical with no emotion whatsoever.

"But what does that mean?" Frustration makes my voice rise. "She'll walk again, right? I mean, she's not…"

"Paralyzed?" She shakes her head. "Don't know without running more tests. We just don't have those kinds of resources here."

"I don't understand."

"Old Richmond. They should be able to help you in the capitol." Now done with her check of Sienna, she walks toward the door. Halfway across the room, she says over her shoulder, "That's where they took the others in your group."

"The others? You saw them?"

She nods. "Yeah, some of them were pretty banged up. Some with third-degree burns. We don't have that kind of care facility. We're only an outpost." Suddenly realizing what she said, she clamps a hand over her mouth. "I think I've said too much." She hurries from the room before I can stop her.

An outpost. Interesting. Colt made it seem like he was in charge, but, apparently, the real puppet master is at this capitol place. If it's anything like our Capital, that's also where the corruption occurs.

Sounds like Old Richmond is where I need to be.

I don't realize I've fallen asleep, slumped over Sienna's bed, her hand in mine, until Colt enters the room and says, "Looks like you could use a good night's sleep."

I sit up quickly, wiping my mouth in case there's any drool. A leader is supposed to be on point at all times. I can't be sleeping on the job.

"It's been a while," I admit.

"You wanna cot?" Colt asks. "You swear you have no feelings for this girl, but it's clear you don't want to leave her side."

"I'm worried about her. That's all. But yes, a cot would be great."

Colt turns to leave, and I stop him. "Colt? Where are my friends? The others who were with me?"

Colt hesitates before motioning for me to follow him. I give Sienna's hand a quick squeeze, promising her I'll be right back.

We head down the hall before he stops in front of another room. I try to turn the knob to go in, but it's locked. That's when I notice the set of keys swinging from Colt's belt loop.

Colt taps the glass, and I peer inside the room. Zane is dressed in white, just like me, just like Sienna, and is lying peacefully on the bed. He's hooked up to an IV and several other machines.

"What's going on?" I demand.

Colt doesn't respond, only leads me to another room where he does the same thing—taps the glass. I peer inside this one. It's Nash in the bed this time, hooked up to an IV. Colt doesn't take me to the next room, but I already know I'd find Chaz in the same position.

I grab Colt by the collar, shoving him forcefully against the wall. "What the hell is going on? Speak. Now."

*Fearless*

"Relax, Trey. I promised you I'd take care of your friends, and I am. They were all severely dehydrated, and they needed rest."

"Why are they locked in there? Doesn't seem very *hospitable.*"

"It's to ensure their safety. If they're disoriented and wander around, they may end up somewhere they're not supposed to be. I can't be responsible for something one of my men might do."

"Why am I not in one of those beds, then?" I accuse. "Huh? I'm sure I'm dehydrated, and Lord knows I'm exhausted. And do you really want to see what I'd do to one of your men if they laid a hand on one of mine?"

Colt removes my hands from his collar, and I let him. "You're the leader, Trey. Which means you have to make the hard decisions. You don't have the luxury of rest. You can't afford to be disoriented. Everything hinges on your capacity to lead. Surely you must have realized that by now."

Colt speaks the truth. I know everything rests on me. But sometimes I get so tired, so frustrated. Over and over we are torn down, decimated, and just when I think we'll rise from the ashes like the phoenix on my back, we are ripped apart once again. I'd like to think I'm like a phoenix, able to rise again and again, no matter how many times someone strikes me down. But, lately, I'm not so sure. I'm barely hanging on. Sometimes I just want someone else to make the decisions for me. Someone else to take the burden and feel the pain.

"But," Colt continues, "if you want to escape, if you want to rest, I can make it happen. Just a little prick, a little bit of fluid, and you'll be out. Say the word."

As tempting as it is, I can't. I want to trust these people, but I don't. I know nothing about them, other than the fact they blow people up when they get too close to their wall. The moment I lose my faculties, I've given them the upper hand. And that's never gonna happen. I'd rather die before losing control of a situation.

Besides, I won't leave Sienna when she needs me. When she wakes up, she needs to see a familiar face in this unfamiliar place.

"Thanks," I say. "But no thanks."

Colt clasps me on the back. "Sure thing. But if you change your mind, let me or one of the nurses know." He leads me back to Sienna's room.

When I see her there, her body so small and fragile against the bed, I know I've made the right decision. There'll be time for sleep later. Right now, this is where I need to be. Watching over her. Protecting her.

I'm not leaving her side. Ever.

# 49

## Sienna

Voices morph around me, like I'm submerged under water and they're talking above the surface. The words are distorted. I try to lift my right leg to push myself up, but it won't budge. I command my left leg to move instead, but it's nothing but a dead weight attached to my body.

It's in that moment I remember. Everything I've lost. The people I love who I'll never see again. The home I can never return to.

Forcing my eyes open, I see Trey talking to some woman I don't recognize. The door opens and shuts as she leaves the room. I take in my surroundings as my heart rate accelerates to the speed of an oncoming train.

Where am I?

The last thing I remember is riding in the ATV with Zane. We were in the middle of nowhere, mountains rising in the distance. How did we get here?

And where exactly is *here*?

I try to croak out a sound, but my mouth feels like I've swallowed a desert. I groan instead.

Trey is immediately by my side. He touches my face, my arm, my hair, all the while thanking a God I know he doesn't believe in. I've never seen him so concerned. And he's never looked at me so tenderly before. Zane is usually the one who allows himself to be so exposed. But right now, Trey's emotions are stripped bare and right at the surface.

When I do manage a word, it's the only one I can think of. "Wa—ter," I wheeze.

"Right. Of course," Trey says. He hurries to the sink, then fills a cup with water. When he returns, he raises the head of the bed and holds the cup to my lips as I sip, dribbling it down my chin. He wipes the excess water with a tissue.

"At least I know you'll be able to take care of me when we're old and gray," I joke, my voice still raspy.

I expect Trey to smile at my attempt at a joke, but he doesn't. His eyes are full of worry.

"How are you feeling?" he asks.

"Like I've been run over by a truck. A half dozen times." I lick my lips. "What happened? Where are we?"

Trey takes my hand, bringing it to his lips. "We made it to Pride."

I glance at the stark white walls. "Why am I in a hospital room? Did something happen?" Panic clubs me in the chest. "Chaz? Zane? Are they okay?"

Trey nods. "They're fine. But there was… an accident. The ATV drove over a landmine and flipped. You were hurt pretty badly."

An image flashes in my mind. An explosion. The crunch of metal. A scream, likely from me.

I squeeze my eyes closed at the memory. When I open them, I ask, "But Zane is okay?"

"A few cuts and bruises, but he's fine."

Trey removes the blanket from my lower body. I'm wearing the same white clothes he is. He hesitantly touches my bare feet. "Can you feel that?"

I shake my head as fear, cold and quick as a snake, slithers up my spine.

His fingers move to my legs, pressing on them. I hold my

breath as he reaches my knee. "How about that?"

I shake my head again. "What happened?" I whisper.

Trey covers me again with the blanket before taking my hand in his. "Don't worry." His lips rest against my forehead. "We'll figure this out. And we'll know more once we get to Old Richmond."

"Old Richmond?"

"That's where the others are. And where you can get better care."

The machine above my head beeps, and my arm tingles where the IV is inserted.

As I stare at Trey, he turns into two—no, *three* people. I close my eyes because so many Treys give me a headache, even if they are nice to look at. I'm suddenly so tired. Too tired to talk or think or breathe. Snuggling into my pillow, I allow my mind to still.

Every time I wake, Trey is there with his worried face and dimpled chin. I'm usually half in this world and half in dreamworld, so I really don't know how many days it's been when someone enters the room and says, "Transport's ready. The president is awaiting your arrival."

Trey thanks the guy, then whispers in my ear. "Time to go, love. I promise I won't leave your side."

My eyes are closed, so I murmur a nonsensical reply.

The next thing I know, we are bump, bump, bumping down a hall or a ramp or something uneven. There's the sound of whirring—and wind. Lots and lots of wind. It lifts the blanket and rustles the sheets of my moving bed. I picture myself twirling in the wind, the breeze lifting my skirt... Wait, I'm not wearing a skirt. Never mind.

I focus on a different dream instead. This one has Trey

in it. And his shirt is off. My fingers trail down his bare back, outlining the phoenix on his shoulder blade. When he leans in to kiss me, his lips are grainy and taste like sand. Suddenly, I have a mouthful of sand.

I wake up sputtering and coughing, the feeling of sand in my mouth still lingering.

"You okay?" There's those worried eyes. Trey leans over me. Our surroundings are different now. The whitewashed walls of the hospital room have been replaced with gray and metal. So much gray and metal. It looks like we're in the inside of a flying saucer, complete with arched ceiling, wires, and exposed pipes. Of course, I'm not sitting in a seat, but strapped to a cot-type bed that has an IV pole and everything. I suddenly feel *very* exposed, lying here in my white pajama-clothes, or whatever these things are called.

"Where are we?" I whisper.

"This your first time in an airplane?" a man calls out from where he lounges in a seat against the wall, a gun resting on his lap. Well, that's inviting.

Not.

My eyes focus on Trey instead. "Are we in an aerodyne?"

Trey nods. "But they call them airplanes here."

"We haven't officially met," the man with the gun says. At first, I think he's talking to Trey, but when I rotate my head to see him, he's staring right at me. "I'm Colt." His smile is crooked, and it's more smirk than smile. "You must be Sienna."

I glance up at Trey, seeking reassurance.

"It's okay," he says. "Colt's been taking care of us. He's a good guy."

"Hi," I say to Colt.

Zane, Chaz, and Nash file onto the airplane, wearing the strangest clothes. They look like something out of a Wild West movie, complete with big belt buckles, blue jeans, and plaid shirts. Zane keeps tugging at the collar of his shirt like it itches him. I turn back to Trey. He's wearing something similar.

Nash and Chaz shuffle past me, Nash pausing long enough to give my shoulder an awkward pat and Chaz stopping to squeeze my hand.

"Hey, girl. You hangin' in there?"

"Barely. You?"

"Barely." He squeezes my hand one more time before releasing it to find his seat.

When Zane sees me, he comes over and kneels by my side, his eyes worried. "Sienna? Are you okay?" His eyes flit to my legs, then up to Trey.

"We'll know more once we reach Old Richmond," Trey says, but based on the look he's giving Zane, I feel like they've had this conversation already.

Zane leans over, brushing his lips across my forehead. "I'm sorry I don't have any healing serum for you. But not to worry, I'm going to do everything I can to recreate Re0Gene 2.0."

I try to bend my right leg so I can prove I don't need the serum, but, of course, it won't budge. Moving my left leg turns out to be just as futile.

"Thanks, Zane."

Zane manages a smile, but it's a worried one, and pats my hand before finding a seat next to Chaz.

It's weird. I know I should feel something about my lower body shutting down on me, but I'm as numb as my legs are. Why should I care that I can't feel my legs when my entire family is gone? Some people might say I'm lucky to be alive, but am I? Am I really?

I'm not so sure anymore.

Colt rises from his seat, tipping his hat. "Say hello to Old Richmond for me. I haven't seen her in years."

"Old Richmond?" Chaz asks from the other side of the aerodyne.

"Yes, sir," Colt answers. "That's where the capitol is located now. Little more than a hundred miles from the original capitol." He puffs his chest out with pride, and I think I now know why this province is called Pride. It's cause everyone here's got a great deal of it.

"The original capitol," Trey repeats. "You mean when there were a bunch of States instead of Provinces, and everyone was united under one government?"

"Exactly." Colt inclines his head at all of us, then heads for the door. He's halfway out when he leans in and says, "Zeke, here, will take care of you if you need anything. Enjoy your flight." A man with dark hair and a beard slips in before the door automatically seals behind him.

I've obviously never been in an aerodyne before, and when we take off, my belly drops to the floor as I clench the sides of the cot. My ears pop as we climb higher and higher. Trey is sitting in a seat beside me and he grabs my hand, squeezing it tight.

"Trey," I whisper over the roar of the engines, "can you tell me a story?" My dad used to tell me stories when I was little and had trouble falling asleep. And right now, I need something to connect me to him, to my family, to home. All I have left are my memories.

"A story, huh?" Trey chuckles. "Can't say I'm the best at telling stories."

"Please try?"

He lets go of my hand and exhales slowly. "Okay, let's see here." His fingers drum against his knees. "Once upon a time there was a girl named... Serena. And she loved a boy named... Trip."

"I like where this is going already."

"But they couldn't be together because there was a wicked... queen... who wanted Trip dead."

I frown. "This doesn't sound so great."

He kisses my forehead. "Hang on, I'm getting to the good

part."

"One day, they were out for a walk in the woods when Trip declared his undying love for Serena."

Nash is a few seats away and pretends to retch on the floor. "We can hear you, you know," he mutters.

Ignoring him, Trey continues. "But right after Trip told Serena he loved her, the wicked queen snuck up on them and chopped off his arm."

"Trey! That's awful."

Trey shrugs. "Anyway, Trip, his arm dripping blood, grasped his sword in his other hand and skewered the queen like a kabob."

I groan.

"But Serena, having had an extensive amount of medical training, took Trip back to her house and bandaged his arm. They decided to get married the next day. Because Trip knew, even though he'd lost an arm, he'd gained the most important thing—the girl he loved and the ability to be with her forever."

The smile I give Trey is small but real. "That was a great story. Thank you."

Trey pushes the hair away from my eyes. "We've been fighting our own wicked queen for a while now. Wouldn't you say?"

"Yeah, we have." I swallow hard as images of my father, my mother, and my sister fill my mind. "When will it end? When will this be over, Trey? I don't know how much more—" I shift away as my eyes swim with tears.

"Hey. Don't shut me out now."

I turn back to him as the tears slip from my eyes. I try to wipe them away, but he beats me to it, his thumb stroking each cheek before touching my chin. "We will fight the wicked queen," he says, "and we will win. I can promise you that."

We've lost so much. It would be easy to curl up and quit. But as I glance around the airplane at the people I love—Trey,

Zane, Chaz… even Nash—I realize something. We don't have to be blood to be family. They're my family now. With them, I can get through anything.

# Acknowledgements

As always, there are many people I must thank for helping me get this book out into the world. I'd be lost without the entire CTP team—so glad they have my back. Many thanks to Marya Heidel for her cover designing talent, to Rebecca Gober for her savvy marketing ways, to Courtney Knight for her book interior designing skills, and to Melanie Newton for her social media prowess.

A big thank you to my editor, Cynthia Shepp, for her dedication to making this book shine. And to my proofer, Pamela Renfroe, for her quick eye.

It wouldn't be an acknowledgements page without a shout-out to my critique partners, Leandra Wallace, Beth Ellyn Summer, and Michelle Mason. Your insight, suggestions, comments, and questions were invaluable. Love you all!

I have to also recognize my Charlotte YA Authors group. Your love and encouragement is everything. And to all my Pitch Wars peeps, I'm so grateful to be a part of such an awesome writing community that supports and uplifts each other.

To my parents and siblings, especially my brother Shannon, for sharing my books with everyone he meets. You're the best!

Of course, what kind of person would I be if I didn't thank my wonderful husband. You've been through this entire publishing journey with me. You've seen my highs and my lows and still love me in spite of them. Thanks for listening to my rants, calming my fears, and letting me cry when I need to. This publishing business is harder than I ever thought, and I thank you for being by my side the whole way. Love you.

To my children who have become self-sufficient when Mom is away at a conference or author event, thank you. Thank you for letting me live my dream and knowing that I'll always come home to you.

Most of all, thank YOU, my wonderful readers. Thank you for loving the first two books enough to read the third. If you've left a review or shared one of my books with a friend, then double thank you. You deserve all the awesomeness in the world!

# About the Author

**K**ristin Smith is the author of the best-selling young adult novel *Catalyst* and its sequel, *Forgotten*. When she's not writing, you can find her dreaming about the beach, beating her boys at Just Dance, or belting out karaoke (from the comfort of her own home). Kristin currently resides in the middle-of-nowhere North Carolina with her husband and five sons. To read more about her obsession with YA novels or her addiction to chocolate, you can visit her at kristinsmithbooks.com.